THE CAROUSEL PAINTER

This Large Print Book carries the
Seal of Approval of N.A.V.H.

THE CAROUSEL PAINTER

JUDITH MILLER

THORNDIKE PRESS
A part of Gale, Cengage Learning

GALE
CENGAGE Learning

Detroit • New York • San Francisco • New Haven, Conn • Waterville, Maine • London

GALE
CENGAGE Learning

ALL RIGHTS RESERVED
Thorndike Press® Large Print Christian Historical Fiction.
The text of this Large Print edition is unabridged.
Other aspects of the book may vary from the original edition.
Set in 16 pt. Plantin.
Printed on permanent paper.

LIBRARY OF CONGRESS CATALOGING-IN-PUBLICATION DATA

Miller, Judith, 1944–
    The carousel painter / by Judith Miller.
      p. cm. — (Thorndike Press large print Christian historical
    fiction)
    ISBN-13: 978-1-4104-2131-9 (alk. paper)
    ISBN-10: 1-4104-2131-7 (alk. paper)
    1. Large type books. I. Title.
PS3613.C3858C37 2010
813'.6—dc22   2009039726

Published in 2010 by arrangement with Bethany House Publishers.

Printed in Mexico
1 2 3 4 5 6 7 14 13 12 11 10

DEDICATED TO

My son, Justin . . .
for the determination
to achieve your dreams.

CHAPTER 1

April 10, 1890
Collinsford, Ohio

I perched on the edge of the brocade settee while Mrs. Galloway stared at me as though she'd discovered some new species of life. A curious look. One that made me feel as though I needed to check my appearance in the hallway mirror. Had the identity of Carrington Leigh Brouwer completely vanished on the journey from France? Possibly I'd sprouted horns. I considered touching my head to ensure that my suspicions were incorrect, for I'd never felt so uncomfortable in my life.

The very thought of stubby protrusions poking out from beneath my unfashionable straw hat caused me to force back a giggle — my compulsive reaction to unpleasant situations. I'd giggled at my mother's funeral when I was ten years old. Last month I'd done the same thing when they placed my father in his grave. I've been told it's a survival behavior used by many children. But at twenty-one years of age, I was no longer a child, and I doubted such conduct would endear me to this dour-faced woman. Then again, I wasn't certain there was anything that would please Mrs. Galloway. Her lips appeared to be permanently fixed in an upside-down U.

She rang a small brass bell that brought a servant scurrying into the room. The maid didn't look much older than me or any more pleasant than Mrs. Galloway.

"We'll need tea, Frances. And tell Thomas I need to speak with him."

The girl mumbled before turning on her heel.

Mrs. Galloway's thin eyebrows dipped into a scowl. "Good help is impossible to find nowadays. Did you find the same to be true in Paris, Miss Brouwer?"

I forced myself to smile at the woman. "Please call me Carrington — or Carrie, if you prefer."

"A family name, I assume?"

"No, from a book my mother read."

Her look of expectancy vanished, and her thin lips tightened into a knot. She must have toyed with the notion that I had descended from people of wealth and distinction. I coughed to hold back a giggle that had risen to the back of my throat. Mrs. Galloway would be horrified to discover how little I knew about my ancestors. And what I did know would make her hair stand on end.

"Well, someone should have mentioned to your mother that Carrington sounds like a boy's name."

Mrs. Galloway's abrupt comment put a halt to my meandering thoughts. I considered telling her my name was quite acceptable for a girl, but before I could respond, a gray-haired man wearing dirty work pants and a frayed shirt appeared in the doorway. It was probably good that the workman's appearance squelched my reply. Otherwise, Mrs. Galloway would think me impudent as well as a descendant of questionable ancestry.

The spry-looking man swiped his palms on his denim trousers. "Frances said you wanted to see me. I was out in the —"

Mrs. Galloway waved the man into an abrupt silence. I assumed he must be Thomas.

The older woman's frown deepened, and she pointed toward the front of the house. "Go out and get those trunks off the front porch and take them upstairs to the spare

9

bedroom. There isn't enough space in the bedroom for that crate. You'll have to put it elsewhere."

"I can put it in the gardening shed if you like. Should be enough room in there."

"No!" I shouted the response without thinking. Now they were *both* staring at me as though I'd grown horns. "Wh-what I mean is," I stammered, "that crate contains my paintings. My father's canvases." I waited, but neither of them appeared to understand. "I need to keep the crate indoors — with me — out of the weather."

"Well, it won't fit in the bedroom, and I can't set it in the middle of the parlor, now can I?"

I momentarily considered telling the woman the parlor would do just fine, but such a remark would probably land both the crate and me in the gardening shed. Why hadn't Augusta explained to her mother that I would be arriving with a crate that contained a few of my father's paintings? Mrs. Galloway was gaping at me as though she expected some sort of response.

"If you could place them somewhere in the house, just until I can make other arrangements, I would be most grateful."

"Well, there's simply nowhere that I can think of," she said as Frances walked into the room carrying a tea tray. "Oh, I know. Push the crate into that space under the stairs, Thomas."

"But that's where I keep *my* belongings," Frances said.

Thomas glanced at Frances and nodded. I supposed it was common for servants to lend support to one another, but since we'd never had servants, I couldn't be sure. One thing was certain: I'd made no friends since arriving at the white frame house on Marigold Street.

Mrs. Galloway's glare stalled any further objection. "Under the staircase, Thomas."

Frances shot an angry look in my direction that nudged me to action. I didn't want the paintings shoved into the gardening shed, but intruding on the maid's storage space wasn't fair, either. "Surely there must be some other . . ."

Mrs. Galloway raised her hand, closed her eyes, pursed her lips, and gave a slight shake of her head. In that moment I decided Mrs. Galloway had a bit of a dramatic flair hidden beneath her ever-present frown.

"I'll hear no more," she announced. "The crate will be stored beneath the stairs until other arrangements can be made. For your sake, Frances, we'll hope that is soon."

I thought Mrs. Galloway hoped it would

11

be soon for her own sake, as well. Except for ordering tea, she'd done nothing to make me feel welcome. "When do you think Augusta will return?" I inquired once the servants had disappeared.

"She's off shopping for a new pair of shoes, so there's no telling. However, I do hope it will be soon. I have a Ladies Aid meeting in an hour. As I recall, your letter said you wouldn't arrive until tomorrow or the next day."

I had already apologized for my unexpected appearance at her home. Didn't Mrs. Galloway realize I'd had no control over the ship's early arrival in port? To me, it had made good sense to catch the first available train to Ohio rather than to rent a room in New York City. To Mrs. Galloway, my early appearance had created an unwelcome interruption. I didn't want to explain that my decision had been based upon the necessity of keeping my expenses to a minimum. Passage on the *Gloriana* had eaten up most of my scanty funds. Other than the few coins that remained in my reticule and my father's crated paintings, I'd been cast adrift without financial resources. Not that my father's paintings could be considered a financial resource.

Like his contemporaries, my father had

occasionally sold a painting or two, but it had been art students like Augusta who had provided the bulk of his income. Even with his teaching, there had been more times than not when the rent had been paid late and the food meager. Augusta had been Papa's most recent student, and she'd left Paris months ago.

Mrs. Galloway folded her hands in her lap and rolled her lips into a tight seam. Other than offering to catch the next train out of town, I wasn't certain anything I said would please her. I truly hoped she would attend her Ladies Aid meeting. I'd be much more comfortable outside of her presence but dared not say so. "Augusta missed you dreadfully while she was in Paris," I tried, flashing a smile. "But I'm confident you already know that."

Mrs. Galloway's dour expression evaporated for a moment. "And it seems she missed you as soon as she returned to Ohio. I must say I was shocked when Augusta told me of your plans to come for a visit." Her smile was as weak as the tea she poured into my cup. "I was dismayed that she would send such an invitation without first requesting permission. I do believe my daughter forgot all proper etiquette and good manners while living in France."

There was now no doubt Mrs. Galloway was unhappy to have me as a houseguest. I didn't know how to respond. Besides, I felt as though a wad of cotton had taken up residence in my mouth. I swallowed a sip of tea and hoped it would help. It didn't.

The older woman stirred a spoonful of cream into the pale brew. "How long do you plan to remain in Ohio, Miss Brouwer?" Little finger in the air, she lifted the cup to her lips and took a sip.

"Forever, I suppose."

Mrs. Galloway sputtered and then coughed. I wasn't sure if I should slap her on the back or relieve her of the teacup before the warm liquid spilled onto her silk gown. Since Mrs. Galloway didn't appear to be a woman who would appreciate a slap on the back — at least not by me — I decided upon the teacup.

She removed a lace-edged handkerchief from her sleeve. After one final cough, she dabbed her eyes. "I believe I didn't hear you correctly. I thought you said *forever.*"

I bobbed my head, but then I noted the look of alarm in her eyes. "But not *here,* of course. I plan to find work and move out on my own as soon as possible."

"Work? Move out on your own? Young ladies of good reputation do not live alone,

Miss Brouwer. And what type of work would you perform? When Augusta told us you would be arriving for a stay, I assumed you had family somewhere in this country."

I wanted to throttle Augusta. She'd not told her parents about my circumstances. I cleared my throat and laced my fingers together in prayerlike fashion. "My apologies, Mrs. Galloway. I assumed Augusta had told you that I am without any relatives. My father was a talented artist, but he left me with nothing more than two paintings and enough money for my passage to America."

There! I'd said it. The truth was out.

Mrs. Galloway picked up her fan and flapped it back and forth with a vengeance. Wisps of her mousy brown hair rose and fell in the artificial breeze. She sucked in her narrow cheeks and suddenly she resembled a prune — a prune with flyaway brown hair. I swallowed a giggle. *I must remain calm. I must remain calm.* I repeated the words in my head while Mrs. Galloway continued to fan herself.

When the hour chimed in the distance, the fanning ceased and Mrs. Galloway jumped to her feet. "If you'll excuse me, I must go upstairs. I'll be late if I remain . . . any . . . longer." Her sentence ran down like a clock that needed winding.

"*Oui,* I'll finish my tea and relax until Augusta returns." Mrs. Galloway's wrinkled brow served to remind me I was no longer in Paris. "I mean, *yes,* I'll finish my tea." I sighed as Mrs. Galloway and her frown disappeared up the steps.

Leaning back, I crossed my ankles and took in my surroundings. Mrs. Galloway had obviously done her best to keep pace with the latest décor. Every flat surface in the room had been covered with vases, figurines, silver-framed pictures, candlesticks, or potted ferns. Several small tables were draped with fringed or lace-edged cloths and topped with porcelain jardinières and multicolored glass-shaded lamps. The room was far too crowded for my liking, but who was I to judge? I was accustomed to the sparse furnishings in the loft above a small French bakery.

Hoping to discover a more comfortable position, I wriggled into the cushions but met with little success. The divan felt as though it had been stuffed with bricks. One look at the chairs positioned near the front window and I decided it was time for a change of seats. They appeared much more inviting. I'd have a view of the front porch and could see Augusta when she arrived.

The ring of a bell drifted from upstairs

and was soon followed by muffled footsteps racing down the hallway. Mrs. Galloway had likely summoned Frances to help her dress. What must it be like to ring a bell and have someone run to do your bidding? I couldn't imagine. I couldn't even picture what it would have been like had my mother lived longer, or how it would have felt to have a father answer my questions or shower me with affection.

A carriage slowed in the street, and I bent forward, hoping it would stop and Augusta would appear, but the buggy continued onward. Leaning back against the cushion, I revisited memories of my own dear mother. Mama had always made me feel special, but since her death, I'd experienced an aching loneliness — a need to belong and feel a part of something other than myself. Papa had tried his best, but it was art that had consumed his every thought. He'd loved me in his own way, of course, but I always believed I was an inconvenience in his world. I interrupted his creativity with my requests to walk in the park or play a game of checkers.

I'd written to tell Augusta of his death, and then her letter had come with an invitation to become a part of the Galloway family. In truth, the letter hadn't exactly suggested a branch on the Galloway family tree, but Augusta had offered a place to stay for as long as needed. To me, that was almost the same thing. I had longed to return to America for many years, having been gone for ten.

The very thought that I might become part of her family had provided me with ample reason to accept. My experience thus far was quite different from what I'd anticipated. I could only hope matters would improve.

CHAPTER 2

"Carrie!"

I awakened with a jolt, not knowing where I was. It took only one look at Augusta to settle my mind. I jumped out of my chair; at least I tried. My right leg remained asleep, and jagged pinpricks raced through the extremity. I hobbled the short distance that remained between the two of us and enjoyed the warmth of Augusta's embrace — and the fact that she had enough strength to hold on to me until my leg would co-operate and carry my weight.

She leaned back. "It is so good to see you." She gave my arm another gentle squeeze and took a backward step. "I see you've maintained your lovely figure."

I didn't tell her it was difficult to gain weight when there wasn't much money for food. Instead, I said, "And it appears you've dropped several dress sizes since leaving France. Let me take a look at you."

Arms extended, she swirled in a giant circle. Her thick auburn hair had been pulled back in a severe coiffure that accentuated her angular features. She completed a final turn and pressed her palms to her waist. "Giving up those rich French pastries has helped. I think my dress size is even smaller than yours."

The belief seemed to please Augusta, and I certainly couldn't argue the point. There was no doubt her waist was at least an inch or two smaller than my own. "And you've fashioned your hair in a different style," I said.

She touched her fingers to one side of her head. "Do you like it? Mother says it's becoming, but I'm unsure."

I shook my head. "I prefer a few curls around your face. This makes you look far older than your nineteen years."

"And it gives my face a horsey appearance, doesn't it?" She turned sideways to show me her profile and pointed to her raw-boned features. "Don't dare try to deny it." She hurried to the mirror across the room and loosened several wispy curls, permitting them to encircle her face before returning for my response.

I gave a firm nod. "Much more appealing."

She wrinkled her nose in impish fashion. "If I possessed your delicate features and gorgeous blue eyes, I wouldn't have to worry about hiding my face."

We'd had this discussion on many occasions when Augusta lived in France. Much to my discomfort, she had constantly compared her appearance to my own. She'd coveted everything from my blue eyes and finely arched brows to the golden highlights in my brown hair. Even more disturbing, she'd considered my upturned nose my most beautiful feature. Strange, because I'd always considered it far too small for my oval face.

"I can see I've made you uncomfortable. I'll do my best to avoid such talk in the future." She squeezed my hand. "I'm delighted you were able to arrive earlier than expected." Her gaze lingered on my hat, and I didn't fail to note the twitch in her lips.

A quick look in the hallway mirror reflected the reason for her amusement. My straw skimmer had tipped askew during my impromptu nap. I did my best to push it into place, but the attempt only caused several hairpins to drop to the floor. I unpinned the hat and lifted it from my head, which proved another mistake. Several unmanageable curls escaped and cascaded across my forehead. "I'm a mess."

"You are not a mess. You are beautiful. And most women I know would pay a fortune for those lovely curls of yours. I know I would."

I chuckled and pushed the hair from my forehead. "If that's the case, let's cut them off and I'll sell them. I could certainly use the money."

Augusta's eyes turned serious. "You need not worry about money. You can stay with us for as long as you like. We're going to have great fun. We'll be just like sisters."

I could feel myself longing to curl around a stray branch of the Galloway family tree, but I quickly chided myself. I could never become Augusta's older sister, neither by blood nor through friendship. Not now. Not ever.

During her time in Paris, Augusta's aunt Evangeline had permitted us to associate at will. Evangeline Proctor had considered me a proper companion for her niece. But that would not be the case here in Ohio. It had taken but a few minutes for me to realize Mrs. Galloway and Evangeline Proctor were complete opposites. Mrs. Galloway would never accept me as her daughter's equal, but there was no need to mention such matters right now.

Instead, I clasped Augusta's hand tight within my own and led her to the uncomfortable divan. With little urging, my friend disclosed the particulars of her life here at home. Some of the details had already been conveyed in her occasional letters to me, but much was new information. I was, however, taken aback by her rather formal behavior — something I'd not observed in Paris.

While living in France, Augusta had been impulsive and carefree. Here in Collinsford, she appeared to worry about propriety. During warm afternoons in Paris, we had thought nothing of removing our stockings and walking barefoot in the grass or wading through an occasional puddle. On cooler days, we had strolled along the narrow streets eating crusty hunks of bread from the downstairs baker's shop. On occasion we had even managed to cajole the owner of a nearby cheese shop into giving us free slices of the nutty-flavored Emmental he featured in his store. Something about Augusta's demeanor told me she would never do such things in this city. The realization dampened my spirits, and I wondered if I'd made a terrible mistake by coming here.

Augusta studied me with her inquisitive gray eyes that reminded me of Stormy, the silvery cat I'd left in the care of the baker's wife. Stormy hadn't seemed to mind when I plopped him on Madame Leclair's wide windowsill and kissed him good-bye. The baker's wife said he'd be a nice addition. What Madame Leclair didn't say, but I already knew, was that she wanted a mouser. She'd be disappointed. Stormy was a fat, lazy cat who'd come to expect his food delivered in a china bowl each day. He'd never become a mouser — unless, perhaps, she starved him. That might force him to action, but I hoped she wouldn't resort to such harsh tactics.

Thoughts of the animal evoked a twinge of melancholy, and I blurted, "Do you have a cat?" Two tiny frown lines appeared between Augusta's eyebrows. No doubt she was thinking I'd lost my mind. Here she was in the midst of revealing her hopes to find the perfect suitor, and I asked about a cat. "I'm sorry, but I've been missing Stormy." I'm not certain my explanation allayed her concerns over my mental condition, but at least she smiled.

"We do, but Mother won't let him in the house. She isn't fond of cats, so Boots spends most of his time out in the garden with Thomas. Except when it's too cold. Then he's sent to the cellar. He isn't friendly like Stormy." Augusta shifted her position and leaned a little closer. "So what do you think?"

I narrowed my eyes as if contemplating my response to Augusta's question while my mind raced to recall what I was supposed to answer. I'd been only half listening throughout her commentary on life in Collinsford. I could feel the beginnings of a giggle, so I swallowed hard and said, "I'm thinking."

"Don't be silly. A simple yes or no is all that's required." She grinned. "But if you say no, I'll be forced to keep on until you change your answer."

"In that case I suppose I might as well say yes." I did wish I knew what I'd just agreed to, but I supposed time would tell.

With Augusta's help, I unpacked one of my trunks before her mother returned from the Ladies Aid meeting. I was pleased there hadn't been sufficient time to attack the others before we were summoned to the supper table. Given Mrs. Galloway's earlier comments, I figured I'd be repacking and moving out as soon as she could shuffle me out the door. My stomach growled with hunger, but I wasn't looking forward to enduring any more of Mrs. Galloway's scrutiny.

Sometime while Augusta and I were upstairs, though I didn't know exactly when, Mr. Galloway had returned home. At least I assumed the man standing in the downstairs hallway was Mr. Galloway because his appearance hadn't alarmed Augusta.

He stepped forward and offered a broad smile. "You must be Carrie," he said. "Welcome to our home." He glanced at his daughter. "Augusta has been anxiously awaiting your arrival. We're pleased you've safely arrived."

His warm greeting was a welcome surprise. However, if his wife was anywhere within earshot, I was sure that Mr. Galloway would be reprimanded later this evening. Once the family gathered around the table, Mr. Galloway thanked God for our food and my safe journey to Ohio. From the look in Mrs. Galloway's eyes, I had my doubts that she concurred. Not that I believed she wished me injured in a train wreck or lost at sea; she just didn't want me in her house — at least not for long.

"Augusta tells us that you are an extremely talented artist," Mr. Galloway commented while passing me a bowl of cubed potatoes swimming in butter and parsley. I accepted the bowl and helped myself to two small pieces of potato. I didn't want Mrs. Galloway to think me without manners. Mr. Galloway frowned and shook his head. "You'll starve to death with that tiny portion. You're far too thin as it is. Take another helping of potatoes." He pointed into the bowl. "And choose those larger pieces."

I complied but kept my head bowed when I passed the bowl to Mrs. Galloway. I didn't want to see her scowl.

Mrs. Galloway took the bowl from my hand. "I imagine Augusta was exaggerating or Mr. Brouwer wouldn't have been charging such exorbitant fees for art lessons. Isn't that correct, Carrie?"

"No. Well, yes . . . Well, I mean, I don't believe I'm as talented as my father, but I don't feel his teaching fees were excessive. He charged much less than many of —"

"There. You see, my dear? I knew she couldn't be as talented as Augusta suggested."

The woman's comment was stated with an authority that defied rebuttal, but Augusta wasn't deterred. "Carrington is extremely talented. One day people will pay a fortune for her paintings. Even her father said she possessed greater talent than his own." Augusta swiveled toward me. "Didn't he, Carrie?"

"Oui," I mumbled.

"That's no more than a father's pride in his child," Mrs. Galloway replied.

"I *do* have talent." The words slipped out with far too much pride and bravado. I wanted to scoop them up like the parslied potatoes and shove them into my mouth, but that wasn't possible. To make matters worse, I looked in Mrs. Galloway's direction. Her pale eyes reflected either shock or anger. Turning away with a jerk, I immediately experienced a painful crick in my neck. I refrained from rubbing the aching tendons, figuring I deserved a bit of punishment for my sassy remark.

"I'd like to see some of your artwork," Mr. Galloway said.

Although I didn't know if he truly wanted to see my artwork or if he was merely attempting to keep some semblance of peace during the meal, I was thankful for his intervention.

"What do you enjoy painting? Do you prefer portraits or still lifes?" He looked directly into my eyes as though he genuinely wanted to know.

"I enjoy both. And animals, as well," I said. "One of my favorite paintings is of my cat, Stormy. I gave it to Madame Leclair for taking him in when I left France." I nearly added that I missed him very much but remembered Augusta's mother wasn't fond of cats.

"I'm sure you miss him," Mr. Galloway replied.

"Yes," I whispered. Mr. and Mrs. Galloway seemed a strange match. He so pleasant and kind — she so disagreeable and harsh. How had such opposites decided to marry each other?

"Did you stop by to see how the house is coming along?" Mrs. Galloway asked her husband.

He nodded and continued to eat his supper. I'd learned from Augusta that her parents were building a new house in the area of town known as Fair Oaks. I thought their existing house quite lovely, and certainly large enough for their family. Augusta told me her mother wanted a house in Fair Oaks because that's where the *right* people lived — people who were wealthy enough to be listed on the social register. The idea of building a house just so you could live next to rich people seemed silly to me, but who was I to make judgments on such matters?

"And? What was the progress?" Mrs. Galloway was clearly impatient with her husband.

"There will be a small delay due to the plumbing for the bathroom."

Mrs. Galloway leaned forward. I thought the lace on her mauve gown might dip into her buttered potatoes, but she stopped short. "*How* small?" she hissed.

"Some of the pipes have to be reordered. We received the wrong size."

"And whose fault is that?"

He shrugged. "Does it really matter?"

"It matters to me. If it's the builder's error, then we need to reduce his fee, and if it's the manufacturer's mistake, he needs to decrease the charges for the materials." She pushed her plate aside. "You may recall that I have a party planned. The invitations have already been sent out. If I have to cancel, I'll be the laughingstock of Fair Oaks before we've ever moved into our new home."

"I —"

Mrs. Galloway interrupted her husband with a glare. "And don't say I told you so, Howard."

"I wouldn't think of saying such a thing, my dear. However, I do believe your guests will understand if the party has to be rescheduled. I'll go over first thing in the morning and remind the men that they need to do everything in their power to meet the deadline."

If I hadn't been present at the table, I think Mrs. Galloway would have told her husband he needed to do more than talk to the builders tomorrow morning. Instead, she clamped her lips together and remained silent until Frances entered the room and asked if we were ready for dessert.

Frances had served each of us a slice of lemon pound cake and was returning to serve coffee when Augusta said, "Carrie promised she'd come to the party so that I can introduce her to our new neighbors in Fair Oaks."

My dessert fork slipped from my fingers and landed with a muffled thump on the linen tablecloth. I had never agreed to attend a party in Fair Oaks or anyplace else for that matter. Why would Augusta say such a thing? Even if I hadn't told her, she should be able to see that her mother wasn't pleased by my presence. Both Mrs. Galloway and I glared in Augusta's direction. At least I'd discovered something the two of us could agree upon. She didn't want me at her party, and I didn't want to attend.

"I don't recall that conversation," I said.

"And I don't recall giving you permission to extend invitations without prior permission." Mrs. Galloway looked down her nose at Augusta.

Augusta ignored her mother's remark and frowned at me. "You *did* agree, Carrie. This afternoon when I told you I'd badger you until you said yes."

So *that's* what I'd agreed to while thinking about Stormy. "It sounds as though the party may be postponed, and I don't know where I'll be living then. It may be impossible for me to attend." It was a feeble attempt to try to save Augusta from her mother's ire.

"But you promised to attend, and even if the party is postponed, you'll still be living with us. Won't she, Father?"

"She is welcome to . . ."

Mrs. Galloway shook her head with a vehemence that made me stare in wonderment. How many pins had she used to hold her hair in place? If I had shaken my head with even half that intensity, my unruly locks would have spilled over my forehead like a waterfall. Yet not one strand of Mrs. Galloway's perfectly coiffed hair fell out of place. It was probably afraid to, I thought. A giggle began to tickle the back of my throat. *Oh please, not now.* This wasn't the time for a smile, much less a giggle. I grabbed my glass of water and gulped.

"By the time our new house is finished,

I'm sure Carrington will be well established in her own home. She tells me she's planning to look for a job and begin a new life . . . somewhere."

The gulp of water and Mrs. Galloway's curt response had doused my urge to laugh. Even though Augusta's mother didn't say so, I knew *somewhere* meant far from Marigold Street or their new house in Fair Oaks. Hadn't she earlier condemned the impropriety of such an independent way of life? But that was before she'd learned of my unimpressive lineage and the fact that I was homeless. Had she expected me to secure a job and locate a place to live during the past three hours?

"Carrington arrived in our home only hours ago. There is no need to speak of work or moving to her own home. She is our guest." Mr. Galloway's stern look silenced his wife.

My discomfort mounted, and I longed to flee from the room. My appearance at their home had created this tidal wave of emotions, and I felt I should say something to smooth the rough waters. I forked a piece of the pound cake and chased it around the dessert plate until it broke into a thousand tiny crumbs. "I do want to find a job. But I'm somewhat uncertain how I would go about securing one." The words hung in the air.

Mrs. Galloway shifted in her chair and defied her husband's warning look. "Perhaps if you tell us your qualifications, we can help. I know of several ladies in Fair Oaks who are hiring domestics."

"Mother!"

"I am attempting to help, Augusta."

Mrs. Galloway glanced at me. I was expected to take up her defense. "Don't be angry with your mother, Augusta. I asked for help." The lemon cake no longer held any appeal, and I pushed it aside. "I fear my abilities keeping house would fail miserably. I have no experience."

"With proper training, I'm certain you could do well."

Mr. Galloway cleared his throat. "There is plenty of time to consider your future, Carrie. You and Augusta have much to talk about, so if you'd like to be excused . . ."

Augusta pushed away from the table and signaled me to follow. After rushing upstairs, she waved me into the bedroom and closed the door. "I do hope you'll forgive Mother for her boorish behavior. She's bent upon impressing folks here in Collinsford and gaining access to a higher echelon of New York society. I know it's silly, but she fears any hint of unsavory gossip will besmirch the Galloway name and ruin our opportunity."

"Opportunity for what?"

With a sad smile, Augusta said, "She lives for the day when she'll see the Galloway name on the New York social register. Being *somebody* is what Mother lives for, and any unforeseen circumstance sends her into one of her moods. Before inviting you, I should have explained your circumstances in detail, but —"

"But you knew she'd call a halt to your invitation?"

Augusta's forlorn look affirmed my suspicions. Mrs. Galloway considered me a broken rung on her climb up the social ladder.

"Please forgive me, but I desperately wanted you to come to Ohio. And I'm delighted you're here, no matter what!" She thumped one of the pillows for emphasis. "Mother's attitude will soften toward you. I'm sure of it."

I didn't share Augusta's confidence — not in the least. Immediately sensing my lack of conviction, Augusta continued her litany. And though I offered forgiveness a multitude of times, she wouldn't cease. Eventually I gave up and permitted myself the luxury of daydreaming.

My thoughts returned to Paris, and I was wondering if Stormy realized I'd deserted him when Augusta grabbed my arm. "You're not listening to a word I'm saying." We were lying across Augusta's pale yellow satin bedspread. Even though we'd been careful to take off our shoes, I knew Mrs. Galloway would be annoyed if she walked into the room and discovered us. Thoughts of the unpleasant woman peering into the room stirred me to action. I pushed myself up until my legs dangled over the edge of the bed and my toes rested on the floor. I wanted nothing more than a good night's sleep. The voyage had been rough, and my nights had been filled with more worry than sleep. And the train hadn't proved much better. Instead of purchasing a ticket for one of the expensive Pullman cars, I'd traveled in one of the less expensive and very uncomfortable coaches. No matter how I had arranged myself in the seat, each time I nodded off, my head snapped forward and wakened me with a jolt.

"I'm sorry. After a good night's sleep, I think you'll find me much better company."

"Oh yes, of course. I should have realized you're tired. I should let you get to bed. I'm so sorry."

Augusta's words were enough to propel me off the bed. I grabbed my shoes, bid her a quick good-night, and scuttled down the hallway before she could apologize again.

Once I'd slipped between the sweet-smelling sheets, I expected sleep to come quickly. But my mind played tricks on me and flitted from one thought to the next. I tried to recall what I had learned about Mrs. Galloway when Augusta was living in France but soon realized there had been little mention of the woman. Instead, Augusta had spoken of her father and brother.

In retrospect, I suppose I hadn't questioned her because it didn't seem important at the time. After telling her my mother had died when I was ten and hearing that Augusta's mother was very much alive, we hadn't talked of them again. Rather, it had been our fathers that we had compared and discussed. And I'd heard a good deal about Augusta's brother, Ronald, as well. I'd been jealous until she told me how he'd teased her when she was a little girl.

Yanking the skirt of my nightgown free from beneath my legs, I rolled onto my side. The bed was far softer than the thin mattress I'd used in the loft, yet even the comfort of the bed didn't convince me I'd made a wise choice. I should have remained in Paris and taken time to make a sound decision. Then again, there had been only two choices. Remain in Paris and hope to find work or accept Augusta's invitation. Papa's friends shared the same bohemian lifestyle. They could offer no help and had encouraged me to return to America, where a fine family awaited me. If only they knew!

Deep inside, a stab of longing pierced my being. How I missed watching Papa stand in front of his shabby wooden easel with a palette in one hand and a paintbrush in the other. I missed his impatience when he awakened to a day without sunshine. I missed his rare words of approval. His praise had been reserved only for my painting. And because he'd never noticed much else about me, I'd cultivated what talent I possessed like a gardener nurturing tender sprouts.

I was certain I'd never be as good as he, but I was compelled to try. I mimicked his technique until the day he said true artists worked to discover their own style. Still, I admired how each stroke of his brush would caress the canvas with bold splashes of color and then fade into haunting shadows, draping his work in mystery. In the last years of his life, he continually labored toward perfection, never pleased with his work, always convinced he could do better. If only he hadn't died.

I stared into the darkness that lay beyond the bedroom window. A distant star twinkled. Was God out there in that vast emptiness looking down on me? Or maybe my mama could draw back the curtain of heaven and see me in this strange new place. I knew Mama was in heaven because when Papa hadn't been within earshot, she had talked to me about God. Even though Papa hadn't approved, Mama and I attended church when we lived in New Hampshire. He never came with us. He said God was for weak people who needed a crutch to get through life. Mama didn't agree. She said believers were the strong ones because they had faith in something beyond what they could see and feel. I tended to agree with Mama. At least until she died. Since then, I wasn't so sure. But I did want to believe *someone* loved me.

CHAPTER 3

The following morning Augusta announced that the two of us would be taking a tour of Collinsford. She'd be leading the tour, and I would be the only tourist. I explained I'd slept very little the previous night and was weary from my travels, but to no avail.

Augusta took a military stance in front of the mirror and, with the authority of an officer leading troops into battle, jabbed a hatpin into her flower-festooned hat. We locked glances in the mirror. "The only way you're going to become comfortable living in Collinsford is to learn your way around town. I think you'll be surprised when you see the size."

"Just don't become angry if I fall asleep in the carriage." I leaned against the front door. "Besides, I observed a great deal of the town on my ride from the railroad station."

After a final look in the mirror, she turned

around. "The wagon would have traveled along the outer edge of town. You didn't see the things we're going to see today. Besides, I want to show you something very special."

I didn't argue. There was a determined look in her eye, and I knew I wouldn't win. She pointed to my hat, and after I'd fastened it on top of my head, we went out the door. Once inside the carriage, I listened with half an ear while Augusta spouted the wonders of Collinsford. With breathless excitement, she expounded upon the many fine dress shops and the fact that they were always well stocked with the latest fashions. I didn't mention such information was useless to me, since I didn't even have enough money to purchase life's necessities.

Augusta straightened her shoulders. I could hear the pride in her voice when she told me that Collinsford held the distinction of being the largest city in Ohio, as well as the seventh largest city in the entire country. You would have thought she'd built it with her very own hands. Then she boasted of the city's proximity to Lake Erie — a wonderful place for a respite from the summer's heat, especially for those unable to leave home for the entire summer. Though I doubted I'd ever have the time or financial resources to visit Lake Erie, I agreed that it sounded lovely.

A streetcar rumbled down the cobblestone road, and Augusta used the opportunity to further boast of the city's attributes. "The streetcar tracks crisscross a great deal of the city, making travel quite simple."

She stared at me, obviously expecting a response, and I did my best to proclaim the innovation absolutely wonderful. I had to admit the city was much larger than I'd anticipated. Yet Collinsford was nothing like Paris. Nor was it anything like the small New Hampshire village where I'd occasionally gone shopping with Mama. And though it was interesting to hear about Lake Erie and see the fine stores along Liberty Avenue, they wouldn't have any effect upon my life. I wouldn't be summering at the shore or purchasing fancy dresses to attend teas and spring parties.

"Close your eyes. We're almost there and I want to surprise you."

I was pleased to comply with her request. She still didn't comprehend how much I longed for a restful nap.

"You can open them now," she said. When I didn't immediately respond, she nudged her elbow into my side and raised her voice at least an octave. "Look!" She pointed to the carriage window.

I forced my eyes open and peered out the window. A massive white marble structure that vaguely resembled pictures I'd seen of the Greek Parthenon loomed in the distance. The sight was enough to capture my attention and erase any thoughts of sleep. "What is that?"

Augusta grabbed my hands and bounced forward on the carriage seat. "You're going to love this. It's the Collinsford Museum of Art. The city voted to build the museum to encourage civic pride and artistic culture. We're the first city in Ohio to complete our museum. It's been open for only three months." She leaned closer. "It cost over a million dollars."

The moment Thomas opened the carriage door, we stepped down and hastened toward the museum entrance. For the remainder of the morning, we meandered through the gallery exhibits and viewed the rooms filled with paintings. I studied each canvas with a critical eye and decided few of them equaled my father's work. Though some would say my opinion was tainted because of the familial relationship, I know that isn't the case.

Years of traipsing through art galleries and museums with my father and his friends taught me to recognize exceptional art —

and my father's art was exceptional. Unfortunately, the world never had the opportunity to discover him.

"I knew it would cheer you to come here," Augusta said as we prepared to depart.

There was no doubt Augusta's intent had been virtuous. But instead of heartening me, the visit left me longing for my father and feeling even more alone. I didn't have time to dwell on such thoughts for long.

My other surprise was lunch at the Camellia Tea Room. I did my best to appear comfortable, but the formal restaurant was patronized by the socially elite, and I was out of my element. I truly appreciated Augusta's kindness, but I would have much preferred leftover roast beef on slices of thick homemade bread while sitting in the park — preferably without shoes and stockings. I sighed with relief when we finally exited the place, thankful I hadn't dropped my fork or spilled tea down the front of my dress.

I glanced upward toward the windows in the three- and four-story buildings that surrounded the restaurant. "Does your father work in one of these buildings?"

Augusta nodded. "A few blocks down the street." She tipped her head to one side and looked out from beneath the brim of her hat. "We should surprise him with a visit. Want to?"

My choices were two: shop in the variety of stores that lined the busy Collinsford business district or visit Mr. Galloway's office. The choice was simple. Augusta gave the carriage driver directions, and within a few minutes we were in front of a four-story brick building.

"Here we are." She locked arms with me, and we entered the front door. "His office is upstairs," she said, leading me toward a flight of marble steps.

When we arrived on the second floor, we walked down the corridor and stopped in front of a door with thick rippled glass that reflected light but didn't permit a view inside. Hanging on the wall to the right was a small black plaque with the words *Howard Galloway & Company* printed in gold letters. Below the name was a gold fist. The extended index finger pointed toward the door. I wondered who the "and company" was, but there wasn't time to ask before Augusta opened the door and the two of us entered.

A matronly woman looked up when we entered. Her graying hair was pinched into a tight bun that rested on the center of her head like a sparrow's nest. Though severe, the hairstyle was no match for the piercing look we received.

"Good afternoon, Miss Galloway." The thin-lipped greeting was less than welcoming, but Augusta didn't appear to notice.

"Good afternoon, Miss Markley. We're here to see my father. Is he in?"

The woman pulled a pencil from the bird's nest and traced it down an open page on her calendar. "He is, but he has an appointment at the carousel factory." She looked at the clock hanging near the door. "If he's going to arrive on time, he'll need to leave in five minutes."

Augusta grabbed my hand and pulled me past Miss Markley's desk. "Oh good. He can take us with him. Won't that be fun?"

The question was directed at me, but Miss Markley jumped to her feet and stepped in our direction. "I don't believe it's a place for young ladies. Let me tell your father you're here."

Augusta waved the older woman back to her chair. "No need. Go on with your work, Miss Markley." Augusta continued to pull me toward a door at the other side of the room.

For some reason I'll never know, I glanced over my shoulder and was met with Miss Markley's fiery eyes. I was certain they could have burned holes in my dress. Hoping to diffuse the situation, I offered a weak smile and shrugged. Miss Markley clenched her fingers into rigid fists. My gesture had made matters worse. "Miss Markley's unhappy," I hissed at Augusta.

"I think she was born unhappy," Augusta whispered in reply. "She'll be fine when she sees that Father is pleased by our visit."

I hoped Mr. Galloway would be pleased. Otherwise we faced the possibility of our dresses or hair being singed by another one of Miss Markley's scorching glares. Augusta tapped on the door. She didn't wait for a reply before entering. Mr. Galloway appeared momentarily perplexed, but a broad smile immediately erased any sign of confusion.

He pushed back from his desk and stood to welcome us. "What brings you lovely young ladies to my office?"

"After visiting the museum, we stopped for lunch and then decided to come by and say hello. Miss Markley tells me you're going to the carousel factory. We'd enjoy going with you."

He hesitated. "I think you would much prefer a visit to Faber's Department Store, wouldn't you?" Reaching into his pocket, he withdrew his money clip and peeled back several bills.

Augusta shook her head. "We don't need money for shopping. Both of us would rather go with you and see the factory. We promise to stay out of the way. Besides, you've told me over and over that you'd give me a tour. This is the perfect opportunity."

While Augusta continued her plea, I surveyed Mr. Galloway's office. A bank of windows lined two full walls of his corner office, and light flooded the room. Papa would have loved this place. He could have painted wonderful pictures here. Dark walnut crown molding emphasized the high plaster ceilings. The room was filled with bookshelves, a long library table, several chairs, and Mr. Galloway's desk. I wondered what he did in this room all day long. Papers were strewn across his desk, and a book lay open on the library table, but those told little of the work performed here. I was accustomed to seeing tangible evidence: a partially painted canvas or sketches drawn on thick paper and spread out across the floor. Here there was neatness. No feeling of creativity.

"Carrie?" Augusta was standing beside me with a quizzical look in her eyes. "Are you ready to go?"

"Forgive me. I was daydreaming." I hurried after Mr. Galloway, for I didn't want to be left behind to face Miss Markley on my own.

I thought Mr. Galloway would take his buggy and meet us there. Instead, he joined us in the carriage. "I'll come back for the buggy later," he said.

The thought of visiting the factory excited me. Perhaps because the one time Papa had painted my picture, I had been sitting on a carousel horse. That was back when Mama was alive — when we lived in New Hampshire. I know we didn't have much money, but we'd left home in Grandpa's wagon to go on a Sunday afternoon picnic. We traveled for what seemed like forever, but I was only five years old, so it may not have been all that far. When we stopped at the park for our lunch, I remember Papa was surprised to hear music. The three of us went to explore and find the band. After a short hike, we came upon a small group of men playing near a carousel with beautiful horses. Mama said we didn't have money for such silliness, but Papa shook his head and sat me on a huge white horse with flaring nostrils and a flowing mane. Once I had settled into the saddle and grasped the leather straps, he and Mama sat down on the grass. The music began, and while the carousel circled around and around, Papa pulled out his sketchbook and drew a picture of my horse. Not me, just the horse.

When I asked him why he hadn't drawn me in the sketch, he assured me I'd be sitting on the horse when he finished the painting. And I was. He even remembered I'd been wearing my soft blue dress with the crocheted lace collar. I had declared the picture a work of perfection. At five years old I thought my life was perfect, too. Fifteen years later, I'd readily admit that my life is far from perfect.

The carriage jolted to a stop in front of a sprawling two-story frame structure. Nothing fancy like the buildings downtown, but even with the doors closed against the surprisingly cold April winds, I sensed something exciting awaited inside. Strange, yet it seemed carousel horses had created a link between my deceased father and Mr. Galloway. In that moment I liked Mr. Galloway all the more.

My heartbeat perceptibly quickened when we entered the building. The smell of wood and paint drifted toward me like a welcome embrace, and I strained to see what lay beyond the wall blocking my view. Before I could capture a glimpse, Mr. Galloway herded us into an adjacent room. The small space was filled with a straight-backed chair and a large paint-stained desk. Dust covered the windowsills as well as all the other spaces not covered with books or papers. Augusta pulled her skirt close, and the two of us stood near the office door while Mr. Galloway shuffled through the disarray.

A stocky man with a thick black mustache and heavy eyebrows stepped to the door. "Anything I can help you with, Mr. Galloway?"

Augusta's father pressed his palms on top of the desk. Elbows locked, he leaned forward and met the man's steady gaze. "The contracts? Better yet, where is Josef?"

The worker balled his fingers into a fist and pointed his extended thumb over one shoulder. "He went to the train station to check on the wood shipment. They delivered yellow pine, of all things. Josef wanted to see if the orders had been mixed up at the train station and someone else got the basswood."

Mr. Galloway pushed himself upright and continued shuffling the paper work. "I suppose this will throw us even further behind with our orders. Am I right, Ed?"

The man twisted one end of his mustache between his thumb and index finger. "Unless Josef locates the wood, that's probably the way of things."

"Ah, here's what I'm looking for," Mr. Galloway said, more to himself than to any of us. He folded the thin stack into thirds and tucked the papers into a pocket of his suit jacket. "Come along, ladies. You're going to be stuck with me as your tour guide, but we can't remain long. Since Josef isn't here, I want to return to my office and complete some unfinished tasks." Mr. Galloway looked at the sturdy worker. "Tell Josef I'll stop to see him on my way home this evening."

The man nodded. "I'll be sure and do that. And I can show the ladies around, if you like."

"Thanks, Ed, but I'm sure you have work that requires your expert attention." Once the worker headed down the hallway, Mr. Galloway edged around the desk and motioned us toward the door. "If you ladies are ready, we'll begin our tour."

Augusta lifted her nose in the air and sniffed. "What is that awful odor?"

"I think that's the glue you smell," her father replied.

My excitement mounted and I came alongside Mr. Galloway. "They create the carousel animals in pieces and then glue them together?"

He gave an appreciative nod. "You're beginning to understand. The head and neck are carved from a large piece of wood by one of the master carvers." He pointed toward a pile of legs and tails surrounding one of the worktables. "The legs and tails are carved separately by journeymen carvers. The apprentices form the body by gluing pieces of lumber into a big box with a hole in the center." He pointed to pieces of wood held by the metal clamps. "The glue must be perfectly dry before the pieces can be sanded and readied for carving of the body. When all of the pieces of the animal have been carved, they're assembled with wooden dowels and more of that hot glue that caused Augusta to wrinkle her nose." Mr. Galloway grinned at his daughter. "Once the horse is assembled, the master carver adjusts the neck and mane to the body with some final carving techniques."

"I don't know why the glue stinks. Are you certain it isn't something else?" Augusta asked.

Her father chuckled. "The glue is made from animal hides. We have to keep it heated at all times or it won't secure the wood. After a while you don't notice the smell."

"I don't believe that for a minute. Do you, Carrie?"

"Hmm? What did you say?"

Augusta gave a dismissive wave of her hand. "You're daydreaming again."

"No, it's just that there's so much to see. I don't want to miss anything."

The room was alive with the sounds of men's voices, the thuds of mallets striking wood, and the clank of metal clamps being lifted to hold the pieces of wood in place. Men wearing heavy canvas aprons stood at large workbenches fashioned from heavy planks held aloft by thick slanted legs. It appeared the tables had been proportioned at varying heights depending on the size of each man. They were carving on the large chunks of glued-together wood, shaping horses' heads or bodies. Tails, both carved and horsehair, rested on benches across the room. Heads in varying degrees of completion sat on the floor awaiting the carver's finishing touches.

Carving tools of every shape and size hung in individual racks beside each carver's station. Sunlight danced off the gleaming blades.

I hurried forward and came alongside Mr. Galloway. "Carving requires many more tools than I expected."

He stopped and waved me toward one of the older men. "This is Mr. DiVito, one of our master carvers. Miss Brouwer was admiring your carving tools, Gus."

The older man gave a curt nod. "Is not all I have." He pointed to a wooden tool chest beneath his bench. "All mine — nearly one hundred. Took me a lot of years to buy them. A workman is only as good as the tools he owns."

I nodded and smiled at him. I'd heard my father say the same about his paintbrushes.

Observing the various stages, from simple pieces of poplar and basswood to beautifully embellished horses, amazed me. With each strike of a mallet, the steel-bladed chisels and gouges cut into the wood, defining or intensifying the features. The workers glanced away from their work only long enough to nod at Mr. Galloway.

I grasped Mr. Galloway's sleeve as we approached a giraffe that was nearing completion. "What a magnificent animal. Such beauty."

"He's our first. Josef's design." There was a hint of pride in Mr. Galloway's voice. "Children will beg to ride on that giraffe, but I want to make sure this first one is just right. We need the painting to be as perfect as Josef's carving."

I stretched my neck, hoping to capture a glimpse of the painters at work. "Where do you paint the horses? I don't see any signs of painting."

"Ah, we do all the painting in a large room at the rear of the building. We don't want wood shavings or dust in the same room where we have wet paint. We'd end up with ruined finishes." He grasped his watch chain and removed the pocket watch from his vest. "I believe we're going to have to call our tour to halt, ladies. We can return another day if you'd like, so you can see the rest of the factory." His lips lifted into a crooked smile, and he wrapped Augusta's shoulder in a fatherly hug. "I can guess what *your* answer will be."

Augusta laughed along with him. An unexpected pang of jealousy attacked me, and for a moment I wanted to jump between them and share her father's affection. We'd neared the door when one of the workers called out to Mr. Galloway. He was waving a paper in his hand. He raced toward us and came to an abrupt halt directly in front of us.

"Josef said to give you this if you stopped by, but nobody told me you were here."

"Thank you, Franklin. I'm glad you caught me. We were just leaving."

Franklin thrust the folded note at Mr. Galloway. "I doubt you'll be pleased with the news." Without further comment, he performed a perfect about-face and marched off.

I didn't know which I wanted to do more: remain and tour the paint shop or hear the letter's mysterious content. I didn't do either — at least not then.

CHAPTER 4

When we sat down to supper that evening, it appeared as if Mr. and Mrs. Galloway had exchanged personalities. In an animated and convivial manner, Mrs. Galloway entertained us with news of the friends she'd visited in Fair Oaks earlier in the day, while Mr. Galloway remained silent and downcast.

Once the platters and bowls had circled the table, Mrs. Galloway tapped her finger on the edge of the table. "Did you hear what I said, Howard?"

He looked up from his plate and blinked his eyes in rapid succession. "I'm afraid I wasn't listening." The moment he made the admission, his neck disappeared beneath his shirt collar like a turtle retreating into its shell.

Given his wife's usual temperament, I understood the desire to become invisible. But tonight it seemed nothing would annoy

Mrs. Galloway. Even in light of her husband's admission, her spirits soared. "I said that Laura Wentworth has agreed to host our housewarming party if our house isn't completed in time. Although it would be highly unusual to host a housewarming at someone else's home, it gives me an excellent option, since the invitations have already gone out."

Augusta picked up a roll and broke off a tiny piece. With painstaking care, she buttered the portion. "But won't the guests go to the wrong house?" She popped the piece of bread into her mouth.

If my foot would have reached far enough, I would have kicked Augusta beneath the table. The question would likely send Mrs. Galloway into her typical querulous state. I held my breath and waited for the response.

"We've already decided upon a solution. Since their home is only a short distance away, I'll have Thomas stand at the end of our driveway and direct the guests to the Wentworths' home." She placed her open palm across her heart. "Leave it to Laura to come up with a brilliant solution. Isn't it perfect?"

I kept my eyes trained on Augusta to make certain she joined in as I bobbed my head. If she showed any sign of disagreement, I would slide down in my chair until I could land a well-placed kick on her shin. Fortunately, Augusta nodded her agreement.

"A wonderful idea, Mother. Who knows — you and Mrs. Wentworth may set a new precedent for future housewarming parties in Fair Oaks."

Mrs. Galloway preened at the possibility. "You may be right, Augusta. What do you think, Howard?"

"Whatever you decide is fine, my dear."

Mrs. Galloway's lips tightened. "What is wrong with you this evening, Howard? Are you ill? You haven't touched your supper."

"I'm fine." As if to disprove his wife's observation, Mr. Galloway took a bite of his green beans.

"You are *not* fine. Something is wrong." She pinned her husband with an impatient stare. "I want to know what is bothering you."

Mr. Galloway leaned heavily into his chair. "The day has been difficult. Each time I think I'm making progress with the carousel factory, I'm besieged with another problem."

"Such as?" Mrs. Galloway raised a perfectly arched eyebrow.

"We're behind schedule. I hired an additional carver two months ago thinking my problems would be solved, but since his arrival, our orders have continued to mount. Word has spread, and it seems everyone wants our horses."

Mrs. Galloway cut a piece of roasted chicken. "I would think you'd be pleased."

"I am, but it creates even more of a backlog. Today I discovered we'd received a shipment of pine. We can't use soft wood. We'll lose additional days while we wait on the shipment of basswood." Mr. Galloway patted the pocket where he'd placed the letter earlier in the afternoon. "Then I received a resignation from my finest painter. He's returning to Germany to be with his ailing parents." He sighed. "I understand his need to go home, but . . ."

Mrs. Galloway brightened, probably pleased that the bad news had nothing to do with her new house in Fair Oaks. "I'm certain you'll be back on schedule before the end of the week."

Mr. Galloway sighed and speared another green bean while Mrs. Galloway prattled on and on about plans for the housewarming party and how happy she'd be once they moved to Fair Oaks. It was as though her husband hadn't aired his difficulties. When she finally took a bite of dessert, I seized my opportunity. "I believe I can help you with one of your problems, Mr. Galloway."

From the weary look on his face, I could see he'd prefer peace and quiet, but I couldn't oblige. I might not have another chance to propose my idea — at least not in these surroundings. In order to meet with success, I would need Mrs. Galloway. The fact that I wanted Augusta's mother as an ally nearly sent me into a fit of giggles, but I pinched my arm until pain replaced any urge to laugh.

When her husband didn't respond, Mrs. Galloway scooted forward on her chair. "How could *you* help solve a business problem?"

I was being put in my place, and for a moment I wanted to retaliate. But if I was to win this battle, I would need Mrs. Galloway. "I would like you to employ me to paint your carousel horses."

Mrs. Galloway held two fingers against her mouth as if contemplating her husband's response. Her eyes glistened with expectation. In that moment I knew she'd become an unwitting ally.

"That's the most ridiculous suggestion I've ever heard!" Cheeks flushed, Augusta slapped her linen napkin onto the table.

I'd expected such a reaction from Mr. Galloway, but not from my friend. Earlier in the afternoon we had spoken of my need to find a job and move elsewhere. She'd even acknowledged her mother wasn't keen on my presence in their home. Though I hadn't mentioned working at the carousel factory, Augusta had agreed to help me seek work. Now, with a possibility in the offing, I had witnessed her startling betrayal.

I flashed a quick look in her direction before turning toward Mr. Galloway. He tipped his head. His tolerant smile made me feel like a little girl who had announced her wish to become a princess. But this wasn't a fairy tale, and I wasn't a little girl. I had to convince him that I could provide an excellent solution to at least one of his problems.

"Before you make up your mind, let me point out that I have excellent skills, and I believe my painting would create an even greater demand for your horses. I know you'll be pleased with my work." A weight settled on my chest while I awaited Mr. Galloway's response.

"I don't doubt what you've said, but there aren't any women working in the factory. I don't believe it would be suitable," he said.

"You're exactly right, Father. It would be more appropriate for Carrington to paint portraits and still lifes. We could help her arrange a showing of her work."

"I don't have any work to exhibit, Augusta. And preparing for an exhibit would take years." Though I'd exaggerated my timeline, I hoped to elicit a response from Mrs. Galloway. I didn't have to wait long.

The older woman shifted in her chair and tapped a fingertip on the table. "Carrington has a valid point regarding an exhibit. As for the portrait idea, perhaps some of our friends might step forward and engage her services, but the income wouldn't be dependable. From what Carrington has told us, there are many starving artists — even in Paris."

The woman was cruel! If I hadn't needed her help to promote my cause, I would have responded in kind. "Then you agree that your husband should offer me the position?"

"I don't generally interfere in Howard's business decisions, but your suggestion does have merit. It appears that both of you would benefit."

"Mother! You can't be serious. I cannot believe what I'm hearing. Did you hear Father? He said no other women work there."

Mrs. Galloway shrugged. "Someone must be first. Isn't that right, Carrington?"

"Oui. Yes. And I'm willing to be that person." I turned to Mr. Galloway. "I hope you'll listen to your wife and give me an opportunity. You won't regret hiring me."

I could see the indecision in his eyes. "I don't want to create problems at the factory, but —"

"Orders need to be completed, Howard. Isn't that what you said? Carrington can help meet that goal. You don't have any other qualified painters begging for work, do you?"

Mrs. Galloway had plowed over Augusta's objections and taken up my cause with a fervor that could have matched Elizabeth Cady Stanton's arguing for women's rights. Mr. Galloway glanced first at his wife and then at his daughter. His brows knit together, and his eyes shone with concern. It was obvious he didn't want to choose sides.

I leaned forward, silently imploring Augusta to look at me. "You know I must go to work as soon as possible," I whispered.

"I know. Silly me. I had hoped you could live with us, and our friendship would continue to grow." A haunting ache lingered in her words.

"Our friendship won't end because I live somewhere else." I straightened in my chair and forced a smile. "Besides, you'll soon be engaged and marry some eligible bachelor. Then what will I do?"

Augusta shook her head. "I don't think that's going to happen in the near future."

Mrs. Galloway clucked her tongue. "You've received several invitations to attend parties in the coming months. If you'd put Mrs. Higgenbrook's etiquette and dance classes to use and quit hiding behind the potted plants the minute you arrive at a party, we'd already be fitting you for a wedding gown."

Augusta splotched pink from bodice to hairline. "Mother! Do cease such talk."

"I'm only saying . . ."

Mr. Galloway cleared his throat. "It seems we've strayed from our initial discussion. From what Augusta has told me about your painting ability, I'm certain you would bring a great talent to the carousel factory. And I can see this as an answer to my dilemma."

"Of course you can. I told you —"

He waved his wife into silence. "However, I do worry about a young woman surrounded by workingmen. They are good men, but at times their language and behavior can be offensive." Mr. Galloway rubbed his jaw and appeared to ponder the idea. "I doubt they would change because a woman is in the vicinity. If you object, it could create animosity, and they might retaliate or quit."

I held my breath and waited for him to continue.

Finally he dropped his palm atop the table and looked at me. "You're hired."

Two simple words, but they were the ones I needed to hear. The words that would change my future. The words that would give me the ability to live under another roof. I didn't know who was happier: me or Mrs. Galloway.

"When can I begin?"

"Why don't we wait until Monday. That way Augusta will have a couple more days to visit with you." He appeared relieved when there was no objection.

Mrs. Galloway stirred a spoonful of sugar into her coffee. "We can make a carriage available so you can locate a place to live. And we'd be pleased to pay your rent for the first few weeks, wouldn't we, Howard?"

"Yes, of course. But she could also live here until she's comfortable living alone in the city. And what if the job doesn't prove to be what she expects? She'd need to return here. It seems to make more sense to hold off on any move."

I held up my hand in protest. "I know I'm going to be very happy working at the factory. You need not worry about me." I inhaled a quick gulp of air before continuing my argument. "If I could navigate the streets of Paris, I'm certain I can find my way around Collinsford."

His nod was barely noticeable, a mere dip of his chin. "You and Augusta can search for your new living accommodations. When you find a place, Thomas can deliver your baggage while you're at work."

"You're very kind," I said.

"In the meantime, the two of you should enjoy yourselves." He turned toward me. "You'll wish you had this freedom once you've been working for a few weeks."

The following morning I donned a navy blue skirt and white blouse. After securing my straw hat in place, I took one final look in the mirror. "Proper attire for seeking an apartment," I muttered to my reflection before exiting the room.

One glimpse of Augusta's soft green day dress and feather-bedecked hat and I questioned my choice of attire. There was no time to change, and even if there had been, nothing in my trunks would suit any better. Last year we had walked the streets of Paris clad in our incompatible clothes: Augusta wearing the latest fashion while I walked alongside clothed like a scullery maid. Even though she'd constantly pleaded to purchase clothes for me, I'd accepted only one time. Father had scolded me severely, but he'd gone the next day and purchased fabric for two new skirts.

Augusta and her mother bid me good morning when I sat down at the breakfast table. Thereafter, except for Mrs. Galloway's occasional remarks, we ate our breakfast in silence. I suspected Augusta wanted to make sure I knew she was still unhappy with my decision. Once she'd eaten the last bite of her toast and sipped the remains of her tea, I pushed away from the table. "Shall we go?"

A curt nod was her only response. She remained aloof as we walked to the carriage. Thomas shifted his weight from one foot to the other while he awaited direction, but Augusta stared silently into the distance.

"Take us to the area surrounding the carousel factory, Thomas. If you see any signs for a boardinghouse in the vicinity, please stop," I directed.

He tipped his gardener's cap. "Yes, miss," he said before helping us into the carriage.

During the drive, I did my best to draw Augusta into conversation. With each attempt, she refused to give me any more than a nod or curt response. Finally I scooted forward and clasped her hand. "I know you're angry. You don't hide your feelings very well." I tried to sound cheerful. "Surely you agree that there is no other choice for me."

Augusta's fingers relaxed within my grip, and her angry eyes softened. "I know. But it doesn't make me happy."

The tightness in my stomach gently eased. "The only thing that will change is my address. We will always be dear friends, and if your mother doesn't object, you can come visit me."

"And you can come visit me, as well. I'm going to hold you to your promise to attend the housewarming party. Ronald will be home from college, and he's bringing his friend Tyson along."

"Tyson? The fellow you talked about when you were in Paris?"

Color flooded Augusta's cheeks, and I knew I'd remembered correctly.

"No matter what I've said about him in the past, he truly is a nice enough fellow. And Mother approves of him. The Farnsworths live in New York City, and their family is on the social register."

I should have known the social register would be enough of a draw to garner Mrs.

Galloway's approval when selecting a suitor for her daughter. Then again, who was I to judge? I had no expertise in such matters.

Still, I did recall a number of comments Augusta had made about Tyson while living in Paris. Comments about his boorish and ungentlemanly behavior. On several occasions he'd treated her with little respect, canceling their plans to go off with another woman. I couldn't understand her interest in this man, but she seemed willing to forgive and forget. I wouldn't question her decision, but it didn't mean I approved. "Then you should have a wonderful time at the party."

Even my lackluster tone didn't dampen her enthusiasm. She clapped her hands and bounced forward on the carriage seat. "Only if you promise to come. I'll ask Ronald to act as your escort, and I have a dress you can alter and wear. I'll pack it in your trunk."

Augusta flashed me a smile that said she'd resolved any possible reason for my refusal. Now that her mood had lightened, I didn't want her spirits to plummet. When the carriage jerked to a halt, I offered a silent prayer of thanks that I could defer my answer until another time.

"This looks promising," I called to

Thomas. The gardener-turned-driver hurried to the side of the carriage and pulled open the door. I squinted at the posting on the front railing of the clapboard house. The signage didn't reflect whether there were any vacancies.

Augusta and Thomas agreed to wait at the carriage while I questioned the owner. My inquiry didn't take long. The housekeeper informed me they had no openings. "We've a waiting list as long as my arm. It's the fine cooking. The men are willin' to pay extra to live here," she proudly added.

"Could you tell me where I might find a room for rent?"

She balanced a broom against the doorjamb and propped a hand on her hip. Straining to one side, she peered across the street. "Around here?"

I could hear the misgiving in her voice. Why would someone with a fine carriage and driver be seeking a room in the factory district? "Someplace within walking distance of the carousel factory," I said.

"You'll not find much of anything open. The workers from the factories hereabouts fill 'em up as quick as they empty." She hesitated. " 'Cept for Minnie Wilson's place. She's always got empty rooms." The woman's lips curled in disgust. "Horrid food.

The woman can't boil a potato that's fit to eat. Her boarders stay only until they can find themselves someplace else to live."

After I'd secured Mrs. Wilson's address, I thanked the woman and turned to leave.

"If you rent a room at Minnie's, you better come back tomorrow and get your name on our waiting list," she called after me.

I waved and thanked her again, envisioning the horror awaiting me at Minnie Wilson's boardinghouse.

CHAPTER 5

The carriage stopped in front of a tidy white frame house. Flower boxes punctuated the wide windows, and a thick wood railing fronted the broad porch. My fear diminished a tad. A sign hung from the porch railing and announced in bold black lettering that we'd arrived at Wilsons' Boardinghouse. Directly beneath the boardinghouse name, the word Vacancy had been painted on a removable piece of wood that teetered back and forth in the breeze.

"Here we are. Would you like to come with me?" I glanced over my shoulder at Augusta.

She agreed, but if she felt any jubilation at my find, she kept it well hidden. "I don't think this is a good location. These houses are occupied by factory workers. You won't be safe here."

I looped arms with Augusta. "You forget that I'm a factory worker, too. Trust me. I'll be fine. Now let's see what Mrs. Wilson has to offer."

Augusta tugged on my arm after I'd knocked on the front door. "What is that terrible smell? It's as vile as that awful glue in the carousel factory." She wrinkled her nose and looked over her shoulder. "Do you think it's coming from one of the factories? You'll never be able to tolerate it." She clasped a hand to her bodice. "And you'll be forced to keep your windows closed in the heat of summer. How will you survive?"

Just then the front door popped open. There was no doubt the smell was coming from inside the snug dwelling. An apple-cheeked woman, nearly as broad as she was tall, greeted us with a smile that matched her size. She seemed oblivious to the odor.

"How can I help you two young ladies?" She stepped to the side and waved us forward. "Come in, come in."

I ignored Augusta's frown and proceeded across the threshold. "You can wait in the carriage if you prefer," I whispered over my shoulder.

Augusta shook her head and remained close on my heels as Mrs. Wilson led us into the parlor. While I explained my situation to Mrs. Wilson, I heard Augusta inhale a huge gulp of air. A minute or two later, a loud whoosh escaped her lips. Both Mrs. Wilson and I turned to stare.

"Breathing through the mouth in large gulps helps to clear the lungs of impurities," Augusta said.

I couldn't believe she managed to keep a straight face.

"I've never heard that before," Mrs. Wilson said. "But I'm always willing to try something new." She sucked in a mouthful of air and clamped her lips together in a tight fold. Her face soon turned the shade of a ripe persimmon. I was thankful when she clasped a hand to her chest and exhaled a gush of air. "I do believe you're right. This deep breathing *is* cleansing."

Without warning an irrepressible giggle hit the back of my throat. I turned toward the door, covered my mouth with one hand, and feigned a cough. I swallowed hard and forced myself to regain control. "May I see the room, Mrs. Wilson?"

"Silly me. Of course." She waved me toward the hallway. "I hope the smell in here isn't too bad. I tried my hand at frying cabbage a little while ago. It was a complete disaster."

I offered what I hoped was a sympathetic nod. Yet why anyone would even want to fry cabbage was beyond my comprehension. I hoped if I moved in, Mrs. Wilson would give up on the idea of cooking that particular dish.

"Cabbage isn't as easy to cook as you might think," she continued. "I burned my first attempt, but I had another head of cabbage, so I boiled that one." She stopped at the bottom of the steps. "The pot boiled dry on my second attempt, so that head got a little crispy on the bottom. Maybe the crispy part will taste like fried cabbage."

There was a lilt to her voice, and it was clear Mrs. Wilson believed she'd achieved a level of success. My giggle returned full force. I clamped my lips together and pinched my nose between my thumb and forefinger. The technique stifled any laughter and also eliminated any odor of burned cabbage, but I'd soon need to breathe.

"There's an empty room on this floor, but you'd have to share the bathroom with my two gentlemen boarders. If you don't mind another flight of steps, there's no one else on the third floor, and you could have a bathroom for yourself."

A bathroom! I couldn't believe my good fortune. "I'd prefer the third floor." I reached behind me and squeezed Augusta's hand. "I'm surprised to learn you have indoor plumbing." For a bathroom all to myself, I would have danced up the remaining flight of stairs. Besides, I'd be even farther away from the odors emanating from the kitchen.

Mrs. Wilson stopped at the end of the hall and leaned on the banister leading to the next floor. "My Herman, God rest his soul, thought bathrooms would be the answer to renting every room in our boardinghouse." She clucked her tongue against the roof of her mouth. "As you can see, he was wrong. Not to say Herman didn't mean well, but I still haven't made back what it cost. And he's been dead more than three years now." She clung to the railing and hiked herself up several steps. "Three years. Doesn't seem possible."

A stitch of guilt niggled at my conscience for taking such pleasure in Mrs. Wilson's bad fortune. I salved my conscience with the knowledge that my rent money would help pay for the bathroom.

We stopped in front of a third-floor door that had been painted to match the white woodwork. A tiny brass frame had been nailed to the door. Inside was a card with the room number and a line for the occupant's name. Mrs. Wilson withdrew a ring of keys from her apron pocket. She pushed the keys around the metal loop until she met with success.

"Here it is," she said, her blue eyes twinkling. She shoved the key into the lock, turned the knob, and pushed open the door. "You can see what you think. It'll be a little musty from being closed up for so long. If you decide you want it, I'll air it out before you move in." Mrs. Wilson stepped back and rested her arms across her broad waist.

Augusta followed me inside. The room was bigger than I'd expected. A large wardrobe sat opposite the bed, and what appeared to be a comfortable chair was positioned near one window. It was a corner room and would provide good light. Although a desk would be nice, there wasn't adequate space.

Augusta crooked her finger and I crossed the room. "You're going to rent it, aren't you?" she whispered.

I nodded. "I'll have my own bathroom," I said, keeping my voice low.

"Unless someone else moves into the other room. Besides, Mrs. Wilson can't cook. You'll starve to death," she hissed.

"It's a lovely room, don't you think, Augusta?" I asked in my normal tone.

Mrs. Wilson stepped forward, her large form filling the doorframe. "I'm glad you like it. It would be wonderful to have another woman in the house. The men are nice, but they tend to talk about work all the time."

"And I surmise you'd like someone who's able to discuss the finer points of food preparation and such," Augusta said, a half smile lurking behind her cheeky remark.

"Exactly," Mrs. Wilson said. She pointed to the brass frame on the door. "Shall I write your name on the card, Miss Brouwer?"

"Oui, please do."

"Are you French?" Mrs. Wilson beamed. "I've never met a person from France before."

"I'm sorry to disappoint you, Mrs. Wilson, but I'm not French. I lived in France for a number of years."

I ignored Augusta's grunt of displeasure as she edged her way past me. "I think you'll be sorry," she whispered. Giving Mrs. Wilson a look that said *You need to move,* she strode toward the door. "I'm going outside for some fresh air. I'll wait for you on the porch."

If Augusta's comment had embarrassed Mrs. Wilson, she gave no indication. But she did remove a limp handkerchief from her pocket and fan the air. "It *is* a bit warm up here, isn't it? The third floor always seems a tad warmer. Heat rises — that's what my Herman, God rest his soul, always said."

I nodded in agreement. Partly because I had learned long ago that heat rises and partly because, after three long years, Herman Wilson's soul needed to be put to rest — just in case God hadn't already seen to the task.

Using the pad of her index finger, Mrs. Wilson prodded the identification card out of the brass frame. "I'll print your name on the card before you move in."

I held on to the banister and clattered down the steps, feeling quite pleased with myself. I'd set aside my fears, obtained a job, and rented a place to live. I was certain I'd made the correct decision. By the time I bid Mrs. Wilson good-bye, the tightness in my stomach had completely disappeared. Now if only the smell of burned cabbage could do the same.

The mood at supper was a mixture of sorrow and joy: Augusta's disappointment was offset by Mrs. Galloway's exhilaration. Throughout the meal, Mr. Galloway did his best to maintain a degree of loyalty to both wife and daughter. I didn't think he was managing to please either one. Augusta attributed her bad humor to my looming departure. Mrs. Galloway credited her jubilant demeanor to an invitation to join the Fair Oaks ladies for tea next week. There was no way to know if Mrs. Galloway's explanation was true, but I had my doubts.

A lull settled over the table, and I decided to use the time to advantage. "There is one hurdle remaining before I can move." I hoped Mrs. Galloway would rise to the bait.

My anticipation intensified when her lips drooped into her now familiar frown. "And what might that be?" The sparkle had disappeared from her eyes.

"My paintings that you've so graciously stored beneath the stairs. I can't possibly leave them here indefinitely, yet there's insufficient space in my room." I looked at Augusta for confirmation of my dilemma.

A bob of her head caused wisps of auburn hair to dance across her forehead. "And that's *another* reason why you should stay here until you can find a place that's more suitable. There's plenty of time. We won't be —"

"Your paintings won't present any problem at all. You can arrange to have the crate stored at the factory. They'll be safe from the weather, and there's more than adequate space, isn't there, Howard? Since you'll be working at the factory, it's a perfect solution."

When he didn't immediately respond, she pinned her husband with an icy stare. "Well? Isn't it, Howard?"

His wife's voice had risen an octave or two, but Mr. Galloway appeared unperturbed when he glanced in her direction. "I was waiting to make certain it was time to speak."

The frown lines surrounding Mrs. Galloway's mouth deepened, and she expelled a loud sigh. "Please. Speak." She folded her arms across her waist and jutted her clenched jaw.

"I will locate a place to store your crate the next time I visit the factory. Until then, we'll keep the paintings stored beneath the stairs."

Before anything further could be said, Mrs. Galloway recaptured control of the conversation. "There. You see? Your problem has been solved. And you need to give Mr. Galloway the address of your boardinghouse so he can stop and pay your rent for several weeks." Her convivial temperament had returned.

"Thank you so much, Mr. and Mrs. Galloway. I believe I can manage to pay the rent, but I appreciate —"

"We won't hear of it, will we, Howard?"

"My wife said we won't hear of it, and that means we won't hear of it. You can tell —" he hesitated a moment — "Mrs. Wilson, wasn't it?" He arched his brows, and I nodded. "Tell Mrs. Wilson that I'll stop by the first of the week."

"Thank you," I said.

A stitch of guilt assaulted me. Even though I remembered Mr. Galloway's earlier offer to pay my rent — after all, who could forget such a thing — I had never intended to accept.

When I'd tossed my bait into Mrs. Galloway's pool of solutions, I had only wanted a place to store Papa's paintings. But I'd hooked much more. At the moment I didn't feel particularly proud of myself. If Mama were alive, she'd give me a sound scolding. For the remainder of the meal, I didn't say a word.

Mrs. Galloway excused us from the table and then announced we would spend the evening going through Augusta's old clothes. "I know there are many items that she hasn't worn for more than a year, and you can make good use of them." She waved Augusta and me toward the staircase. "This way, you won't need to spend your wages on clothes and such. You'll want to save as much as possible so that you won't be dependent upon others for help in the future."

Mrs. Galloway hadn't laid a hand on me, yet the sting of her words hit like a sharp slap — the impact so painful I touched outstretched fingers to my cheek. The biting remark had effectively shredded any remnant of my earlier guilt.

The older woman yanked dresses and skirts from a closet — this was the first house I'd ever seen with one of those — and Augusta rifled through a chest of drawers in search of stockings, nightgowns, and unmentionables. While I remained framed in the doorway, clothing flew toward the bed like a volley of badminton birdies.

By the time they'd completed the task, mounds of clothing adorned the bed. I stared at the heaping array. "You can't possibly have anything left in your closet. Please, put it back. I don't need all of this." I took a tentative step into the room and spread my arm in a sweeping gesture. "There isn't space in my room for all of this."

"With a bit of organization, I'm sure you can make space." Mrs. Galloway smiled at me, but there was no warmth behind it. "I know you didn't have a mother to teach you manners, Carrington, but rebuffing those who offer help isn't considered proper etiquette."

My embarrassment was now complete. Flashes of burning anger and humiliation seared me. Beneath my pale skin, heat flooded my cheeks in unrelenting waves. I hoped my eyes reflected the plea for help that lodged in my throat. And that Augusta would notice.

"I'm sure you're weary after your long day, Mother. I'll help Carrie fold and pack these things. As I recall, you and Father were invited next door for a visit with Mr. and Mrs. Barton this evening. I'm sure Father would like to spend the evening in your company."

I couldn't imagine why Mr. Galloway would ever want to be around his wife, but I was thankful for Augusta's suggestion — and even more thankful when her mother agreed.

"I'll send Thomas to retrieve one of the trunks from the cellar, and you two can pack the clothing in there." After one final inspection of the stacked garments, her cold eyes settled on me. "If nothing else, you'll be better dressed than any other woman in The Bottoms."

Once Mrs. Galloway cleared the hallway, I

leaned across the mound of nightgowns. "What's The Bottoms?"

"Ignore my mother. She judges people based upon where they live. That's why she's so anxious to move into our new house. She badgered Father until he agreed to build the house in Fair Oaks."

Poor Mr. Galloway. I could only imagine what he must have endured. "The Bottoms is where I'll be living — where the factories are located. Am I right?"

"Yes." Augusta's eyes dimmed. "Are you sorry you came here?"

"No, of course not. Your father is giving me a wonderful opportunity. I believe I'll take great satisfaction in painting the carousel animals. And if I'm given an occasional opportunity to paint a portrait, that will be a good thing, too."

Thomas arrived outside the bedroom door and waited until Augusta motioned him inside. "You can put the trunk beside the dresser, Thomas." She thanked him and then waited until he was out of earshot. "It's my hope that word of your talent will spread and you won't be in the factory for long. I don't want to sound like my mother, but I shiver at the thought of you working among all of those unrefined men."

Scooping up an armful of nightgowns, I

dropped them into the trunk. "You forget that I am not the daughter of wealthy parents. For years, my father was a simple farmer who painted when time permitted. Once we were in Paris, he no longer farmed, but he wasn't a man of wealth or education."

"But his reputation among well-known artists gave him a position of honor."

I snorted. A most unladylike reaction, yet the notion that my father held a position of honor required a snort. Yes, my father's talent was admired by his peers and members of the art community, but he hadn't achieved a position of honor. He wouldn't have been teaching unexceptional art students if he'd been esteemed by Parisian society. Yet I would never say such a thing to Augusta. Besides, I would have had to interrupt her prolonged criticism of my unladylike snort.

Instead, I retrieved a dress the shade of ripe cranberries from the heaping pile on the bed. "Will this be acceptable for church services tomorrow morning?" I held it close to my body, enjoying the feel of the cool, slick silk against my outstretched hand.

"Yes, of course. Let me look in the closet. I have a hat with ribbons that are a perfect match." Before I could object, she ducked into the depths of the closet. I couldn't understand her muffled remarks, but moments later she backed out of the small space. With a triumphant glint in her eyes, she held the hat aloft. "I told you. It's perfect." She thrust a sand-colored hat adorned with cranberry taffeta in my direction. "Here. Try it on."

I didn't object, for it was evident I would meet with little success. I snugged the hat onto my head and jabbed a pin through the woven, pale yellow straw. When I turned to receive Augusta's appraisal, she waved me to the hallway.

"Hurry, there's someone downstairs."

"But . . ." I pointed to the hat.

"Come on!" she urged.

At any moment I expected her to bounce up and down and yank me along by the arm. "What's the hurry? Won't Frances answer the door?"

I was only a few steps behind her when we arrived at the top of the staircase. At that very spot, without the least bit of warning, Augusta came to an abrupt halt. Unable to slow my momentum, I plowed into her backside and sent her plummeting like a sack of potatoes. The spectacle was not pretty. Arms akimbo, she slid and toppled. *Thud. Thud. Thud.* With each strike, her petticoats, pantaloons, or stockings came into full view.

She landed with her body turned toward the spindled banister, her face hidden from view. Terror clutched my throat. My breathing turned shallow and I forced myself to inhale. What if she'd broken an arm? What if I'd knocked her unconscious? *What if she's dead?* I clattered down the steps and dropped beside Augusta. I slapped my palm across my mouth to hold back the sound of a dreaded giggle.

When I was certain any threat of laughter was under control, I leaned close and whispered her name. Ever so slowly she turned to face me. A hint of purplish blue tinged her prominent cheekbones, but she was alive. Relief flooded over me like a cleansing rain, and I exhaled a deep breath. "Is anything broken?"

"I don't think so." She struggled to free one arm from between the spindles and righted herself. Before we could further assess her injuries, we both turned toward the sound of a man's laughter and light applause.

"A fine entrance, Augusta. I do hope this was a practice session for your performance at the Midland Theater."

I had no idea who this man was, but I wanted to throttle him!

CHAPTER 6

I couldn't believe my ears. I thought I'd heard Augusta say the name Tyson.

"Tyson Farnsworth?" I turned away from the tall, broad-shouldered young man standing in the foyer and hissed my question at Augusta. She nodded up and down, but immediately touched her fingers to her head. "Your head hurts?"

"No, but you should remove your hat."

"My hat?" If the only thing concerning Augusta was the fact that I was still wearing a hat, the fall had surely affected her brain. I held three fingers up and displayed them in front of her face. "How many fingers do you see?"

"Don't be ridiculous. Five," Augusta said while she pushed my hand away.

Panic. That was the only word to describe the cold fingers that had clamped tight around my heart. I wished Tyson would step forward and take control, but when I managed a sideways glance in his direction, I knew I was on my own. He had propped himself against the wall with his arms folded across his chest. He was the boorish, ungentlemanly fellow Augusta had described to me in Paris — and more. But right now I didn't have time to deal with Tyson's lack of sensitivity.

"Look again!" I held up three fingers and waved my hand back and forth.

Augusta giggled. I could feel my panic mushroom. I was the one who laughed at inappropriate times, not Augusta. Pushing my hand closer, I looked directly into her eyes. "Tell me how many fingers!"

"Three fingers. Three this time and three the last time." She tipped her head to one side and grinned. "Had you worried, didn't I?" She clutched her arm around her waist and burst into a gale of laughter.

"That wasn't funny, Augusta!"

My emotions reeled. I didn't know whether to cry from embarrassment or join in her laughter, stalk outside or remain in her house, let relief wash over me or chastise her with harsh words. Before I could make my final decision, Augusta grasped the banister railing and attempted to stand. She groaned.

"I'm not falling for that trick again." I

looked at her and smirked.

Tyson pushed off from the wall and propelled himself toward the stairs. In three long, easy strides, he transformed into a knight in shining armor, rushing to Augusta's rescue. He bent forward, assisted her to her feet, and held her around the waist as she descended the final three steps. "Here, Augusta, let me help you into the parlor."

With her back hunched like a withered old woman, Augusta leaned heavily on Tyson's arm and hobbled past me. She reminded me of the little old ladies who shuffled through the park while clinging to their grandsons' arms.

Tyson glanced over his shoulder and shot me a look. He'd decided I was no more than an inconsiderate slug. I could read it in those icy blue eyes. How dare he? Not once had he stepped forward to help when Augusta lay sprawled on the stairs. What was he doing here, anyway? Wasn't he supposed to be at school with Augusta's brother? I clenched my jaw to hold back the angry words burning in my throat.

I marched into the parlor and faced Augusta. She was sitting on the sofa, calmly arranging the pleats in her raspberry and charcoal gray dress. While I stood waiting to unleash my frustration, she held me at bay and formally introduced Tyson Farnsworth. She didn't realize there was no need for formal introductions. The chameleon had already shown me his full array of colors.

The moment the formalities had been concluded, I did my best to interrupt Augusta. To my consternation, all attempts were squelched while she regaled Tyson with far too many details of our friendship. To the untrained observer, we would've appeared to be a convivial group enjoying an evening visit. And with the exception of Augusta's bruised eye and messy hair, she appeared the perfect hostess. But this was all a game, and I wasn't in the mood for such childishness.

When she wound down long enough for me to get a word in, I didn't hesitate. "I can see the bruise beneath your eye, but I want to know if you've suffered any other injuries, or if this was all a ploy to frighten me."

She pointed to the empty cushion on the settee. "Sit down here," she said before turning toward Tyson. "Would you be so kind as to go to the kitchen and ask Frances to fetch me a wet compress for my eye?"

"Yes, of course. Anything else? A cup of water or perhaps some tea?" The questions slipped from his tongue like warm molasses.

I thought Augusta would swoon at his sticky-sweet offer. She gazed at Tyson like an adoring schoolgirl. Granted, he did possess the piercing blue eyes she'd so often mentioned, but I also detected an icy aloofness that caused a cold chill to spiral down my spine. I wanted to nudge her from her state of silliness, but I remained silent until Tyson strode off toward the kitchen.

"What are you doing?" I hissed. "I can already see that he's counting you as his latest conquest." I wrinkled my nose in disgust. "If he'd ever harbored any doubt of your affection, your fawning behavior has erased all doubt."

With a wave of her hand, Augusta silenced me. "We don't have long until he returns. My body aches. Come morning, I imagine my back and legs will match the color beneath my eye. But I can use this to advantage. The Lilac Ball is the weekend after our housewarming. I want an invitation from Tyson."

I couldn't believe my ears. Augusta was finagling for a dance partner while I worried she'd been maimed for life. I locked my fingers together and squeezed hard, or I might have considered wrapping them around Augusta's neck.

"You're going to make a fool of yourself.

And what is he doing here, anyway?"

"I'm not certain. I think it must be providence."

She gave me one of those moony-eyed looks I'd seen earlier. If she weren't injured, I'd be tempted to shake some sense into her. "I don't like him. He has shifty eyes and a cold heart. And you've obviously forgotten we discussed him in Paris. You said he was rude and inconsiderate. I believe those are the words you used to describe him."

Augusta pulled back as though I'd landed a direct blow. "People change, you know. Besides, you don't even know him."

"I know his kind."

Augusta tipped her head and sniffed. The picture she presented reminded me of her mother, and I cringed.

"You don't know any more about men than I do. I detect a genuine change in Tyson. He's kindhearted and appealing."

At the sound of footfalls in the hallway, I leaned closer. "Don't say I didn't warn you."

Tyson strode into the room carrying a bulging linen cloth in one hand and a towel draped across his arm. He looked like a waiter preparing to serve dinner. "I had Thomas chip some small pieces of ice from the block in your icebox," he proudly announced. "I've had my share of black eyes, and ice works better than cold water. Keeps the swelling down."

I immediately surmised that any black eyes suffered by Tyson Farnsworth were due to his wretched behavior. I made a mental note to add that to the increasing list of reasons why I considered him a bad choice for Augusta. Who would want to pursue a man who boasts of black eyes and fisticuffs?

Yet even that comment didn't faze Augusta. When he applied the ice-filled cloth to her cheek, she placed her fingers over his hand and gave him a lopsided smile. My stomach clenched as I took in the scene. Something needed to be done to stop this nonsense.

"I'm sure your arm is tired, Tyson. I'll be glad to relieve you." I reached to grasp the cloth, but Augusta clasped my wrist with her free hand.

"I'm fine." Tyson glanced over Augusta's head and winked at me.

My cheeks felt as though they'd been scorched by a hot poker. The gall of this man was beyond belief. He was a dishonorable scoundrel. I glared in return and decided it was time to attack.

"What brings you to Collinsford, Tyson? I thought you and Ronald were still attending college classes."

Now it was his turn to glare at me. I offered what I hoped was a sweet yet somewhat smug smile in return while Augusta sat between us, oblivious to the silent exchanges swirling around her.

"My classes ended a full week earlier. I was going to go home, but my parents are presently traveling. Ronald convinced me I should come to Collinsford and he'll join up with me as soon as he can." Tyson bent closer to Augusta. "He did write and tell your parents I was coming, didn't he?"

Augusta's fingers tightened around Tyson's hand, and several drops of water dribbled from the tea towel. "No need for concern. My parents will be delighted you've arrived early. Mother was extremely pleased you'd be here for the housewarming."

"Does your early arrival mean you'll depart soon after the housewarming?" I asked.

Augusta pinched my arm with agonizing intensity. If I hadn't clamped my bottom lip between my teeth, I would have squealed in pain. The most I could do was force her fingers from my arm and attempt to maintain a snippet of restraint and demure composure.

He lifted his shoulders into a straight line. "I haven't decided when I'm going to leave. What about you, Miss Brouwer? Any plans for the future?"

"None that I care to discuss at present." I pointed to the dripping cloth. "Looks like the ice needs to be replaced."

My comment wasn't well received, but I didn't care. I had successfully avoided Tyson's interrogation.

Last evening, before Mr. and Mrs. Galloway returned home from their visit with the neighbors, I had retreated to my bedroom. In retrospect, it was a cowardly act. Yet I knew I couldn't bear Mrs. Galloway's scrutiny. While Augusta hadn't held me responsible for her bruises, I wasn't certain Mrs. Galloway would be so generous — especially if the bruising hadn't disappeared in time for the housewarming.

When I arrived at the breakfast table, Mrs. Galloway offered a terse greeting. I cringed when Augusta entered the room. The bruise had darkened and some of the swelling still remained. She looked like she'd been on the losing side of a tavern brawl.

Mrs. Galloway reached across to examine her eye. "You need to dust additional powder on your cheek. And take care to choose a hat with a full brim that will drop across your forehead."

I lowered my eyes and pretended to examine the pattern of the tablecloth. By tomorrow I'd be moved out. I knew the timing would please Augusta's mother even more than me. I uttered a silent thank-you when Mr. Galloway entered the dining room.

"I knocked on Tyson's door. Seems he's not feeling well and asked to be excused from church services."

A likely story. I didn't believe for a minute that Tyson was sick. However, both Augusta and her mother were overwrought with concern. I expected one or both of them to rush upstairs, sit by his bedside, and offer to hold his hand. Ridiculous. He had been perfectly fine last night. The chameleon wanted to sleep late and avoid the Sunday sermon. I would have preferred avoiding church, too, but not for the same reason.

I swallowed a forkful of scrambled eggs and envisioned my introduction to the Galloways' acquaintances: *Hello, this is Augusta's friend Carrington Brouwer, who recently returned from France. Carrington is the one responsible for those nasty bruises on Augusta's face. She pushed our dear Augusta down a flight of stairs last night.* My appetite disappeared.

I continued to chase pieces of egg around my plate until Mrs. Galloway announced we must finish up and be on our way. After I helped Augusta pat another layer of powder on her swollen cheek and choose a hat that I hoped would mask the bruise, we descended the stairs — with me in the lead. Whenever approaching a flight of stairs in the future, I resolved never again to follow behind Augusta. My father would have considered the decision silly and useless — akin to closing the barn door after the horses had escaped. That saying had been one of Papa's favorites. I felt weepy at the remembrance. Holding a fisted hand to my lips, I coughed to hold back the unbidden tears.

Because we arrived at the church somewhat late, our entrance required only one or two introductions before we arrived at the Galloways' pew. I could only hope we would escape as easily. From all appearances the added face powder and hat were working well. Augusta wasn't receiving any gaping stares, but I doubted whether anyone could gain a good view of her. She'd been squished between her mother and me.

After the Scripture reading the preacher announced his sermon topic: forgiveness. I prayed Mrs. Galloway would hearken to the preacher's words and the remainder of my time with the family would be somewhat bearable, but Tyson's presence would surely add to the awkwardness of the afternoon.

While the preacher opened his Bible and looked out over the congregation, I settled against the back of the pew and prepared for the sermon. It was sometime during the beginning of the preacher's message and the final amen that I convinced myself Tyson was primarily responsible for Augusta's fall. If he hadn't unexpectedly arrived at the front door, she wouldn't have plummeted down the stairs. In all likelihood, church wasn't the proper place to be mitigating my guilt, but it eased my conscience to assign at least a portion of the fault to him.

After church I used the ploy to advantage. When Mrs. Galloway pointed to me as the culprit responsible for Augusta's bruised face, I didn't hesitate to add Tyson's unexpected arrival into the explanation. After that, an accidental fall was the only explanation given. Mrs. Galloway didn't appear willing to assess any responsibility to Tyson.

Augusta pulled me aside while her parents visited outside the church. "Don't be offended by Mother's comments. She's embarrassed by my appearance and fears someone might believe Father inflicted my bruises."

My stomach plummeted at such a thought. "I never considered such an idea. How could anyone think your father would —"

"There's cruelty in more homes than you might believe. Even among the folks who show up at church every Sunday. Of course that's not true of my father, but Mother always believes people will think the worst." She grasped my arm, and we walked toward the carriage. "She thought I should remain at home this morning, but Father wouldn't hear of it."

Augusta released my arm and hoisted herself into the carriage. Her face had tightened into a grimace.

"You're hurting much worse than you've been letting on, aren't you?"

"I'm a little sore, but it will pass soon enough. Don't say anything to Mother. I'm hoping Tyson is feeling better and the three of us can go out for the afternoon."

The thought of spending an afternoon with Tyson held no appeal, but I didn't argue. I'd wait and see how he was faring when we got home. If Augusta's plan took shape, I'd find some way to excuse myself.

The ride home was surprisingly pleasant. The churchgoers had accepted the explanation given for Augusta's bruises, Mrs. Galloway was in good humor, and the weather was surprisingly warm for an early spring day in northern Ohio. Augusta would have added Tyson's arrival as another reason for the pleasant mood. And I suppose it was. For everyone but me.

Augusta was careful to hide any sign of pain as we walked up the steps and into the house. Frances stood in the foyer waiting to relieve us of our wraps. Augusta removed her lightweight cape and handed it to the maid. "Has Tyson come downstairs?"

Frances nodded. "He has. He said to tell you that he is feeling better."

"Where is he?" Augusta raised on tiptoe and peered down the hallway. She obviously hoped to see Tyson emerge from the dining room.

Frances scrunched her brow. "He said to tell you that he decided to return home and see his parents for a short time."

"That's it? He didn't say anything else?" Augusta's voice had taken on a shrill tone.

Frances looked toward the ceiling and tapped her index finger against her lips. "Oh. Yes. He said he'd be back in time for the housewarming."

Immediate disappointment clouded Augusta's eyes, and I squeezed her hand in a show of support. Although I had harbored no desire to spend the afternoon with Tyson, his disappearance was the cause of my friend's pain. At that moment I disliked him even more.

I couldn't help but wonder what had precipitated such a hasty departure. Not for a minute did I believe he'd gone to visit his parents. Only last evening he'd told me they were off traveling. Tyson's behavior left me to draw only one conclusion: He was up to no good.

CHAPTER 7

I would have preferred to leave the Galloways' house quietly on my own the next morning, but Augusta vehemently disagreed. She insisted upon eating breakfast with me, instructing Frances to pack a lunch for my noonday meal, and riding along in the carriage with Thomas and me. Her company would have been appreciated had she not been so gloomy.

From the time we sat down in the dining room for breakfast until I bid her good-bye at the carousel factory, Augusta lamented Tyson's departure as well as my move to The Bottoms. Had I not been resolute in my refusal, she would have followed me into the factory to watch me paint. She'd avowed her father wouldn't mind in the least. Though I didn't doubt her claim, I'd shuddered at the idea. Being the only woman in the factory would be difficult enough. But if I arrived with a friend in tow — especially when the friend's father was the owner — the workers would never accept me.

When Augusta bid me farewell, it was with a promise that she and Thomas would deliver my trunks to Wilsons' Boardinghouse before they returned home. She offered to have the driver call for me after work so that we could eat supper together at her home. I declined. The sadness in her eyes was almost enough to make me change my mind. Instead, I promised to join her another evening. Although obviously unhappy, she mumbled her agreement. Thomas had stopped the horses a short distance from the factory. I didn't want the workers to see me arrive in a fancy carriage.

Once Augusta departed, I squared my shoulders and strode toward the factory door. A stiff wind caused an unexpected chill, and I pulled my cloak tight around my neck. Had I realized what a drop in temperature the breeze would create, I'd have tucked a pair of gloves into my pocket. Bending my head against the wind, I continued onward. But the closer I got, the slower I walked. A number of men brushed past me and hurried toward the door, obviously eager for the warmth inside the factory. If I dallied much longer, I'd be late for my first day of work. So I inhaled a deep breath, forced one foot in front of the other, and pulled open the door.

I took a quick survey of my surroundings. Now that I was an employee rather than a visitor on a brief walking tour, the place looked different, although the pungent smell of glue remained. A man with graying hair and stooped shoulders stood near a desk not far from the entrance. I decided he must be Josef Kaestner. Mr. Galloway had told me Mr. Kaestner would be expecting me.

The workmen entering the factory stared at me as though I'd grown a second head. My heart slammed against my chest and hammered a reverberating beat that ascended and pulsated in my head. There really was no reason for apprehension, yet I could barely swallow as I closed the short distance to greet the older man.

"Good morning." My voice squeaked like an untrained bow being drawn across taut violin strings.

The man appraised me with wary brown eyes and a single nod of the head. "Morning."

"Mr. Kaestner?"

"Nope." He continued to sift through the papers on the desk.

"Nope?" I hadn't meant to mimic him, but his response had taken me by surprise.

He tilted his head to one side and gave me a hard look. "That's what I said. Nope." Lifting a pencil from the desk, he pointed to the area where I'd seen men carving on my previous visit. "He's back with the carvers. He expecting you?"

"Yes. Should I go back there?"

The man dropped the paper work onto the desk and shook his head. "I'll go get him. Name?"

I pointed my index finger at my chest. "My name?"

"Unless you want me to give him someone else's."

"Carrington Brouwer," I croaked. My arch enemy, the ever persistent and unmanageable giggle, rippled at the back of my throat, begging for release. I tightened my lips together and fought against the threatening laughter. For a moment I thought I might explode. It wasn't until the man turned to walk away that I released my breath. Before I could clasp my hand over my mouth, a snorting guffaw escaped.

The man stopped and looked over his shoulder. "You say something?"

I held a hand to my mouth and forced a cough into the gurgling laugh. "A tickle in my throat," I sputtered, silently condemning myself for my lack of control.

He grunted and swatted the air as if to let me know I was an unwanted irritation, a pesky fly upsetting his busy routine. The action was unnecessary: He'd already succeeded.

I drew in a deep breath of air and pursed my lips before I pushed the air from my lungs. Midbreath, my throat constricted, my stomach convulsed, and a loud hiccough escaped. *No! Not now!* Not the hiccoughs. Hadn't the giggle been enough embarrassment?

When I was a little girl, Papa had instructed me to hold my breath whenever I had the hiccoughs. The remedy had never proved particularly successful, but maybe just this once it would work. I pinched my nose together, opened my mouth, and sucked in air until I thought my lungs would explode. Another spasm hit my throat and stomach, but I continued to hold my breath. Without exhaling, I opened my mouth and forced a little more air into my lungs. Another hiccough. Still pinching my nose, I exhaled one long breath, drew in more air, and held it in my lungs. Maybe this time.

"*Gut* morning!"

The voice that boomed in my ears bore a distinct German accent. Startled, I jumped and swiveled. I didn't know who was more surprised — me or the man staring at my thumb and index finger tightly positioned on either side of my nose. Heat scalded my cheeks as I released my hold.

"Sorry I am if I gave you a scare. Mr. Morgan said you wanted to see me, *ja?*" He continued to stare at me, his brow furrowed as though he'd never before seen a woman.

I shook my head. "No. I wanted to see —" Before I could finish, a loud hiccough erupted and echoed into the cavernous room. My embarrassment was complete. I wanted to flee.

"Now I see why the nose you were holding," he said. His chocolate brown eyes twinkled with amusement. "My *mutter* always told me a good scare would frighten the hiccoughs away."

"I don't think that works, either. I was frightened when you walked up behind me, but I still have the hiccoughs." I clasped my hand over my mouth to hold back the noise of another attack. I waited a moment and then said, "I need to speak with Josef Kaestner."

He touched his index finger to his chest. "That is me. Josef Kaestner."

My remaining smidgen of self-confidence evaporated like the morning mist. "Y-y-you?" I stammered. "*You're* Mr. Kaestner?"

This man was far too young to be in charge of Mr. Galloway's factory. He appeared to be no more than five or six years older than I.

While he glanced toward the paper work in his hand, I studied him. His eyes closely matched a chocolate brown thatch of unruly hair that had been trimmed close around his ears. I didn't have to tip my head back very far to look him in the eye. He wasn't tall, but his angular features seemed to create an illusion of height. His thick fingers bore a number of nicks and scars, and his rolled-up shirtsleeves revealed muscular forearms. I did my best not to stare but found it impossible.

After dropping the papers on his desk he looked up as though he'd forgotten I was in the room. "Ja, I am Josef Kaestner." He exaggerated his mouth and pronounced the words slowly, enunciating each syllable in a loud voice. Apparently he thought I was dense or hard of hearing.

"Then you *are* expecting me. I'm the new artist." Seeing the confusion that shone in his eyes, I quickly corrected myself. "The new painter — for the carousel horses."

Mouth agape, he stared at me for what felt like five minutes or more. Though it was probably less than a minute, it seemed like forever before he pulled a slip of paper from his pocket and gave me a fleeting glance.

"*Nein.* The only painter I am to see is Mr. Brouwer."

"I'm Mr. Brouwer. I mean, I'm Carrington Brouwer, *Miss* Carrington Brouwer." Mortification rushed over me. What kind of woman agreed she was a man? Only me! My response had been as clear as a church bell tolling the hour. At least I had plowed onward without so much as a hiccough or giggle. Fear and embarrassment had combined to snuff out my normal pesky interruption, even if only for the moment.

Mr. Kaestner traced his fingers along his clean-shaven jaw and took another look at the paper. His eyes narrowed and he shook his head. "This cannot be correct. In this factory, we have only men."

I bit my tongue, for a sharp retort wouldn't serve me well. "I am a well-qualified artist, Mr. Kaestner. I'm certain you'll be pleased with my work."

"An artist?" He motioned me toward the office I'd recently visited with Mr. Galloway and pointed to a dust-covered chair. I removed my handkerchief and swiped the seat before I turned and sat down. He stood nearby with his arms folded across his broad chest. He'd been watching my every move, and his look told me I'd just made a mistake: I'd confirmed that proper women didn't belong in a dust-laden factory inhabited by men. Now I'd have to prove him wrong.

He sat down without wiping his chair. "Tell me what it is you know about this work we do."

I had to muster a large dose of inner conviction to appear unruffled. Mr. Galloway had already hired me, but it seemed I would be required to convince Mr. Kaestner of my qualifications. He jiggled his leg at a dizzying speed while I detailed my training and accomplishments.

Though it took great perseverance, I refrained from grabbing his knee and holding it in place. What would he think if I should reach forward and grasp his leg? Such improper behavior was out of the question, but I did direct a frown at the bouncing appendage several times. Mr. Kaestner seemed not to notice. I decided he must be bored with my recitation. Once I'd finished, I leaned back in the chair and met his intense brown eyes. He didn't appear particularly impressed.

"In Paris with the artists you trained and painted portraits? Nothing else?"

"And still lifes," I added. He'd obviously

worked hard to lose his German accent. For the most part he'd succeeded, but he hadn't mastered the language completely — not yet.

"And the still lifes," he repeated. His eyes registered confusion. "The portraits and still lifes we do not paint in our factory, Miss Brouwer. We paint on the wood, not canvas. In our factory there is little freedom for what I hear you artists call 'creative expression.' Here you paint what the carver makes for you." He continued to jiggle his leg. "This training of yours, it does not qualify you to paint the carousel animals. But what can I do? Mr. Galloway has already hired you."

"I beg to differ, Mr. Kaestner. I believe you will find me well qualified for any task you present."

His leg stopped the incessant bouncing. "I am a wood-carver. That does not mean I can build a house. Both use wood; both take special talent and training, ja? The two, they don't change places." He crisscrossed his fingers. "Your talent and training, they do not make you good for painting the carousel animals."

He looked at me as though his argument had won the advantage. Well, this wasn't a game of lawn tennis, and I didn't think he'd won at all. Far from it. "I suggest you set me to work, and we'll see whether I have the skills required to meet your expectations."

He pressed his palms against his thighs and pushed up from the chair. "For this, I already know the answer, Miss Brouwer. It is an experienced carousel painter I need, not a picture artist." He motioned me forward. "Come with me."

Picture artist. I wasn't a *picture artist.* I considered correcting him but knew it would serve no helpful purpose.

"First I will take you through to see the factory and how this place we operate. Then I think you will agree it is not gut for a lady to work here."

I didn't tell him I'd already been on a partial tour with Mr. Galloway. Besides, I'd seen very little on my earlier visit. Mr. Kaestner opened a door. "This is the wood mill. Where we cut and prepare the lumber," he shouted. The clattering squeal and groan of the huge overhead belt and pulley system created a deafening noise. I clapped my hands to my ears to muffle the noise.

The smell of fresh-hewn wood flooded the room, and I inhaled deeply, enjoying the reminiscent scent of childhood walks in the New Hampshire woods. Several shipments of lumber had arrived, and young men were straining under the weight of the loads they were stacking near the double doors that led outside. All of them were young and strong, and I wondered if this was the place where Mr. Kaestner had first developed his muscular arms. Across the room I recognized the older man who had greeted me upon my arrival. He was shouting orders, and I decided he must be the supervisor. The men who operated the machines appeared at least ten years older than those shouldering the lumber. Survival of the fittest, I decided. Those who survived years of lifting the heavy lumber were finally promoted to the machinery.

My shoes scrunched in the carpet of wood shavings that dusted the floor. Although the men appeared oblivious to the noise of the machinery, they'd clearly noticed me. And from their furtive glances, I knew my appearance was causing discomfort.

Once we'd exited the wood mill and Mr. Kaestner closed the door, I uncovered my ears. "The wood mill has more workers than I imagined."

"Our orders continue to increase. We now have fifty-two workers in this factory. Fifty-three if I count you."

He didn't sound thrilled to be adding me

to that number.

"Over here is the machine shop, where we make and repair the gears and other assembly parts. We hire our own mechanics, so they are all well trained. Sometimes they must travel and help assemble the carousels we ship."

"So you ship carousels from this factory?"

"Ja. Where else would we ship them from? We build the carousels, we sell the carousels, and we ship the carousels — sometimes to cities here in America, sometimes to India or Australia. Sometimes even to South Africa."

Once again he spoke in a slow and deliberate manner. Mr. Kaestner truly believed I was a complete dolt. Yet how could I fault him? My question had been ridiculous. I was astonished to learn there were orders from as far away as South Africa and India, but I didn't mention my surprise. I wasn't sure I should say anything else during my tour. Although we didn't enter the machine shop, Mr. Kaestner opened the door and gave me a brief peek. Only a few of the men looked my way — all of them frowned, and I was pleased we didn't go inside.

Mr. Kaestner pointed toward the stairs. "Upstairs, that is where we store extra animals until they are needed — we call it the holding pen. Right now we do not have many extras up there. Also upstairs is the upholstery shop, where the chariots are padded to make them more comfortable. You can see that another time. Next we will go through the carving shops, the glue shop, and the paint shop."

"Of course," I mumbled, hastening to keep pace.

"In here we have the carvers — apprentices, journeymen, and master carvers. Some do not speak English so well. Unless the men come to us with great experience, they begin as apprentice carvers."

It seemed Mr. Kaestner wasn't going to miss any opportunity to point out my lack of training to work here.

One of the young apprentices spoke to me as we entered the woodcarving shop. I smiled and acknowledged him. Then several others nodded. I hoped they would remain as friendly when they discovered I was a new employee. I had expected to spend more time in the carving shop, but Mr. Kaestner rushed me through without explanation. He didn't even hesitate in the glue shop, though I didn't mind bypassing that particular area.

When he came to a halt outside the door leading into the paint shop, he rested his hand on the doorknob. "I am puzzled. The men, some of them seemed to know you."

"I toured a portion of the factory a few days ago with Mr. Galloway and his daughter, Augusta," I said, attempting to capture a glimpse of the paint shop through the glass window. Mr. Kaestner's shoulder blocked my view.

"The Galloways, they are your friends?"

The timbre of his voice caused me to look away from the door and meet his eyes. There was little doubt he'd been taken aback by this latest revelation. And it didn't appear the news pleased him. "Augusta Galloway was my father's art student for several months."

"So that is why Mr. Galloway has given you this job. It is not because you are qualified or even suited to the work. You are here because Miss Galloway is your friend."

I wanted to argue that he had jumped to an incorrect assumption — at least partially incorrect. But from the set of his jaw, I didn't think he'd tolerate any disagreement. I held my breath and wondered if he would permit me inside the paint shop or order me off the premises. My insides churned with a desire to scream *Open that door and let me in.* Instead, I clenched my lower lip between my teeth and waited. When Mr.

Kaestner finally turned the knob and pushed open the door, I released my lip. The metallic taste on my tongue signaled I'd drawn blood. I withdrew a handkerchief from my pocket and silently chastised myself.

When we finally entered the painting room at the rear of the building, my pulse quickened. The scent of paint and varnish hung in the room like a welcoming friend.

There were prancing horses, bucking horses, standing horses, and several other animals in differing poses that were partially hidden from view. A beautiful swan chariot awaited paint, and I hoped I would be permitted to work on it. I envisioned the beauty I could add if given the opportunity. Mr. Kaestner placed his index finger and thumb inside his mouth and somehow produced a shrill whistle.

A tall man with a receding hairline popped up from between a rack of the carousel horses and waved. "Be right there!" he shouted. Moments later he loped toward us with a long-legged stride. "Sorry to keep you waitin', Josef. Needed to take care of my brush. Don't want paint dryin' in the bristles." He gave me a quick nod of acknowledgment before continuing. "Don't tell me we got more problems."

This man was obviously astute at reading Mr. Kaestner's moods.

Mr. Kaestner grunted. "This is your new painter." He gave a quick tip of his head in my direction. "Henry, meet Miss Carrington Brouwer. Miss Brouwer, this is Henry Tobarth. Mr. Tobarth supervises the paint shop. Your work he will assign, and then he will tell me if it measures up. If your work does not his approval get, then you must move to the other room, sand down the animal, and start over."

Although I wasn't entirely sure what it meant to sand down and start over, I knew I could do it. But from the look on Mr. Tobarth's face, he didn't possess that same confidence. He appeared either confused or disgusted; I wasn't certain which. His smile had disappeared, and his forehead was lined with more creases than a pleated ruffle.

"Whoa! Hold up here. I ain't so sure I understand." Mr. Tobarth shifted his weight to his right leg and raked his fingers through his thinning hair. "Ain't no women workin' in here."

"There is one woman now. Mr. Galloway hired Miss Brouwer. A friend of the family, she is."

Although I'd thought it impossible, the creases in Mr. Tobarth's forehead deepened.

"A woman *and* unskilled." I couldn't tell if his shoulders or his mouth drooped more — I think it was a tie.

"Not unskilled. I have —"

Mr. Kaestner held up his hand and pierced me with a sharp look. "You are right. A woman she is, and unskilled she is. You must instruct her like any other untrained painter. For this, I am sorry, Henry. We had agreed to hire a skilled painter."

Mr. Tobarth's earlier finger-combing had resulted in strands of hair sticking up like a rooster's comb. His eyes bulged as he glanced back and forth between Mr. Kaestner and me. Then the tiniest of smiles began to form at the corners of his mouth. "This is some kind of joke, ain't it?"

"Nein, Henry. I had no choice. Miss Brouwer is a friend of Mr. Galloway's daughter, and he has hired her to work as a painter."

My chest tightened. Mr. Kaestner's response was laden with disgust, and the frustration in Mr. Tobarth's eyes was pitiable. Neither one seemed to care that I was present for this discussion of dread and dismay.

"But we've turned away three men because they was unskilled. Now you're tellin' me I gotta teach an unskilled wo-wo-lady?" He shook his head. "This don't make no sense." He pointed a thumb toward the back of the shop. "The men ain't gonna be happy with this, neither."

Mr. Kaestner gave a nod. "The men, they do not run this place. Do your best to train her. Mr. Galloway wants her to become a good painter."

"And I wanted someone who was already a good painter," Mr. Tobarth mumbled as Mr. Kaestner turned and walked off. "Come on, Miss Brewer."

"Brouwer. Carrington Brouwer," I said, doing a quickstep to keep up with his long-legged stride. "And I do have some experience, Mr. Tobarth."

He stopped in his tracks. "How come you didn't say so?"

"I did. But Mr. Kaestner chose to discount my abilities. I hope you won't do the same." Fearing he might not pay heed, I clicked off my talents like beads on an abacus. Unfortunately, when I finished, Mr. Tobarth didn't appear any more impressed than Mr. Kaestner had.

He didn't comment at all. His lips twisted into a halfhearted smile as he pointed toward the unpainted carousel horses. "You'll start over here in the primer area." We passed by several men who stopped painting and stared at me.

Mr. Tobarth waved in their direction. "Get back to work. We're behind on orders as it is. Ain't none of you got time to be standin' around gawkin'." The older man's command was all it took to steer the workers back to their painting.

I followed behind him and came to a halt when he pointed to a space that I guessed would be my work area. "Is there someplace I can store my cloak and personal belongings?" I held up my reticule, a bag containing the lunch Frances had packed for me, and my sketch pad.

"The men toss their coats wherever they find a nearby free space — same with their lunch." He glanced around the area with a befuddled look on his face.

"I'll just put them over here," I said. He appeared grateful to be relieved of the problem.

Over the next half hour Mr. Tobarth explained my duties: I would go into the adjacent room and begin with the first rack of four horses. I was to wipe them down with a clean, dry cloth until every one of them was free of even the tiniest speck of sawdust.

"They need to be smooth as a baby's bott—" He stopped abruptly. A stain of crimson splotched his cheekbones, and he looked away. "Get 'em good and smooth — like glass." I didn't think it was possible for wood to feel as smooth as a baby's bottom, and I'd touched glass that wasn't particularly smooth, but I assured Mr. Tobarth I would make him proud.

"When you have all of them clear of sawdust, we move the rack in here, and you begin with the first coat of primer. You got to use long, steady strokes, and whatever you do, remember you got to apply all the paint with the grain of the wood." He reminded me about the grain of the wood at least three times.

"While those dry, you go back to the other room and begin wipin' down the next rack of horses. And so it goes. The rack gets moved back and forth. Wipe, paint, wipe, paint. The primer will help you see the imperfections in the wood. Each horse has to get at least two coats of primer. Dependin' on the carver and the wood, some will need to be sanded and primed four or five times. After that, the horse gets its primary color."

"So I must do the sanding, also?"

"Until you learn how we complete the paintin' process and understand how smooth the wood has got to be, you're gonna be doing your share of sanding.

Later, if you're still here, you won't have to do the sanding."

From the sound of his voice, I knew he didn't expect me to be here long enough to meet that requirement. "Do I apply the primary color, too?" I didn't think I'd ever be excited about such a dull possibility, but I hoped to move ahead as quickly as possible. I didn't tell Mr. Tobarth, but I wanted to be working alongside him painting all of the beautifully carved detailing — as well as adding a few embellishments of my own.

He wagged his head. "That'll come later, if . . ." He didn't finish the sentence. He didn't need to.

While he stood watch over my ability to wield a dustrag, I began wiping down the first horse. Mr. Tobarth said these were outside-row horses, so they were more ornate than some of the others I'd be working on later in the day.

"The inside rows of horses ain't so fancy," he explained.

When I'd completed wiping one side to my satisfaction, I walked around the horse and studied the animal for a moment. "Come look, Mr. Tobarth. The carving isn't completed on this horse."

In two long strides he was beside me. He looked at the horse; then he frowned at me.

"It's finished."

"No," I said. "Look at the other side. He forgot to carve the flowers and the —"

"We only do the intricate carvin' on the side that faces the outside — that's what we call the romance side. We paint the inner side of the horse to match the carvin' on the romance side. Ain't no need to worry yourself with that. The carvers know what they're doin'. Just wipe and prime."

I didn't recall if the carousel horse I'd ridden so many years ago had been carved on both sides or only one. I wanted to believe it had been as beautiful on one side as the other, but it probably hadn't. The one-sided process was more expedient, but it somehow seemed like cheating — like painting a bowl of fruit and leaving out the oranges or the grapes. Later in the morning, when I was satisfied the horses had been wiped clean of all possible sawdust, I signaled Mr. Tobarth.

He returned to my side and slowly circled the rack while sliding his palm over the bodies and down the sleek legs. He used a clean cloth and swabbed between the thin ridges of carved hair that created the horses' manes. When he finished the task, he grunted approval, helped me move the rack into the other room, and handed me a container of milk paint to prime the horses.

A pungent odor filled my nostrils, and I tilted my head away from the bucket. "It smells sour."

Mr. Tobarth bent his head over the open bucket. For a moment I thought he might stick his nose inside. I pictured him with the milky white substance covering his face. He'd look like a circus clown or perhaps resemble one of the mimes I'd seen perform in Paris.

He raised his head and touched his index finger to his nose. "You got a good sense of smell, Miss Brewer. The paint is sour. I'll get a fresh bucket."

"BrOUWer." He looked at me as though I'd lost my senses. "My name is Brouwer, not Brewer," I explained.

"Brouwer, Brewer," he mumbled. He shook his head and walked off.

A few minutes later he returned and hung a fresh bucket of primer on a thick spindle attached to the rack. "Go ahead and start paintin'," he said, thrusting a wide-bristled paintbrush into my hand. "Don't forget to keep with the grain of the wood. And no runs," he cautioned before heading off. "I'll be back to check on you later."

From my vantage point, I could see two other men in the paint shop. I couldn't tell for sure, but it looked as if one was using glossy black paint on his horse while the other was stippling a buff-colored horse with charcoal gray. I stared in their direction several times, but whenever I caught one of them looking at me, he immediately turned away. I wondered how long they had been required to clean and prime horses before moving on to their current jobs. Even more, I wondered if Mr. Tobarth would introduce me to them. Probably not before our lunch break, especially since both Mr. Kaestner and Mr. Tobarth were concerned about getting the orders completed.

I had finished the first coat of primer on two of the horses when Mr. Tobarth approached and told me I'd need to work faster. "We'll need the swan chariot for this carousel." He pointed to the large double-seated chariot that had been moved into the wiping room. "Once you've completed these horses, set them aside to dry and begin wiping down the chariot."

"Before the other rack of horses?"

"Yup, before the other rack of horses." He blew out a long sigh that caused his chest to collapse like a deflated balloon. Mr. Tobarth's irritation was, quite obviously, complete.

I dipped my brush in the primer and offered a silent thank-you when I heard the shuffle of his retreating footsteps. I hadn't completed priming the rack of horses when a loud buzzer over the door sounded to announce the noonday break. I waited to see where the men would settle with their lunches and then picked up my sack and approached them. When they saw me walking toward them, they scattered like mice fleeing a sinking ship.

CHAPTER 8

Work on the chariot hadn't gone quickly. I finally resorted to a clean paintbrush to remove the final sawdust from the intricate carving that decorated the show side of the massive piece. Mr. Tobarth still hadn't declared it ready for primer when the final buzzer over the door sounded. I didn't need to be told it was the end of the workday. My arms and shoulders ached, and a dull, throbbing pain hammered my low back. The constant bending and stooping had taken its toll. Mr. Tobarth had offered me a stool, which I'd used for a portion of the day, but reaching overhead had created a pain of its own.

I pressed my palms against my lower spine and arched my back before removing my canvas work apron and donning my cape.

Mr. Tobarth watched from a distance, and when I neared the door, he said, "You'll get used to it, if you last long enough." His tone carried no malice, but I was certain he was watching for my reaction.

I gave a nod. "I'll see you in the morning." I don't know if that was the response he expected — or wanted. I stifled my desire to ask if I'd performed as well as other workers on their first day of wiping and priming. Mostly because I was afraid of the answer. I trudged toward the factory exit, feeling the men's hard stares boring into me. I didn't look up, for I feared seeing anger in their eyes. One day I would have to face those fears, but this wasn't the day. First I must summon some courage.

Eager for a friendly face, I picked up my pace. The sun had made a nearly full descent, and the early evening sky was filled with shades of burnt orange and gray when I arrived at the boardinghouse. Mrs. Wilson bustled from the kitchen with a smile that wrapped from ear to ear. Her gray hair was pinned in a lopsided bun that made her all the more endearing.

"Your trunks arrived and they're safely in your room." She tipped her head closer, and the bun slipped another notch. "Ralph was home for the noonday meal, and he helped the carriage driver carry them upstairs. I don't think he was any too happy when he discovered you'd taken a room on the third floor." I had no idea who Ralph was, but he and Thomas were probably suffering with back pain, too. "I imagine you want to freshen up before supper. We'll eat in half an hour." She reached into her apron pocket and withdrew a key. "You'll need this to get into your room."

"Thank you, Mrs. Wilson. I'll be back down in half an hour."

"In case you were wondering, Mr. Galloway sent payment for your rent with his driver." Without missing a beat, she continued. "Hope you like pork chops."

The selection wasn't my favorite, but thankfully she didn't wait for a response. I climbed both flights of stairs and was certain Thomas and Ralph had been less than pleased to carry my belongings all the way to the third floor. After washing up, I surveyed the trunks. There wouldn't be time to make much progress with them before supper. And the thought of leaning over them and removing the myriad items made my back ache all the more. I'd rest for the short time remaining before supper and unpack this evening.

Instead of taking time to unlace and take off my shoes, I removed an old piece of newspaper from one of the wardrobe drawers and spread it at the foot of the bed.

Careful to keep my shoes on the paper, I eased against the pillow.

I remember thinking the mattress was quite comfortable, but that was the last thing I recalled before being startled awake by rapping at my door. "Miss Brouwer. You in there, Miss Brouwer? We're waiting supper on you."

Trying to clear my foggy brain, I forced myself upright. A man was shouting my name. I forced my caked lips apart. "I'm in here." I croaked the response through a sleep-filtered haze. Outside, darkness had descended.

"Miss Brouwer? The pork chops are getting cold. You coming?"

Pork chops. I was at the boardinghouse. "I'll be right there," I called to the unknown man on the other side of the door. I heard muffled footsteps retreat down the hallway. I couldn't take time to check my appearance. No telling how long the others had been waiting.

Patting my hair, I rushed down the stairs. The smell of fried pork and sauerkraut assailed me as I hurried along the hallway and entered the dining room. Struck dumb, I stood inside the doorframe with my mouth gaping open and my thoughts spinning like a whirlpool. My breath caught in my throat.

"Good evening, Miss Brouwer."

The man didn't appear surprised by my entrance, though he didn't appear pleased, either. I nodded. "Good evening, Mr. Kaestner." I wanted to run screaming from the room. Of all the boardinghouses in The Bottoms, why was Mr. Kaestner renting a room in this one? Surely with his position as manager of the factory, he could afford finer accommodations. Before I could take stock of the situation, Mrs. Wilson waved me into the chair opposite Mr. Kaestner.

The older woman took obvious pleasure in introducing me to Ralph Lundgren. Not only was he a fellow boarder, but Mr. Lundgren had been responsible for awakening me from my nap. He was also credited with helping Thomas lug my trunks up the two flights of stairs. I thanked him profusely for his acts of kindness; he waved off my words of appreciation as a shade of beet red stole across his cheeks. I'd obviously embarrassed the kind man.

Mr. Lundgren had an unruly head of brown hair and ears that were far too large for his head. In his favor, he had kind brown eyes and a pleasant smile that he generally directed at Mrs. Wilson.

"And you already know Josef, don't you?"

"Yes," I murmured. "I apologize for delaying supper."

Mrs. Wilson dropped into her chair with a thud. "Don't you worry one little bit, Carrie — may I call you that? Seems more friendly." She didn't wait for my answer but continued on. "This isn't like those boardinghouses where there's ten or fifteen folks. We're like a small family, aren't we, Ralph?" Though she didn't give him an opportunity to respond, I had already figured out that Mr. Lundgren would agree with anything Mrs. Wilson said. "Why don't you say the prayer tonight, Ralph."

I bowed my head, but I only partially closed my eyes so I could peek across the table at Mr. Kaestner. Ever so slightly, I tipped my head upward and raised my eyelids until his face came into full view. His intense brown eyes were riveted on me. What was he doing with his eyes open? I slammed my eyelids shut and tilted my head forward until my nose nearly touched my plate.

After the prayer I was careful not to look in Mr. Kaestner's direction. I was successful until the pork chops, fried potatoes, and sauerkraut had circled the table. It had been no small task cutting a bite of meat from the pork chop, but I finally managed. I'd just begun to chew when Mrs. Wilson asked about my day.

"Tell me all about it," she said. "I've never been inside the carousel factory, although I certainly enjoy riding the lovely horses. Or at least I used to when I was a little younger and somewhat slimmer."

"You could ride on one of the chariots," Mr. Lundgren said. "Do you make those beautiful chariots at the factory, Miss Brouwer?"

I didn't know why he was asking me. Mr. Kaestner was far more qualified to answer questions about the factory. Mumbling around the piece of pork chop in my mouth, I offered an affirmative response. I chewed and chewed, but the piece of meat wouldn't disappear.

"We've gone and interrupted. I promise we won't cut in again." Mrs. Wilson held an index finger to her pursed lips and directed an admonishing look at Mr. Lundgren.

Hoping no one would notice, I clasped my napkin to my lips and expelled the rubbery piece of meat inside. One glimpse at Mr. Kaestner's face revealed he'd figured out exactly what I'd done. I felt like a student caught cheating on an examination. Heat spread through my chest, crawled up my neck, and exploded across my cheeks. I lowered my eyes as quickly as I'd raised them, my embarrassment complete.

Mrs. Wilson touched my arm. "We're waiting, my dear."

I offered a quick recapitulation of the day's events, leaving out the part about being shunned by the men and the fact that I'd been hired without Mr. Kaestner's approval. "My work was quite different from what I've experienced in the past, but I believe I'm going to be quite happy at the factory." I stole a look at Mr. Kaestner, but his face was a blank canvas, void of all expression. What a relief it would be if I could pick up a brush and paint a smile on his lips and dot a gleam in his eyes.

Mrs. Wilson stabbed her fork into the mound of sauerkraut. "What do you think, Josef? Did Carrie do a good job today? I'd think you'd be relieved to have another painter in the shop." She pointed the tines of her fork toward him. "Why don't you look pleased?"

"Another painter, he quit this afternoon. I traded one painter with a year of training for a woman with no experience at all. I am told the work Miss Brouwer completed today was acceptable. But slower than the men, she is."

His critical tone caught me by surprise. Was it my fault if another worker decided to quit? A fire ignited deep in my belly. Perhaps indigestion played some part in the burning sensation, but Mr. Kaestner's snappish remark was doubtless the primary culprit.

"You seem to be implying it is my fault the painter quit." I pushed the words through clenched teeth.

He dug his fork into a lump of fried potatoes and balanced several broken pieces on his utensil before he looked up. "Ja, you *are* the reason, Miss Brouwer. With a woman, he refused to work."

Mr. Kaestner's words collided with my fear. If he fired me, how could I survive? The burning sensation exploded like fireworks. An intense heat scorched the back of my throat, and I grabbed for my glass of water. I swallowed a large gulp, but it didn't douse the fire. I couldn't decide what would be worse: facing angry-eyed men each day or not having a job.

Mrs. Wilson's cheery inquisition had come to an immediate halt, and the room was now as silent as a tomb.

Finally Mr. Lundgren tapped his finger on the edge of the table. "I say if a woman can do the work, why shouldn't she? I wouldn't mind having a few women working alongside me over at the glass factory. I get tired of looking at scraggly bearded men all day long." His chuckle rang a little hollow, but he was doing his best to smooth the waters. "Maybe I should make a suggestion to my boss, Mr. Gottlieb."

Mr. Kaestner gave him a sidelong glance. "Mr. Gottlieb might think different, but women — ach! Problems they can cause."

Mr. Lundgren shrugged. "So can men, just a different kind. Good managers learn how to handle all kinds of people, particularly them that's got good skills."

I bit back my anger at Mr. Kaestner, grateful Mr. Lundgren had come to the defense of womankind.

Mr. Kaestner's right eyebrow twitched. "So you are thinking it is because of me this painter quit today?"

"I'd say it is nobody's fault, but the least the fella coulda done was give Miss Brouwer a chance to prove herself. He probably wouldn't have lasted long anyway. Men that fly off the handle can always find something or someone to make 'em angry. Right?"

I crunched a mouthful of undercooked potato. The grinding echoed in my ears while I waited for Mr. Kaestner's answer.

"For the other men, I cannot speak."

"But you can speak for women!" The stinging retort was out of my mouth before I could clamp my jaw.

He reeled back as though I'd landed a blow, but he didn't respond. I chased a piece of potato around my plate, stabbed it with my fork, and popped it into my mouth.

"Thank you for the food, Mrs. Wilson. I must return to the factory this night. If you will excuse me, ja?" Mr. Kaestner pushed away from the table.

"I have pie for dessert," she said.

He patted his stomach and offered a faint smile. "Too full, I am."

Obviously, Mr. Kaestner had a problem telling the truth. He'd eaten less than half of the food on his plate, and I was sure he couldn't possibly be full. I wanted to confront him, but I refrained. Such talk might lead to words that would hurt Mrs. Wilson's feelings. Besides, who could say what turn the conversation would take? He might say more about the additional problem I'd created at the factory.

"We can wait to have dessert until you return," Mrs. Wilson said.

"Nein. I will be late. I promised Henry I would dapple two of the horses."

"You paint, Mr. Kaestner?"

His left eyebrow cocked, and I knew he'd detected my surprise. He stood and pushed his chair under the table. "I was hired as an apprentice when I went first to work in a carousel factory. We had to learn many jobs, even if it was a carver we wanted to be. I did what I was told because we needed food for the table. I carried wood. I sanded. I primed. I dappled — everything but the fancy painting like —"

"It's good someone gave you an opportunity to learn all those skills," I said.

He turned and walked off. There was no indication he'd heard the plea in my voice. I doubted whether anything I could say would change Mr. Kaestner's attitude. He didn't want me in the factory.

When I heard the slam of the front door and was certain Mr. Kaestner had departed, I leaned toward Mrs. Wilson. "I'm surprised Mr. Kaestner doesn't live in a fine house or take rooms in one of the lovely hotels in Collinsford. Strange that a man in his position would live among the workers, don't you think?"

Mrs. Wilson wiped the corner of her mouth with her cloth napkin. "When Josef first arrived, I asked him the very same question." She tapped her finger to the side of her head. "Curious how we think alike." She giggled.

"And what did he tell you?"

"He said he would be saving his money for investment."

"Investment in what?"

"I didn't figure it was any of my business. I was glad he wanted to take a room with me. I've been even more pleased that he decided to remain. Josef is a good boarder, and saving money is a good thing."

"Yes. Indeed it is." I forced down a small piece of the apple pie. Like the potatoes, the apples were undercooked. "If you'll excuse me, I believe I'll go upstairs."

Mrs. Wilson nodded. "Of course. You have all that unpacking to take care of. I'd be happy to help you once I finish the dishes."

"I wouldn't think of it. You have more than enough to keep you busy for the evening." I scooted away from the table and bid Mr. Lundgren and Mrs. Wilson a good evening.

Inside my bedroom I stared at the trunks and decided I'd remove only the items I would need over the next few days. No need to unpack everything. I'd likely be leaving as soon as Mr. Kaestner convinced Mr. Galloway the presence of a woman was far too great a liability.

CHAPTER 9

The next days passed without further incident. None of the other employees quit, but no experienced painters had applied for the vacated position, either. Each night, Mr. Kaestner and Mr. Tobarth worked late in an attempt to meet the demands. Though I expressed my willingness to join them, Mr. Kaestner always turned down my offer. I don't think Mr. Tobarth agreed with the decision, but he didn't argue.

Mr. Lundgren had finished giving thanks for our meal on Friday evening when Mrs. Wilson pulled a note from her apron pocket and passed it across the tureen of lumpy gravy. "Mr. Galloway's carriage driver brought this for you, Carrie. He said he'd stop by tomorrow morning for your response." Mrs. Wilson's clear blue eyes remained riveted on the sealed envelope.

"Thank you, Mrs. Wilson." I placed it on the table beside my plate.

"We can wait until you've read it," the older woman said.

Her voice exuded such anticipation that I couldn't deny her. I slid my finger beneath the seal and withdrew the note. "It's an invitation to supper after work on Saturday evening and to church on Sunday morning. Augusta has invited me to visit the zoo with her on Sunday afternoon."

"Oh, isn't that nice. Will you spend the night at the Galloways'?"

I nodded and replaced the note inside the envelope. "Your Sunday should prove less taxing with one less to cook for."

"Two less," Mr. Kaestner said. "I will be working Sunday afternoon and evening. If you will pack me a lunch, to work I will take it."

Mrs. Wilson's eyes clouded. "You're going to work on the Lord's Day? Oh, I don't think that's a wise idea, Josef. We all need a day of worship and rest. I think you should reconsider."

His fingers tightened around the handle of his fork. "I will go to church before I go to work, Mrs. Wilson. I pray God will understand my problem. Until we can find a good painter, I must step in and complete the work."

I thought Josef's crooked smile insincere,

but Mrs. Wilson seemed not to notice. "You work far too hard, dear boy. I have been praying that exactly the right person will come in and apply for that position."

"And the other jobs, too. Before all my men quit," he added.

I straightened in my chair. "Others have quit?"

He rested his palms on the table and pushed himself away from the table. "Two men in the woodshop — one that carves the rims and one who is learning to measure and cut, to glue and clamp the wood."

"And that's *my* fault, too?"

His left shoulder dropped a notch and he shoved his hand into his pocket. "They did not say your name, Miss Brouwer."

He turned and strode off before I could ask further questions, but the implication had been clear. Whether or not the other workers said my name, Mr. Kaestner blamed me. If this continued, I would lose my job for sure.

I excused myself from the table and went upstairs to pack for my visit with Augusta. Though I couldn't tell her of my concerns, it would be good to escape for a short time and pretend life wasn't so difficult. Even if more men quit tomorrow, I wouldn't be at the supper table to hear Mr. Kaestner's report. Yet I wondered how much he'd told Mr. Galloway. Was this invitation more than what it seemed? Perhaps the visit had been arranged so that Mr. Galloway could privately tell me I couldn't return to the factory. My earlier pleasure dissipated, and a heavy lump settled in its place.

Sitting on the edge of the bed, I gazed out the window and down the street toward the factory. I could see the glow of light from inside and wondered if anyone other than Mr. Tobarth and Mr. Kaestner had to work late because of me. *Because of me.* Maybe I should resign. That would solve the problem for all the men. Yet they weren't leaving their jobs for good reason. They were quitting simply because a woman had been hired to work there. Loneliness and rejection plagued my thoughts like unwelcome friends. Right now, it would be easy to walk away, but I shook my head. No. I wouldn't give in — not yet, anyway.

The following day when the noonday buzzer sounded, the men gathered together for their lunch. All except Mr. Kaestner, who remained in his office, and Mr. Tobarth, who continued to paint while he ate his sandwich. The workers sat in a circle, hunched forward, while they shared both food and conversation. Every once in a while, one of them would steal a look in my direction and just as quickly turn away. Let them think and say whatever they wanted. Wedging my drawing pad on my lap, I pulled out my pencil and sketched a picture of the huddled men. They weren't going to intimidate me.

During the remainder of the day, I did my best to keep up with the horses that came in from the woodshop. It seemed as if the men had decided they would hurry through every bit of their work to create a large buildup in my area. Either that or they'd been holding back horses for several days and decided to overwhelm me on the final day of the week. Mr. Kaestner would surely think me less capable than the man who'd previously worked in this position. But there was nothing I could do.

When the buzzer sounded, I removed my apron and hung it on the nearby hook. Once the men were on their way, I gathered my belongings and hurried out of the building. Except for Mr. Tobarth and Mr. Kaestner, I'd decided it was best to maintain my distance from the other workers. It seemed some of the wives were unhappy that I was working in the vicinity of their husbands. At least that's what Mrs. Wilson had heard at the market on Wednesday. I didn't want to be accused of forcing my friendship upon any of them or stirring up trouble.

I picked up my step, eager to get home, wash up, and change my clothes. Rounding the corner near the end of the block, I jumped backward when a woman and young child stepped into my path. I shifted sideways, but she matched my movement. "Excuse me," I said. Gathering my skirts, I attempted to sidle around her, but she once again blocked my path.

Her dark eyes glistened with anger. "You need to find work elsewhere. A factory full of men ain't no place for a woman to be workin'. Not unless she's lookin' to steal someone else's husband." She hissed the words from between clenched teeth.

I clasped my hand to my bodice and instinctively shook my head. "I'm not searching for a husband. I need the work to support myself."

Her gaze traveled up and down the length of my body and came to rest at a spot beneath my chin. "There's proper places for a lady to work, but the factory ain't one of 'em. Go help in one of the fancy dress shops or work as a maid for some of the rich folks. There's men who need the factory jobs. Men who've got families to feed."

"I much prefer painting. I'm not much of a seamstress. Besides, there's currently a vacancy at the factory, and no one has applied for the position."

"That's 'cause you're workin' there."

I felt as though I'd been doused by a cold glass of water, and I swallowed the giggle that threatened to erupt. This woman wouldn't think a fit of giggles funny — not in the least. I inhaled a deep breath. "If a man's family is hungry, my presence in the workplace should be of little concern."

"Well, the wives don't want you in there, neither. You think we like the idea of our men ogling the likes of you all day?" She poked her rough index finger toward my nose. "We know your kind."

Hiking my skirt, I rushed across the street, eager to escape. When I'd left the Galloway house last Monday morning, I hadn't thought I'd be excited to return so quickly. I'd been very wrong.

Mrs. Wilson greeted me the minute I walked in the door. "Are you certain you don't want at least something light to eat? Something to tide you over until supper?"

I assured her I'd be fine, but she followed me up the steps, chattering all the way. By the time we arrived at my room, she was puffing. I didn't know why she'd followed me up the stairs, and she clearly needed to rest. Her cheeks were bright red. Perspiration lined her forehead and upper lip.

Pointing to the chair across the room, I waved her forward. "Do sit down, Mrs. Wilson. I'll go to the bathroom and wash up while you catch your breath." Thankful I'd set out my clothes before leaving for work, I picked up the skirt and shirtwaist.

"That will be fine," she wheezed. Retrieving Augusta's invitation from the bedside table, Mrs. Wilson fanned the paper in front of her face. The limp piece of paper flipped and flopped, but couldn't stir much air. "Would you open a window before you go, dear?"

"Of course." After raising the window and propping it with a wooden slat, I hastened down the narrow hallway. If I didn't hurry, Thomas would arrive and I wouldn't be ready. I didn't want to keep the Galloways waiting — especially Mrs. Galloway. If supper was ruined, it would be my fault, and I certainly didn't need anything else added to my list of faults.

The small bathroom proved more of a challenge than I'd expected. As I twisted to remove my work dress, a metal hook on the back of the door scraped across my shoulder, and before I recovered from the stinging pain, I knocked my elbow into the wall and banged my hip into the washbasin. At this rate, I'd arrive at the Galloways' looking as though I'd received the worst of it in a boxing match.

"This will have to do," I muttered, still fastening my skirt on my return to the bedroom. The bathroom acrobatics had left my hair in complete disarray, but I doubted there would be time to do much more than stab a few hairpins into place. As I opened the wardrobe to remove my shawl, I glanced over my shoulder at Mrs. Wilson. I was glad to see that her complexion had returned to its normal hue. "Did you need to speak to me about something in particular?"

Mrs. Wilson folded her arms across her ample chest. "I'm not one to carry gossip, but —" She glanced toward the window, as though she expected an eavesdropper to be standing on the roof.

"But *what,* Mrs. Wilson? Have you heard some disturbing news?"

My wavy reflection stared back at me in the mirror. The quality of the looking glass was certainly inferior, but the mirror alone couldn't be blamed for my unkempt appearance. Comb in hand, I pulled the loose strands upward and jabbed them into place with hairpins.

"I heard a few women talking at the meat market today." She shook her head and offered me a pitiable look.

"And?"

"The men are planning to meet with Mr. Kaestner and demand that you be fired." She pressed the folds of her apron beneath her thick fingers. "It may be just idle talk, but they don't like their husbands working with an unmarried woman."

My stomach lurched and I clasped a hand to my midsection. Mrs. Wilson had confirmed what I'd heard only a short time ago. Once again I felt the need to defend myself. "The only man I'm around is Mr. Tobarth, and he's old enough to be my grandfather." If Mr. Kaestner was threatened with additional walkouts, he'd push Mr. Galloway to dismiss me. The thought was enough to send my stomach from a lurch into a complete flip-flop.

"I shouldn't have told you. Now I've gone and ruined the rest of your day, haven't I?"

I patted her shoulder. No need to tell her I'd already had my day ruined by one of the angry wives. "It's fine. Better that I know." At the sound of a carriage, I stepped to the window. "I think that may be Augusta. I don't want to keep her waiting."

Mrs. Wilson pushed up from the chair,

her knees popping like firecrackers. "You sure you don't want to come back here to spend the night? You could go to church with Mr. Lundgren and me and then go to the zoo with your friends."

"Thank you, Mrs. Wilson. Why don't we plan on next Sunday? I've already promised Augusta."

"I know you've been here less than a week, but I'm going to miss you this weekend. It's nice having another woman around the house."

Her smile warmed my heart, and my stomach settled a little, too. I was fond of Mrs. Wilson and said so, but I didn't mention her less-than-stellar cooking. After closing the window, I grabbed the handles of my bag and clattered down the steps. Mrs. Wilson followed close behind. Going down the steps proved much less strenuous for her.

A knock sounded at the front door as I began my descent to the first floor. I could see a man's suit jacket through a small portion of the window not covered by Mrs. Wilson's lace curtains. Likely Thomas, although I'd never seen him in anything other than his old work pants. I yanked open the door.

"Hello, Carrington."

"Tyson? What are you doing here?" My

suitcase slipped from my fingers. It bounced against my leg and made an unexpected landing on my big toe. My screeching caused Tyson to take a backward step. If he'd taken one or two more, he'd have fallen backwards off the porch. A sight I would have relished!

While I hopped on my good foot, Mrs. Wilson hurried into the parlor. Dragging a wooden chair into the hallway, she pointed at the seat. "I'll remove your shoe and see if you've done any damage to your foot."

Tyson stepped closer and tapped his watch pocket. "We're expected back for dinner very shortly."

I bent my knee and tucked my foot out of Mrs. Wilson's reach. "We don't have time. I'll check it once I arrive at the Galloways'. I'm certain it's all right." I stood and did my best to erase the older woman's concern. "See?" I stepped down on the foot and forced a smile while I inwardly winced. "I'm perfectly fine, and Mr. Farnsworth will carry my suitcase to the buggy."

Though I had no desire to hold Tyson's arm, it was the only way I could keep from hobbling down the steps to the buggy. We'd made it to the front gate when Mr. Kaestner appeared. His fleeting look of disapproval annoyed me. Granted, I was leaning heavily against Tyson's arm, but I was injured.

I stepped into his path to forestall him. "I'd like to introduce you to Mr. Tyson Farnsworth. He is a friend of the Galloway family."

"And of *you,* it would seem." His gaze rested on my proximity to Tyson as he extended his hand. "Josef Kaestner," he said. "Pleased to meet you, Mr. Farnsworth. Please excuse me; I don't have much time."

There was a bite to his words, and I wondered if it was because I was going off to enjoy myself while he worked, or if it was something more. Perhaps the men had already asked for a meeting with him.

"Come along, Carrington." Tyson patted my hand in a much too familiar manner. "We don't want to be late."

His possessive mannerisms annoyed me. "Do stop your fawning. I'm holding your arm for support, nothing more. And where is Augusta?"

Tyson held my waist far too long while assisting me into the carriage, and I would have slapped him had Mrs. Wilson not been watching from the porch. Once he took up the reins and clucked at the horse, I waved and was surprised to see Mr. Kaestner watching from the front window. The curtain dropped back into place when he saw me looking. He appeared most unhappy, and I wondered if I would have a job on Monday morning.

"Augusta hadn't finished dressing, and she asked that I come for you. She thought it a great imposition, but I was pleased that Thomas was off on an errand. It gives us time to be alone."

"And why would we want to be alone? It's Augusta who finds you an interesting suitor."

"And I find *you* interesting," he boldly proclaimed.

"Mr. Farnsworth! Augusta is my dear friend, and I find your comment highly improper."

He winked and tipped his head close. "*Do* you? Then this must remain our little secret. Promise you won't tell."

His mocking tone confirmed what I already knew. Augusta would believe whatever he told her — she was besotted with him. I was growing increasingly uncomfortable in his presence.

"Tell me about your new job, Carrington."

"I'd rather hear what prompted your hasty departure during your last visit." I folded my hands in my lap, eager to hear his excuse. "As I recall, you mentioned going home to visit your parents."

"Frances confused my message. I told her I was going to visit my parents. Either I failed to properly explain or she misunderstood that I was going to visit them at Long Branch — in New Jersey. Mother loves the shore and is visiting friends."

"And you've returned so soon?"

He cocked his head and looked at me from beneath hooded eyes. "You sound as though you don't believe me." He placed his palm across his heart while holding the reins in his other hand. "Do tell me I've misjudged you before you break my heart."

"I don't know why anything I say should break your heart, Mr. Farnsworth. I will admit that I think your quick recovery and ability to travel to New Jersey quite amazing."

"If you give me a chance, I believe you'll discover I possess a number of astonishing talents."

"I'm not interested." I wanted to tell him that he was no gentleman, but I held myself in check. Tonight I would attempt to broach the subject with Augusta. She needed to open her eyes and see that Tyson Farnsworth wasn't a man who would make her happy. Not now. Not ever.

CHAPTER 10

That evening at dinner my foot was soaking in a basin of cold water beneath the table. I thought it most inappropriate, but Augusta had insisted. So there I sat, passing a bowl of creamed corn while my toes iced in a pan of frigid water. The idea of a dinner guest with her foot in a basin of water was simply unbelievable — especially at Mrs. Galloway's proper dining table. I dared not look at the frowning matriarch or I'd break into a fit of giggles.

"Tell us about your new job in the carousel factory, Carrington. I know Mr. Galloway has been eager to hear how you've been faring." Mrs. Galloway cut a bite of roast chicken and then peered down the table toward her husband. "Haven't you, Howard?"

"I would be pleased to hear what Carrington thinks of her work thus far, if she cares to tell us."

Mr. Galloway's words contained a kindness that permitted me an escape, but I feared avoiding the subject might give him cause for concern. Concern that he might discuss with Mr. Kaestner. I didn't want to do anything to speed that possibility. I still remained hopeful the men at the factory would eventually accept me and there would be no need to report any difficulty to Mr. Galloway.

With everyone at the table now looking in my direction, I decided to push forward, though I refrained from detailing any problems. "If all goes well, I'll be learning to dapple the horses next." Having my foot submerged in ice water made it impossible not to shiver, but I did my best to keep my voice from shaking.

Mr. Galloway's brows dipped ever so slightly. "I understand the men have been somewhat reluctant to accept you among their numbers."

So Mr. Kaestner had already talked to Mr. Galloway. I should have known he wouldn't wait. Mr. Kaestner would be the most impatient to be rid of me. After all, he was the one required to work late into the night and on his day of rest.

"There are some who don't like a woman working in the factory," I said.

Mr. Galloway took a sip of coffee. "So I've been told. I believe we've had several employees use your employment as the reason for their resignations. We'll soon need to address the situation."

Mrs. Galloway perked to attention and scooted forward on her chair. Apprehension lurked in shadows of her pale gray eyes. "Address it *how?*" There was a note of urgency in the question.

"We can't operate a factory without employees. We seldom have skilled craftsmen apply, so each new worker must be trained. That process takes time, which we don't have. We're already behind on our orders." Mr. Galloway sent a fleeting glance in my direction. "Josef dispatched word that one of our journeyman carvers who specializes in making bodies is unhappy and threatening to quit. Then one of the men who has been working in the roundhouse ever since we opened walked out. Two hours later an apprentice, one of our legmen who'd shown great promise, said he wouldn't be returning."

Tyson snickered. "So you hire legmen? Exactly what does that entail? I might be interested in applying."

Mr. Galloway didn't appear amused by Tyson's remark. "I doubt you'd qualify. A legman is an apprentice carver who works for many years carving animal legs before he is considered good enough to become a journeyman. When one of them leaves us and goes to work for a competitor, we've not only lost a legman, we've lost the months or years of training that our journeymen and master carvers have invested in the apprentice. We must find a solution to this dilemma."

I shuddered at the news, but before I could say a word, Mrs. Galloway took control of the conversation. "Such as *what,* Howard? You're not going to ask Carrington to resign from her position, are you?" She sucked in a deep breath but didn't wait for his response. "Because if *that's* your plan, I'm going to object. Those men shouldn't dictate who does or doesn't work in your factory."

"Do stop, Mother. I think it would be a grand idea if Carrie resigned. She could move back here. Then we'd be able to attend the spring socials, and she could come with us to the shore this summer." Augusta clapped her hands. "Wouldn't that be perfect, Carrie?"

Mrs. Galloway's frosty look was an equal for the icy shiver that curled through my body. "I don't think Carrington should give in to the pressures those men are exhibiting toward her. Women have every right to support themselves if that's what they elect to do. You need to take a stand on this, Howard."

Once again Mrs. Galloway had become both an unsuspecting and unforeseen ally. In spite of any hardship it might pose to her husband's business, she was going to make certain my job remained intact. She didn't want me returning to live under her roof. Did Mr. Galloway comprehend the true reason his wife was coming to my defense? Doubtful. He was far too kind to think she'd be motivated by anything other than the cause of women's rights or a genuine interest in my future welfare.

"There are business interests at stake that I'm sure Mr. Galloway must consider," Tyson said, helping himself to another piece of chicken. "He can't permit his business to fail because of one woman, now can he? If that happened, you and Augusta would be unable to purchase those pretty gowns or expensive jewelry you enjoy."

Mrs. Galloway stiffened in her chair. "The carousel factory isn't my husband's only business venture. Far from it, Tyson. We have other investments to sustain our income."

Tyson swallowed a bite of potatoes. "I didn't mean any offense. However, I know men don't like to fail once they invest in a business — at least that's what my father has told me."

"And he's correct, but I think Josef and I can develop an amicable solution for all concerned," Mr. Galloway said, turning to look at me. "And I want you to remember that I don't want you to remain at the factory if you're unhappy. Our home is always open to you, Carrington."

Mrs. Galloway flinched. "She's not unhappy. She didn't say one word about being unhappy, did you, Carrington?"

I wondered which would be the path of least resistance: to return to the Galloways' or remain at the factory. I wasn't welcome in either place. I lifted my cold dripping foot from the water and rested it on the side of the basin. "This past week hasn't been entirely pleasant. And I didn't know other workers had quit on my account. I realize the men are opposed to my presence, but I'm very hopeful that once they see the contribution I can make to the company, they'll accept me." I wasn't certain the wives could ever be won over to my side, so I didn't mention them.

"There you have it!" Mrs. Galloway gave

a firm bob of her head. "Carrington will have no problem once you set things aright with the men. You simply must go in there on Monday morning and assert yourself. Women have a right to earn a living in places other than a schoolhouse or dress shop. You must let them know who is in charge."

At the moment I longed for a towel and warm stocking more than a fight for women's rights. My toes were freezing, and I didn't want to plunge my foot back into that basin of cold water. But if I dripped on Mrs. Galloway's fine Aubusson carpet, I'd not soon be forgiven. My foot teetered on the edge of the basin as I leaned forward to signal Augusta.

From that point on, everything seemed to move in slow motion — like thick, cold molasses. The basin tipped over, water sloshed on the carpet, Mrs. Galloway shrieked, Augusta jumped up to help and tipped over her chair, Mr. Galloway rang the metal bell for Frances, and Tyson did absolutely nothing. I, on the other hand, clutched my throat and bit my lip, but I couldn't stop from laughing.

Mrs. Galloway pinned me with a deadly stare. I needed to get control before she had me committed to the local mental institution. But the longer she stared, the more I giggled. Even with my hand clapped over my mouth, laughter bubbled through my fingers like a babbling brook. My embarrassment mounted with each chortle, yet I found it impossible to stop. Rounding the table in slow motion — or so it seemed to me — Augusta clasped her fingers around my arm in a viselike hold and pulled me up.

"Lean on me, and let's get out of the room before my mother regains her voice," she hissed.

I'm sure we made quite a sight. Me, giggling and hobbling along on my injured bare foot, and dear Augusta, doing her best to brace me up while trying to keep a straight face. We made it into her father's small library, where she literally pushed me into a chair and commanded me to stay put while she retrieved my stocking. I don't know where she thought I might go. I wasn't in any hurry to face her parents, but at least my incessant giggling had ceased. I could hear Mrs. Galloway shouting at Frances. The unhappy matriarch had regained her voice, and I would likely be the next recipient of her wrath.

Before I could further contemplate Mrs. Galloway's fury, Augusta reappeared with my stocking dangling from one hand and a towel in the other. I thanked her while I dried my foot and shoved my toes into the tip of the stocking. "I'm very sorry for what happened. Do you think your mother will forgive me? I've likely ruined her carpet."

"The rug will be fine, and if it's not, it will give her an excuse to purchase a new one. I'll explain your impediment when I have her alone for a few minutes."

I stopped pulling at my stocking. "My impediment?"

"The giggling," Augusta replied. "Mother doesn't understand that you can't control it. I'll explain."

"Oh yes. Thank you." I pointed toward my unshod foot. "My shoe?"

"I thought it might be best to go without your shoe until morning. I want you to be able to go to the zoo." She sat down opposite me. "You do think you'll be able to, don't you?"

"I'll do my best, but you may have to go without me."

"No!" Her eyes shone with alarm, and she clutched my hand. "Mother won't let me go with Tyson unless we're chaperoned. I don't want her coming along. And you know she will. Please promise you'll come."

How could I refuse? I wanted to tell her that she should avoid Tyson, but I knew she wouldn't listen. "I may have to borrow one of your father's walking sticks, but if it means that much to you . . ."

"Oh, it *does*. I knew I could count on you, Carrie. And don't you worry about the carpet or Mother. I'll take care of everything."

My toe was much improved by morning, but not so much that I didn't wince when I shoved my toes into my shoe. Though I had expected Tyson once again to feign illness and disappear, he'd been dressed and at the breakfast table on time. We attended church together, all of us crammed side by side in the pew with Tyson pressed to Augusta's right and I to her left. There was little doubt Augusta was pleased by the arrangement. As for me, I was content to be at the end of the pew, where I didn't have to sit next to either Tyson or Mrs. Galloway. Augusta's mother had spoken to me that morning, but I wasn't convinced all was forgiven. Mrs. Galloway had tapped her foot on the hardwood floor throughout breakfast. I decided either she had a nervous tic or she wanted to ensure that I noticed the rug had been removed. How could I not notice? I truly didn't know what to say. Though I'd offered my apology, I couldn't offer to pay for the rug. I'd never earn enough money to replace such a costly item.

When the sermon finally began, I was quite pleased that Tyson was in attendance. The preacher spoke with eloquence about looking beyond outward appearances and seeing the heart of each person we encounter. He spoke of the Pharisees, and I immediately counted Tyson among them. I elbowed Augusta to make certain she was listening. She sucked in a breath and frowned. It was obvious I'd offended her. Though I'd need to explain my action later, I was sure she'd turn a deaf ear. Augusta had already made it perfectly clear: Tyson could do no wrong.

Our first opportunity to speak alone wasn't until after lunch. At the completion of the meal, Mrs. Galloway interrogated me at length regarding the condition of my foot. Though I told her it was fine, she offered to take my place as chaperone for the trip to the zoo. I declined but could feel her eyes on me as Augusta and I excused ourselves to freshen up for the outing.

My toe ached, but I forced myself to walk as normally as possible. I could limp once we were away from the house. The moment we were upstairs, I apologized for nudging her during the sermon.

"I simply thought the preacher made a valid point. Some people aren't what they appear. They wear one face in public and another in private. I wasn't referring to you."

"Like my mother?" she asked.

That wasn't the response I'd expected. I dropped to the side of the bed and briefly contemplated my answer. "I suppose your mother does have two faces. I think she believes she'll be happy when those wealthy people in Fair Oaks welcome her among their number. But once that happens, there will be something else she hungers for to make her happy. I think we're born with a longing for something more than humans or things can fill, but I haven't yet figured it out. Does that make any sense at all?"

"I suppose, but right now I'm more interested in having Tyson make me happy."

I loosened my shoe and wiggled my toes. "That's exactly what I'm talking about. You're hoping Tyson will fill your empty space and make you happy. But he won't."

Nostrils flared, Augusta planted her hands on her hips and glared at me. "Exactly what is that supposed to mean?"

"The preacher said a person who is beautiful on the inside is a person who would exhibit it on the outside, as well." I met her harsh gaze.

"So you can judge him?"

"No. That's not what I'm saying. Tyson is attractive on the outside, but I think you need to get to know him better. You need to be certain his principles match your own." I tightened the laces of my shoes and cautiously stood. "I just don't want him to hurt you. I'm afraid you'll pledge your love to him and then discover he's one of those wolves in sheep's clothing."

Augusta checked her hair in the mirror and then turned to face me. "You need not worry about Tyson. He'd never do anything to hurt me."

I gathered up my reticule and sketch pad and followed her out of the room. Mrs. Galloway stood in the foyer watching my every move. There would be no opportunity to borrow one of Mr. Galloway's walking sticks before we departed. Such a request would give the older woman ample reason to declare me medically unfit for a day at the zoo. "Enjoy yourselves," she called after us. I half expected her to change her mind and come along.

On several occasions during the carriage ride, I glanced up to see Tyson watching me. When we arrived at the zoo, he squeezed my hand and winked while he helped me down. Augusta had turned and was none the wiser for what he'd done, but my anger was boiling like a teakettle. I considered kicking him in the shin but didn't want to take a chance on injuring my other foot.

We'd proceeded only a short distance when he offered me his walking stick. I was loath to take the thing, but Augusta insisted. Rather than create a scene, I begrudgingly accepted. We'd stopped to look at the elephants, viewed several cages of monkeys, and stared into a watery pool of crocodiles when I finally tapped Augusta's arm.

"I need to sit down and rest. Why don't we see if there are some benches nearby?"

Her eyes sparkled as though I'd given her a special gift. "Of course. I think I saw benches near the lion cages not far from here."

Augusta proved to be correct. We located several benches where I would have a clear view of the lions and tigers. "This will be perfect. I'll sit here and sketch while the two of you complete your tour."

"We won't leave you for long," Tyson said. He touched my shoulder in a much too familiar manner.

I shrugged his hand from my shoulder. "Do take your time. Augusta will vouch for the fact that I prefer to be alone when I draw."

He tipped his hat and grinned at me before offering his arm to Augusta. I didn't know how she could care for such a man. He was a scoundrel of the worst sort, yet she seemed totally unaware. I settled on the bench and watched as they sauntered off. To most they appeared a young couple in love. To me, they were a disaster in the making.

Immediately upon our return, Mrs. Galloway greeted us from the front porch, buzzing about like an annoying fly. As soon as Tyson mounted the steps, she clasped his arm in an overtly possessive hold. It was at that moment I fully realized Mrs. Galloway was awestruck by the Farnsworth name — or money . . . perhaps both. She continued to clutch his arm while she ushered us into the house.

Mr. Galloway looked up from his reading when we entered the parlor. "How did you enjoy the zoo, Carrington?"

"I had a lovely afternoon, thank you."

"Show him your drawings, Carrie." Before I could object, Augusta pulled the sketchbook from my hands and flipped open the cardboard cover. She turned back the pages and shoved the book into her father's hands. "Look at these. Carrie thinks they would make marvelous carousel animals. Don't you agree?"

Mr. Galloway hunched forward and held the book toward the early evening light filtering through the front window. He studied each page far longer than I'd expected, yet his expression remained unchanged. An unexpected uneasiness crawled up my spine as he continued to examine the final drawing. He closed the sketchbook, and as he handed it to me, I could see the excitement in his eyes.

"These are excellent drawings. I particularly like the lion. Do you think you could paint the animals to look like your sketches? I'm sure children would love them."

"Yes, of course," I said, my enthusiasm increasing. "I don't believe the woodworkers would find them any more difficult to carve than the horses, once they became familiar with the patterns. They've already made one giraffe, so I don't think they'd object to trying some other animals."

Mr. Galloway rested his forearms across his thighs. "Once we are fully staffed at the factory, I think we should begin producing some of your drawings. What do you think?"

"I would be very pleased." I wanted to shout for joy and clap my hands, but I forced myself to maintain proper decorum.

"I have several other ideas, too."

"Good! I'll go over these with Josef. I'm sure he'll find them exciting."

Josef. The carousel factory manager's name was enough to set my nerves on edge. I could only imagine what *he* might think when Mr. Galloway arrived with my sketches. "Perhaps you should wait until I've been there awhile longer before you speak to him. I wouldn't want him to think I'm pressing any advantage due to my friendship with Augusta."

Mrs. Galloway scooted to the edge of the settee. "On the other hand, those men need to know that you are the owner and they must do as you say, Howard. I don't imagine your father permits his employees to have any authority in *his* business operations, does he, Tyson?"

Tyson lifted one shoulder into a half shrug. "I have no idea. I care little about business matters."

"Oh?" Her brows knit together for an instant. I wasn't sure if she was perplexed or worried by his response. It took her only a split second to regain her composure before she turned to her husband. "Still, Howard, I think you must be stern with those men, or they will run roughshod over you."

"Agatha, your opinion is quite clear. I think it's probably best if you make the decisions regarding operation of the household and I'll take care of decisions regarding the businesses." Mr. Galloway stood up and nodded toward the dining room. "I do believe Frances is ready to serve our supper."

Although Augusta strenuously objected, I insisted upon leaving as soon as the evening meal was over. Both she and Tyson accompanied me to the boardinghouse. I would have preferred that Tyson remain behind. The driver's company would have been preferable to Tyson's, but at least he stayed in the carriage when we arrived at the boardinghouse.

Augusta stepped inside to bid me farewell. We were standing in the hallway with Mrs. Wilson when Josef thrust open the front door and nearly plowed the three of us to the floor. I don't know who was the most surprised by the incident, but Josef was the first to recover.

He uttered a brief apology and said, "I see you have finally returned from your weekend of pleasure."

"And it would appear you've been out enjoying yourself, also," Augusta replied.

Josef cocked a brow at Augusta's tart response. "You make a mistake, Miss Galloway. I'm back from working at the factory. We are without enough workers, and this makes the long hours for some of us."

Augusta tipped her head to one side. "Perhaps you should better utilize the workers you already have, Mr. Kaestner. I know Carrie's abilities far exceed the work she's currently assigned." Leaning forward, Augusta plunked a quick kiss on my cheek. "Take care of yourself. I expect you for dinner at least once during the week."

I could feel Josef's eyes trained on me. No doubt he thought I'd been complaining to Mr. Galloway. "Please don't plan on me. It's late when I get home from work, and —"

"Then next Saturday evening for sure. You can spend the night again."

I opened my mouth to refuse, but Augusta wagged her finger.

"I won't hear an objection. Thomas will call for you next Saturday evening. You can act as my chaperone again," she whispered in my ear.

"We'll see," I murmured. I didn't want to argue in front of Mrs. Wilson and Josef. I knew I wouldn't win. However, I didn't plan to continue acting as Augusta's chaperone.

Besides, Mrs. Galloway would be delighted to assume the role, since she obviously considered Tyson Farnsworth an ideal match for her daughter. The thought caused an involuntary shudder, and I rubbed the goose bumps that covered my arms.

CHAPTER 11

As promised, Mr. Galloway arrived at the carousel factory early Monday morning. Several hours had passed when one of the workers summoned me to the front offices. I did my best to brush the whitish dust from my clothing and face as I followed along, but I'd been sanding for some time and the dried milky primer had descended upon me like a winter storm.

Josef didn't acknowledge me, but Mr. Galloway smiled and beckoned me forward. "Let me take a closer look and see if it is truly Carrie hiding under that white mask."

I swiped my handkerchief across my cheeks and nose and hoped I'd successfully removed any remnants of the paint. Mr. Galloway's smile gave me hope that this would be a friendly exchange.

"Sit down, Carrie," he said.

This time I didn't bother to wipe the dust before I plopped onto the chair. I wondered if Josef noticed.

"Josef and I have been discussing the men who have recently resigned from their jobs. I wanted to discover the reason."

"It's because of me, isn't it?" My voice cracked as I spoke.

Mr. Galloway's sorrowful smile answered my question. "Not because it's you, Carrie, but because you are a woman. Some of the men are superstitious about women in the workplace. Some say they are uncomfortable having a woman around — they must watch every word they say. Others believe men are entitled to factory jobs because they have families to support." He leaned against the desk and tented his fingers beneath his chin. "Those who are married tell me their wives are unhappy that a woman is working in their midst. And some are opposed simply because they believe the other men will be angry if they don't join the opposition."

"Do you want me to resign, or do you plan to fire me?"

"Neither. I'm not sure Josef agrees with my decision, but I'm not yet ready to succumb. I'm going to advertise in Philadelphia and New York. If we're fortunate, we may locate a few experienced men. And who can say, if those men who quit don't find work,

they may come back and ask to be rehired."
Mr. Galloway tapped the drawing on Josef's
desk. "After I talked with the men, Josef
and I had a good look at your drawings."

Mr. Kaestner's gaze remained fastened
upon the pages. He didn't appear pleased,
but I was eager for a change of subject and
decided to brave the storm.

"What do you think of them?" I ventured.

He shrugged and dropped into a chair
beside the desk. "They are not bad drawings, but they need changes before they will
work for us. A carver's eye is needed for the
best carousel animals."

My thoughts whirled. *Not bad drawings?
Not bad? What would it take to impress this
man?* I curled my fingers into fists and dug
my fingernails into my palms. I needed to
remain calm. "I didn't realize you were an
art critic, Mr. Kaestner," I said in a mea-
sured voice.

He tipped his head to the side and
squinted his right eye as if picturing me in
the sights of his rifle. "I am the art critic
when it comes to carousel animals in this
factory." He looked up at Mr. Galloway.
"Unless it is someone else you are wanting
to take over this duty."

"No, of course not. You're the expert, Josef. I brought these to you for your opinion

because I thought Carrie's unique animals might give us an advantage over other carousel factories." Mr. Galloway's apologetic tone surprised me.

A lock of Josef's thick brown hair fell across his forehead, and he swiped it away with an agitated grunt. While keeping his eyes on Mr. Galloway, Josef flicked his index finger and gently pushed the drawings a few inches away — as though secretly attempting to distance himself from my efforts. But I knew exactly what he was doing.

Why was he so unwilling to receive fresh ideas? Did he fear I'd usurp his position? Surely he knew that wouldn't happen. I had no idea how to carve, and I possessed no interest in learning.

"Right now we don't need more advantage, because we cannot keep up with our current orders. We will fall further behind if we design new animals. There is not time to perfect the designs or draw the templates we would need. The carvers, they would not be able to create with the same speed and skill, and the painting techniques would need time to be decided and perfected. These things, they differ with each new animal. Making changes now is a bad idea."

Mr. Galloway cupped his chin and nodded. "You're right. This isn't the time. But I

184

don't think we should completely disregard the idea of adding these animals once we're caught up with our orders. I like what Carrie has done."

For the first time in many months, I experienced that warm feeling I used to get when Papa praised my artwork. "Thank you for your confidence in me, Mr. Galloway." I flashed a smile and decided the time might be right to request a move from the sanding room. With men quitting, surely my talents could be put to better use. And once the men realized I could make a valuable contribution to the factory, they'd be more likely to accept me. "Since we're so far behind on the painting, Mr. Galloway, perhaps one of the apprentices could sand the horses and I could help with more of the painting. I believe I've already acquired the necessary skills to sand and apply primer."

"I do believe Carrie is right. There's no sense wasting her talent with sanding and priming. Let's get her to work on some of the more technical painting so that we can complete the current orders." Mr. Galloway patted Josef on the shoulder. "I'm relying on you, Josef. With you at the helm and Carrie's talent, I know we're going to make our carousel factory the best in the country."

Mr. Galloway's plaudits were appreciated,

but Josef's leg was bouncing up and down. He'd apparently developed the nervous habit of jiggling his leg to help him overcome worrisome situations — not nearly as embarrassing as my tendency to erupt into fits of laughter. And it was becoming increasingly clear that Mr. Kaestner considered my presence in his factory a worrisome and irritating burden.

Though I thought his attitude less than gracious, I did feel a smidgen of sympathy — mostly because I'd experienced similar difficulties. Well, maybe not similar, but at least I'd been forced into some circumstances I didn't like. "I agree. I think Mr. Kaestner is going to lead the factory toward immense prosperity."

Josef placed his palms on the desk and pushed himself up from the chair. Wariness shadowed his eyes as he walked Mr. Galloway to the door. I, too, stepped toward the exit, but Josef motioned me to remain, saying, "We need to discuss the changes in your work duties."

I didn't miss the edge in his voice but was thankful I'd soon be doing something other than sanding. Josef stepped out of the room with Mr. Galloway. I hoped the men would begin to respect me once they saw I was qualified to paint the horses or perhaps one of the beautiful scenes that decorated the crown of the carousel.

Josef's gait was slow and determined when he returned to the office a few moments later. He gathered my drawings and bounced the edges on top of the stained wooden desk. I wanted to hurdle across the expanse and retrieve them, but I maintained my distance and kept my attention fixed upon the drawings — prepared to leap into action should they slip from his hands. They didn't.

Using two fingers, Mr. Kaestner drew open the lower desk drawer and dropped the pages inside. I could no longer contain myself and leaned forward when he pushed the drawer back into place.

He looked up and met my eyes. "They will be safe in the desk, Miss Brouwer."

"I'd prefer to keep them with me. I can put them with my sketch pad in the other room."

"They will not do us much good in there, ja? If I am to fix your drawings into workable designs, I'll need them available when I find some time for the extra work."

I shrunk back. His emphasis upon the added duties had come through loud and clear. "I'll be glad to help in any way possible," I offered.

"Enough you have done already, Miss Brouwer." He stood and strode out of the room. I hurried behind him, still wiping away the flecks of primer that speckled my face and hair. I managed to hold my head high even though several of the men in the carving shop glared at me as we passed by. Soon they'd understand my employment had more to do with my talent than the fact that I was acquainted with the factory owner's daughter.

He waved me onward. "I'll tell Mr. Tobarth he can show you how to stipple the horses, but first I must stop at the round-house."

I remained close on his heels and followed him inside the circular room where numerous men were busy assembling the crown of a carousel. I took up a position beside the stack of sandbags used to add rider weight to the beautiful carousel horses during the testing process. Mr. Tobarth had explained that each new carousel must be assembled and operated with the added weight before it could be declared fit for shipment to the new owner.

The shipping crates were assembled in a small room off the roundhouse, and from the frenzied hammering and shouts, I guessed the men had fallen behind schedule.

188

An older man with a drooping mustache that matched his downturned eyes stopped as he neared me. "This is all your fault. Why don't you get out of here and go find yerself a husband! If it weren't for you, we wouldn't be short of help." Each venomous word struck home, and I longed to run from the room.

"Get those crates moved to the other side of the room," Josef shouted as he approached. He waved me forward. "Come along."

When we arrived in the paint room, Josef pointed to the far wall. "Stay there while I speak to Mr. Tobarth."

I would have preferred to be present for the conversation between the two men, but I didn't press the point. Standing in the appointed spot, I watched the animated conversation. Mr. Tobarth pointed first in one direction and then another. Like molten wax, the supervisor's facial expressions transformed in slow motion. Josef, however, remained unflappable. Throughout the conversation, his arms remained folded across his chest, his legs positioned in a firm military stance.

Finally, Mr. Kaestner signaled for me to join them. Pasting on what I hoped was a smile, I trod the distance while the two men stared at me. Discomfort inched up my spine.

The smile didn't evoke a response from either of them. Neither appeared happy. Josef was the first to make a move. He dropped his arms from their folded position and pointed to a row of horses. "Mr. Tobarth says he wants you to learn the fancy painting."

I could barely believe what I'd heard. "No stippling?" I asked, just to be certain I hadn't misunderstood.

Mr. Tobarth shook his head. "Gus can take care of the stippling, and we can use solid-colored horses while we're runnin' behind. Right now, I need help with the finish work. You said you know how to paint, so I say we let you prove it." He glanced toward Mr. Kaestner. "I hope my trust in you ain't been misplaced, Miss Brouwer."

So that's why they'd been arguing. Mr. Kaestner wanted to keep me on the dappling or solid painting, while Mr. Tobarth wanted me doing finish work. The thought that I would be painting detail work was the best news I'd had since I'd been hired. "I believe you'll be pleased with the decision, Mr. Tobarth."

Josef turned and walked away, but not before shooting me a you'd-better-be-right look that curbed my enthusiasm.

Mr. Tobarth pointed toward a box of paintbrushes. "You can use those brushes," he said. "And don't let Josef get you down. He never likes to lose a battle — 'specially when he thinks he's right." He walked me toward a beautiful brown horse with tan dappling. "You can get started on this fine fellow." He patted the horse on the rump. "You're gonna have to do above average work to impress Josef, so don't rush. He don't approve shoddy workmanship, and neither do I."

"What happens if my work is found lacking?" I didn't expect such a thing to happen but thought it best to know the consequences in advance.

"You'll have to request a sand-down. Then you'll start over. If the animal's features are weakened too much during the sand-down, you'll have to toss it in the heap."

"Heap?"

Mr. Tobarth pointed to a small pile of wood stacked in the far corner. "Takes too much of a carver's time to try to recapture what once was perfection. Takes less time to just start over. 'Course you'll make no friends among the carvers if they discover one of their horses in that heap. And believe me, they keep an eye on that woodpile."

The thought of ruining any of the animals stirred my fears. The men already disliked me. How would they behave if I ruined one of their horses? I walked around the animal, contemplating exactly what I wanted to do and what colors would be best. The face of a court jester had been carved behind the cantle, and I knew I would have great fun painting him. I ran my hand along the smooth wood, my fingers dipping into the intricately carved crevices that created the horse's flowing mane. A garland of perfect roses and leaves draped downward across the body in perfect symmetry. "Who carved this horse?"

"Mr. Kaestner — one of his new designs. You'll need two to three days for each color to dry and harden. Paint as much as possible on each horse before movin' to the next one in the rack. You can use as many colors as you like, but be sure one color is dry before you touch it with another. If not, the colors will bleed and you'll have a mess."

I swallowed the lump in my throat. I dared not ruin this one. Tilting my shoulders back, I glanced down the row of horses. Given the number of horses that awaited paint, I'd probably end up working on a horse from every one of the carvers. Gathering my courage, I donned my apron, picked up a paintbrush, and gave a firm nod. First, I'd need to decide exactly what colors I wanted to use and where I wanted to begin. I walked around the horse and considered my choices. I'd begin with the center of the roses and use the same color on the jester's hat — or perhaps I should begin by shading the nostrils and eyes. Tapping the wooden tip of the paintbrush against my cheek, I considered several options for the blanket and saddle. They would need to contrast perfectly, and I'd need to layer the shading, which would take several different colors.

Startled by a loud gravelly sound, I dropped the paintbrush and swiveled around to see Mr. Tobarth watching me. He cleared his throat again and pointed to the horse. "I said you shouldn't rush, Miss Brouwer, but I didn't mean you could spend the remainder of the day decidin' on your colors and technique. The woodworkers have given you beautifully carved outlines. I'd think with your artist trainin', you could add the paint without so much thought."

"Yes, of course." I could feel the heat rising into my cheeks. "I think I'm going to begin with the roses."

"Don't think — just paint."

By the end of the day, several of my horses

had been moved to the drying rack. They would require a great deal more work before they would be ready for the final sealants. Still, I was pleased with what I'd done and thought my technique as good as any I'd seen on the other horses. Of course, Mr. Tobarth could boast that he'd done more than double the amount of my work. But he'd been doing this much longer. One day I'd be able to keep up with him. And one day I'd set myself apart and use my creativity rather than simply paint what the carvers had designed.

Josef arrived in time for supper, and I longed to hear what he would say about my accomplishments. By the time he was eating his dessert, I was still waiting. He'd visited with Mrs. Wilson about the spring weather and the flowers she was planning for her garden, and he had asked Mr. Lundgren about work at the glass factory and even requested a set of fresh towels from Mrs. Wilson for the next morning, but he hadn't said one word to me. Not a word!

Deciding to take matters into my own hands, I cleared my throat and smiled at Mrs. Wilson. "I began a new job at the factory today."

"Oh?" Mrs. Wilson's eyebrows wiggled

and gyrated like two arched plumes. "Did you hear what she said, Ralph? Carrie's got a new job at the factory. Do tell us about it."

Mr. Lundgren mumbled his agreement around a bite of dry pound cake. I did my best to remain focused upon Mrs. Wilson or Mr. Lundgren, but my eyes betrayed me and flitted toward Josef. His features were as taut as the strings on Mr. Lundgren's guitar. I immediately regretted my decision, but there was no turning back. Mrs. Wilson and Mr. Lundgren were waiting to hear my report.

With somewhat dampened enthusiasm, I explained how I'd painted roses and saddles and blankets, and the court jester's hat, of course. Mrs. Wilson asked lots of questions, and my spirits soon were on the rise.

"Mr. Tobarth even asked me to add the stripes and final shading to one of the horses he'd been working on for the past two weeks." Pride swelled in my chest as I completed the account. After folding my hands in my lap, I leaned back in my chair and reveled in a feeling of triumph. In retrospect, it had been a very good day.

"And what did *you* think of our Carrie's accomplishments, Josef?" Mrs. Wilson beamed like a proud parent.

Josef pushed his dessert plate away and rested his forearms on the edge of the table. "The work, it was passable." He gave one bob of his head. "Ja. Most of the work *our* Carrie completes is passable."

My elation vanished. *Passable?* Had I heard him correctly? Good sense argued with anger. Anger won and I challenged his comment. "You thought my work merely *passable?*"

"You will get better with practice." He wiped his mouth with the cloth napkin and dropped it alongside his plate.

I took a deep breath before replying, careful to keep a controlled tone. "Exactly what was wrong with my work?"

"On canvas you were accustomed to painting whatever you desired. Now you must learn to follow the craftsman's vision. Most carvers are pleased to see a painter make fancy their horses with some added decoration. But first you should learn the basic techniques." He placed the napkin beside his plate. "And your striping isn't well defined. Mr. Tobarth tells me you refused his suggestion to use a maulstick."

It seemed Josef had scrutinized all of the work I'd completed. Did he want me to fail, or did he check all new painters with such diligence? I decided I'd try to elicit the information from Mr. Tobarth the next morning, but I'd need to be careful in my approach.

"What's a maulstick?" Mrs. Wilson asked. "And why didn't you want to use it, Carrie?"

"It's a long stick with a knob on the end that you can use to steady your hand when painting lines and such," I said, pulling myself back to the present. "I was confident my striping would be straight and steady without using the stick."

"And what did you think when you had finished?" Josef leaned his shoulders forward and looked me in the eye.

The hairs along the back of my neck bristled. Josef wanted me to declare my work hadn't been perfect. Though I had observed a slight waviness in my striping, everything inside me railed against admitting the truth. I feared he would use such an admission against me. Fingers crossed beneath the table, I said, "My opinion remained the same."

"Ach!" He slapped his hand through the air. "You are not willing to admit you failed."

"I didn't fail. I still have much to learn, but Mr. Tobarth said I did a fine job."

"He said you did a fine job for your first

day — that is not the same as a fine job, Miss Brouwer." Josef pushed away from the table and stood. "Your striping will need to be touched up. More time lost. I am going back to work, Mrs. Wilson."

Before I could further argue my case, he turned and stalked off.

CHAPTER 12

The following day I waited until I was certain my conversation wouldn't be overheard. The men ignored me, yet listening ears and whispering lips seemed to repeat everything I said. When I spotted Mr. Tobarth painting the trim lines on one of the horses, I decided the time was right and tiptoed to his side.

"Mr. Kaestner tells me the painting I completed yesterday was only passable and that the striping will need to be repainted."

Mr. Tobarth loaded the tip of his brush with a unique shade of blue, one he'd mixed himself. With one long stroke, he laid down perfectly straight lines and then created triangles along the breastplate of a medium-sized jumper — my favorite of the carousel horses thus far.

"You did a fine job, Miss Brouwer." He lifted his brush, reloaded it with paint, and continued striping. "It was your first day. I didn't 'spect it would look perfect."

I shifted my weight to gain a better view of his technique. "But have you received perfection from the men on their first days?"

"You askin' 'bout the men who've been hired to do paint design or them that's apprenticed first?" He had crouched low to align his strokes while he continued along the front of the breastplate.

"The ones hired to paint design," I said, careful to keep my voice low.

The familiar scent of paint fumes filled my nostrils. I hunched forward to hear his response because I didn't want Louis, the other painter, to overhear our conversation. I hadn't failed to notice his furtive movement along a nearby rack of horses. No doubt he'd be reporting everything he heard to the other men. I wondered if he'd been eavesdropping before leaving work yesterday. Had he heard Josef and Mr. Tobarth evaluate my painting? If so, the men had probably already heard, already discussed, already taken pleasure in knowing my work had been deemed merely passable.

"Your straight-line work isn't up to par."

His brief assessment startled me back to the present.

"You'll get better. Especially if you use a maulstick," he said.

"But *you* don't use one."

"I been doin' this for thirty years. I used a stick when I first started. Ain't no shame in using a tool if it helps you do a better job." He pointed the tip of his brush toward the other room. "The carvers use any tool that helps them create the best-lookin' animal. Painters need to do the same. If we're gonna outshine those Philadelphia and New York factories, we got to be willin' to push our pride aside."

Pride? Is that what Mr. Tobarth thought? That I'm an arrogant woman, unwilling to accept direction? Warmth climbed up my neck and spread across my cheeks. I didn't want to admit he was right, but my refusal to use the maulstick told another story — at least to Mr. Tobarth.

He pushed up from his stooped position and stretched his neck. "If you ain't got no questions, Louis, you can begin workin' on the horse at the end of the second rack. We ain't got time to be wandering around doin' nothin'."

"What's she workin' on?" Louis called out.

"Unless Mr. Kaestner told you to take over as supervisor of the paint shop, it ain't none of your business what she's doin'. Now move that horse and get to work."

A silent cheer reverberated deep inside

my chest and worked its way up my throat. Quickly slapping my palm tight against my lips, I managed to smother the cheer into a throaty cough. I'd learned this particular technique due to my bouts of unexpected giggles throughout the years. My method had come in handy on a number of occasions, though it did have one disadvantage: I often received forceful yet well-intentioned slaps on the back. I'd borne my share of bruises after such episodes.

Mr. Tobarth added a daub of navy blue to the azure and mixed the two colors with his brush. "You think you might want to use a maulstick today?" He glanced up while he continued to stir the bristles in the paint.

"Yes, but I wondered if I could ask you a few questions about Mr. Kaestner."

His lips curved in a lopsided grin. "If you got questions about Josef, why don't you ask him? You live at the same boarding-house."

I leaned close to his ear. "I don't think he likes me."

Mr. Tobarth chuckled. "You think he knows you well enough to decide somethin' like that? You ain't been around long enough for that."

"Some people make immediate judgments." I leaned in just a bit. "Don't you think?"

He shrugged. "I s'pose. But not Josef. He's a solid kind of fella. Takes things slow and steady — studies 'em out. Does the same with people." With practiced ease, Mr. Tobarth drew his brush across the horse and formed a perfect line.

I exhaled a whoosh of air. I'd been engrossed in Mr. Tobarth's every movement and didn't realize I'd been holding my breath. "Have you known Jo— Mr. Kaestner for long? He doesn't say much about himself at the supper table."

"I've known him 'bout six or seven years — maybe longer. He started out in Philadelphia, just like me. I remember when he came to work as an apprentice. Everyone realized right away he had his father's talent."

"His father? He was a carver, too?"

"Prob'ly the finest I've ever known. He taught Josef to wield a mallet and chisel when the boy was no more than four or five." Mr. Tobarth edged his thumbnail along a line of paint. "I doubt his mother woulda allowed such a thing if she'd been around."

"His mother's dead?"

"Far as I know. He's never mentioned her

to me. Neither did his father. Josef's father died about a year before he came to Ohio. After he got out here, he convinced me to leave Philadelphia."

He pointed to a small tin. I retrieved it from the floor and handed it to him. "If you're such good friends, why don't you live at the same boardinghouse?"

Mr. Tobarth stepped back and gave me a sidelong glance before he surveyed his work. "I couldn't take the cooking at Mrs. Wilson's place. She's a fine lady — no doubt 'bout that — but after a couple months, my stomach rebelled, and I moved down the street to Helen Milford's place. Miss Milford's kinda cranky, but the food's good and there's plenty of it."

"There's always plenty on the table at Mrs. Wilson's, too." I felt a sense of obligation to come to Mrs. Wilson's defense. She was, after all, a kind and generous woman.

"That's 'cause no one can stand to eat much of her food." He nodded toward the horses awaiting paint in the nearby rack. "You best get busy on those horses. They ain't gonna paint themselves."

"Can we talk some more during the noon break?"

"If ya like. I'll be right here workin' while I eat."

His parting words were a reminder that I was the cause of the required overtime hours. I wondered if the other workers had ever carried through and asked that I be discharged. I doubted I'd ever know, but I found the worrisome thought abrasive. If Mr. Kaestner had been permitted to hire an experienced carousel painter, one of the opposite gender, the factory might be on schedule. Then again, who could say when a qualified man might have applied? I salved my conscience with that thought, picked up my paint box, and studied the beautiful long-necked stander. The horse was an outside horse — a fancy. That's what Mr. Tobarth called the animals placed on the outside row. I was honored he was permitting me to work on the beauty.

The older man had already dappled the horse's rich brown coat with subtle hues of black and raw umber. The shading delicately enhanced the muscles and tendons to perfection. According to the instructions written on a paper and attached to the horse, the broad saddle straps and reins were to receive a coat of deep green. Once the forest green dried, the scalloped flowers atop the straps were to be painted with emerald green and the centers finished in gold. The effect would be striking.

I squeezed a portion of the Japan paint into a wooden bowl and decided a touch of black would help deepen the color. I added a daub and mixed until I'd achieved the perfect color, but before I could begin painting, Mr. Kaestner signaled me to come to the sanding room. I covered the paint and hoped he wouldn't detain me for long. Worse yet, I hoped I hadn't done anything to get myself in more trouble.

The conversation didn't take long. Mr. Kaestner had examined two of my sanded horses and declared they needed additional work. "You can finish your painting, but then to the sanding you must return."

I could sense the carvers had watched the exchange. They couldn't hear what Mr. Kaestner had said, but I was certain they knew I was being chastised. I longed for another route back to the paint room, but fact was fact. There was no other way. I'd only taken a few steps into the room when one of the men hollered, "Why don't ya go back where ya come from? We don't need no more men quittin' because of you."

"That's right! There's men needin' these jobs. If something ain't done soon, you might be the only one workin' here."

The second shout came from one of the journeymen, a man who would not easily be replaced. I wanted to shout an angry retort but knew it would only make matters worse. I picked up my pace, hoping to escape further angry remarks. My skirts stirred the stagnant air, and the curled wood shavings that layered the floor danced around my shoes. Not one of the men came to my defense. I hadn't truly expected any of them to step forward and take up my cause, but I had secretly hoped.

Shoulders slumped, I donned a mantle of rejection and returned to my duties. Reeling from the men's angry comments, I absently stroked my brush across the reins and applied the dark green paint. Would I ever do anything to suit? If Mr. Tobarth was happy, Mr. Kaestner was unhappy. If Mr. Kaestner was pleased with something I did, Mr. Tobarth found fault with something else. And it had become increasingly obvious the men didn't plan to accept my presence.

"Stop!" Mr. Tobarth grabbed the brush from my hand and pointed at the freshly painted surface.

I lurched backward, mouth agape. My heartbeat shifted to a frenetic pounding tempo, and I gasped for a breath of air.

"Look at what you've done! What did you mix in the paint?"

His thunderous voice boomed in my left ear as I searched for an answer. "I-I nothing . . . j-j-just paint," I stammered.

Neck arched, Louis appeared out of nowhere and peered over Mr. Tobarth's shoulder to examine my brushstrokes. "I guess she's ruined that horse." He shook his head and gave me a how-could-anyone-be-so-dim-witted look. But behind that look, I saw a gleam in his eyes. A gleam that reflected he was the one responsible for this catastrophe. He turned and strode away, leaving me to fend for myself.

Mr. Tobarth grabbed the bowl of paint from my hand. He leaned so close I expected him to have a dot of green paint on his nose when he lifted his head. One thought of the supervisor with a green nose was all it took for a bubble of laughter to rise in my throat and work its way to my nose, my eyes, and my mouth. The explosion was of unheralded proportion. I did my best to cover my mouth or make it sound like a cough, but one look at Mr. Tobarth was enough to let me know I'd failed. Miserably.

"You findin' this funny?"

I shook my head and clapped my hand to my mouth while I swallowed another onslaught of giggles. "No. I do this when I'm nervous," I mumbled from beneath my palm.

Mr. Tobarth's eyebrows dipped low and forced deep creases into his broad forehead. "Then go ahead and get it over with. We'll talk once you finish laughin'." He turned and raked his paint-stained fingers through his thinning hair.

For some unknown reason, his behavior had a calming effect upon me. And although it still took a few moments to regain my composure, my giggling ceased. "I apologize. For both my laughter and the mistake. Please believe me. I didn't put anything in the paint."

Mr. Tobarth listened patiently while I explained the mixing process I'd used; then he asked several questions. Afterward he dipped his index finger into the paint and rubbed it between his finger and thumb. "There's sand in this paint. Someone had to put it in there, and I think I know who that someone is." He turned on his heel and shouted, "Louis! I want to talk to you."

Surely another worker wouldn't intentionally mix sand in my paint and risk the possible ruination of a carousel horse. Would Louis go to such lengths to get me in trouble? Would he be willing to sacrifice the painstaking work of a talented carver?

Would he disregard the cost to his employer? I didn't want to believe he would act in such a manner — so reckless, so irrational, so destructive. Yet someone had tampered with my paints.

My stomach lurched and a wave of nausea assailed me. I stared at the coarse wet paint, wondering what to do. Any attempt to rectify the paint while it was still wet would only cause more problems. I could choose another horse from the rack, but Mr. Tobarth might want me to refrain from further work. I paced back and forth in the narrow space beside the rack of horses. The muffled voices of Mr. Tobarth and Louis drifted across the expanse, but I could understand only an occasional word. A door slammed in the distance, and Mr. Tobarth reappeared.

"We may be able to salvage this without too much work. Once it dries, I'll see if Bill Robaugh can help us out with some sanding on the reins. Choose another horse and let's get to work."

"Did Louis do it?"

Mr. Tobarth grunted. "Yep. He tried to deny it, but I pointed out the sand on his apron where he'd wiped his hands. And I saw him over in your work area when you went into the sanding room earlier. Guess he decided he might as well fess up."

"I'm truly sorry, Mr. Tobarth. The horse is one of the most beautiful in the rack. I'm certain the wood-carver will be unhappy if he finds out I've caused it damage."

"That's one of Josef's horses, and you didn't cause the damage. Louis is the one responsible."

"Now that you've talked to him, perhaps things will improve and Louis won't mind painting alongside me." I could only imagine how difficult it would be to work with Louis in the future. I swiped a sweating palm down the front of my apron. Could things get any worse?

"You ain't gonna be workin' with Louis. Can't afford the likes of him 'round here."

Mr. Tobarth's reply echoed through the silent room. I now realized the slamming door had signaled Louis's departure. My question had been answered. Things could get worse — much, much worse.

When I turned the final corner toward work the following morning, my heart lurched. Twenty-five or thirty men had gathered along the south side of the factory and were staring in my direction. And not in a welcoming manner. Though the morning breeze was cool, perspiration beaded along the outer edge of my bonnet. If I was going to enter the building, I'd have to circle around the men.

Gathering a deep breath, I forced myself to hold my head high. Except for the paint shop, there were men from every area of the factory. And if Louis hadn't been discharged yesterday, he would have likely been at the forefront. I couldn't understand why men from the shipping and freight shop or men from the printshop cared about my presence. I'd said no more than good morning to most of them. Why did my presence among them create so much anger?

One of the younger men from the printshop stepped in front of me. "We want you out of the factory. You're the cause of my friend Louis getting fired yesterday. You made a mess of your work and then blamed him, didn't ya?"

"N-no. That's not true at all." I didn't know whether to defend myself against the false accusations or turn on my heel and run.

"Don't make no difference who did what. There's been nothing but trouble since you walked through the door, and we want you outta here," another man shouted from among the crowd.

A loud cheer of agreement followed, and

a few of the men pumped clenched fists into the air. My stomach clamped in a knot, and the taste of this morning's rubbery eggs climbed up the back of my throat. The thought of disgorging my breakfast in front of the angry men should have had a sobering effect. Instead, a shrill giggle erupted before I could clamp my hand across my mouth.

A man toward the edge of the crowd dropped his lunch pail and lurched toward me. "You think this is funny? Men out of work over the likes of you?" His fiery words seared my lips like a hot poker.

I attempted a backward step, but fear held me captive. I couldn't move, not even an inch. My throat constricted and caused an eerie, unwanted lightheadedness to wash over me. It seemed I was watching from afar as the worker poked his finger beneath my nose and continued his angry assault of words. I was afraid I would faint at any moment.

"What is this noise out here?" At the shouted question, the men turned as if they were standing on one of the rotating carousel platforms. "There is work to be done inside, ja?"

Hearing Josef's voice, I inhaled a much-needed deep breath. The men shuffled toward the entrance, their grumbling whispers hovering overhead like low-hanging thunderclouds. Josef pushed through the crowd and came to my side.

"What did you say to create all this trouble with the men?"

I swallowed a gulp of air. All thoughts of fainting fled from my mind. "What did *I* say? You think *I* started this. Those men were waiting here for me when I arrived at work." I listed the insults that had been hurled at me without giving Josef an opportunity to interrupt. I didn't know which was worse — the men accosting me or being required to defend myself to Mr. Kaestner.

"Ja, they think it is your fault that Louis was fired. Makes no difference what he did. They know Louis would still have a job if a woman had not been working in the factory."

I couldn't believe my ears. "You're taking their side in this?"

"I am not taking sides. I am telling you what they believe. And what they say is true. If you did not work here, we would not have these problems."

"But if they'd just let me do my work and forget I'm here, there wouldn't be a problem, either. Have you thought of that? Don't they bear any fault?"

He grasped my elbow. "I will see you safely to the paint shop, and then I must talk with the men. I hear too many threats that more workers plan to quit, and some say they are planning a walkout. This kind of talk I must stop. We have too many orders that must be filled."

He wasn't going to answer my question. Mr. Kaestner was much more concerned about filling orders than the behavior of his workers. No doubt he hoped to hear me say I would quit, but I couldn't bring myself to do such a thing. Why was it more important that a man earn a living than a woman? Quitting just didn't seem right!

CHAPTER 13

May 3, 1890

There'd been no further incidents since that day outside the factory. Mr. Kaestner had talked to the men, and Mr. Tobarth told me the workers had begrudgingly agreed to take further complaints directly to Mr. Kaestner. I didn't know if he'd received more protests since then or even if the men would keep their word. I did know none of the men had made any overtures toward accepting me. With the exception of Mr. Tobarth and Mr. Kaestner, none of them even acknowledged me.

Though I enjoyed painting, the daily rejection had begun to take its toll. I hadn't gone to visit Augusta since the incident with Louis and wondered if Mr. Galloway had heard I was at the center of yet another mishap.

And although we lived under the same roof, Mr. Kaestner's presence provided me with little insight. He carefully avoided talk of the factory during mealtime at Mrs. Wilson's table. And lately he'd been avoiding talking at all — unless Mr. Lundgren or Mrs. Wilson directed a question to him. He didn't need to worry about me. I wasn't about to do or say anything to provoke him, especially when Mr. Tobarth was willing to answer my many questions.

Shortly after Louis's dismissal, Mr. Tobarth and I had taken to working side by side so that our voices didn't echo every time we spoke to each other. The change had created a more friendly environment — at least in the paint shop.

I mixed a daub of black paint into the dark green I'd placed in the bowl only seconds ago. The process brought Louis to mind. I would once again begin work on the thick reins of the giant horse that had been spoiled by the sand-infused paint. Mr. Robaugh, one of the master carvers, had managed to remove the paint, but in spite of his experienced and careful work, the damage required hours and hours of work. Even then, Mr. Robaugh had been dissatisfied. He'd told Josef the horse couldn't be restored to its original beauty. The sanding made it impossible to create the same depth and beauty in the carving, but Josef had decided it would be better to save the horse and move it to an inside position.

Mr. Robaugh had been among the men who'd gathered outside the factory to taunt me. No doubt he'd told the men exactly how many hours of overtime he'd been required to work in order to restore the horse to usable condition. Strange how they all blamed me instead of Louis. I had tried to apologize to Mr. Robaugh when he'd begun work on the horse. I'd even offered to stay late and help. He'd waved me aside like a pesky fly and told me to leave him alone.

Now only a little more touchup would be required, and Mr. Tobarth said he'd complete that work once I finished the rest of the trim.

I moved a few inches closer to where Mr. Tobarth was painting silver medallions on a jumper. "Has Mr. Kaestner mentioned anyone applying to fill the vacant positions?"

The wiry man tipped his head to the side and eyed his work. "Nope. Ain't heard nothin'." He drew his brush along one edge of the intricate carving. "Saw you in church last Sunday. That's your first time attendin', ain't it?"

"Second," I said. "I didn't see you."

"That's 'cause I sit near the back. Unless I'm late, then I gotta sit closer to the front. Somehow I didn't figure you for a church-going gal, but Mrs. Wilson's a strong influence in gettin' folks out to church."

His comment startled me. Even in the factory I always did my best to act proper. "Why do you say that?"

He shrugged. "Never heard you say anythin' 'bout God or church. Ain't no need to get your feathers ruffled. Didn't mean no insult by it."

I didn't know why his comment bothered me. Probably because I figured knowing the Lord was like wearing a badge. If you knew Him well, people could tell. It hadn't taken me long to figure out that Mrs. Wilson knew the Lord and Mr. Tobarth, too. They both talked about God sometimes. Kind of like my mama had done when I was little and Papa wasn't around.

"What about Mr. Kaestner? He doesn't act like someone you'd see at church, but he attends every week, doesn't he?"

"Josef? Why, he's 'bout as strong in his beliefs as Mrs. Wilson."

"But he works on Sunday," I countered.

Mr. Tobarth rocked back on his heels and laughed. "You one of those folks that's all tied up in worryin' 'bout rules, huh?"

"The Bible says you're supposed to rest on the Sabbath." I knew that was true. My mama had told me.

"You're right about that." He tapped his finger on his narrow chest. "But it's what's in here that's important. To my way of thinkin', folks worry too much 'bout the wrong things."

I didn't want to argue the rights and wrongs of what people thought about others or the judgments they imposed. And I certainly didn't want to argue about the contents of the Bible. I didn't know enough to hold my own in a debate.

"You gonna keep going to church?" he asked.

"When I'm at the boardinghouse, I will. But sometimes — as I'll do today, for instance — I go to visit friends after work on Saturdays and don't return home until late Sunday evening."

He flashed me a lopsided grin. "Over to the Galloways, I'm guessin'."

I turned my focus to the floor, surprised his comment had caused a feeling of shame to ball up and settle in the hollow of my stomach. "Yes," I whispered.

"Ain't no use tryin' to hide anythin' around this place. Everyone knows you and the Galloway gal are friends. Might as well be proud of the fact." He tucked the paint can close to the rack. "Mostly they're just jealous they don't have the same advantage."

"Maybe," I replied, knowing I wouldn't have been hired had it not been for my friendship with Augusta. However, my association with the Galloway family had unearthed its own ever-growing mound of problems — the primary one being Augusta's insistent invitations to visit her nearly every weekend.

Yet I should be grateful. Where would I be without the Galloways and their help? I mentally checked off the many things they had done for me. The job, the clothing, the paid-up rent, the storage of my father's paintings. Yes, where would I be without the Galloways and their help! Occasional visits at their home were nothing compared to the generosity I'd received.

Mr. Tobarth stood up and lifted his brush to shade the ears of his horse with dark umber. "Josef says you got some of your paintings stored here at the factory. I'd like to see some of your work if you're of a mind to show 'em to me one of these days."

There truly wasn't anything that wasn't known by everyone in the factory. They even knew about the paintings. "They aren't my work, Mr. Tobarth. They're the remaining

221

works my father completed before his death."

"So he was one of them famous European-type artists that made lots of money for paintin' bowls of fruit?"

I chuckled at the question. "He wasn't very famous, and he didn't make much money at all. But his work was admired by all of the other artists. They said he'd be famous one day. Unfortunately, death put an end to his work."

His eyes softened. "Death has a way of doing that." He held the paintbrush to his side and stood back to view the shading he'd completed. "But when you know you'll see the people you love in heaven, it helps ease the pain." When I didn't respond, he glanced over his shoulder, his bushy eyebrows curved at a cockeyed angle. "Don't ya think?"

"But what if you don't think you'll see them in heaven? What if someone you love isn't there? And what if they go to heaven and I don't?"

Concern extinguished the customary glint from his eyes. "You sure got a lot of what-if questions. I'm not sure I'm the one to answer all of 'em, but I'll give it a try — at lunchtime. You bring your pail over here, and I'll tell you how you can be sure 'bout where you're going when you die." He stepped forward and deepened the shading on the inside of the horse's left ear. "Right now I need to concentrate on finishing up some of these horses."

"I'll do that," I said. For some reason, his offer had produced an inexplicable feeling of joy. I didn't know if it was because Mr. Tobarth had spoken to me as though we were friends or if it was because I might receive some additional assurance I'd see Mama and Papa when I died.

She'd done it again! Tyson was sitting on the front porch of Mrs. Wilson's boarding-house when I approached after work. Augusta was nowhere in sight. "Where is Augusta?" I asked, walking past him.

"Good afternoon to you, too, Miss Brouwer." I ignored his sarcasm and continued inside. Tyson followed close on my heels. "How long before you're ready? Augusta said you got off work at six o'clock on Saturdays. It's already seven."

"I don't control the amount of work that must be completed in a given day. And if I'm asked to finish something before leaving, I must do so." I glanced over my shoulder. "Some of us *work* for a living."

He slapped his palm against his chest.

"Oh, you've wounded me, Miss Brouwer. I doubt I'll ever recover from your cruel words."

I waved aside his attempt at comedic drama. "Augusta? Is she —"

"Anxiously awaiting your arrival. I told her it didn't take both of us to call for you. She seems to have difficulty getting anywhere on time."

"That must be a recently acquired bad habit. I don't recall her ever being late when she lived in Paris." I rested my foot on the bottom step of the staircase. "I'll be down momentarily. You can wait in the parlor or on the porch. Whichever you wish."

"I'd prefer to come upstairs and help you." He winked and rubbed his palms together.

I had considered Tyson's past behavior offensive, but he obviously needed to understand that I would no longer tolerate his ill-mannered advances. I leaned across the banister determined I would no longer mince words with him. "I find you one of the most boorish men I've ever encountered. You are coarse in both word and deed, and if it weren't for Augusta, I wouldn't give you the time of day. If your crude behavior doesn't cease, I shall speak to both Augusta and her father." His head jerked back. I silently applauded myself, pleased I'd attained the desired impact.

He made a quick recovery and took a step closer. "I've had far more practice at these games of cat and mouse than you, dear Carrington. I suggest you be careful."

I did my best to ignore his ominous tone. "I'm not playing a game. I'm giving you a warning. Stop your offensive behavior, or I'll speak to Augusta."

"I must warn you, I am quite effective where Augusta is concerned."

I stood there blinking, my heart gone eerily still. "If you'd cease your advances, this wouldn't need to become a contest."

He winked — bold as you please — as if I'd never mentioned his behavior, as if my threat meant nothing, as if he held the trump card. I squared my shoulders and marched upstairs. If he tried to follow, I'd push him down the steps without a second thought.

While I washed up and changed my dress, I considered penning a note and sending my regrets to Augusta. I knew she'd be either angry or hurt — probably both. It didn't take long to push aside the idea and return downstairs. My traveling case had been sitting by the front door since I'd left for work early that morning. Tyson had found more than sufficient time to annoy me, yet he still hadn't loaded my bag.

"You are a picture to behold," Tyson said, his voice smooth and soft.

"And you are a boorish cad." I grabbed the handles of my traveling case and started for the door. When we stepped onto the porch, Tyson reached to take it from me. I swirled around in protest and pulled the bag close to my skirt. "I can carry it myself."

"You are quite haughty, aren't you?" He took two long strides to the porch steps and then glanced back at me. " 'Pride goeth before destruction, and a haughty spirit before a fall.' " He grinned, mocking me with his eyes. "Proverbs sixteen, verse eighteen."

"You'll forgive me if I am somewhat surprised by your ability to quote Scripture." I hastened to the carriage, lifted my bag, and slung it inside. "And the fact that you would do so in this situation grieves and offends me. Tell me, Tyson, if I am filled with pride, how do you label your own sin?"

"Me?" He tipped his head close to my ear. "I don't worry about the sin aspect. I worry only about the conquest."

I did my utmost to sit as far away from him as possible. He seemed to find my behavior amusing. How could Augusta think this shallow, loathsome man appealing? During our carriage ride, he did his best to engage me in conversation while I did my best to ignore him. Thankful to see Augusta waiting on the porch when we arrived, I grabbed my bag and stepped down from the carriage without a backward glance.

"You should always wait for the gentleman to assist you," Augusta whispered when I leaned forward to accept her embrace.

"What gentleman? And why are you dressed in that fancy gown?"

She tipped her head to the side and giggled. "Tyson, of course. You should have waited for him to help you down."

"I've grown accustomed to fending for myself over these past weeks. Besides, I'm perfectly capable of getting in and out of a carriage without help. Shall I take my bag upstairs?" I gestured toward her dress. "And you still haven't told me why you're wearing that elegant gown." The dress was beautiful. Fashioned of pale mauve duchess satin and bearing the latest fashionable huge velvet sleeves adorned with lace, the gown would likely be the envy of many a young lady.

"Come along. We need to hurry and get you dressed. I'll have Frances help with your hair. You did bring one of the evening dresses, didn't you? We're going to a party."

A mental image of the party gowns that vied for far too much space in my wardrobe danced before me. "No. Your note said nothing about a party. You and Tyson go on. I'll stay here and rest. I'll find a good book in your father's library. Besides, I'm tired after working all day."

Augusta planted her fists on her hips. "Don't you even think of refusing. We'll find something in my closet that will be perfect. Come along." Like an obedient child, I followed her up the stairs and into the room I'd occupied during my first days in Collinsford. "Wait here. I'll be back before you have time to miss me."

I eyed the bed with longing. If only I could change into my nightgown and slip between the cool sheets to rest and rejuvenate my aching muscles. I dropped to the side of the bed, the soft mattress beckoning me once again to enjoy its comfort. I removed my shoes, lifted my legs onto the bed, and eased my back against the plump pillows. A sigh escaped my lips, and I closed my eyes. An intoxicating scent offering a promise of spring drifted through the window and carried me back to my early years in New Hampshire. Daddy had planted lilac bushes along one side of the house because they were Mama's favorite. Each spring I'd pick bouquets for her. And each spring Mama would tell me lilacs were God's promise of another wonderful springtime. I always agreed.

But the lilacs wouldn't bloom for at least another four or five weeks. Spring had a way of teasing with sunny days and budding flowers, but winter hadn't quite released its hold. The biting wind of the previous morning had been proof of that. The very thought caused me to shiver. I pulled the soft blanket across my shoulders and promised myself I wouldn't go to sleep.

"Carrie!"

Startled, I lurched forward. If I hadn't grabbed the bedpost, I would have landed on the floor. My heart pounded with turbulent ferocity, and I clasped a palm to my chest. "Why are you shouting?" I yelled. I couldn't help myself. Augusta had nearly frightened the life out of me. Her eyes widened, and for a moment I thought she was going to cry. "I didn't mean to hurt your feelings, but I'm right here where you left me."

"But you were asleep."

I didn't know what difference it made if I slept on the bed or if I sat in a chair with

229

my eyes wide open while I waited. It obviously mattered to Augusta. She stood in front of me, satin and lace flowing over her arms in myriad colors.

"I've brought these for you to try. Frances is coming with some more."

"I don't want to try on all of these gowns." I pointed to a charcoal gray offering. "That one will do." Besides, it would match my best shoes. I was thankful my toe no longer pained me. Otherwise, the pointed shoes would have pinched. And I didn't think Augusta would permit my ugly work shoes with a formal gown. The very thought was enough to make me giggle.

"I think this one is better," Augusta said. "And what is so funny?"

"Just a fleeting thought," I replied while Augusta tugged a gown from between Frances's arms and held it against my waist.

One look in the mirror and I gasped. The color was a shade that could only be described as somewhere between fuchsia and purple. It reminded me of a petunia. Even the sleeves drooped like the edges of the trumpet-shaped bloom. I didn't intend to arrive at the party resembling a drooping fuchsia flower.

"No. The gray. I insist." Crossing my arms over my waist, I began tapping my foot, determined this skirmish would not be lost. "Frances can return the other gowns to your room, and you can help me change."

Augusta didn't argue. I don't know if it was the resolve in my voice or my firm military stance, but she piled the gowns into Frances's arms and sent her down the hall. Augusta helped me with my dress, then Frances returned and arranged my hair in a tea-cake coiffure. She draped far too many curls across my forehead, but when I raked my fingers through the fringe, her lips tightened into a knot. There was little doubt I'd offended her, but I didn't intend to go out in public with those drooping tresses hanging in my eyes. They reminded me of the thick trim that decorated Mrs. Galloway's frightful table coverings.

"A bit too curly, don't you think?" When Augusta and I locked gazes in the mirror, I arched my eyebrows.

"It's perfect. We don't have time to straighten it. Besides, curls are in fashion." She selected two aigrettes and shoved them into the curls. "Perfect."

In my estimation the coiffure was far from perfect, but I thanked Frances for her help. She frowned in return. Apparently my words didn't ring true. Then again, it may have been my exercise in finger-combing that had offended her.

Before there was time to further consider her behavior, Augusta grasped my hand and pulled me toward the bedroom door. It was when we stopped to gather our wraps from the nearby chair that we heard Mrs. Galloway's screams.

CHAPTER 14

While we raced down the hallway, I pushed the curls off my forehead, thankful I could finally see where I was going. Had anyone observed Augusta yanking on my hand while we hurtled toward her mother's room, we would have been declared completely mad. Augusta rushed to her mother's side, but I skidded to a dead halt just inside the door. To say Mrs. Galloway's appearance was startling would be an understatement. How her facial features could contort into such an unattractive assemblage was beyond my comprehension.

Augusta clutched her mother by the shoulders and begged to know what was wrong. Mrs. Galloway gasped great gulps of air and waved her arms toward the dressing table. Clasping a hand to her heart, she exhaled several indistinguishable sounds before screeching, "My necklace is missing! My diamond and sapphire necklace. The one your father gave me for our anniversary."

She collapsed into Augusta's arms and continued her zealous weeping while I stood frozen in place, my mouth gaping like an open door. I didn't know what to say or do. The woman appeared inconsolable. I decided her flair for the dramatic had once again taken over. Augusta was having little effect, so hoping to lend aid, I stepped forward and reached to open one of the drawers in the mahogany jewelry box.

Mrs. Galloway shifted toward me with the speed of a cat pouncing on prey. "Don't touch a thing!" she shrieked.

Hand trembling, I jumped back. "I wasn't . . . I didn't . . . I only hoped to help. I thought perhaps you had placed your necklace in a different drawer when you last put it away." I stifled the gurgling onset of a hysterical giggle.

"Do you think I would keep a valuable necklace in a simple jewelry box? The necklace was in my husband's safe." She tapped a velvet case sitting on her dressing table. "In this box. The necklace is gone," she hissed.

I edged toward the door. "Would you like me to fetch Mr. Galloway?"

"Yes. You do that," she said between sobs.

Relieved to be away from the frenzied woman, I rushed down the stairs toward Mr. Galloway's library — and directly into the arms of Tyson Farnsworth. I silently chastised myself for not watching where I was going.

"To what do I owe this privilege?" He held me close, the warmth of his breath causing me to lean backward.

"Let me go. I must speak to Mr. Galloway at once." I yanked away, but not before his fingers traveled down my back in a bold and frightful manner.

The thought of slapping his face flitted through my mind, but such a reaction would only add to the current havoc taking place in Mrs. Galloway's room. The woman couldn't handle another problem at the moment — nor could Augusta. Tyson followed behind me. I didn't know why. Either he was checking to see if I'd told him the truth or he planned to offer his assistance. Knowing Tyson, I didn't think it was the latter.

After I located Mr. Galloway in the rear garden talking to Thomas, I relayed the details. He motioned me to follow while he continued to ask questions. Tyson remained close on my heels, and I watched while Mr. Galloway examined the safe in his library for any evidence of foul play.

"I know I opened the safe to place the deed inside only an hour or so before retrieving the jewelry box. I thought I'd locked it, but it's possible I could be mistaken." He rubbed his forehead and stared at the floor. "I simply can't be certain," he mumbled. "Why don't the two of you wait in the parlor while I go up and speak to my wife."

I wanted to oppose Mr. Galloway's suggestion. But any objection would call for an explanation and further turmoil, so I followed behind the older man until we reached the parlor. The moment Mr. Galloway was out of sight, Tyson lunged toward me. His teeth gleamed like porcelain daggers. I needed a plan. A plan that would put some distance and several large objects between us. After a glance over my shoulder, I swiveled around and dashed to the other side of the settee. I felt like Little Red Riding Hood with the wolf poised and anxious to devour his prey.

Tyson snickered and followed. "No need to run and hide. There's no one watching. Why don't you come over here and sit with me? I'd like to talk with you about your life in France and your father's paintings."

Ha! He no more wanted to talk about my life in France or my father's artwork than he wanted to perform a day of manual labor. Did he think me a fool? That I would immediately rush to his side like an unsuspecting child? I remembered well what had happened to Red Riding Hood.

"I prefer to remain here. Why don't you sit down and tell me about your time in college and how you plan to make a living now that your schooling is complete."

Surprisingly, he dropped into the chair and laughed. "I don't think your innocent ears could withstand an accounting of my college years." He leaned forward and rested his arms across his thighs and smirked. "Would it surprise you to know that a fine fellow like me was dismissed from college because of his unwillingness to abide by the rules?"

"Not in the least."

He laughed, a little too loudly. "That's what I like about you, Carrington. You say what you think. But let me —"

Before he could finish, Augusta bounded down the steps and settled into a chair beside him. His piercing blue eyes remained fixed upon me, and an unexpected shiver spiraled down my spine.

Augusta grasped Tyson's arm, and he looked away. "Poor Mother. I believe she has finally calmed a bit. Father told her he would replace the necklace, but it won't be the same as having the one he presented to her on their anniversary. She's determined the thief be apprehended."

"I couldn't agree more. And we should all do whatever is necessary to discover who the culprit may be." Tyson tapped the arm of his chair and stared at the rug. Moments later, he lifted his head with a jerk. "I know! We need to determine the last time your mother saw the necklace and then compile a list of any possible suspects."

I wondered if Tyson had been reading some of Allan Pinkerton's detective novels and now fancied himself a sleuth of sorts. Or perhaps he hoped to impress Augusta or Mrs. Galloway with his ability to retrieve the necklace or apprehend the culprit. Surely he realized he didn't need to do anything more to win Augusta's affections. As far as I could tell, Mr. and Mrs. Galloway thought him the perfect escort for their daughter. I thought his idea rather silly.

"I'm certain your father will want to contact the police," I said. "They're familiar with the proper techniques to solve a crime."

Tyson stabbed me with a menacing sneer. "There's no reason we can't begin to compile information before they arrive." He turned to Augusta for validation. She leaned into his arm and bobbed her head in agreement. I wanted to shake her into reality but knew my efforts would prove fruitless.

"He's right, Carrie. I'm sure the police would be grateful for any help we can give them."

"I disagree. I think they would choose to gather the information themselves and then tell us what we can do to assist them." I truly didn't know what the police would prefer, but I wanted Augusta to agree with me.

"Admit you're wrong, Carrie. You're simply permitting your pride to take over. Tyson is correct this time," Augusta said. Tyson preened like a cat that had just lapped up a bowl of cream. He knew he'd won.

Augusta's words stung. That was twice in recent days that I had been called prideful. Couldn't she see this had nothing to do with pride? I was trying to save her from a scoundrel of the worst sort.

"Do you truly believe I'm prideful?" I wasn't certain I wanted to hear the answer, yet I couldn't resist asking. Was the fact that I couldn't resist asking a matter of pride, too? Would Augusta agree with Mr. Tobarth's assessment of me? A jumble of thoughts tumbled around in my head while

I awaited her judgment.

"Maybe a little," she said. Her voice was tentative, and she couldn't quite look at me. Her gaze rested on my chin. I wanted to tell her she should have the courage of her convictions and look me in the eyes when she said something so hurtful. *Prideful?* I considered some of the things I'd said and done since arriving in Collinsford. I had to admit there might be a minute possibility others thought I possessed a slight attitude of superiority.

There was the incident in which I'd defended my artistic ability and told Mrs. Galloway I was a talented painter. I'd been somewhat prideful when I'd told Mrs. Wilson about painting stripes on horses at the factory; and I'd been defensive when Josef hadn't been impressed by my painting qualifications. And, of course, there was my refusal to use the maulstick. There probably were other incidents I couldn't think of at the moment. Still, there were many other people I considered much more arrogant and prideful than me. How could Augusta turn on me? I didn't need to ask, for I already knew the answer. She wanted to please Tyson.

And please him she did. While Augusta hurried off in search of paper and pencil for his list, Tyson smirked at me. "You should have known she would side with me, dear Carrie."

A rush of fear surged through my body. He was playing a game with me, and I didn't know the rules. Truth be told, I didn't even know the game.

"Ah, here is Augusta with paper and pencil. Now, let's see. We need to determine who was in the house when you first discovered the necklace was missing."

"There's no way to determine when the necklace was removed since Mrs. Galloway had placed the jewelry case in Mr. Galloway's safe," I countered.

"Then we must begin by determining the last time the necklace was seen."

Tyson's attempt to adopt the role of detective was most annoying. "Wouldn't you need to speak to Mrs. Galloway in order to gain that information?" I asked.

"Mrs. Galloway or the person who carried the case to the safe," he said, with a glint in his eye.

"Oh, you are so clever," Augusta cooed.

I considered countering the silly comment but held my tongue. Mr. Galloway was leading his wife down the stairs. I'd wait and see if he judged Tyson clever or if he'd prefer to have a policeman investigate. Mrs.

Galloway settled in one of the upholstered chairs. Her complexion had turned the shade of cold ashes, and I feared she would swoon if further confusion arose.

Deciding to be on my best behavior, I waited for Augusta or Tyson to make the first move. Tyson didn't disappoint. Quicker than a bird taking flight, he detailed his plan to capture the culprit. I couldn't believe my eyes or my ears. Both Mr. and Mrs. Galloway offered him their undivided attention. Why didn't they simply contact the police? I stared out the window, half listening, annoyed by the entire scene. Several children were playing jump rope out front, and I soon found myself absorbed in their game of double dutch. Their ability amazed me. I'd never been much good at jump rope — even with a single rope, but the *slap, slap, slap* of the two ropes and the laughter of the girls mesmerized me.

I'd been lulling in a self-imposed stupor when I heard Tyson say, "From what you've told me, the only stranger in your home since you last saw the necklace is Carrington."

I snapped to attention as if I'd been whapped by a cold, wet towel. "Excuse me? *What* did you just say? Are you accusing me of theft?" I imagined that my eyes were now bulging like a giant frog — or was it a toad with those protruding eyes? "Surely I misunderstood." My voice croaked like a bullfrog. It took only the fleeting thought of frog eyes, toads, and croaking to send me into a fit of giggles. I couldn't stop. Tears trickled down my cheeks while Mr. and Mrs. Galloway stared at me. They appeared disgusted by my behavior, and I did my best to hold my breath and gain control.

"She doesn't mean to be rude," Augusta said. "You recall she does this when she's upset."

"Or when you have feelings of guilt?" Tyson leered across the room and cut me with a steely look.

Fear overtook me, and the laughter stopped midgiggle. There was no doubt in my mind that he was accusing me of stealing Mrs. Galloway's necklace. How *dare* he? Would Mr. and Mrs. Galloway think I would do such a thing?

"You don't believe him, do you? I have never stolen anything in my life." I hesitated and quickly recanted. "Except a few slices of bread from Leclair's Bakery one day when I was very hungry," I admitted. "But nothing else. And why would I steal from the very people who have done the most to help me?"

They didn't respond. They were all staring at me as though they considered me a suspect. All except Augusta. In her eyes, though, I detected a hint of worry.

Finally I said, "I think you should call the police. Then I'm certain the true thief will be caught."

Mr. Galloway immediately concurred, though Tyson did his best to convince him the police couldn't do any more than he'd already accomplished. While Augusta took her mother upstairs to lie down until the police arrived, Mr. Galloway departed for the police station, leaving me, once again, alone with Tyson.

"Why are you doing this? You know I would never steal from the Galloways."

He shrugged before dropping into a nearby chair. "All things considered, you *are* the most likely suspect. The servants have worked here for years. You're the only unknown component in the equation. I truly believe the police will draw the same conclusion."

Tyson was pleased with himself. I could tell by the way his chest expanded when Augusta returned to the room — as if he'd been anointed with some special power that I couldn't comprehend. Maybe he was right. I certainly didn't understand why the

Galloways had listened to him accuse me of stealing before they decided to contact the police. And now I was concerned Mr. Galloway would tell them I was the prime suspect. They might not even look for the real thief. I tried to calm myself by remembering one of my father's admonitions about never borrowing trouble. It didn't help.

Augusta did her best to act the proper hostess while we waited, but I suspected she had allied herself with Tyson. She was fawning over him, and she couldn't meet my eyes. Every time I caught her looking at me, she glanced away. What would it be like to be locked up in a jail, I wondered? Would I giggle or cry when they slammed the door and tossed me into a dank cell with nothing more than bread and water?

I was contemplating the idea when Mr. Galloway entered the house accompanied by a short, bald man with a tiny mustache that curled on each end. He didn't look like a policeman, but Mr. Galloway introduced him as a detective with the Collinsford Police Department. I didn't know whether to be pleased or frightened when Mr. Galloway informed us Detective Nelson Lawton had been with the Pinkerton Agency for a year before joining the Collinsford Police Department. The detective immediately corrected him.

"Nearly two years," Detective Lawton said. He appeared eager to impress us with his competence. "Let's begin at the beginning."

Not wanting to laugh at the tiresome remark, I curled my lips inward until I was sure they had completely disappeared from sight. Mrs. Galloway was summoned from her room, and once again the routine questions were asked — and answered, mostly by Tyson. I seemed to be the only one who noticed he had taken over as the self-appointed authority on all that had occurred. I also noticed Detective Lawton giving me sidelong glances each time Tyson mentioned my name.

I pressed my hand down the gray silk dress and imagined myself twirling around the dance floor. I'd had no particular desire to attend this evening's party, but even a stuffy dance would have provided more enjoyment than Detective Lawton and his copious questions.

After all, what difference did it make where I was born, and why did he need every address where I'd lived for my entire life? He wrote down the information as though his very life depended on it. As I watched him, I had the fleeting notion that perhaps *my* life depended upon what he was writing. Instead of thinking about the dance, I wondered if I should be constructing a defense.

"Tell me, Miss Brouwer, did you have access to the necklace in question?"

"I don't think so. I mean, I lived here for a time — as a guest of the Galloways — until I secured my own living quarters."

"Hmm. And from what you've told me, you're currently living in The Bottoms, isn't that correct?"

He made it sound as though living in The Bottoms was a crime in and of itself. "I live in a boardinghouse close to my work, and it is, as you say, located in The Bottoms."

"So it is safe for me to assume you are living on a small income?"

Oh, he was thinking that because I was poor, I had a motive to steal from the Galloways. Well, he wasn't fooling me in the least! "I am living on an adequate income, but even if I were starving, I wouldn't steal from the Galloways."

"Except for perhaps a few slices of bread?" Tyson asked.

I wanted to reach across the distance that separated us and smack the grin from his face, but I forced myself to remain calm and offered the detective a sweet smile. At least I hoped it was sweet. I was having difficulty getting my lips to cooperate. "I don't think a couple slices of bread taken from my landlady's bakery equates to stealing a valuable necklace," I countered.

"No, it doesn't. But if a suspect shows a propensity toward such behavior . . ." The detective's incomplete sentence hung in the air like an unspoken accusation.

CHAPTER 15

When I arrived at work Monday morning, I removed my coat and sat down at my work area. I was more than thankful Mr. Tobarth didn't ask about my weekend, for I wanted all memories of the previous days to flee from my mind. Dwelling on what I now considered a horrid visit wouldn't resolve anything.

With my paints before me, I studied the variety of colors. I wanted the perfect shade to stripe my horse. My eyes flitted from one hue to the next, but soon the paints mocked me. The colors floated before my eyes like a multitude of vibrant silk gowns — like the gowns worn by Mrs. Galloway's female guests on Saturday evening. I cringed at the thought.

Strange how I'd been initially delighted to go and visit the Galloways. I'd been eager to escape my difficulties at work and step into their problem-free world. But within hours of my arrival, I'd wanted to flee their home and return to The Bottoms. The remainder of the visit had been disastrous. Mrs. Galloway had insisted upon attending the party after Detective Lawton departed.

Mr. Galloway had vehemently advised against the idea, but his wife would not be denied. She was determined to increase the social stature of the Galloway family, and this was a party where all the right people would be in attendance. Those she wanted to impress. Those she wanted to infiltrate. Those she wanted to *be.*

Though I kept my opinion to myself, I, too, thought she should remain at home. There would be other opportunities to gain favor among the members of Collinsford's upper class. However, Mrs. Galloway had won the argument. We all attended the party.

I think she enjoyed making an entrance. She was most pleased to explain her pasty complexion, her near fainting spell, and the tragedy that had befallen the Galloway household. The dowagers gathered around and offered sympathy as they listened to her tale of woe. Instinctively they clasped a hand to their own heavily bejeweled necklines or wrists.

Mrs. Galloway's cheeks gradually took on color as she basked in their attention. She obviously believed a stolen necklace had established her as a member of polite society. I had my doubts. Though my understanding of societal rules was limited, I thought it would take more than a piece of stolen jewelry to penetrate the ranks of the prune-faced women.

The evening was further marred by Tyson and his snide remarks. I did my best to avoid him, but when Augusta brought him to my side and insisted the two of us enjoy a dance, there was no escape. I questioned him at length about why he was casting blame in my direction. At first he feigned ignorance, but when I persisted, he said I shouldn't have spurned him. Spurned him? His reply was ludicrous. He was Augusta's beau. If only Ronald had come home from college and I'd had a proper escort, I could have avoided dancing with Tyson. He held me much too close, and when I pushed away, he snickered.

Trying my best to push the memory from my mind, I picked up a maulstick. I'd decided on a subtle shade of creamy yellow to stripe the navy blue blanket flowing from beneath the horse's saddle.

"Nice work."

I hadn't heard Mr. Tobarth approach. I turned and looked up. "Thank you."

"I see you decided on usin' a maulstick after all." He bit his lip between his teeth, and the veins on either side of his neck protruded like two ropes. "What's your opinion now that you've tried usin' it?"

"You were right. It helps a great deal."

He gave a firm nod of his head, apparently pleased by my response. After selecting a brush and paint, he took his place nearby and set to work on the jumper. "Good weekend at the Galloways'?" he asked.

I'd told him about my plans; now I wished I hadn't. I didn't want to carry tales of what had happened. Yet I wondered if news of the theft would be in the local newspaper. Would my name be listed as a visitor at the Galloways' home? If Tyson had his way, he'd have me listed as the number one suspect.

"Not so good." I related the barest of details and was thankful when Mr. Tobarth didn't ask a lot of questions.

"You go to church with the Galloways when you visit?"

I nodded. "Over at Community Central."

We had, in fact, gone to church on Sunday. All of us. Even Tyson. I hadn't heard much of the sermon. I'd been too busy worrying about going to jail for a crime I didn't commit. "Do you think God lets good people suffer and bad people get away with things?"

Mr. Tobarth chuckled. "I think there's lots of good people who suffer. Jesus was perfect. He suffered and died on the cross for our sins, didn't He?"

"Yes, but it doesn't seem right that good people should suffer, does it?"

"Nope. But this here's what the preacher calls a fallen world. When Adam and Eve sinned, evil came into the world. Kinda turned things upside down and makes it hard for us to understand when good people get hurt. But the devil's out there prowlin' around, doing his best to cause pain and confusion."

"Still, it's hard to accept that good people can be accused and punished for something they didn't do."

He stood and carefully painted a glint in his horse's eye, then turned and looked at me. "You talkin' 'bout yourself or just in general?" With the stroke of his paintbrush, the animal had taken on a personality of its own. It looked kind and gentle. Like the carousel horse I'd ridden when I was a little girl.

"Both," I said. "Do you think if people pray, God turns things around?"

"If you're askin' do I think prayer works, the answer is yes. But if you're askin' do I think God always give us the answer we want, the answer is no. We're not supposed to understand everything that happens in this world, but one day it will all be clear to us."

"I see," I muttered, but didn't really see. I wanted Mr. Tobarth to tell me God would answer my prayers in the way I had asked. I wanted to know the real thief would be found. I wanted to know I wouldn't go to jail. Maybe all the bad things in my life would be made clear when I died, but I didn't want to wait that long — and I wasn't ready to die, either!

For now, I needed to concentrate on my painting, but I determined to give the matter of answered prayer more thought while I ate my lunch. I continued painting in earnest and was surprised when the buzzer sounded. I gathered my lunch pail and sketch pad, just in case I found myself unable to concentrate on prayer or God, and headed outside. Ignoring the bench, I settled beneath a big old tree. After spreading the cloth napkin across my paint-splotched apron, I took a bite of my sandwich. Did other people have problems concentrating on God? Did their minds wander when they attempted to pray? Surely I wasn't the only one. Then again, maybe I was. If I'd grown up spending time in prayer, maybe I wouldn't find it so difficult to focus my thoughts on God. If I could concentrate on my painting, surely I could train my thoughts to remain upon God in the same manner.

I hadn't heard the shuffle of feet or noticed the women approach until they were standing directly in front of me. There were four of them in all — strangers. Two held young children by the hand, while one was much older with withered skin. She'd covered her gray hair with a multicolored scarf that had been knotted beneath her chin. She waved a thin knobby finger at me and shouted something in a language I didn't understand.

Instinctively I reared back. Splinters of rough tree bark bit into my shoulders, but I remained plastered against the sturdy trunk. Hoping to dispel what was obviously some misunderstanding, I forced a feeble smile. The women glared in return. My gesture of friendliness had only made matters worse. The older woman took another step toward me with a menacing glint in her eye.

Perhaps if I spoke to them in a kind manner, it would help. "It's a lovely day, isn't it?" My palms turned moist, and I could feel beads of perspiration forming across my upper lip. Who were these women, and what did they want? "May I help you?"

The middle-aged woman grasped the old woman by the arm and shook her head. The old woman touched her fingers to her lips, then pointed at me. The younger of the two nodded. "We want you should stay away from our husbands. Only one kind of woman wants to work with the men." Her words bore a heavy accent, but there was no doubt to their meaning. The three other women nodded their approval of the message, though I doubted the old lady understood what had been said.

"I am a good person. I need work to buy food."

"Bah!" The middle-aged woman curled her lip and flung a dismissive wave in my direction. "We speak for the wives. We want you to leave this place."

The hunched old woman muttered and spit on the ground. I thought it must have been a curse, and I wanted to tell her I didn't need any more trouble in my life, but the look in her eyes was enough to seal my lips. I didn't even breathe until all of them were out of sight. Only then did I toss the napkin into my pail and push to my feet.

My hands quivered as I wiped my damp palms down the front of my work apron. So much for my time of meditation and prayer.

Mrs. Wilson was aflutter when I returned home from work on the following Saturday. She stood outside, a floral apron tied around her thick waist while she paced the length of the porch. By the time I neared the front steps, she was wringing her hands together.

"Is something wrong, Mrs. Wilson?" I knew it was a silly question, but I hoped my bright smile and even tone would soothe her. Cupping her palm, she waved me forward as though she could scoop me up the stairs and onto the porch. I hurried my step. "Tell me what's happened," I said.

"A policeman was here," she whispered. "He said he was a detective. He was asking questions about you."

I sighed and dropped onto one of the porch chairs. I didn't need further trouble. Two more times during the week, wives, mothers, and children of the workers had stood across the street and stared at me during my lunchtime. Now the detective had come calling. And he certainly hadn't wasted much time. Would my difficulties never end?

"Are you in trouble, Carrie? He wouldn't tell me anything, just kept asking questions."

Lifting my nose in the air, I sniffed and jumped up from the chair. "Something's on fire, Mrs. Wilson."

"Oh, dear me, I put a chicken on to fry and forgot all about it when I came out on the porch to watch for you."

Smoke filled the hallway, but as it turned out, the only damage was to the chicken. I flapped a dish towel at the billowing smoke while Mrs. Wilson did her best to remove the charred crust and salvage some of the meat, to no avail. That night, supper consisted of potatoes and creamed peas. Neither Mr. Lundgren nor Josef complained. I think they were thankful the potatoes were lump free. It had taken more instruction than I'd expected to teach the woman how to make a decent white sauce for the peas and properly mash potatoes, but she'd mastered both. At least for tonight.

After the dishes had been washed and I was alone with Mrs. Wilson in the kitchen, I quizzed her about the detective and what questions he'd asked. They'd been much the same as he'd asked me, and I decided he was simply attempting to catch me in a lie.

Of course Mrs. Wilson expected an explanation. I did my best to give her a brief account, but one question led to another. By the time we'd finished our talk, it was nearly bedtime. "I trust you won't say anything about this to the others?"

She patted my arm. "You can trust me, Carrie. The question is, can you trust that Tyson Farnsworth?"

"I don't think so, but Augusta thinks he's almost perfect. I haven't been able to convince her otherwise."

Before Mrs. Wilson could question me further, I hurried upstairs and prepared for bed. I tried to pray, but I didn't know exactly what to say. I finally ended up with a jumble of words that made little sense. I told God I was sure He already knew my problems, and I'd appreciate it if He would grace me with a solution that eliminated any prospect of jail. Sleep came quickly, but my dreams were filled with frightening episodes that included a trial at which Tyson Farnsworth was the judge. He sentenced me to fifty years in jail. I awakened myself shouting, "I'm not guilty!"

I was thankful my third-floor bedroom prevented my cries from carrying to the lower floors. If the others heard, none of them mentioned it at breakfast. The usual Sunday breakfast had been prepared — scrambled eggs, crispy bacon, and burned toast. There was little conversation during the meal, but all four of us were dressed in our Sunday best.

Once the meal was completed and the dirty dishes stacked in the kitchen, Mrs. Wilson removed her apron and pinned her hat in place. After a glance in the hall mirror, she gave an affirmative nod. "I believe we're ready for church." She grasped Mr. Lundgren's arm and motioned to Josef. "You can escort Carrie."

I don't know who was more surprised, Josef or me. And I don't know whose features took on more color. Josef's cheeks turned a deep crimson shade, and I felt as though a fire had been kindled in each of mine. However, Josef didn't hesitate before offering his arm. Fingers trembling, I took hold and was surprised by the strength I could feel beneath the navy blue sleeve of his jacket. Strange that holding his arm created a feeling of safety. We walked the short distance to church with Mrs. Wilson and Mr. Lundgren in the lead — as though we'd been doing this for years.

"Your painting, it is improving," Josef said after we crossed the street.

"It is?" His words were a soothing balm to my wounded spirit, and my heart thumped an extra beat. I'd been longing for someone's approval, especially since the incident at the Galloways'.

"Ja. You are learning gut from Mr. Tobarth." Strands of thick brown hair fell across his forehead, and he pushed them back in place with an impatient grunt. "Another painter was hired yesterday. Monday, he begins to work with you and Henry."

"Oh, that *is* good news."

He bobbed his head. "Ja. He has worked in Philadelphia like Henry and me. He is an old friend and a gut worker. Lucky we are to get him."

"Does he know about me?" My heart hammered in my chest, but I wanted to know what to expect on Monday morning.

"For sure I told him we had a lady working in the paint shop. He wanted to know if you were pretty." A laugh rumbled deep in his chest.

With a sidelong glance, I asked, "And what did you tell him?"

"I told him ja, you are pretty, but he is to keep his eyes on the horses and not on you. Also I told him you are looking for a rich husband." He shook his head. "Rich, he is not."

I couldn't believe my ears. He'd made that remark as casually as if he'd said the sky was blue. I dug in my heels and skidded to a halt.

"Something is wrong?"

"Yes, something is wrong! How could you say such a thing about me?"

"Is the truth, isn't it? You are all the time going with the Galloways to those fancy parties. Is to find you a husband, ja?"

I dropped my hold on his arm and firmly planted a fist on each hip. "That is so far from the truth that it makes me want to laugh. I don't like going to those silly parties, and I am *not* looking for a husband."

Pointing to the church, he said, "We will be late. I don't like to be late for church." He bent his elbow and glanced at my fist. "We will go now?"

I took hold of his arm and marched alongside, hoping my thumping feet would let him know just how much he'd annoyed me. How had he come to such a conclusion? And he didn't even give a proper response when I said I wasn't looking for a husband.

I walked a short distance farther before I repeated, "I am *not* looking for a husband." For some reason I wanted him to acknowledge I was content with my status as a single woman.

He remained silent until we were walking

up the front steps of the church. "It is time for us to be thinking about God, ja?"

My insides churned. He was avoiding my question because he didn't believe me — I was sure of it! We sat down in the pew as if we belonged together. I wondered what Mr. Tobarth would think if he saw us. And what if some of the other workers and their wives saw us? What would *they* think? The wives would probably be pleased. If Josef were my beau, they'd no longer consider me a threat, and maybe they'd cease their intrusions during my lunch break. On the other hand, the men might dislike me even more if they thought Josef had taken a romantic interest in me.

I peeked at him from beneath the brim of my straw hat. His head was bowed, and his lips were moving ever so slightly. I wasn't sure if he was praying, but his eyes were closed. This must be one of those times when he thought about God.

I bowed my head and decided I should do the same. I tried to focus on God, but my thoughts flittered like a restless bird bounding from branch to branch. The organist hit a sour note, and I thought about how I wished I could play the piano; I thought about Josef's soft brown eyes and why they suddenly seemed to look deep inside me; I thought about why he assumed I wanted to get married; I thought about everything but God.

When the organist finally struck a loud chord that signaled the service would soon begin, Josef lifted his head, and I followed his lead. What had he prayed about? Or had his thoughts wandered like my own? Not likely. Mr. Tobarth had said Josef was a devout believer. Unlike me, Josef probably had no trouble keeping his focus upon the Almighty.

Although I hadn't managed to remain focused during the early portion of the service, I did sit up and take note during the sermon. The preacher spoke about Stephen and how he'd been wrongly accused. I thought of Tyson and the blame he'd been casting on me. It gave me little assurance when I heard the preacher say that Stephen had been stoned to death. Maybe I *would* end up in jail!

"A gut sermon the preacher gave us today," Josef said as we departed the church.

"Not so good for Stephen," I said.

Josef extended his elbow. I attempted to disguise my awkward feelings and grabbed hold. "Maybe not so gut for Stephen, but it teaches us a lesson that we must be willing to hold fast to our beliefs."

"I'm not so sure. Stephen was telling the truth, but God allowed those men to stone him to death. If you're telling the truth and you ask God for protection, don't you think He should answer your prayer?"

Josef leaned down and picked up a scrap of paper that had blown across the church-yard. "Maybe God doesn't give us what we are wanting, but I think our prayers, they are always answered." He crumpled the paper and shoved it into his pocket. "Some-times we must suffer."

I didn't like his answer. It was much the same as what Mr. Tobarth had told me. I wanted Josef to agree with me. Even more, I wanted God to remove Tyson Farnsworth from my life. And beyond that, I wanted God to make sure I didn't go to jail. Maybe I didn't have the strength to be a Christian. I couldn't summon the slightest desire to suffer.

Before I could question Josef further, Mrs. Wilson scuttled to my side. Her feather-bedecked hat was much too large for her head, but it made her all the more endear-ing. "I've a surprise for the two of you," she said.

I held my breath and waited. Though she meant well, sometimes Mrs. Wilson's sur-prises turned out to be more of a curse than a blessing.

"What kind of surprise?" Josef asked.

"We're all going on a picnic together. I have a lunch ready back at the house." She waggled her finger. "I don't want to hear any excuses. It's a beautiful Sunday afternoon, and it will only be better if we're outdoors with good food."

Josef grinned at Mrs. Wilson. "Such a kind offer. How can I refuse?"

I noticed Josef didn't mention the food portion of Mrs. Wilson's invitation. I agreed to attend. Not because I expected a fine feast, but because I hoped to further explore God's method for answering prayer requests. And because I wanted to learn more about Josef. The curt behavior I'd experienced at the factory had disappeared. I wondered if my initial impression of him had been mistaken. Perhaps he wasn't as sullen and unfriendly as I'd suspected. Or perhaps this was his Sunday behavior.

Before we left the house, I picked up my sketch pad and tucked it into a bag with the Bible my mother had given me — just in case an opportunity arose to discover those much hoped for answers about prayer and suffering.

Mrs. Wilson had arranged the afternoon and took great pleasure in directing our activities until we'd completed our picnic lunch. She was packing the leftovers when Josef pointed to my sketch pad. "You are drawing more carousel animals?"

I withdrew the tablet and flipped back the cover. He looked at the drawing and then at me. I couldn't tell for sure what he thought. "Very gut, this is."

His words warmed me like a welcoming fire on a cold winter day. I hadn't expected him to think much of the drawing. When I'd been hired at the carousel factory, he had been unimpressed with my previous art training. And this sketch was a portrait of my mother. A simple picture that I'd begun to draw in the evenings because my memory of her features had begun to fade. I wondered how it was possible that such a thing could happen. She had given me life, nurtured and loved me, yet my mind played tricks on me when my pencil touched paper. To forget what she looked like seemed unfaithful.

Josef tapped the page. "This is someone you know?"

My voice hitched in my throat. "M-my mother," I said. "She's dead."

Josef removed the sketch pad from my hands and examined the picture more closely. "Your mother, she was very beautiful." Lifting his head, he studied me until I squirmed under his scrutiny. "You have the same eyes as your mother." He touched his finger to his chin. "And the same chin, too, I think. A picture of someone you love is nice to have. My mother, she is dead, too." A hint of sadness hung in the air.

"Do you have a picture of her?" I asked.

"No, but I have gut memories of her. She liked to laugh. Fun we had in our house when she was there." His eyes had taken on a glassy, faraway look.

I remained silent, watching and understanding; he had returned to one of those happy times he'd mentioned, one of those times when his mother was alive. His features had softened, and the hint of a smile played on his lips. There was a gentleness about him I'd not previously noticed. Then again, we'd never been alone or talked so intimately.

Mrs. Wilson and Mr. Lundgren had strolled across the park toward a small pond, where children were skipping rocks and one or two were making valiant attempts to catch a fish with their poorly fashioned fishing poles. They weren't having much luck, but they didn't seem to mind. Their laughter rippled across the expanse that divided us and pulled Josef back to the present.

"To be young and untroubled is a gift we don't appreciate until it's gone," I said.

His brows furrowed over eyes that shone with concern. "You are troubled much?"

I picked at a blade of grass and finally pulled it from the ground. "I suppose I'm more troubled than ever before in my life."

An uncomfortable silence spread between us. He likely believed I was referring to problems at the factory. No doubt he wanted to tell me I could relieve my troubles by going to work somewhere else. Little did he know that my problem was much more serious than the muttered insults I endured at work. But I couldn't share my secret with Josef — not now.

Mr. Lundgren called out for us to join them, and I jumped to my feet. For now, I could withhold my secret. But what if the police detective came to the factory and wanted to question Josef? What would he think of me when he learned I was suspected of being a thief?

CHAPTER 16

On Monday morning I received an introduction to the new painter, Gunter Schmitt.
All concern over Gunter's willingness to
work alongside a woman evaporated the
moment I met him. A shock of sandy hair
fell over one eye, and he possessed an air of
sophistication. I wasn't certain if it was the
hair over his eye or his self-assured manner.
Perhaps a little of each. Instead of hesitat-
ing to shake the hand of a woman, he
reached out and grasped my hand in a
friendly manner. When he didn't drop his
hold, I noticed Josef nudge him in the side.
He grinned and released my hand with an
effusive apology.

After Josef had given Gunter a tour of the
factory, the two of them returned to the
paint shop. Josef motioned to the rack of
elegantly carved horses awaiting the painter's brush that would bring them to life.
Gunter inspected some of the horses that

had been partially painted and were ready for their next application.

Stooping around one of the horses' heads, he signaled and complimented me on my work. Once again, Josef nudged him, but Gunter laughed and finally chose one of the horses that I had begun. A giant white jumper I had planned to embellish with a pink and white blanket. I had decided upon pink as the primary color for the carved roses, with leaves of deep green and a garland of pale blue highlighted with gold. Pink would make it the perfect choice for any little girl who wanted to ride a carousel horse. I doubted Gunter would use such a color scheme.

Mr. Tobarth set him up to work on his other side. I supposed it was to keep one eye on me and the other on Gunter. I strained forward when he began to prepare his paints. I didn't see any pastel shades in his mix.

He ran an appreciative hand down the horse's body. "A fine paint job," he said.

Mr. Tobarth bobbed his head. "That's Carrie — Miss Brewer's work."

"Brouwer," I whispered. *Why can't he remember my name?* Sometimes I thought he knew how much it annoyed me and did it on purpose.

"I mean, that's Miss Brouwer's painting — and Josef's carving," he added.

Gunter arched his back and rested his elbows across his thighs. "I think you'll like what I can add to the horse."

Though I had already pictured the completed horse in my mind, I nodded. No matter how good his work, it wouldn't be what I had planned. I knew exactly what that horse needed to make it beautiful. Deciding it would be best if I didn't watch, I concentrated on the flowing blanket draped across my horse's back. Still, I couldn't help but occasionally sneak a glance down the line. He'd started with the roses; he was painting them a pale red — not the shade I would have picked, but at least he hadn't chosen to paint them yellow or white.

When the bell sounded for lunch, I leaned toward Mr. Tobarth. "I have a few church questions for you."

He arched his brows. "Church questions or questions about the Bible?" he asked as we headed outdoors.

"About the Bible, I guess, but more about God not taking care of the people who believe in Him."

"Thought we covered that in our earlier conversation."

I nodded. "We did. But in the sermon on

Sunday, the preacher talked about Stephen and . . ."

He touched my arm. "I was there — don't need a repeat."

"I don't understand God's letting Stephen die. If someone accuses you of something and it's a lie, why should you be punished?"

His forehead wrinkled for a moment. "Are you talkin' about Stephen, or is this somethin' personal?"

I didn't want to reveal my encounter with the detective, but I didn't want to lie, either. "Mostly about Stephen. If you can make me understand about him, then it would help me understand when things happen in my life."

He didn't look completely convinced. "It's true God allowed Stephen to die, but He rewarded Stephen even before he died. Didn't you hear when the preacher said Stephen saw the heavens open up and Jesus was standing at the right hand of God?"

"Um-hum," I said, still waiting for more. I didn't doubt that seeing Jesus at the right hand of God was a wonderful thing, but Stephen still died. I couldn't be certain, but Mr. Tobarth's eyes looked as if they were filled with pity, because I still didn't understand.

"Here's the thing of it, Carrie. After Stephen saw heaven, there ain't no way he'd want to stay here on earth. Not after seein' what was waitin' for him up there."

"Oh," I whispered. "I see." None of what he'd said helped my situation. I removed the ham sandwich from my pail and took a bite.

I was still chewing the overcooked piece of ham when Mr. Tobarth said, "Lots of the saints suffered 'cause of their beliefs. Paul was thrown in jail and suffered somethin' fierce to defend his faith."

If Paul had gone to jail and suffered, it didn't look like I could expect God to save me from a jail cell. The hairs on the back of my neck prickled to attention, and the bite of sandwich stuck in my throat like a wad of cotton. I gulped water from my cup to help push it down. After several swallows, it landed in my stomach like a heavy weight.

Mr. Tobarth nodded toward the women who had taken their position across the street. "From the looks of those women, I'd say they're mighty unhappy to see you out here. How long has this been goin' on?"

I shrugged. "Not too long. I told them I wasn't looking for a husband, but I guess they don't believe me. They want me to quit."

"I could try goin' over and talkin' to them,

if you think that might help."

"I doubt it would do any good." I stood, gathered my lunch pail, and headed inside. I considered waving to the women but decided such behavior, even if intended as a friendly gesture, would ignite further anger.

At the end of the day, I found myself walking toward the door with Gunter, and he asked if I was in need of an escort home.

"An escort is right here for her," Josef said, stepping out of his office. "We live in the same boardinghouse, so is not necessary for you to worry about Carrie's safety."

"Carrie? I thought she was *Miss Brouwer."* Gunter slapped Josef on the shoulder. "Then I will walk with you and *Carrie.* Your boardinghouse, it is on the way to where I live."

Josef grunted. He didn't appear pleased by Gunter's decision and walked at my side, forcing Gunter to follow behind. A few weeks ago, his behavior might have angered me, but today I found his desire to protect me reassuring.

After I prepared for bed, I pulled out my mother's Bible and settled in the chair. I thumbed through the pages until I came to the book of Acts. That's where Mr. Tobarth told me I could begin to read about Paul and his suffering. The more I read, the more I marveled at the change in Paul and his willingness to suffer for his faith. Like Jesus, he forgave those who persecuted him. I wasn't sure I was up to such a task, but I prayed and asked God to give me the strength and proper words if the police should believe I was guilty of stealing Mrs. Galloway's necklace. I also prayed He would give me greater understanding of the Bible, because I didn't know how anyone could live a Christian life — at least not all the time. I fell asleep reminding myself to ask Mr. Tobarth how people accomplished such a feat.

The following day at lunchtime, Mr. Tobarth accompanied me outside. I was pleased the women weren't across the street today. I hadn't yet figured out their schedule. One day they were out in force, and the next none of them appeared.

"I read the book of Acts," I said.

"What did you think?" He removed an apple from his lunch pail and rubbed it on his pant leg. I didn't think his pants were all that clean, but the apple had a nice shine when he finished. He crunched his teeth into the fleshy fruit and chewed with gusto.

"It was . . ." I hesitated, uncertain how to express myself. "It made me think quite a bit."

Mr. Tobarth took another bite of his apple and waited.

"Paul was a very good man, and he suffered a lot, but after reading some of what he says, I've decided it's much harder to live a Christian life than I thought."

"Now, that's a fact. Becoming a Christian — that's the simple part. We can reach out and take the gift of eternal life that we've been offered, but tryin' to live right and follow the example we've been given — that's not so easy. Once we become believers, we need to offer our best — can't do no more than that. You keep readin' what else Paul has to say." He continued to gnaw on the apple and then tossed the core into the trash.

I wasn't sure I wanted to hear any more of what Paul had to say, especially if it was about suffering. But I did agree to continue reading. Mr. Tobarth said Paul had a lot of good instruction for Christians. I hadn't been looking for more rules to follow — I wasn't even sure I could do justice to the ones I'd read so far.

He stood up, his signal it was time to return to work. "Ain't none of us perfect, but bein' a Christian means you always try to do the right thing, no matter what. An' ask God to help you."

That sounded like quite an order, but if my life continued on its current path, I'd have plenty of opportunity to put some of the teachings into practice. Or at least I could try.

I did my best to sort out my thoughts throughout the afternoon, but mostly I wanted to tell Gunter he wasn't using the proper colors that I'd envisioned for the white horse. While I had come to accept the red he'd decided upon for the roses, I was having difficulty with his remaining choices. He'd used bright primary colors of yellow and blue for the blanket and garland. And he'd used emerald green for the leaves and stems instead of forest green. To make matters worse, he hadn't properly shaded the leaves. They would have looked much better with hints of umber and dark brown. What was he thinking?

By day's end, it had taken all the restraint I could muster to hold my tongue. As I walked by the rack of carousel horses, I took an extra moment to study the proud white jumper and lamented what could have been. Fortunately, Gunter had walked toward the front door a few minutes earlier. Otherwise,

278

I fear my discipline would have vanished.

"He has a lot of talent with a paintbrush, don't he?"

I spun around and nearly fell into the rack. Mr. Tobarth was eyeing Gunter's horse with obvious admiration. What should I say? Both Mr. Tobarth and Josef thought Gunter an excellent painter. Choosing my words carefully, I said, "His techniques and choice of colors are different from mine, but I'm certain he will prove an excellent addition to the factory."

"Yep. I'm sure glad to have his help."

Not wanting to discuss Gunter or his painting any further, I took extra time cleaning my brushes. Mr. Tobarth finally removed his work apron and retrieved his hat. He waved in my direction, bid me good-night, and strode toward the door. Once he'd departed, I moved with greater speed and soon was on my way home.

I'd gone only a short distance when I heard Josef call my name. I turned to see him racing toward me. Moments later, he came to a panting halt beside me. "I thought you had walked home with Gunter."

Why he thought I'd be walking with Gunter, I didn't know. "He left about fifteen minutes ago. I needed to clean my brushes."

He settled into an easy stride, yet he

wrung his hands together like a frightened schoolboy. After several stammering attempts, he tried again. "Has . . . um . . . do you . . . are you . . . the community picnic, did Gunter ask you?"

His question confused me. It took a moment for me to unscramble what he'd said. "Oh!" I said when I finally understood. "You want to know if Gunter asked me to attend the picnic on Sunday." I shook my head. "No, he hasn't." I didn't add that I wouldn't have accepted the invitation.

Josef's shoulders relaxed as he exhaled a low whistle from between his pursed lips. "Then would you be my, could I be your — To the picnic, would you go with me?"

I didn't realize I'd been holding my breath until I, too, exhaled a whoosh of air. Mrs. Wilson had mentioned the community picnic shortly after I'd moved into the boardinghouse, but I hadn't paid much attention. If she was alone this evening, I'd gather the details. "I'd be pleased to attend with you."

"Ja? You will?"

"Of course." Why did he seem so surprised? I'd already told him I wasn't attending with Gunter. Maybe he thought I had plans to go to the Galloways' for the weekend. Or did he think I was planning to attend with Mr. Tobarth? The idea made me giggle.

His brows dipped and his smile disappeared. "What is funny?" he asked.

It was apparent he thought I was laughing at him. "I was thinking about something else. About Mr. Tobarth," I quickly added.

"What about Mr. Tobarth is funny?"

"I was just thinking about him attending the picnic." Before he could say anything, I continued. "He thinks Gunter's choices of paints for your giant jumper are excellent. Have you seen it?"

Tiny lines deepened across his forehead. "The horse?"

I sighed. "Yes. Have you seen it since he began working on it?"

"Nein." His brow remained furrowed, and he shook his head. "A good job, he will do. Gunter is a fine craftsman, very skilled."

"But the colors are wrong," I said. "They should be what I decided."

He stopped midstep and tipped his head to one side. "You became the boss when I wasn't looking?"

"No, of course not. I don't mean to be forward, but I had an exceptional palette planned for that horse. He has used bold, bright colors."

Josef seemed to be studying me as we

continued toward home. "And what did you want?"

I immediately detailed my plans for him. He listened and nodded while I told him the colors and shading I would have preferred.

"Pretty, those colors would have been." My heart swelled with pride until he said, "But pretty Gunter's colors are, too. Ja?"

Mumbling my agreement, I did my best to hide my disappointment. I had hoped to win him to my side, but removing Gunter's bright red roses or yellow garland would be out of the question. I don't know what I had hoped to accomplish. Maybe Mr. Tobarth was right about me and my pride. Maybe I just wanted Josef to agree with me in order to boost my own ego.

"For you, I will carve another big jumper that only you will paint, ja?"

"Or maybe you will carve one of the animals I sketched, and I can paint it?" The minute the words were out of my mouth, I wanted to take them back. I'd managed to dim the sparkle I'd seen in his eyes only moments ago. Why couldn't I be content with what he had offered? "But another jumper would be good, too," I said, grasping his arm.

"Ja. We will see."

From the bow of his head and the dejected tone, I knew my words had stung. His carefree mood had disappeared as quickly as sunshine on a cloudy day. My stomach did a quick flip-flop. "Tell me about the picnic," I urged, giving his arm a slight squeeze.

He did his best to sound jovial while he described the affair, but when we climbed the stairs and entered the boardinghouse, his earlier lightheartedness had not returned, and my stomach hadn't settled, either. I hoped he would forgive me, but I wasn't certain if an apology would make things better or worse — so I decided against broaching the subject further. Maybe I would apologize tomorrow, or maybe at the picnic, or maybe not at all.

Mrs. Wilson explained that the picnic was an annual affair at Collinsford Park and had been going on for the last fifteen years or so. Most folks in the community would attend. The festivities included games, a picnic, and boat rides for those who cared to spend a few extra coins and enjoy a ride on the lake.

The older woman had been pleased to share information about the picnic, but when I mentioned that I would be preparing the picnic lunch for Josef and me, I sensed my hastily spoken words had hurt her. "I only wanted to save you the extra work," I said, hoping she would understand. "I'd be glad to prepare food for you and Mr. Lundgren, too."

My explanation hadn't been entirely truthful, but I couldn't tell her I preferred my own cooking. That would be downright cruel. When I'd weighed the effects of being completely honest against stretching the truth, stretching had won. I hoped Jesus would understand, because I didn't see any way to handle the situation with complete honesty. Each evening I'd continued to read more of Paul's letters to the churches, and I was becoming more and more convinced I couldn't do all those things he spoke about that made people good Christians.

Mrs. Wilson patted my shoulder. "We'll work together on our lunches. That way we can learn from each other. What do you think?"

Relief flooded over me, and I bobbed my head in agreement. "Yes, that would be great fun." Her warm smile was enough to convince me that all had been forgiven.

On Saturday evening Mrs. Wilson and I worked together on our preparations for the picnic that would take place after church the next day. By the time we completed the task, I was more than ready for bed. I did my best to read from the Bible, but my eyes wouldn't stay open long enough for me to complete more than a verse or two before they drooped shut. I finally closed the Bible, uttered a brief prayer, and crawled between the sheets.

The following morning I was pleased when the preacher said he was going to talk about joy. However, when he used Paul and Silas as examples, my personal joy took a downward plunge. I'd read about the two of them and how they'd prayed and sung hymns in jail. I doubted whether God would send an earthquake to shake down the walls of my jail cell. And if He did, I doubted I'd be like Paul and Silas and just sit there. I think I'd be so happy to have the walls fall in that I'd run as if the devil were hot on my heels.

When the sermon ended, I breathed a sigh of relief. I hoped the preacher would move on to some other book of the Bible next week. After the benediction was finally given, I was only too happy to hurry out the church doors.

Folks didn't stick around to visit. Everyone was in a hurry to get home, change clothes, gather up their baskets of food, and join the fun. The day was perfect — warm with just a slight breeze. On the way home, we walked past several houses with flowering lilac bushes. Their sweet perfume reminded me of my mother, and I wished I could pick a few of the blooms and take them home with me.

"Come along, Carrie. We've got to hurry if we're going to be on time for the street-car." Mrs. Wilson had turned and was waving me forward with a feverish zeal.

I wanted to argue that it would take only a few minutes to complete our preparations. We'd finished most everything before we'd departed for church. But arguing would only use up the precious time Mrs. Wilson hoped to save. Besides, Josef was tugging me along, so I had little choice.

As I'd predicted, we completed our tasks in record time and were some of the first to arrive at the park. Mrs. Wilson scuttled toward the pavilion to reserve space at one of the tables, and picnic basket in tow, Mr. Lundgren followed behind. I followed Mr. Lundgren, and Josef followed behind me. We must have looked like dutiful sheep following our shepherd.

The older woman stopped only briefly before locating the table she wanted. She pointed with her right hand and waved us forward with her left. "Right here," she said. "This is where we'll have our lunch." Josef placed our picnic basket alongside the one carried by Mr. Lundgren, and Mrs. Wilson gave a firm nod. "This is a good spot. We'll be in the shade."

"I brought a blanket and thought it would be nice to eat under a tree near the water," I said. "But we'll leave our basket here for now."

"You young people can get up and down on a blanket, but folks my age can't get up once we get down there." She chuckled. "But if that's what you want to do, that's fine with us. We'll sit at the table to eat our food."

The four of us left the pavilion and joined the other folks who'd arrived. Soon several of the men were leading groups of varying ages in sack races and relays. Mostly the children participated, but before long some of the adults joined in the fun, and those of us watching became a cheering section for our favorites. The crowd continued to increase in size, and eventually Josef and I were standing shoulder to shoulder.

"Could I interest you in joining me as a partner in one of the relays?" asked a voice from behind us.

Our lips were only inches apart when Josef and I turned in unison. Behind us, Gunter was grinning wide enough to cause crinkle lines along the edge of each of his deep brown, sparkling eyes. Josef visibly stiffened at the sight of his old friend, and all visible signs of pleasure vanished from his face.

"Carrie is with me. To the picnic, we came together." As if to emphasize his position, he held his head higher and was now looking down at Gunter.

Gunter's relaxed demeanor and lazy grin remained intact. He shrugged his shoulders. "Because she came with you does not mean she can't be my partner in one of the games." He extended his hand to me. "Come. To stand around and watch is not fun. Is much more fun to join in."

I shook my head. "I am with Josef, but thank you for the kind invitation. And we are having a very nice time. The games are fun to watch, but I don't care to participate. If I did, I'm certain Josef would willingly act as my partner."

Gunter didn't appear deterred. He leaned against a nearby giant oak tree and folded his arms across his chest. His rolled-up shirtsleeves revealed his muscular arms to advantage. "Then here I will stay, too. I will enjoy the games along with the two of you." He flashed another wide grin. "I hope you have enough food in your basket for three. I'm famished."

Mrs. Wilson took a backward step. "Did I hear you say you're hungry?"

Gunter nodded. "I'm hoping my friend Josef is going to invite me to share lunch with him."

"Oh, Carrie didn't pack enough for three, but I have more than enough in my basket. You follow Carrie and Josef up to the pavilion, and they'll show you where we're sitting."

Gunter quickly accepted the invitation. It was only later when he realized Josef and I were going to be lunching elsewhere that he tried to escape Mrs. Wilson's invitation. But the older woman wouldn't be deterred. Before Gunter could make an escape, she had him seated beside Mr. Lundgren with a checkered napkin on his lap and a heaping plate of food in front of him.

Josef and I laughed as we spread our blanket on a grassy spot not far from the lake. "I think Gunter is unhappy with both of us," I said, offering Josef a roast beef sandwich on buttered brown bread.

"He should not be interfering in our day." He took a bite of the sandwich, and his eyes widened with obvious surprise. "This is gut."

"Thank you." His compliment pleased me and caused a stirring deep inside that I hadn't expected.

"You made this?"

"Part of it," I said.

Although I couldn't take credit for the roast beef, I'd given Mrs. Wilson some hints on how to roast meat without a stringy or tough result. She'd done an excellent job. Even the bread she'd made on Saturday morning was tender. We had worked together on the desserts and the biscuits she'd insisted would be needed to go along with her homemade preserves. We each packed a glass jar of lemonade with chunks of ice and extra slices of lemon for added tartness, then wrapped it in newspaper to keep it cold.

"All has very fine taste," Josef said.

He held out two cups while I unwrapped the jar of lemonade. When I'd filled them both, he handed one to me and then took a drink. "This is nice and cold." He pointed to the newspaper. "That is a gut idea, ja?"

I laughed and agreed. Conversation came easily during our lunch, and I was surprised yet pleased by Josef's openness. He told me how Mr. Galloway had visited him in Philadelphia and convinced him to come to work in Collinsford. I hadn't realized until that moment that Josef owned a small interest in the carousel factory and that he and Mr. Galloway hoped to one day expand and become the largest carousel factory in the country.

"Maybe one day a carousel from our factory will sit in this very park." His eyes shone with excitement.

"It sounds wonderful, Josef. I'm sure your hard work will make all your dreams come true."

He lightly touched my hand. "Someone beside me to share the dreams is needed to make it very gut."

I didn't know what to say. Was he simply making an offhand remark, or did he mean something more? Understanding Josef had become increasingly difficult. I was hardly qualified to judge his intent. My emotions had been in a constant state of upheaval since the first day I'd set foot in Collinsford.

CHAPTER 17

Friday and Saturday,
May 23 & 24

Now that Gunter had joined us in the paint shop, Mr. Galloway and Josef were eager to meet the deadlines for each order. Since his arrival, we had worked at a rapid pace to complete the horses, and a rack was now ready for final inspection. I waited in anticipation while Mr. Tobarth paraded around the horses like a general inspecting his troops.

I'd grown to admire Gunter's ability with a brush, but he didn't take the time to shade or thoughtfully consider his color choices. Otherwise, I'd not been able to find fault with his work. Yet I hoped Mr. Tobarth would declare my horses of finer quality. Gunter apparently didn't care, for he'd gone to eat his lunch with Josef. On several occasions while walking home with Josef, I'd mentioned how important I considered the color choices and shading. He never actually voiced his thoughts, but he listened intently to what I said. I was certain he agreed with me, for he'd inquired about the techniques I had used in the past when painting portraits or still lifes.

Mr. Tobarth scrutinized each of the hooves and the horses' flowing manes. Then he stroked his hand along the bodies and gave attention to the eyes and nostrils of each of the carved animals. He grunted and nodded while he examined the flowers, the shields, the garlands, and the occasional dog or fox carved behind the cantles.

Finally he stepped back from the rack and stroked his jaw. "These are all good. I'll have Josef give 'em a final look-over, but I can't find a thing wrong with any of 'em." Running his hand down the neck of a giant jumper, he said, "Josef will be relieved to hear all of yours passed my inspection."

Relieved to hear *my* horses passed? I blinked away the tears that unexpectedly blurred my vision.

Mr. Tobarth gently patted my shoulder. "I know you were worried what with your lack of proper trainin' and all, but I can't find much to complain about with your work." He ambled back toward the rack and rested his hand on one of horses. " 'Course we knew we could depend on Gunter for his usual excellent work."

I deflated quicker than a balloon losing air. From what Mr. Tobarth said, both he and Josef had considered Gunter's work excellent and mine merely passable. Fiery anger wrapped its hot fingers around my spine and jabbed me like a burning poker. I wanted to shout that I was the better artist. A sharp jab stopped my rebuttal and pricked my conscience — *pride!* Why did I always want to be best? Why couldn't I be pleased when someone else received a compliment or did something better than I did? I should be happy for Gunter and delighted we'd completed our order on schedule.

"You done a fine job, Carrie. Once you begin to paint at a faster pace, it'll be hard for anyone to outshine your work."

Mr. Tobarth's praise eased my pain, but soon an unbidden sadness crept over me. I had never understood these strange feelings of pride and jealousy, but I wanted to rid myself of them. I'd been praying God would remove them from my life, but my prayers hadn't been heard — or if God had heard them, they were still on His waiting list.

That afternoon I worked with less enthusiasm, but I did pray with more fervor. I wanted to become a person who didn't envy others. After all, life wasn't a competition, it was a personal journey — that's what Mr. Tobarth had told me when he'd first mentioned my problem with pride. I knew he was right, but that didn't make it any easier.

When Gunter ambled across the expanse and into the sanding room to instruct one of the men working on a horse, I glanced around the paint shop. Only Mr. Tobarth and I remained. I took a moment to watch him draw his brush in a perfectly straight line before beginning to fill in the reins with a deep chocolate brown. His steady hand amazed me. He must have felt my gaze on him, for he turned and looked over his shoulder.

"Not happy with what I had to say earlier, are ya?" There was a glint in his eyes.

I considered telling him I was just fine, but then I admitted my disappointment. "I don't want to be jealous. I've even prayed about it, but God hasn't answered my prayers."

He chuckled. "You are the most impatient gal I've ever met. You keep on prayin', and God will answer. But be prepared — He may send some things your way you ain't expectin'."

I wasn't sure what Mr. Tobarth meant, but Gunter returned to his work area, and our discussion ended as quickly as it had begun. When the bell sounded at the end of the day, there hadn't been a chance to question him further. Removing my apron, I decided I might ask him tomorrow.

Crossing the threshold into the main work area, I could see Josef waiting for me. He laughed and joked with the workers passing by on their way out the door. His easy manner and ability to both supervise and work alongside the men amazed me. He didn't seem to suffer from feelings of pride or envy.

We'd talked more and more during our walks to and from the factory, and each day I could feel myself growing fonder of him. And each day I hoped his feelings matched my own.

His smile broadened when I approached. "Did you have a gut day?"

Had I? In some respects it had been a very good day, yet in others not so good. "I accomplished a lot."

The answer was enough to satisfy him. "I heard today about a dance at the pavilion in the park. Tomorrow evening, it will be." He wiggled his finger back and forth between the two of us. "Pleased I would be to have you attend with me."

My stomach roiled, and a sick feeling washed over me. "Oh, Josef. I would love to go with you, but I've already promised to attend the Galloways' housewarming party tomorrow evening. I'll be there until Sunday. Could we —"

"Nein! Pretend I did not ask." He locked his shoulders and formed his lips into a tight, thin line. Shades of red splashed his cheeks and trailed down his neck. There was no doubt my refusal had embarrassed him. "You go. Enjoy with the Galloways their fancy party and fancy friends. I can see this is what you like." I grasped his arm, but he pulled away. "Save for those fancy men, your smiles and friendly behavior."

His words lashed with the sting of a horsewhip. I stared at him in amazement. I'd never before seen Josef behave in such a manner. This man I had recently considered the perfect Christian had lost control of his temper — out on the street with people passing by. I couldn't believe his behavior. I wasn't certain if it was my gaping mouth, for I'd gone slack-jawed, or the staring passersby, but Josef's features slowly relaxed as he regained his composure.

"Sorry, I am, for my, my . . ." He drew circles in the air with one hand.

"Bad behavior or outburst?"

"Both. Sorry I am for all of it. Accept, please, my apology."

The anger that had flared in Josef's eyes only a short time earlier had been replaced with shades of sadness. Hoping to raise his spirits, I pasted on a smile and said, "And here I thought you were almost perfect." We continued to walk toward home.

"Perfect, I am not. My faults are many, and my temper. *Ach!* With this I have the greatest trouble." He shook his head and looked down at his scuffed shoes. "Even my prayers to change, they go unanswered."

I could barely believe my ears. Josef didn't receive immediate answers to *his* prayers? "That happens to me, too," I said. "I pray and pray, but still God hasn't changed me."

He nodded with understanding. "Is gut you pray about your pride."

I stopped midstep. "Why did you assume this was about my pride?" Granted, Mr. Tobarth, Tyson, Augusta, and Mrs. Galloway had all mentioned my pride, but now Josef acted as though my issue with pride was a matter the entire city of Collinsford regularly discussed.

He shrugged. "Is very clear that with your pride, you still have problems." He hesitated a moment.

"You're right — I *still* have a problem. Just like your prayers about a bad temper, God hasn't answered my prayers about pride.

What do you do when God doesn't seem to hear your prayers?"

"Wait and keep praying is the only answer I can give you. When God is ready, He will answer. But work to make ourselves better, we must do. God will help us, but He isn't the only one who must do the work. With that I am not so gut." He touched his hand to his chest. "Anger does not please God, so work on this I must."

"Maybe we can help each other," I suggested. "When you see me acting prideful, you could signal me. And if I see you beginning to exhibit signs of anger, I could do the same."

"What is this signal you speak of?"

"It can be anything we decide upon."

We both grew silent and considered the idea. It would need to be something other people wouldn't question.

"I know! We can pull on the ear," he said, yanking on his right earlobe.

"I suppose that would work," I replied, pleased that we now had a common bond — even if it was only pulling on our ears.

The following afternoon Josef and I walked home together. Assuming he would spend the evening sitting on the front porch with Mr. Lundgren and Mrs. Wilson, I asked,

"Do you have plans for this evening?"

A thick lock of hair dropped across his brow when he bobbed his head. "Ja. I will go to the pavilion with Gunter."

My mouth was so dry the air caught in my throat when I tried to swallow. I was certain my hearing hadn't failed. Josef was going to the dance — without me. I could picture the scene in my mind. The single young ladies would throng around him, eager to have the manager of the carousel factory lead them onto the dance floor, each one hoping to win his heart. But I couldn't object. I had refused his invitation.

I did my best to smile, but I doubted it was any more than a lopsided grimace. "I'm sure the two of you will have a nice time."

"Would be nicer with you along, but Gunter said he would help to find me some dance partners."

I gritted my teeth. Leave it to Gunter to offer help where it wasn't wanted — at least not where *I* wanted it.

Josef stopped on the porch when we arrived at the boardinghouse. "Out here I will sit until supper. The weather is nice." He opened the screen door for me and then stepped back toward one of the chairs.

"I must go in and complete my packing."

"Ja. You need to finish. For me there is

time enough after supper to get ready."

I nodded and climbed the stairs to my room. Why had he reminded me of his outing! Now I must fight both jealousy and pride. While I placed my clothes on the bed, I did my best to remain focused on what I would need until my return tomorrow. As frequently as I packed, I should have memorized a list of the items, but it seemed I always forgot something. Of course, Augusta easily came to my rescue with whatever was needed. While I packed several combs for my hair, I considered Mrs. Galloway's missing necklace. Perhaps I would learn that it had been returned to her. Not likely, but I could hope.

I'd closed the latches on my travel cases only minutes earlier when Mrs. Wilson called upstairs to say Mr. Lundgren was on his way to help me. Before I could object, Mr. Lundgren popped into sight, his unruly brown hair flying in all directions. "You just point me to the baggage, and I'll get it down those steps."

He entered my room, and I motioned toward the corner. Refusing my offer to carry one of the bags, he hoisted one in each hand and led the way downstairs. Josef jumped to his feet as Mr. Lundgren stepped outside and dropped the two valises on the porch.

"Why didn't you call me to help you, Ralph? I would have carried the bags downstairs." Brows furrowed, Josef directed his frown at me.

"I told him I would carry one, but he insisted."

"Next time you will call me to carry your cases, ja?"

After assuring Josef I would do so, I thanked Mr. Lundgren. The older man waved off my offer of a coin for his help and hurried back inside as if to escape argument. I was just about to sit down in the chair beside Josef when I remembered I'd left my reticule upstairs.

"I'll be back in a moment." I strode inside and hesitated at the flight of stairs. At the moment, I wondered if having my own bathroom was really worth climbing to the third floor. Exhaling a giant breath, I climbed the first flight. No sooner had I arrived on the third floor and entered my bedroom than I heard a carriage arrive.

I'd given Augusta strict orders that I no longer wished to have Tyson call for me, that his constant appearance without her had given rise to questions. She didn't inquire any further but had promised I need not worry; she would accompany Tyson in the future. I stood at my window and looked out, eager to see if Augusta had kept her word. I expected to see her step out of the carriage. Instead, a handsome young man I'd not seen before opened the door, hollered something to Thomas that I could not distinguish, and stepped down. I leaned forward on tiptoe and rested my forehead against the bedroom window, hoping to see Augusta. My excitement bubbled like a boiling kettle. I could only assume she had given Tyson the mitten and this was her new beau. But the handsome gentleman closed the door and strode toward the front steps alone. Perhaps she'd spied my baggage on the porch and decided to wait in the carriage. She wouldn't dare send a stranger to escort me!

Grasping the banister with my hand, I flew down the two flights of stairs, the soles of my shoes sliding from step to step like a sled on ice. I braced myself and held tight as I slid down the final flight. But my hold wasn't firm enough to avoid a collision with the handsome gentleman who happened to enter the front door at the exact same moment.

He managed to remain upright as I catapulted into his arms. I looked into blue eyes that shone like sunshine on water. His smile was every bit as engaging as his sparkling eyes. "You must be Carrington," he said.

His words broke the spell, and I reluctantly took a backward step and removed myself from his embrace. "Yes, Carrington Brouwer." My voice warbled like a dying bird, and I cleared my throat. "And *you* are?" This time I croaked. From bird to frog — that should impress him. I swallowed hard and stifled a rising giggle.

"I am Ronald Galloway, Augusta's brother." His grin returned and he bent forward into a grand bow that made me chuckle. Returning to an upright position, he said, "I am very pleased to make your acquaintance. My sister speaks of you often."

"Does she? I hope it's all good."

"*Very* good, but she failed to tell me of your beauty. I will soundly chastise her for that oversight."

"Ja, I do not know how anyone could forget to speak of Carrie's gut looks."

There was no way of knowing exactly when Josef had entered the foyer. Ronald had completely blocked him from view until he'd stepped to the side as he spoke.

Ronald jerked and glanced over his shoulder. Evidently he'd not known Josef was standing behind him, either. With a slight turn of his body, he extended his hand. "I don't believe we've met."

He accepted Ronald's hand. "No, we have not met. I am Josef Kaestner. For your father, I manage the carousel factory."

"Ah yes, I remember. You're the German fellow he hired in Philadelphia."

Josef's jaw clenched at the remark. "I am American citizen. Not born in this country like you, but still I am American."

His tone was harsh and anger flashed in his eyes. From his spread-legged stance and curled fists, I wondered if he might punch Ronald in the nose. "Josef! Could I impose upon you to tell Mrs. Wilson I am leaving?"

When he looked at me, I yanked on my left earlobe, but the gesture had little effect. Thankfully, Ronald didn't seem to notice that Josef was glaring at him. I was certain Josef desired an apology, but it didn't come. His complexion changed from pinkish red to magenta, and I wondered if he might explode like an overcooked beet.

"Josef!" I hadn't meant to shout, but my tone gained the attention of both men, who suddenly looked in my direction. There I stood — tugging on both my earlobes like a bell ringer heaving the ropes in a church tower. Josef relaxed ever so slightly. Ronald

stared at me as though I'd completely lost
my senses.

CHAPTER 18

Once we were on our way, Ronald didn't hesitate to quiz me about my strange behavior. I didn't want to betray Josef's confidence, yet I could hardly tell Ronald I was trying to enlarge my earlobes. They were already the size of my thumb tip, and no young lady desired large earlobes!

Rather than tell him an outright lie, I lapsed into a rambling account. By the time I uttered the final word, he appeared thankful to have me clamp my lips together. My response rendered him both speechless and bewildered. With my task accomplished, I settled back against the leather carriage seat.

We'd traveled approximately a mile when Ronald tentatively inquired about my portrait painting. I surmised he feared another lengthy, incoherent response, but this time I answered with clarity and brevity. My reply had the desired effect. His pinched features and rigid posture completely disappeared.

"Perhaps some of the guests at Mother's housewarming would be interested in sitting for a portrait."

"With my work at the factory, I don't have time. But in the future I may return to painting on canvas instead of wood."

"That's right! Augusta told me you paint the carousel horses in Father's factory." He looked at me for a moment. "Fascinating."

"Exactly what is so fascinating? That I work in your father's business, or that I paint horses?"

"Both. It's difficult to imagine a young lady working in a carousel factory — or any factory for that matter. Are there others of you?"

He made it sound as though I belonged to some strange organization. I thought of his mother and how she'd stared at me that first day I'd arrived. I'd even been wearing this same hat. Ronald was staring at me in much the same manner — as if I had horns poking from my head. I surreptitiously touched my hat just to make certain.

"I'm the only woman working in the factory at this time, but I imagine there will be more in the future. Who can say what changes will take place. I'd like to think that your father or Josef would consider hiring other women if they were qualified to perform the duties."

"So you've encountered no problems with the men or the work?"

How should I answer his questions? I didn't want to tell him that Louis had mixed sand with my paints and been discharged; nor did I care to tell him that many of the men had threatened to walk out shortly after I'd begun work, and most of them still wouldn't speak to me. On the other hand, I could hardly say I'd been welcomed with enthusiasm.

"It has been challenging. Painting the horses is much different from painting on canvas. Still, I find the work much to my liking."

He tipped his head back against the seat and chuckled. "I can't imagine my sister or any other woman I know ever saying she enjoys work."

I shrugged. "One does what is required. I feel fortunate I am able to paint."

To avoid further questions, I decided to pose some of my own and inquired about Ronald's schooling. I listened with interest while he told me his studies were focused upon business so that he might one day properly take his place alongside his father. While I was listening to Ronald's explanation, it occurred to me that this would be the perfect opportunity to discover a little more about the chameleon.

"And what about your friend Tyson? Is he enrolled in the same course of study?"

I'd done my best to carefully phrase the question so I didn't appear overly interested in Tyson. I didn't want Ronald thinking I'd set my cap for Augusta's beau. Fortunately for me, Ronald was pleased to furnish a plethora of information. I learned that Tyson had entered college with the intention of becoming a lawyer, a profession his father had chosen for him. And his earlier arrival in Collinsford hadn't been because his classes had ended or because of his rowdy behavior. Rather, he had been dismissed from school due to bad grades. In fact, he'd been barred from taking the final exams.

"So you told him to come to Collinsford and you'd join him when you finished classes?"

"We never discussed that, but you can never tell about Tyson. He's an impulsive sort of fellow. Of course, we all think the world of him." Ronald chuckled. "I do believe he's been putting some of his classwork to good use, what with the theft of Mother's jewelry. I think he imagines himself some sort of sleuth who is going to solve the crime."

"And do you believe he's making progress with his investigation?"

"I have no idea. I say let the police do their work and find the culprit."

I nodded my agreement, yet I wondered if the police were aware of the many lies Tyson Farnsworth had been telling since his arrival in Collinsford — or if they cared. They would probably think the fabrications had nothing to do with the missing necklace. And they'd probably be right. Yet the fact that he was doing his best to point the police in my direction made me wonder why he'd lied about so many things.

Augusta and Tyson were waiting in the foyer when we arrived. This was my first visit to the Galloways' new home in Fair Oaks, and Augusta immediately offered a tour. I was amazed by the gardens and the abundance of lush greenery, but Augusta explained her mother had hired several gardeners to work on the plantings while the interior work was being completed. Leave it to Mrs. Galloway to have nothing less than a perfect lawn and blooming flowers for her housewarming party. And she was more than a little relieved that she wouldn't have to have the party at the Wentworths' home after all.

The house was beautiful, much larger than

I thought necessary for a small family, and ostentatious enough to make Mrs. Galloway the envy of at least a few wealthy friends. Having heard informal suppers were considered the trend among members of high society during the summer months, Mrs. Galloway had decided to follow suit. While I was certain the others had eaten, I'd had nothing since lunchtime and was famished, but to mention such a fact would be rude.

Later, when Augusta and I went upstairs to dress, my stomach growled in protest. Augusta touched her fingertips to her cheeks. "Goodness, Carrie! Your stomach sounds like an approaching thunderstorm. Let's get you dressed so you can go downstairs and get something to eat." She motioned toward the door. "Mother has a number of new servants, but any one of them should be able to help you."

It would have been simpler to have a tray brought upstairs, but such a request would have been an imposition. And Mrs. Galloway didn't need the servants otherwise occupied. The older woman was scurrying around as if her very life depended upon making a good impression on the residents of Fair Oaks.

The dress I had chosen was a pale yellow silk with bell-shaped sleeves of silk velvet in a deeper shade. The dress reminded me of blooming buttercups. Augusta declared the gown a perfect shade for my complexion.

"Don't forget to come back up for the ostrich feather fan, and I have some feathers I'll place in your hair. They will be perfect."

Caring little about the fan or the feather hairdressing, I crossed the room while waving my agreement. At the moment, I wanted a slice of bread or piece of cheese to stave off the hunger pangs. Rushing down the back stairs, I signaled one of the recently hired maids. The dear girl took my plight quite seriously and led me to the kitchen, where I was offered much more than bread or cheese. It was impossible to eat all she placed in front of me, but I did my best, even eating a second tea cake. I offered profuse thanks and headed for the back stairs. I needed my corset loosened before the evening's festivities began. Otherwise I'd surely burst!

To my dismay, the stairway was blocked by several butlers who pointed me toward the other exit. There wasn't time to argue. Augusta would soon be coming down to help her mother greet the guests. Grasping a handful of silk, I hiked the skirt of my gown and rounded the corner with all the speed I could muster. I should have been watching more closely, but my mind was focused upon my corset when I collided with Tyson outside Mr. Galloway's library.

My elbow landed in his midsection with a powerful blow that would have tested a pugilist. When I heard an immediate whoosh of air, I wondered if I'd knocked the breath out of him. I leaned in close to his doubled-over form and listened for the sound of his breathing. Arms wrapped around his stomach, he leaned against the doorframe. He was still on his feet, so I assumed I hadn't killed him.

I didn't realize I'd been holding my own breath until I needed to exhale and inhale before I could speak. "Can you breathe?" My voice caught in my throat. He wasn't dead, but what if I'd caused a terrible injury? What if he didn't recover? Augusta would never forgive me. I felt the blood drain from my face and thought I might faint. I couldn't be certain if it was fear or the tight corset, but I didn't want to swoon.

Tyson gave one nod and slowly tipped his head far enough to drill me with an angry glare. "That . . . was . . . unnecessary."

That he was well enough to be angry gave me assurance I hadn't mortally wounded him. And his unwarranted accusation infused me with renewed strength. I stood tall and squared my shoulders.

"If you think that was an intentional act on my part, it only reflects how little you know about me. I would never do such a thing."

Using the doorframe as a support, he straightened. Still clasping his waist, he looked at me. The anger suddenly disappeared from his eyes and was replaced by a look I couldn't quite discern — as though he'd had a revelation of sorts. No matter the reason, I was thankful his anger had dissipated and offered yet another apology, even though he was as much at fault as I.

I don't know if Tyson accepted my apology. There wasn't time for me to wait. If I didn't soon get upstairs and have Augusta untie my corset laces, I was going to faint or expel the contents of my stomach on the highly polished Italian tile, a debacle for which Mrs. Galloway would not soon forgive me. The idea of such an occurrence created a tickle in the back of my throat. Only the pressure of my corset stayed a fit of giggles.

I signaled one of the maids to bring Tyson a glass of water and hastened upstairs, where I was confronted by a pouting Augusta.

There was no time to placate her. "Unfasten my dress and loosen my corset before I faint." When she didn't move, I added, "Or I'm going to disgorge the contents of my stomach on your dressing table." That brought her across the room in record time.

The pout remained, but she nimbly loosened my garments. The relief was immediate. I inhaled and then exhaled a cleansing breath of air. "That feels so good. You can't imagine the pain I've suffered since going to the kitchen. I *can* tell you the food your mother plans to serve at the party is absolutely marvelous."

Augusta didn't seem to care about the food or my discomfort — only that we were going to be late making our appearance at the front door. I did my best to send her without me, but she insisted the maids were busy and there was no one to help with my dress. With genuine misgiving, I turned and inhaled — but only a little.

"The corset needs to be taut or the dress isn't going to fasten. Take another deep breath."

I pretended to inhale but simply could not bear that unyielding piece of feminine misery pressing on my ribs for the remainder of the night. If the dress didn't fasten, I'd remain in the bedroom. Augusta could say I was ill, which wouldn't be far from the truth!

Undeterred by my lack of cooperation, Augusta continued her efforts. She yanked and tugged and finally exclaimed, "There! I've got the dress completely fastened."

I sighed. At least exhaling air helped a little. Of course, exhaling required that I inhale. Therein lay the difficulty. I could only hope that the food would soon digest and I'd feel a smidgen of relief. Perhaps that was why the Bible warned against gluttony. I would ask Mrs. Wilson rather than Mr. Tobarth. Explaining my difficulties to a man would be highly improper — and embarrassing. The thought of mentioning undergarments to Mr. Tobarth made my stomach lurch. I held my palm to my mouth.

"You're not going to . . ."

I shook my head. "No. I'll be fine. Just give me a moment." I knew I'd feel better if I could empty my stomach, but Augusta was motioning me toward the door.

Both Ronald and Tyson were waiting in the foyer. Tyson stood with his palm resting across his waist. His thumb was tucked into his vest pocket, and I couldn't be sure if he was assuming a gentlemanly posture or if his stomach still ached. He frowned in my direction, but I pretended not to notice.

Ronald extended his hand when I reached the final step. "You look absolutely lovely, Carrie."

"Isn't that the dress you wore to the concert earlier in the month, Augusta?" Tyson peered at my gown and then looked at Augusta for confirmation.

"No! I wore a deep gold silk with embroidered flowers on the bodice." Augusta's brow puckered. "You said it was the most beautiful gown you'd ever seen."

Tyson recoiled at the stinging remark, and a sense of self-satisfaction wrapped around me like a warm coat. Unfortunately, my smug reaction collided with the distinct feeling God would disapprove of my haughty attitude. I did my best to erase the high-and-mighty feelings, but it was difficult. I held out a glimmer of hope that Augusta would see Tyson as I did — a boorish cad who couldn't be trusted.

Tyson tugged on his vest and assumed a look of arrogant sophistication. "I was merely confused. You have so many lovely gowns, and you look gorgeous in every one of them." Tyson's placating tone had the effect he'd obviously hoped for: Augusta preened and grasped his arm.

His quick recovery and Augusta's response obliterated my earlier optimism. My friend was a hopeless romantic who couldn't see beyond Tyson's good looks and smooth words.

"Shall we go for a stroll in the garden?"

Ronald's question interrupted my thoughts. "You don't have to remain here and greet the guests?"

"Mother said that she and Augusta would handle those duties and I should circulate among the guests as they came out to the garden." He grinned and leaned closer. "She told me to be particularly careful that I didn't turn you loose among the guests. Something about you being prone to fits of laughter." We crossed through the parlor and out the doors leading to the garden.

Not for a minute did I believe my giggling was the reason Mrs. Galloway wanted me under Ronald's constant scrutiny. I was certain she feared my family background and lack of social graces would prove embarrassing. We had neared a fountain with a statue of a woman pouring water from a pitcher when a frightful thought brought me to a sudden halt.

What if Mrs. Galloway asked Ronald to remain close because she thought I'd been the one who had stolen her necklace? The possibility caused a stabbing pain in my head, and I instinctively touched my hair.

One wiggle of a feather pinned in my coiffure and I realized the smarting had been caused by a hairpin rather than my worrisome idea. Still, the thought nagged at me.

As the guests entered the garden, Ronald moved among them, making proper introductions and carefully guiding the conversation to something other than me. Mostly he talked about himself — the rowing team, the debate awards, his excellent grades, his future plans, and how pleased he was to be working alongside his father during the summer. I found the information interesting the first one or two times, and then it turned tiresome.

While he repeated the litany to yet another couple, I glanced around the garden. My knees turned to jelly as I locked gazes with Detective Lawton. What was *he* doing here? He tipped his head in recognition, and his bald head shone in the waning sunlight. I'd been holding my breath, and when I exhaled, the stays in my corset gripped my midsection like a legion of iron fingers.

When I finally was alone with Ronald, I inquired about the detective's presence. "It was Detective Lawton's idea. He thought the party might prove a perfect opportunity to discover the identity of the thief or thieves, though I'm not certain why. You do know that later that night Mother discovered two of her rings missing from the safe, as well."

His comment set my heart pounding. No one had mentioned any missing rings to me. Had the information been intentionally withheld? Was this some sort of ruse? Were they planning to catch me in a trap? Was the detective watching for a reaction? I did my best to remain calm. "No. Augusta must have forgotten to mention the rings. Is your mother certain nothing else was taken?"

Ronald shrugged. "I don't know, and Mother is of little help providing facts. She's hopeful the detective will soon sort things out."

It was obvious the subject of Detective Lawton and the missing jewelry didn't interest him in the least. He was soon making another introduction and recounting his many collegial accomplishments.

As the party progressed, I lost sight of the detective. By the time the last of the guests left, I realized I had managed to stay away from him the entire evening, and for that I was most grateful. The moment I could pull Augusta away from Tyson, we went upstairs. I couldn't wait to remove my gown and corset.

I had hoped to ask her about the missing

rings, but her ongoing litany about Tyson prevented me from doing so. My eyes grew heavy as she droned on, and once I donned my nightgown, I decided the questions could wait until morning.

I was the only guest at breakfast. Tyson remained abed, claiming illness, which didn't surprise me. It was, after all, Sunday morning. I wondered if he would do another disappearing act while we were attending church.

Mrs. Galloway took center stage and throughout the meal rehashed the previous night's events. It seemed her greatest worry was whether she'd be judged acceptable to join the rank and file members of Collinsford society — especially those living in Fair Oaks. "Laura Wentworth says I have nothing to worry about, but you can never be certain." She took a bite of her coddled egg and stared down the table at her husband. "The guests all thought it rather exciting that we had a detective hidden among the crowd. Did Detective Lawton have anything to report?"

"Agatha! You weren't supposed to tell anyone who he was." Mr. Galloway's stern tone and angry look surprised me. "How do you expect him to make any progress with his investigation?"

"I'm sorry, but they all thought it quite fascinating. I told them to act as though he was simply another guest." She took another bite of her egg and pinned Augusta with a critical eye. "What is the matter with you this morning, Augusta? You're particularly quiet. Are you ill?"

Augusta assured her mother that all was well, but I suspected she'd hoped Tyson would appear and escort her. Once we'd completed breakfast, we were off to church. Minus Tyson.

We had settled in the Galloways' pew when I turned to say something to Augusta and noticed Detective Lawton sitting across the aisle, several rows back. He was alone, and once again he tipped his head in recognition. What was he doing here? I didn't believe the detective lived in Fair Oaks. I whispered my surprise to Augusta, who simply shrugged and appeared indifferent. Obviously she was still lamenting the fact that Tyson had remained abed. Would she never come to her senses?

But this wasn't the time to be thinking about Augusta or Tyson. I needed to keep my focus upon God so that I would receive the message He had for me. Both Mrs. Wilson and Josef told me they always prepared their hearts by meditating before the sermon. As usual, my thoughts were difficult to restrain. They wandered back to Tyson and Detective Lawton, but I soon managed to gain control of my roving worries and prayed that God would speak to me through the pastor's message.

The preacher stepped to the pulpit, and I straightened my shoulders, giving him my full attention. When he announced he would speak from the book of Daniel, I gulped. I knew a little about Daniel and his bravery facing those lions, and that wasn't a sermon I wanted to hear. Facing lions wasn't high on my list — I'd seen them in the zoo with their ferocious teeth and powerful jaws. The lion I'd sketched for the carousel factory revealed the brawn and fierceness of the animals. Today I wanted to hear something that would soothe my discomfited soul.

The preacher looked out across the congregation, and I was sure his gaze rested upon me when he said, "I'm not going to preach about Daniel today. Instead, I want you to learn a lesson from Shadrach, Meshach, and Abednego."

My insides looped tighter than a seaman's knot. He was going to preach about that fiery furnace. Right then and there, I decided hearing about lions would be less frightening. Many years ago my mother had read to me the story about Shadrach, Meshach, and Abednego. I'd stayed away from the fireplace for quite some time after that. But now I forced myself to remain attentive while the preacher told how the three men stood firm in their beliefs, wouldn't bow down to false gods, and were thrown into a blistering oven. As a child I hadn't given much thought to the faithfulness the three of them exhibited, but now I was amazed. How had they managed to stand so firm in their faith?

"But what does this mean to us? We don't have to face a fiery furnace." The preacher posed the question, and I waited, along with the rest of the congregation, to hear the answer. I'd learned that church wasn't like school. The preacher always answered his own questions. That permitted me some relief, because I didn't always know the answers, and I didn't want him to call on me. The reverend cleared his throat, and I looked up.

"It means that sometimes we're thrust into another kind of fiery furnace. A furnace created by people who unfairly accuse or punish us. And when that happens, we need to stand fast in our belief that God will deliver us."

When I glanced up, the preacher was pointing his thick index finger in my direction. I shuddered. I didn't want God to test my faith. He should test people like Mrs. Wilson or Josef or Mr. Tobarth. People who would be willing to face roaring lions or a scorching fire.

"You must remember that God's power is available to us in all of the struggles of life. God's presence is with us in the troubling and frightening trials we face. We can go forth knowing that He is with us in our suffering."

I wondered if that meant I should be prepared to suffer if I was accused of stealing Mrs. Galloway's necklace. I removed my handkerchief from my reticule and dabbed my forehead. The sanctuary had become uncomfortably warm.

When we stood to sing the final hymn, I leaned close to Augusta. "It's very warm in here, isn't it?" I snapped open my fan and flipped it back and forth with a vengeance.

She frowned at me as though I'd lost my mind. "No!" She pointed to the fan. "You're flapping that thing as though you're trying to start a fire."

Her comment stopped my fanning midflutter. I tucked the object into my reticule and followed her out of the church, still thinking it terribly warm.

I wasn't surprised to learn that the chameleon had disappeared during our absence. The maid handed Augusta a note. In it, Tyson apologized for the hasty departure, said he was feeling much better, and would return Monday afternoon or Tuesday morning at the latest.

"He's probably gone to see a doctor and doesn't want to worry me," Augusta said when we were alone.

"You may be right." I didn't believe he was going to a doctor and neither did she, but if it saved her embarrassment, I would play along. "You look tired, and I have laundry that needs my attention at home. I hope you'll understand that I must leave early."

"Laundry? On Sunday afternoon?"

I shrugged. "The Lord knows I must complete my laundry when time permits. Sunday may be the day of rest for some, but for those who work six days a week, there is work at home that needs attention."

She didn't argue, and for that I was grateful. I readied my belongings and, after thanking Mr. and Mrs. Galloway for their hospitality, instructed the recently hired liveryman to take my luggage to the carriage. With the opulent home and all of the newly engaged domestic help, I decided business must be very good for Mr. Galloway. Perhaps he and Josef would be able to move forward with the expansion of the factory sooner than anticipated.

When I stepped across the threshold onto the porch, I was surprised to see Ronald waiting for me. "I couldn't let you return home unaccompanied," he said.

I wanted to tell him I wouldn't be alone. There was, after all, the carriage driver. I wondered if Augusta had encouraged him; she'd mentioned on several occasions Ronald and I would make a perfect match. I, on the other hand, didn't agree. Though his manners were impeccable and his looks appealing, we had nothing in common. He'd been the perfect gentleman, but once we'd arrived in Fair Oaks, he had bored me with nothing but talk of himself. In his defense, I'd decided that was what the social set did at these gatherings.

During the carriage ride home, I plied him with several questions surrounding the missing necklace and rings, as well as Detective Lawton's appearance at church, but he remained as uninterested today as he'd been last evening.

When we arrived at the boardinghouse, I

saw Josef sitting on the front porch between Mrs. Wilson and Mr. Lundgren. His right knee was bouncing in a gyrating motion. Nothing good had ever happened when Josef bounced his knee in this fashion, and I hoped there wouldn't be a repeat of Friday evening's encounter.

I held my breath while the carriage driver removed my luggage. But before Ronald or I could greet him, Josef jumped up from his chair and crossed the porch in long determined strides. He entered the house, and behind him the screen door banged against the wooden doorframe in three short cracks.

CHAPTER 19

For the remainder of the afternoon, Josef was nowhere to be seen. I washed my clothes and, after hanging them on the lines, peeked around the corner of the house hoping to catch a glimpse of him, but to no avail. On one of my trips up and down the stairs, I thought I heard him in his bedroom. I refrained from asking Mrs. Wilson if she'd seen him, for I didn't want her to think me overly interested in his whereabouts.

At suppertime Josef took his chair across the table as though his earlier disappearance had been a normal occurrence. Neither Mrs. Wilson nor Mr. Lundgren mentioned his perplexing behavior, so I didn't, either. Mr. Lundgren thanked God for our food, and Mrs. Wilson passed the meat platter. The pork roast appeared to be cooked to perfection, and I said so. Mrs. Wilson beamed. "I followed the instructions you wrote down for me last week."

Mr. Lundgren took a bite and nodded his appreciation. "Maybe you should write down instructions every day. This is mighty tasty."

Josef forked a piece of meat onto his plate. "Your time at the Galloways' was gut?"

The question caught me off guard, and my attention shifted from the platter of meat to his intense stare. The look was powerful enough to make me want to turn away, but I held fast, unwilling to surrender to the urge. "Their new home is lovely. The party was well attended and the food excellent. I ate so much my stomach hurt all evening."

His eyes softened at the admission. "You could not dance?"

"There was no dancing at the party, only eating and talking to people. It was a party for the Galloways to entertain and visit with their new neighbors."

"And to show off their fancy house, ja?"

"Mrs. Galloway is very proud of her new home." I'd leave it at that. The Galloways had been good to me, and I didn't want Josef or anyone else to think me ungrateful. "And how was the dance you attended?"

"Was gut. Lots of dancing and music. Lots of ladies — and men. Many people."

"And did you dance with a lot of the

ladies?" I wanted to stuff the question back in my mouth the moment I'd uttered the final word.

He grinned and there was a twinkle in his eye. "You are worried one of those ladies will win my heart?"

Mr. Lundgren winked at Mrs. Wilson, who giggled in response. They were obviously enjoying the exchange.

"I'm not worried, merely interested."

"Ja, you are worried. I can see it in your eyes." He pointed to one of his own chocolate brown eyes and grinned.

A sudden surge of anger battled within. I didn't want Josef making assumptions about my feelings for him or for anyone else. However, with the three of them laughing, I decided it would be better to join them rather than argue the point. The truth was, I *had* been worried some attractive young lady would steal his heart. I just didn't want Josef to know it!

When we finished supper, I went outside and sat on the porch. A short time later Josef joined me. "Is a nice evening."

I agreed but then added, "My worry over those ladies at the dance is not as great as your concern over Ronald Galloway." I knew I should let the matter rest, but I'd given in at supper and couldn't resist revisiting the topic.

Instead of becoming irritated, Josef nodded. "You are right. That Ronald Galloway is someone to worry me. He has money and knows fancy people. For you, he could make a gut husband."

"He would make a good husband for someone, but I don't think it will be me. He is very nice, but he has met a young woman he cares for very much. Besides, his parents would never think I was a good match for him."

"This person was at the party?"

"No. He met her only recently and hasn't introduced her to his parents yet. He's told only Augusta — and she told me."

Josef appeared to be digesting my response. "I do not think Mr. Farnsworth is gut man for your friend Augusta. Mr. Galloway likes him?"

I explained that Tyson's family was old money and Mrs. Galloway wanted Augusta to marry into a social status higher than their own. Josef nodded, though I don't think he completely understood. I would have preferred to tell him about the missing pieces of jewelry and my concern that I was a suspect, but I feared speaking about it just yet. I had been praying something would happen that would vindicate me.

Our conversation slipped back to familiar ground when I inquired if he'd made any progress with my drawings of the zoo animals. "Ja. When I have time on Sunday afternoons and sometimes in the evening, I have been drafting the plans."

My pleasure mounted at the news. I thought he'd completely pushed aside the concept. "Which drawing are you working on?"

He smiled and a slight gleam reflected in his eyes. "Would be more excitement if you wait and see."

My enthusiasm waned. "Wait and see? I get to approve the final plans, don't I? They're my drawings, after all."

The sparkle vanished from his eyes, and his smile disappeared. I hadn't meant for my words to sound harsh, but I'd obviously insulted him.

"There again the pride comes, ja? Mr. Galloway puts me in charge of his carousel factory, but you cannot trust me for this?"

I'd wounded him — of that there was no doubt. But they were my drawings, and I wanted the animals to be perfect. The eyes and mouths needed to be exactly right, and the bodies should be sleek and reflect motion — not staid or tired. I wanted my carousel animals to be ones that would enthuse children — ones like the beautiful white horse that had excited me when I was a little girl.

"Is it wrong to want perfection? When you carve, you strive for perfection. Does that make you proud, or does it make you an excellent craftsman?"

His brow furrowed slightly. He appeared to be considering what I'd said. I waited, wanting to give him as much time as necessary to weigh my response.

"You are right. A man — or a woman — needs to do the best work possible. This, the Bible tells us, ja?"

Why was he asking me? He possessed Bible knowledge. I was a veritable newcomer to daily Bible reading and prayer. But I nodded. Jesus surely approved of hard work and diligence. He'd certainly exhibited those qualities to a greater degree than any mortal.

"Then what I have done, you can see. But construction and carving I know, so you do not get the final word." He looked deep into my eyes. "You agree?"

Either way, I wouldn't have complete control, so I might as well agree. At least I would see what he'd accomplished thus far. "I agree. Where are the drawings?"

"I will get them. They are in my room."

He glanced toward the sky. "The sun is going down. We will look at them on the dining room table."

I followed him indoors and sat down at the table. I should have known my presence there would evoke questions from Mrs. Wilson. She peeked around the corner from the kitchen. "We've already eaten supper, Carrie. Have you forgotten so soon?"

I giggled at the question. "No. I'm waiting for Josef to bring some drawings downstairs."

That was all it took for Mr. Lundgren to join in the conversation. Soon they were both seated with their folded hands resting on the table. Josef's gaze settled on me as he came to an abrupt halt in the doorway.

"We all are going to look?"

I shrugged. "I believe so."

His smile radiated warmth, and in one fleeting moment, I decided he was the kind of man who would make a good husband. I touched a hand to my cheek and could feel heat emanate like a smoldering fire. *What brought that idea to mind?* Certainly he was a fine and talented man. Mr. Tobarth had convinced me of that shortly after I'd arrived at the factory. But I hadn't spent my life dreaming of love and marriage. Why was I thinking about Josef Kaestner in such a manner? I silently warned myself to erase such thoughts. Papa said marriage could smother dreams, and I wasn't prepared to extinguish mine.

"Your cheeks are flushed, Carrie. Are you feeling unwell?" Mrs. Wilson's brow knit in concern.

As though on cue, both of the men turned and stared. The fire reignited, and I could feel beads of perspiration prickling my scalp; soon they'd trickle down my forehead and cheeks.

I picked up a piece of paper and fanned with ferocity. "I'm fine — just a little warm."

Josef reached across and touched my hand. "Be careful! That is one of the sketches."

Startled, I released the piece of paper and watched it flutter to the table. Mrs. Wilson retrieved the sheet and gave it an admiring glance before pushing it toward Mr. Lundgren. "Look, Henry. It's beautiful, isn't it?"

I stretched my neck to gain a view and had to agree that Josef's changes appeared excellent. Mrs. Wilson slid the paper across the table. I nodded in agreement and smiled. "It *is* excellent."

"Is sometimes gut to let another person have control, ja?"

"Sometimes," I said, my voice as thin as the piece of paper. I wasn't about to totally commit to the concept. Who knew what he would do with my drawings if I agreed.

His chest puffed a hairsbreadth. If I hadn't been watching for his reaction, I would never have noticed. Did he think I was releasing all control over my drawings to him? I couldn't let that happen. Scooting to the edge of my chair, I said, "It is also good to continue contributing to your work once it's begun."

"Ja. And we will begin with this one as soon as our orders for the current carousel have been completed next week." He withdrew a drawing and handed it to me. "I have already enlarged it. What do you think?"

The magnificent lion I'd drawn looked back at me with gleaming eyes, his mouth open wide to reveal the huge teeth and powerful jaws from my original sketch. Visions of Daniel in a lion-filled den surrounded by the ferocious creatures suddenly appeared before me. I clutched the paper tight between my fingers and swallowed hard.

"Do not press so hard. Your fingers will make a hole in the paper." Josef's voice was warm and gentle. "You like it?"

"It is beautiful, but I wonder if we should

do one of the other animals first. Perhaps the zebra."

"Zebra? Nein." Josef shook his head. "This is the one Mr. Galloway wants first."

"It will be grand. I'm sure of it," I said, nodding my approval.

I told myself that by the time the lion was carved and painted, my problems with Tyson, the necklace, and Detective Lawton should be resolved. Then the lion wouldn't matter. Or would it? Would the image of a lion forever be a reminder of Daniel's faithfulness, and would it compel me to follow his example? I should never have sketched that lion!

At noon on Tuesday I took my lunch outdoors and settled in my regular place beneath the tree. At first I thought I might be fortunate two days in a row. The women hadn't appeared on Monday, and they weren't present when I first walked outside. But I'd barely begun to eat when a group appeared. It was the same women who'd approached me the first day. They stood across the street staring at me, and my discomfort increased with each bite of food.

I gulped down the final bite of my jam sandwich and shoved the apple back into my lunch pail. I'd eat it later. Going back to work early would be more enjoyable than enduring angry stares. I picked up my sketch pad, but before I'd gathered all my belongings, the women and two children crossed the street and marched in my direction.

My pulse quickened. I glanced toward the rear entrance to the building and attempted to gauge the distance. Could I outrun them? The thought disappeared as quickly as it had arrived, and panic seized me in a stranglehold. My breathing turned shallow; my heartbeat reverberating in my ears like a pounding drum.

The woman who had spoken to me on the first day approached while the others remained near the street. "Why you still work here?"

My mouth felt as dry as dust. Though I tried, not one word escaped my lips. The woman appeared to take my silence as a challenge and grabbed my arm. Before I could offer resistance, she yanked me over to where the other women stood near the edge of the street. One of the children clung to her mother's skirt and peered at me with downcast lips and widened eyes. The other, a young boy of two or three, hunkered down to pet a stray cat.

Fear clutched me in a terrifying embrace.

I wanted to scream for help but couldn't form a sound. Instead, I remained firmly planted, unable to move a muscle or speak a word while the women hurled questions and insults. Their eyes were filled with undeniable hatred. Unable to bear their looks, I tore my gaze from the old woman and focused on the little boy gently stroking the cat.

He seemed unaware of the tumult that swirled above him like a gathering thunderstorm. Without warning, the cat lunged forward and raced into the street. Arms outstretched, the boy ran after the furry animal and into the path of a lumber wagon. The women's angry shouts hung on the afternoon breeze as I broke through their ranks and sped toward the boy. Grabbing him around the waist, I hoisted him from the ground and pulled him close to my chest.

My skirts caught between my legs, and we fell to the street. I heard the rip of fabric as I frantically rolled to my side, barely escaping the wagon wheels. The boy shrieked in my ear as I hugged him close. "You're all right," I wheezed.

"Kitty," he cried, wrestling to free himself.

I couldn't be certain, but he appeared to be unscathed. Before I could check him for

wounds, the women and wagon driver surrounded me. Once assured neither the boy
nor I had come to any harm, the driver
shook his head. "You ain't much of a
mother, lettin' the boy run out in the street
like that." He jerked around and headed off
to his wagon.

The boy's mother gathered him into her
arms and fluctuated between kissing his
tear-stained cheeks and rebuking his bad
behavior. The child appeared totally confused.

The old woman grasped my arm and
spoke to me. I couldn't understand a word
she said, but her eyes had softened, and the
words were gently spoken. One of the other
women stepped near. "She is thanking you
for to save the boy's life." She pointed to
the boy. "Her grandson."

I nodded to the old woman. "You are
welcome."

The women began talking among themselves, and finally the one who had taken on
the role of interpreter turned to me. "We
want to say we are sorry for the way we treat
you, but we worry our men will —" She
pointed to her eye. "They see you are pretty.
They will think you make better wife than
us." When I didn't immediately respond,
she grasped my hand. "We worry when

women come to work in factory. Is not a good thing if our husbands are around other women all day long."

"Your husbands aren't working near me. I work in the paint shop and rarely see them. I give you my word, I have no interest in any of them. Please believe me."

The older woman waited while the interpretation was given and then gave a firm nod and spoke to the other woman.

"Grandmother Nina says that since you have saved the boy's life and you give us your word, we will trust you. She will speak to the other women and say to stay away."

"Tell her I said thank you very much. I won't betray her trust." I'd barely completed my thank-you when the old woman grasped my shoulders and planted a kiss on each of my cheeks. Then she spit on the ground beside us.

I flinched and attempted a sideways step, but she held fast to my shoulders. She pointed at my lips and then toward the ground. "You!" she commanded.

Stunned, I looked at the other woman. "She wants me to spit?"

"It will seal your pact," she said. Though I was aghast at the thought, I didn't want to do anything that might shatter our tenuous agreement. Closing my eyes, I puckered my lips and spit.

CHAPTER 20

As Josef predicted, the carousel we'd been working on had been completed and was prepared for shipment on Saturday morning. "Now I can begin the lion," he announced with great excitement at supper that evening. I think he expected to see me exhibit more fervor, but it was Mrs. Wilson and Mr. Lundgren who became his primary enthusiasts.

"I can only imagine how thrilled you must be to think of painting the lion, Carrie." Mrs. Wilson turned toward Josef. "She does get to paint it, doesn't she?"

"Ja, of course. Unless she wants Mr. Tobarth to assist her." His reply was muffled by a mouthful of creamed peas.

"I prefer to paint it myself, but I won't hesitate to ask Mr. Tobarth for his advice." I glanced toward the grandfather clock sitting in the far corner of the hall — a wedding gift from Mr. Wilson's mother. That's what

Mrs. Wilson had told me during my first week at the boardinghouse. Removing the napkin from my lap, I placed it on the table and pushed away. "If I'm going to be ready in time for the concert, I'd better go upstairs."

Josef's eyes crinkled with his broad smile. "Ja, you want to look as gut as the man who walks beside you."

Mrs. Wilson giggled and waved her napkin at Josef. "She's going to look beautiful. No one at the concert will give you a second glance once they get a look at Carrington in her finery."

"With that I will not argue," he said.

Keeping my gaze fastened to the tips of my shoes, I hurried toward the stairs before they could see my embarrassment. Other than the community picnic, this evening would be my first formal outing with Josef. Though Mrs. Wilson and Mr. Lundgren would also be in attendance, they'd mentioned several times that they would be sitting with the older folks close to the bandstand. "They're mostly hard of hearing," Mrs. Wilson had said.

I smiled as I remembered Josef's invitation last Wednesday. He'd fumbled for the proper words and taken a backward step, as if additional space were needed to buffet my response. When I had immediately agreed, his jaw dropped and his mouth opened wide enough to capture a swarm of gnats. I had been required to clear my throat several times before he finally acknowledged I'd spoken.

He had expected to hear that I'd be spending another weekend with the Galloways, but he didn't tell me that until the following day. I didn't divulge that the Galloway family would be visiting friends at the New Jersey shore — all except Mr. Galloway. Nor did I divulge that I'd been invited to go along.

At Augusta's insistence, Mr. Galloway had granted permission for me to miss several days of work, but I had declined. I thought the idea of seeking a special favor improper. Her father had appeared relieved. I'm certain he'd been worried how he could justify my absence to Josef or any of the other workers should they inquire. When I'd discovered Tyson Farnsworth was going with the family, I was thankful I would be in Collinsford.

I selected one of the simple dresses Augusta had given me, one that I particularly liked in a pale rose shade. Instead of frills or ruffles, the dress had been styled with an elegant simplicity that I thought understated and particularly flattering. This wasn't a concert where the women wore fancy dresses or gowns like those I'd seen at the Galloways' home. And I didn't want to stand out in the crowd. The wives of the factory workers now tolerated the fact that I worked in the factory, but it didn't mean they liked me.

I tied a black ribbon around my neck and placed two small flowered combs in my hair. Those, too, had belonged to Augusta. She discarded her clothing and accessories as frequently as petals dropped from flowers, and her mother encouraged the practice. Another glance in the mirror and I decided my appearance would have to do. We would be late if I continued restyling my hair.

Why was I fussing so, I wondered as I rushed toward the stairs. Josef saw me every day, and most of the time I was wearing a paint-spattered canvas apron with my hair in complete disarray. I didn't worry over my appearance at the factory, so why now? Why did I want to impress him this evening? *Because you care for him.* The words were so clear that I spun around to see who had spoken them. No one was there, and I silently chided myself for such silliness.

Josef was waiting in the foyer when I descended the stairs. The evening sunlight shone through the front door and danced on his still-damp hair. His suit was the plain dark blue one that he wore to church each Sunday. The moment I neared the bottom step, he held out a small bouquet to me.

"Thank you." I wondered if I would have to hold the stems for the entire concert. Spying Mrs. Wilson's vase in the parlor, I said, "Why don't I tuck one of these flowers in my hair and place the rest in water so they won't die? That way, I can enjoy them in my room for several days."

Josef concurred. "They will be better in the water. I should have thought . . ."

"No, please. I'm delighted with the flowers. They are perfect."

He followed my gaze to the vase and hurried to retrieve it from the other room. "I will fill this with water, and then we will go."

In a few minutes we were on our way. Mrs. Wilson and Mr. Lundgren had departed some time ago — to be certain they could sit up front with their friends. The park wasn't far, and by the time we arrived, the members of the orchestra were warming up their instruments. "I'm glad I didn't cause us to be late."

"Being late for concert is not so bad. Not like being late for church."

I nodded, remembering how Josef disliked being late for Sunday services. With a smile that spread from ear to ear, Mrs. Wilson waved her limp handkerchief overhead. She and Mr. Lundgren had secured seats in the second row, where they had an excellent view of the band shell. From that position, they wouldn't miss a thing.

Josef stood beneath a large oak tree and looked toward the benches surrounding the front of the stage. "Would you like me to see if there are any seats, or would you rather remain here in the shade?"

Even from our distant vantage point, it was abundantly clear there were no remaining seats. People were packed in tightly together row after row.

"Right here is fine."

I held two corners of the blanket; together we spread it beneath the heavy branches of the ancient tree. Josef extended his hand to assist me to the ground and then dropped down at my side.

"Not so fancy as the parties you attend at the Galloways', ja?"

"No," I agreed. "But this is very nice. I'm pleased to be here with you."

"For sure, you are?"

I giggled at his surprised look. "For sure, I am."

The conductor took center stage, welcomed the crowd, and announced the concert would now begin. From where we sat, I saw him turn his back to the audience, lift his baton high in the air, and with an air of authority, signal the musicians to begin. I had expected a makeshift group with little time to practice and little musical ability. I was mistaken.

When I scooted back to lean against the trunk of the oak, Josef signaled me to wait. He removed his suit jacket and placed it behind my back. "Your dress, it might get dirty or rip on the bark of the tree," he said. "I would not want to be the cause of your beautiful dress being spoiled."

Though I'm sure he wondered about my expensive clothing, Josef never inquired. I didn't know if Mrs. Wilson had explained the gowns were Augusta's castoffs. If she hadn't, he'd surely assumed by now that I'd been the beneficiary of my friend's outdated clothing.

The crowd remained seated and attentive until the intermission. When the musicians returned and began playing, the children were first to begin dancing on the covered wooden platform that surrounded the outer perimeter of the bandstand. Soon others joined them. I could feel Josef watching me, and my stomach tumbled with anticipation.

He lightly touched my arm. With his eyebrows arched high on his forehead like two question marks, he tipped his head toward the platform. "You like to dance, ja?"

At my slight nod he jumped to his feet, extended his hand, and with a gentle tug, helped me to my feet. Then he shrugged into his suit jacket and offered me his arm. While we strolled toward the platform, I was overcome by an inexplicable and strange sensation. I couldn't understand my reaction. It was as if I were drawing strength from Josef's sturdy arm. My feet seemed to float across the grass, and I felt safe at his side. *Is this what love feels like?* I wondered. *Surely not.* I couldn't love someone I barely knew. I ventured a sidelong glance at Josef's profile. He possessed a quiet strength that I admired. *You simply respect him,* I told myself.

He slowly pulled me into his arms for the first dance. My pulse quickened, and a surge of heat coursed down my arms, leaving my palms wet and my body trembling beneath his strong hands. We circled the floor, and Josef held me close while my heart hammered a message that spoke of much more than respect — my heart spoke of love. *I must regain control of my emotions,* I thought. Yet I knew I could not.

When our third dance came to an end, we were standing near Mr. Lundgren and Mrs. Wilson. I'd been surprised to see the older couple take to the dance floor, but they appeared to be having an enjoyable time. Mr. Lundgren suggested a change of partners, and when the music began, I circled along the platform with him. I'd been watching the small children and nearly toppled into him when he came to an abrupt halt.

I looked up and was struck dumb at the sight of Detective Lawton with his hand on Mr. Lundgren's shoulder. "May I be so bold as to break in and finish this dance with Miss Brouwer?"

Mr. Lundgren appeared momentarily confused but quickly recovered. "She's a fine dancer, but I'm in need of a glass of that lemonade." Before I could object Mr. Lundgren strode off toward the refreshment booth on the other side of the pavilion. No doubt the detective's sly use of my name had caused Mr. Lundgren to think I'd be pleased to dance with the man who'd cut in.

Although Detective Lawton held me at a proper distance, his mere presence at the concert set me on edge, and a shiver danced down my spine. There was no reason to play coy with the investigator. He was here for only one reason — me.

I worried what Josef would think when he saw me dancing with this stranger. If I could hurry the process, perhaps the detective would depart. "What is it you want, Detective? I've already answered all of your questions."

"Lovely dress you're wearing," he replied. "I'm surprised you can afford such quality on the pay you receive at the factory."

The inference as well as his tone annoyed me, but I wanted to be rid of him, so I explained where I'd gotten it. "If you don't believe me, you're welcome to check with Miss Galloway when she returns from the shore."

"So you know the family is gone?"

"Of course. I was invited to accompany them, but I couldn't be away from my work." I met the detective's intense stare with one of my own. "Do you truly believe I stole Mrs. Galloway's jewelry?"

"I'm not certain what to believe. You're the most likely suspect. No one else who has had opportunity to steal the jewelry is in need of money. And you were in the house the only time the safe may have been left open."

I wanted to point out there were members of the household staff who were in greater need of money than I, but I wasn't about to point a finger at them. "I've heard tell that some people commit crimes not for the money but for the excitement it creates. And you surely know there are people who put on an appearance of wealth but are really suffering financial problems."

"You are an astute young lady, Miss Brouwer. Are you referring to anyone in particular?"

"If I were in your position, I would be very interested in Tyson Farnsworth."

He tipped his head back and looked down at me. His bulging eyes and rather flat nose put me in mind of a walrus. And his somewhat rotund figure added to the mental image.

"Really? And why do you think Mr. Farnsworth could prove to be a viable suspect?"

"For one thing, he lies. More than you can even imagine." With fine-tuned precision, I enunciated the final two words. I wanted to make certain the detective understood Tyson Farnsworth didn't merely experience an occasional slipup in his stories. The man was a well-seasoned liar.

When the detective asked for verification, I told him of Tyson's expulsion from college and his concealment of that detail from Augusta and her parents. "Tyson told us he'd finished school a week earlier than Ronald Galloway, but Ronald told me Tyson had been expelled and forbidden to take his final exams."

"Anything else?"

I bobbed my head, eager to continue. "He also lied about being sick in order to avoid church services. Then he feigned a miraculous recovery and told the maid he'd gone home to visit his parents. Oddly enough, the evening before he'd said his parents were traveling. In fact, that was the reason he'd given for coming to Collinsford unannounced." I also cited Tyson's departures on the two weekends when I'd been a guest at the home. "Did he mention those excursions to you?"

"Please remember that I am the one asking the questions, Miss Brouwer."

I was pleased to see that the detective appeared taken aback by my revelations, and I decided to press my position. "If I were the detective assigned to this case, I would talk to Tyson's family and inquire why he's spending his summer in Collinsford rather than at home. At the very least, you'd think he would be working alongside his father in the family's business, wouldn't you?" I asked with arched brows.

He appeared to be considering what I'd told him, but when he didn't reply, I grasped his hand a little tighter to squeeze out a response. He startled at the pressure and met my eyes. "Mr. Farnsworth has as many suspicions about you as you seem to have about him."

"Can I assume you'll investigate my theories as closely as you have his?"

He chuckled. "Mr. Farnsworth and his family are well acquainted with the Galloways, while you're more of a newcomer into their lives. Except to confirm you don't have the jewelry in your possession, I haven't been able to investigate you very well, Miss Brouwer."

I didn't know how he had determined I didn't have the jewelry hidden in my room, but I didn't want to ask. No need to give him further reason to doubt me. But something in my demeanor must have revealed my interest, for he grinned and said, "I searched your room after you and Mr. Kaestner left the boardinghouse."

Before I could discover how he'd acquired a key to enter my room, the music stopped and the crowd swirled around us. I'd begun to question his entry into the boardinghouse and didn't see Josef standing nearby.

"This man is a friend, Carrie? I heard him say my name, yet I do not know him."

I startled and glanced over my shoulder and into Josef's eyes; they had turned ominously dark. I wondered if this meeting would bring my short-lived friendship with Josef to a halt.

Stretching forward, the detective offered his hand. "Detective Nelson Lawton, Collinsford Police Department."

Josef wasn't quite so quick to extend his hand, but he finally reached out when the detective took another step toward him. "Josef Kaestner, which you already know."

The detective nodded. "Manager and part owner of the carousel factory."

Josef glowered. "How do you know this?" He glanced in my direction.

"I didn't tell him," I said, feeling the need to defend myself.

"Mr. Galloway told me who you are and where you live — primarily because I was questioning him about Miss Brouwer."

Josef's attention shifted back and forth between the detective and me. "You have some special reason for asking these questions?"

"I do, but it might be better if Miss Brouwer explained. Right now, I need to go back to the police station and investigate some information Miss Brouwer has given me."

Josef watched the detective until he disappeared in the waning evening light and then turned back to face me. "We can sit on the blanket while you tell me."

My hands were sweating and my heart pounded beneath my rose-colored bodice as Josef escorted me across the grass. Once the police had become involved, the Galloways had given up control of the investigation. Why had I suggested the police be contacted? If I'd kept that thought to myself, Mr. Galloway would have probably received a payment from his insurance company, and life would have continued as usual. Instead, the matter remained under investigation.

I'd observed the worry in Josef's eyes — or had it been suspicion? How much should I reveal? My thoughts twisted like a tangle of crochet thread.

The conversation didn't go as well as I'd hoped. Because I didn't want to tell him I was the primary suspect in the investigation, I zigzagged around most of Josef's questions. I did tell him Mrs. Galloway's expensive necklace and rings had been stolen, and the police had been contacted at my suggestion. That much was true, and it made me sound more like a partner in solving the crime than a suspect. By the time the conversation ended, Josef seemed convinced I was helping the detective solve the crime — and I said nothing to change his mind.

Later that night when I returned to my bedroom, I considered everything I hadn't told Josef. I should have been completely honest with him. What was it I feared? Did I believe he, too, would consider me the best possible suspect? Surely after spending time with me over the past month and a half, he wouldn't so quickly judge me. After all, neither the detective nor Tyson had convinced the Galloways I was a thief — and it certainly wasn't from lack of trying.

Yet I hadn't wanted to divulge Tyson's unwanted advances to Josef. He would surely confront the wealthy young man. I could see it unfold before my eyes. The two men would argue; Tyson would feign ignorance; and the moment Josef was gone, Tyson would run to Augusta. He would tell her I had been secretly attempting to win his attentions. Instinctively I covered my ears. Moments later a tear trickled down my cheek. Augusta was desperate for Tyson's affection. She'd made it clear she hoped to marry him. In her current state of mind, he could convince her of anything. Our friendship would lie in ruins. A flash of pain seared my brain. I massaged my temples and asked myself why it mattered what Josef thought.

The investigation had nothing to do with my performance at work, and my employment was the only thing Josef controlled. *And perhaps my heart.* That nagging thought had returned every day since it had first flitted through my mind late last Sunday night. Now that seed of thought had taken root and sprouted tendrils. Long taut vines that constricted each time I made a decision or spoke a word that affected my relationship with Josef. *I must be careful to protect my heart.* Over and over, I repeated the phrase. I hoped it would safeguard me from pain.

CHAPTER 21

June 7, 1890

A week later Josef and I were walking side by side after work and were nearing the boardinghouse. "You could still change your mind and tell Miss Galloway you have other plans," he said. "I could, but she would be slow to forgive. They are leaving for the summer months to enjoy the cooler weather at the home of friends in the Thousand Islands. We won't see each other until they return in early September."

"Augusta must always come first? Do you think she chooses you over Mr. Farnsworth?"

Without looking, I could see the disappointment in Josef's eyes, just as I could hear it in his voice. Unable to give him an answer that would satisfy either of us, I offered a shrug in reply. He deserved more, but I didn't want to be dishonest. Even more, I didn't want to wound him with hastily spoken words.

Instead of continuing up the steps to the boardinghouse, he grasped my elbow. "If it is so important that she see you before she goes to this summer place, do you not think she could come here to visit with you on Sunday afternoon?"

There would be no escape, but nothing I said would please him. "I have given my word that I will attend, Josef. She is my friend, and I can't break my promise. You would expect the same from me, wouldn't you?"

His beetled brow told me he was at least considering what I'd said. Finally he nodded. "Ja, I would expect that. But I would do the same for you. I do not think Augusta does this. She is selfish with you."

He was correct in his assessment of Augusta. She did expect me to be at her beck and call, and I didn't think she'd ever change her plans on my account. I'd never asked her, but I knew it would require a matter of life and death if my request infringed upon her time with Tyson.

"You're correct. She is selfish, but this is a farewell party of sorts. And if you want my company, I will be at your side for the remainder of the summer concerts and dances."

"That would be gut. And when Augusta comes home from her summer island, you will be strong and can tell her no."

I studied him for a moment and gave a firm nod. Convinced I must make a change in my relationship with Augusta, I determined to take control of my own social life — beginning tomorrow. "I'd better hurry, or I'll not be ready when Augusta arrives for me."

Josef laughed and shook his head. I knew what he was thinking. The Galloways would send a carriage, but Augusta wouldn't be inside. Though she promised to come, she always sent someone in her stead. Josef's laughter rang in my ears as I hiked my skirt and scaled the two flights of steps to my room. Who *would* arrive this evening?

I hadn't organized my clothes before leaving for work. Now I needed to decide what I would wear. At least I wouldn't be spending the night, so I didn't need to pack a bag. Since the Galloways planned to depart on Sunday morning, I had a perfect excuse to return home when the party ended.

I managed to complete my toilette quickly, and as promised, Mrs. Wilson scaled the stairs and laced me into my corset. I'm not certain which one of us was breathing heavier when she finished. Dropping into the chair beside the window, she mopped her forehead with a corner of her apron.

"We've finished the task none too soon. Your escort has arrived." She leaned closer and peered down at the street. For a moment I thought she might stick her head out the open window. "Driving a roundabout rather than the big fancy carriage." Her brow tightened into a frown. "It's that detective from the police station. What was his name again?"

I closed the distance in record time. Holding the fullness of my skirt aside, I stepped close to Mrs. Wilson and peeked across her shoulder. My heart skipped several beats before it raced into double time. In a silly effort to slow the quickening thud within my chest, I placed my hand on my bodice. It didn't help.

"Carrie?" Mrs. Wilson was staring at me, her eyebrows resembling two thin question marks. "What is his name? Larson?"

"No, it's Lawton." In an effort to avoid further questions, I crooked my finger at the older woman, retrieved my reticule from atop the bureau, and stepped to the door as rapidly as my gown would permit.

Mrs. Wilson pushed up from the chair. Her breathing remained labored, and it was obvious she didn't want to face the two flights of steps that awaited her. No matter she would be going down rather than up — she declared either way was a chore at her weight and age. She followed behind and clung to the handrail as we made our descent.

"Why did they send the detective to escort you?" she hissed when we reached the first landing.

Glancing over my shoulder, I touched my index finger to my pursed lips. "Shh. He'll hear you," I whispered.

"Don't be silly. He's out on the front porch. How can he hear us all the way up here?"

I continued my descent and was far ahead of Mrs. Wilson when I turned around and said, "Trust me. He has excellent hearing. Take your time. There's no need for you to greet him."

Those words were all it took for the older woman to step lively. "I don't want the detective to think I'm impolite, Carrie."

"We must be brief. I don't want to be late. I promised Augusta I would arrive in time to help her with her hair."

The older woman clucked her tongue. "She has a maid but still expects you to help her. I believe Miss Galloway needs to think of someone other than herself."

"Augusta frequently styled my hair when I was staying at their home."

The only sign that Mrs. Wilson heard me was a soft grunt.

Fortunately, Detective Lawton refused her invitation to step inside. Mrs. Wilson frowned at his negative response, but I breathed a sigh of relief.

Once we were on our way, I turned to the detective. "Is there some particular reason that you're acting as my driver, or did you request the duty?"

"With the Galloways preparing to leave for the summer and the crime still unsolved, I wanted the opportunity to speak with you alone and make certain you're not planning to leave Collinsford."

My muscles tightened and I gripped the edge of the seat. He still considered me his prime suspect, and that annoyed me in the extreme. After advising him I had no plans to leave Collinsford, I expressed my irritation. He merely shrugged and tweaked one end of his mustache, obviously unmoved by my outburst. I found his silence maddening.

Once I'd settled myself, I decided to try again. "If it wouldn't be a betrayal of your position, I would appreciate knowing if you've investigated anyone else with the same zeal you've directed toward me."

"I have."

I stared at him and waited. He didn't say anything more. "You have? That's it? You have nothing more to add?"

"No." He shook his head.

I wanted to shout that I deserved more of a response but knew it would serve no purpose. The detective didn't plan to divulge the results of his investigation — if, in fact, he had investigated anyone other than me, which I truly doubted. I folded my hands in my lap, tightened my lips into a thin line, and decided I, too, would remain silent.

Save for the clopping horses' hooves, the remainder of the ride passed in disquieting silence. When we arrived at the Galloway residence, the detective assisted me down. "If you decide to travel outside of Collinsford, you should advise me prior to your departure." Dark pinpoint pupils bored into me while he awaited my answer.

"You will be the very first person to know."

"Sarcasm doesn't become you, Miss Brouwer."

"I must admit that being suspected of a crime brings out the worst in me." I took a side step around the detective. "Now if you will excuse me, I'm expected inside."

Hurrying, I made my way up the stairs to Augusta's room, which had the look of a baggage room at the railroad station. Trunks lined the walls and flowed out into the hallway. "I'm surprised your mother would entertain on the evening prior to your departure for the summer," I said.

"The servants are the ones who suffer, not Mother." Augusta leaned close to the mirror and pinched her cheeks. "I always appear too pale, don't you think?"

"I never thought so, though you may be a bit pale this evening." I closed the distance between us and picked up the hairbrush. "Has the detective made any further progress in locating your mother's jewelry?" I drew the brush through her hair in long, steady strokes while watching her reflection in the mirror. To me, Detective Lawton had claimed to be making no progress, but who knew what he'd reported to the Galloway family. He might be closing in on his suspect, and if it was me, I wanted to know! When Augusta didn't respond, I tugged on a strand of hair.

"Ouch! Do be careful, that hurts." She touched her fingers to her head as though she'd been mortally wounded. "The last I heard, there was nothing to report. Tyson mentioned he thought you could very well be the most likely suspect, but I didn't hesitate to tell him such an idea was utter nonsense." Obviously embarrassed to relate the information, she turned her gaze away from the mirror. "The detective told my father he'd continue to work on finding the jewelry, but I don't think Father holds out much hope the thief will ever be found."

Fearful she would change the subject, I decided to avoid any mention of Tyson's accusation. "And the detective?"

She shrugged. "He still thinks there's hope — but he's probably afraid to say otherwise. His job could be in jeopardy if he isn't successful solving crimes, don't you think?"

"Possibly," I muttered. Twirling a strand of hair around my finger, I pinned it atop her head.

When I'd completed fashioning Augusta's hair, she looked at me in the mirror. "I'm going to miss you terribly. If you'd agree, I know I could convince Father to bring you along on one of his weekend visits."

I shook my head. "We've already had this discussion. I'll see you when you return in September. Until then, you'll have Tyson to keep you company."

"That's not the same. Besides, he won't be with me all of the time. He has business that requires his attention from time to time."

I wondered what kind of business. From what I'd learned, avoiding work was the only business that occupied Tyson's time.

"Enough of this gloomy talk. Let's go and enjoy ourselves with the others."

Augusta tugged on my hand and drew me toward the door. The sound of music drifted down from the ballroom on the upper floor. Mrs. Galloway had insisted upon a floating dance floor, the kind with layers of ribbed wooden slats that created pockets of air beneath the topmost layer. Dancing on air — that's how I'd heard the floors described. And of course Mrs. Galloway wanted a dance floor that would outshine any other in Fair Oaks. For now, it did. But soon another dowager would outdo her. Then Augusta's mother would need to purchase something else to make her feel important and accepted. I marveled that Mr. Galloway gave in to his wife's outlandish demands.

Tyson and Ronald were waiting inside the door leading into the ballroom. Tyson quickly swept Augusta into his arms and across the dance floor. I wasn't certain if Ronald truly wanted to dance with me, or if he felt obligated because we'd been left standing alone, but I accepted his offer.

"How are things faring with the young lady who has won your heart?" I asked. "Will I meet her this evening?"

"No. I haven't gained the courage to speak to Mother. She's hoping I'll become enamored with the Wentworths' daughter, Kathryn."

"I've met her. She seems a lovely young woman, but if you're not interested, why not tell your mother?"

He chuckled. "You've been around my mother long enough to know she doesn't take such matters lightly. I'm hoping Kathryn will gather some gumption before I do." He leaned forward in a conspiratorial manner. "She's in love with a young man who lives in Cincinnati. She met him while she was attending finishing school."

"So each of you is waiting on the other to soften the blow." I giggled. "I do think it would be the gentlemanly thing if you would take the lead."

"Being a woman, I'm sure you do. However, Mrs. Wentworth isn't nearly as formidable as my own dear mother. I believe Kathryn will have the easier time of it if *she* deals the first blow."

Shortly before the dance ended, I mentioned Detective Lawton's presence and plied Ronald with several questions. Unfortunately, he didn't tell me any more than I'd already learned — which was very little indeed. When the music stopped, I turned to see Tyson and Augusta standing near us.

Tyson winked at me and took a sideward step. "What do you say we exchange partners, Ronald?"

I couldn't believe Tyson's cheeky behavior. What if someone had seen him wink at me? They might assume I'd been flirting with him. The very thought sent an icy finger crawling down my spine. The moment the music began, he pulled me much too close. In my attempt to push him away, I stumbled on his foot.

He smirked. "Careful or we'll land on the floor. If you want to lie down beside me, I can think of more comfortable places."

I wanted to slap his face. But such action would create a scene that would require explanation. And no matter what I said, Augusta didn't want to hear the truth. It seemed nobody wanted to hear the truth about Tyson Farnsworth.

CHAPTER 22

July 4, 1890

The weeks since Augusta's departure had passed with surprising speed. I hadn't missed the weekend parties at Fair Oaks in the least. Truth be told, I had welcomed the respite. And Josef had stepped forward to fill any void created by Augusta's summertime absence.

My growing friendship with Josef seemed natural; we lived in the same boardinghouse, worked in the same factory, and shared a love of carousels. And with the recent challenges of creating the newly designed animals, we'd even begun discussing the designs after supper each evening. I'd developed a genuine appreciation for Josef's talent, and he constantly expressed admiration for my ideas and work, as well.

While Mrs. Wilson was preparing for the Independence Day festivities, Josef and I were revising our latest design for a leopard.

We had somehow moved from the concept of individual design to working in concert to create the perfectly designed carousel animal.

Mrs. Wilson bustled into the dining room, wiping her hands down the front of her apron. "You two need to put away your work. We need to leave in less than an hour or we won't arrive at the park in time for the mayor's speech. Remember, the streetcars will be crowded today."

I pushed away from the table, not convinced missing the mayor's speech would be such a terrible thing. However, I didn't want to disappoint Mrs. Wilson. She'd been looking forward to the celebration for several weeks and was determined to arrive on time. Two hours ago she'd sent Mr. Lundgren in search of the ideal spot for our picnic. He'd been instructed to find a place with ample shade and close enough to the podium to hear the speeches and see the entertainment that would follow. He'd left the house with a final warning that he'd be required to protect the space from any two-legged intruders who might arrive late and attempt to infringe upon the secured area.

I wasn't certain public land could be staked out in such a manner, but Mrs. Wilson appeared to know exactly how to claim a private space for our picnic. It had been many years since I'd attended an Independence Day celebration, and my own feelings of patriotism had begun to surface during the past weeks. Not since the year before my father and I departed for France had I participated in any meaningful July Fourth celebration. There had been a small gathering of American artists living in France, but those celebrations had primarily consisted of men drinking wine while they discussed their latest paintings. I picked up the drawings and stacked them on the dining room table. Today I would celebrate this country's independence in proper American fashion.

I excused myself and, after a visit to my bedroom for a quick change of attire, returned downstairs. Josef and Mrs. Wilson stood on the front porch. The older woman was staring at the screen door as though peering inside would make me appear. To think she was antsy was an understatement. The moment I stepped outdoors, she grasped my arm and tugged me toward the steps.

"Grab the picnic basket, Josef!" she called over her shoulder while propelling me forward. "We don't want to miss the next streetcar. It's sure to be full."

When we arrived at the stop, Mrs. Wilson's breath was coming in short gasps. She clasped a hand to her chest, and I was thankful to see the streetcar moving toward us. We should have left earlier so that the poor woman wouldn't have had to rush. I silently chastised myself for taking time to change my skirt and shirtwaist. If Mrs. Wilson fainted or suffered heat exhaustion, it would be due to my vain behavior.

The moment we stepped up into the streetcar, I motioned for Mrs. Wilson to take one of the few remaining seats. She patted the seat, and I dropped down beside her. Josef stood in front of us, the picnic basket lodged between his feet.

She pulled out her fan and flapped it with enough vigor that I no longer worried she would faint. When her complexion returned to its normal color, I leaned closer. "Are you feeling better?"

"I'm fine, dear. No need to worry yourself on my account." She waved to several of the ladies sitting near the rear of the car before tipping her head close to my ear. "They'll be surprised when they discover we have a picnic spot saved for us."

Once the car clanged our arrival and came to a stop, Mrs. Wilson waited until Myrtle Cutsinger plodded down the narrow aisle. The heavy-hipped woman leaned forward only far enough to gain a view out the window. "Looks like all the shady spots are spoken for. We'll be toasted to a crisp out in that sun." She tapped Mrs. Wilson's arm with her umbrella. "We should have arrived earlier, Minnie."

"It's always good to plan ahead for these holidays." Mrs. Wilson pushed up from her seat and waved us forward with a wide grin.

Mr. Lundgren was sitting on one of two large quilts spread beneath a large elm tree. We would have an excellent view of the stage as long as folks didn't take up residence in front of us. And if anyone tried that tack, Mrs. Wilson would probably shoo them away. While we laid out our food, the band gathered in the pavilion and prepared for the concert.

An occasional toot or squawk could be heard while musicians warmed up their instruments, but once the conductor signaled, all turned quiet. Then in a magnificent burst of sound, a John Philip Sousa march filled the summer afternoon air. With cymbals clanging and drums beating a clipped cadence, the band continued to play several more patriotic numbers that brought the crowd to its feet. The final march brought the mayor to a makeshift stage that fronted the pavilion. Festive red, white, and blue bunting draped the empty space beneath the platform, providing excellent concealment for the children playing hide-and-seek.

The mayor lumbered up the two steps onto the platform and glanced over his shoulder, no doubt expecting the musicians to step down and permit him the benefit of their shaded pavilion. But they remained perched on their chairs with their attention fixed upon the band conductor. The mayor appeared sorely disappointed.

Folks continued visiting and eating their picnic lunches while he shouted out his plans for the coming year if they would only reelect him to office. His wife and children stood in front of the podium and did their best to arouse applause each time he hesitated and nodded in their direction. When even the mayor's children tired of his speech and took shelter in the shade beneath the platform, he finally signaled to the band conductor.

As cheers emanated from the crowd, the mayor waved his hat overhead as though the cheering were for him.

Mr. Lundgren leaned against the tree trunk with a glass of lemonade and chuckled. "That man would win more votes if he'd just keep his mouth shut."

"Ja. He does enjoy hearing himself talk, that's for sure." Josef sat with his legs bent close to his chest and looked toward the pond not far in the distance.

I followed his gaze and jumped to my feet. "We should go and feed the ducks our scraps of bread. Come, Josef."

Slowly unfolding his legs, he gathered the leftover bits and pieces into a cloth napkin and rose to his feet. He patted his stomach. "I think I ate too much. Now I wish for sleep."

"You ate too much because Carrie prepared most of it last evening," the older woman remarked with a grin. "But she has been giving me some helpful tips, and one day soon, I hope to match her abilities in the kitchen." She didn't wait for a response before turning to ask Mr. Lundgren a question.

Mrs. Wilson accepted her inabilities in the kitchen as readily as she accepted the shortcomings in others. *"We're all just people trying to get along in this world. God gives us different talents. Some can cook, some can sew, some can grow flowers, and some can paint pictures. That's what makes this world a special place."* She'd made the comment to me many weeks ago while attempting to roll out a tough piecrust.

380

In somewhat the same way, I attempted to make each of the carousel animals unique and special — they were alike and yet very different. Perhaps that desire came from God, too, I thought while strolling at Josef's side.

"It has been nice these last weeks to have you always at the boardinghouse," he said.

I giggled. "You mean rather than rushing off to spend time with Augusta each Saturday evening and Sunday?"

"Ja. I understand she is your friend and you enjoy her company, but it is nicer for me when you are here."

His compliment embraced me with an inviting warmth that I could neither ignore nor explain. My heart fluttered in quickstep when he grasped my hand and helped me settle on a bench near the edge of the pond.

"You have enjoyed this time without going to visit the Galloways?" His eyes filled with expectation.

Sunshine danced on his hair and cast shades of umber and bronze among the chocolate strands. "Yes, I have enjoyed my time with you very much."

Though my heartbeat had slowed to a more normal rhythm, I'd suddenly acquired a strange sense of shyness. Each day we shared time together. Why had I suddenly developed such awkward feelings here at the park?

After tossing a handful of breadcrumbs toward several ducks that waddled up from the water's edge, he sat down beside me. Resting his elbows across his thighs, he glanced over his shoulder and met my eyes. "I have a fondness for you, Carrie."

The words had been spoken with ease, yet each one pierced my heart like an arrow hitting its mark. "You do?" I whispered.

He chuckled. "You cannot tell this already?"

I was uncertain how a proper lady should respond but decided I would be truthful rather than coy. I doubted Augusta would agree. "I have been hoping that was true."

"And you are feeling the same way?" His brows arched high on his forehead.

"Yes, I'm feeling the same way."

He leaned back against the wooden slats of the bench with a broad smile splitting his face. "Is gut we feel the same, ja?"

"Yes," I replied. "Very good."

Josef maintained a proper distance during the afternoon, but once the sun had set, he moved close by my side. We watched the fireworks burst overhead and gasped with delight at each explosion. After a particularly large display had illuminated the sky and darkness once again prevailed, Josef pulled me close. The shimmer of moonlight outlined his features. Slowly he lowered his head and covered my lips with a tender kiss. His touch set off an explosion inside my head that rivaled the evening's fireworks. I whispered his name, and once again he took my lips captive, until another explosion lit the sky.

Gently, I pushed against his chest. "People will see us."

Leaning close, he motioned toward several embracing couples. "They are busy with each other. About us, they do not care."

A blast cracked the silence and was soon followed by several more loud explosions that signaled the final display of the evening. I jumped to my feet. "We'd better find Mrs. Wilson and Mr. Lundgren and get in line for the streetcar."

He clasped my hand and pulled me to a halt. "I did not mean to frighten you, Carrie. You don't need to run off."

"I'm n-not frightened." I couldn't hide the tremble in my voice any more than I could hide the fear in my heart. I longed for Josef's affection, yet he didn't know of the accusations against me. And until the detective gave up on finding Mrs. Galloway's jewelry or apprehended the culprit, I couldn't share the tale with Josef — and I couldn't chance losing my heart to him, either.

We walked side by side, and once again he leaned close. "I will not rush you, but I want for you to know my feelings. I don't want Mr. Galloway's son or some other man to steal your heart when I am not looking."

"That won't happen, Josef. I promise."

"Gut. I am glad to hear this."

Mrs. Wilson bustled toward us with Mr. Lundgren following at a close pace. She waved her arm in a giant semicircle. "If we hurry, we'll be able to get a seat on the next streetcar."

Josef took the picnic basket from Mr. Lundgren with his left hand and clapped the older man on the shoulder with his right. "She hurries to get us here, and now she can't wait to rush us home."

Mr. Lundgren pushed his hat back on his head. "Just like a woman."

Josef glanced over Mr. Lundgren's shoulder and grinned at me. "Ja, just like a woman."

Shortly after we arrived at work on Monday morning, I could sense Josef's concern. Even from across the vast expanse of the paint shop, I could tell something was amiss. He remained at a distance, where he wouldn't be detected by the visiting strangers, yet I could see him watching their every move. His attention shifted back and forth, skimming faces among the group.

Who were these men and why had he been excluded? I wondered. Lifting my paints, I moved to the leopard's head.

"Who are they?" I hissed at Mr. Tobarth.

He lifted one shoulder and just as quickly dropped it back in place. "Don't know, but they're sure lookin' things over."

I considered the gathering of men Mr. Galloway had escorted to the rear of the paint shop. They were talking in hushed tones. "None of them are men you knew in Philadelphia, are they?"

Mr. Tobarth's lips curled in a lopsided grin. "None of the fellows I knew dressed like that."

"What about the owners? I'll bet they did." I dipped my paint into a mixture of pale pink I was using to shade the cat's large tongue.

After one tentative step that brought him farther into the paint shop, Josef took another step, then squared his shoulders. Holding a paper in one hand, he walked up to Mr. Tobarth with an assured stride. He didn't look toward the men who had gathered around Mr. Galloway in a semicircle. Drawing near, he stooped down between the two of us and pointed to the blank piece of paper while he talked.

"Those men, I think they are here to purchase the factory," he said.

"How is that possible? You own part of the factory. Besides, Mr. Galloway isn't interested in selling this place. Augusta would have told me if he had such a plan."

"When did you last talk to her?" Mr. Tobarth tapped the wooden tip of his paintbrush against one of his front teeth while he waited for my reply.

"I haven't heard from her since she left a month ago, but I'm certain she would have written and told me."

"If she knows," Mr. Tobarth said. "Her father has been in Collinsford more than he's been with his family out at that summer place. She probably don't have any idea what he's doin' with his business. Long as she has a new dress to wear to the next party, I don't think she'd care what's happenin' here."

Pointing my paintbrush in Mr. Tobarth's direction, I said, "I think I know Augusta better than the two of you. She *does* care and she *would* tell me." I was tempted to emphasize my point by daubing a dot of pink paint on the tip of his broad nose, but the visitors had dispersed and were moving in our direction.

Josef made a great show of folding the paper and striding off toward his office at the front of the building. Soon Mr. Galloway and the group came closer. I wanted to throw a sheet over my leopard so they couldn't see it before it was completed and part of a working carousel. Apparently Mr. Galloway didn't share my concern that someone might steal our ideas, for he pointed out the leopard, as well as the elephant, a mountain sheep, and several partially painted horses positioned in the drying rack. What was he thinking?

Mr. Tobarth remained focused upon his work, looking neither right nor left. Two of the men directed questions to him, but none came my way. In fact, the men stared at me as though I were one of the carousel animals on display — much as Mrs. Galloway had stared at me the first day I'd arrived in Collinsford.

When we departed for the boardinghouse after work, Josef quizzed me at length. He'd discovered very little useful information from Mr. Tobarth. I told him the men had inquired about the length of time it took Mr. Tobarth to paint the carousel animals, his choice of painting techniques, and how many years he'd worked at the factory. Other than that, they'd remained aloof while they circled around for several minutes to watch him paint.

"And they said nothing about buying the factory?"

He'd already asked that same question three times, and each time I gave the same reply. Finally I sighed and came to a halt in the middle of the brick sidewalk. "Do you think I would tell you a lie about such a thing?"

"I hope you would not lie to me about anything. But my concern is great. Not a word did Mr. Galloway say to me before he left the factory with those men." He motioned me to begin walking. "You do not think that is strange?"

"I don't think you should worry. It will do no good."

"This is true, but it is difficult."

I nodded. I knew exactly how difficult. For far too long, I'd been worrying about Mrs. Galloway's jewelry. It had been nearly impossible to cease fretting, but it hadn't done me one smidgen of good. And it wouldn't help Josef, either.

"Why don't we work on the new drawings this evening?" If I could keep Josef busy, maybe he wouldn't worry.

"We are working too much. After supper we should go to the park instead."

I didn't argue. The park sounded much more inviting.

I didn't see Mr. Galloway arrive at the factory the next morning, but around nine-thirty Gus Werner, one of the carvers, came to the paint shop and nudged Mr. Tobarth. "Mr. Galloway just left the factory, and Josef wants to see you in the office." Gus still hadn't accepted me as an equal, and he didn't meet my gaze, but he cocked his head toward the front of the factory, "He wants to see you, too, Miss Brouwer." He stepped toward our paints. "I'll see to your brushes."

Standing up, Mr. Tobarth grunted his approval. I clipped along at a near run in order to keep up with his long-legged stride across the paint room and up to the front of the factory. The minute we entered Josef's office, I knew something was amiss. Josef's leg was jiggling so fast he could have churned cream into butter. He gestured for us to enter the room and pointed for Mr. Tobarth to close the door.

"Sit down, sit down!" He swatted toward the chairs, and the two of us dropped quickly into place.

Josef's behavior disturbed me, but I waited in silence. Apparently Mr. Tobarth sensed a need to remain silent, too, for he sat there as though he'd been struck dumb.

"Mr. Galloway says those men who were here yesterday are very impressed with our new designs." Josef leaned across the desk, his eyes dark and brooding.

Confusion muddled my brain. Wasn't that a good thing? We'd been working at a feverish pace to design something that would bring in more orders and distinguish our factory from those in Philadelphia and Brooklyn. I waited for Mr. Tobarth's response. I did my best to force something from the older man: I cleared my throat, moved my leg close, and poked his shoe. I even jabbed my elbow into his side. He sat there like a lump on a log until I could no longer keep my mouth shut.

"Isn't that what we hoped for?" My voice was paper thin.

Josef leaned across the paper-strewn desk and looked at me as though I'd taken leave of my senses. "They didn't place one order — not one. They aren't interested in purchasing our carousels."

A lump the size of a grapefruit formed in my stomach. "But they looked excited when they saw the drawings and the animals."

"That much I already know." Josef shoved the clutter into his desk and slammed the drawer. If only this problem could be so easily eradicated.

"Didn't Mr. Galloway say anything to you?"

Josef leaned forward and rested his forehead in his palms. "No. When I approached him, he said he would talk to me later. There is something more to this."

Mr. Tobarth scooted to the edge of his chair. "Maybe he needs money and figures the easiest way is to sell your designs and then have the two of you come up with something different for us to make."

I jerked to attention. "They aren't his designs. They are ours — mine and Josef's. How can he sell them?"

"You work for him, and I figure that makes 'em his. He probably feels the same way."

Josef's complexion had turned the shade of the milk paint used to prime the horses. "You think that is it, Henry? He plans to sell our designs?"

"I'm only makin' a guess, Josef. Who can know what those rich businessmen are thinkin'." He looked over his shoulder toward the paint shop. "We can talk 'bout this later. Right now, there's work that needs to be done."

Josef nodded. "Ja. But who can say for how long."

The ominous tone of his voice matched his downcast features. There would be much to discuss this evening.

CHAPTER 23

For the remainder of the week, Josef's worrisome mood prevailed. His downcast disposition even continued throughout the weekend. Nothing I said or did helped. Sunday's sermon taught about casting your cares upon Jesus, a topic I thought particularly appropriate to the problem. Unfortunately, the message had no positive effect upon Josef. By Monday morning, I was pleased to return to the paint shop, where I wouldn't be faced with his discouraged demeanor and negative comments.

The day progressed without incident, and for that I was grateful. No men in business suits paraded through the factory to see our work or look at drawings and designs. Mr. Galloway made no further appearances at the factory. It seemed as though all had returned to normal. It was as though the incidents of the previous week had never occurred. Except when I looked at Josef's face.

At day's end he stood at the factory door, as glum as when we'd entered. I strolled toward him, my lunch pail in one hand and my sketch pad secure beneath my arm. I forced a smile. The muscles in his face didn't move a sixteenth of an inch. I couldn't even detect a slight twitch.

The heavy wood door had been wedged open, and the summer breeze greeted me with more enthusiasm than Josef's sullen features. I inhaled a deep breath, determined to lift his spirits. "Looks like it's going to be a beautiful evening." I tucked a loose strand of hair behind my ear and listened to the silence between us.

"I said, it looks like it's going —"

"Ja. I heard what you said."

He grabbed his lunch pail from where it had been resting on the floor and strode out of the building as though he couldn't get away fast enough. Usually I had to go to his office and force him away from his desk, but not today.

I glanced over my shoulder at the open door. "Who is going to lock the building?" Securing the building had always been Josef's job, unless he was away. Then Mr. Tobarth took charge.

"Henry will see to it," he said.

"Mr. Tobarth is in charge of the factory now?"

"Nein." He coupled his curt response with an annoyed look that let me know he didn't want to discuss the factory, and I wondered if Mr. Galloway had made an appearance sometime during the day. He could have come and gone, and we would have never seen him back in the paint shop. Yet I didn't want to ask. It would only create more discord.

I stopped beside the entrance. "Mr. Tobarth has already left through the rear door."

Josef grunted and kicked the piece of wood from beneath the door. He waited until it slammed shut and shoved a key into the lock. "There! It is locked."

I remained beside the closed door and stared at him, completely dumbfounded by his behavior. When he finally looked at me, I tugged on my earlobe. I hoped the act would lighten his mood, but my attempt fell as flat as one of Mrs. Wilson's banana cakes.

As we neared the boardinghouse, Josef's lips tightened into a thin line. He lifted his nose in the air. "Mrs. Wilson has burned the cabbage again. This, I do not need."

There was no doubt he'd correctly assessed the situation. Even at the front sidewalk, there was no denying the odor. "She didn't do it on purpose, Josef. And you must admit, she's been doing much better over the past weeks."

"She should not take in boarders if she cannot cook."

I grasped his shirtsleeve and looked deep into his eyes. "You need to spend some time with the Lord, Josef Kaestner. You had no trouble telling *me* how I should depend upon God for everything when I faced difficulties. But now that *you* face a problem of your own, you become angry and mean-spirited."

The anger in his eyes softened for a moment but soon returned. I dropped my hold on his arm, turned on my heel, and hurried inside. I didn't want to hear his excuses. Mrs. Wilson's cooking hadn't changed. He had.

The screen door banged behind me, and I heard a pot drop in the kitchen. Maybe it was the cabbage — at least that might make Josef happy. "Is that you, Carrie?" Mrs. Wilson sounded far too happy. I decided it must have been an empty pan that fell on the floor.

"Yes. Do you need some help in the kitchen?"

"I can always use help with my cooking," she said, chuckling. "But that's not why I called to you." She walked down the hallway, wiping her hands on the corner of her apron. "You received a letter today, and I thought you'd want to read it before supper." She stepped into the parlor, picked up the envelope, and handed it to me. I could see the curiosity in her eyes as her gaze trailed the envelope from my hand and into my skirt pocket. "Aren't you excited to see what it says?"

After handing her my lunch pail, I patted my pocket and headed toward the stairs. "It will keep for a few more minutes."

Before she could say anything more, Josef entered the front door, handed her his lunch pail, and circled around me on his way upstairs. "Good afternoon, Josef. Supper in half an hour," she called after him. He grunted in return. "That young man is in a foul mood for sure." Mrs. Wilson clucked her tongue. "And me with burned cabbage to serve him. I doubt that's going to help."

I grinned and continued up the steps. The burned cabbage wouldn't help, but I doubted that even a perfect meal and fine dessert would do much to improve Josef's mood. I stopped at the bathroom, washed up, and then continued down the hall to my bedroom. I'd left the windows open that morning and was thankful it hadn't rained. I was also thankful for the breeze that helped cool the room. Though I enjoyed the privacy of the third floor, Augusta had been right. The room was quite warm most of the time.

I sat down by the window, took the letter from my pocket, and removed the thick contents. While living in France, Augusta had written few letters, most of which had consisted of one hastily scribbled page, so to see so many pages in one letter surprised me. There had obviously been much happening in the Thousand Islands. Perhaps Tyson had proposed. Even on this warm afternoon, the thought made me shiver.

The neatly penned date above the salutation was nearly a month old. She must have begun her letter shortly after their arrival. The first page spoke of the weather and a party the family had attended on their first night. The journey had been quite boring, and she still wished I had come with her. If Josef's mood didn't soon improve, I'd likely be wishing the same thing.

The letter continued on and on, telling of the many parties, but also declaring a growing dissatisfaction with Tyson's absence. Knowing I could read the letter in detail after supper, I skimmed over the next two pages. From what I gathered between the lines, Tyson had been absent as much as he'd been present. Poor Augusta had counted on flaunting him at all of the parties. She was certain his good looks would make the other young ladies jealous. Though I'd told her over and over that looks were only skin deep, she thought Tyson more than a handsome face. He'd convinced her he possessed a kind and generous nature. And the fact that he'd easily won Mrs. Galloway's approval seemed to validate Augusta's view of Tyson.

When I turned to the next page, I straightened in my chair. Augusta was writing about my father. The preceding pages slipped from my lap as I continued to read. Surely she'd made some mistake.

The bell at the bottom of the steps clanged to announce supper. I wanted to read the letter again, but there wasn't time. My heart was racing as I rushed down the steps. Mr. Lundgren gave thanks for our food and had barely finished when Mrs. Wilson arched her brows and tapped my hand. "Anything interesting in your letter?" She passed me the bowl of cabbage, and I handed it to Josef without taking any.

The older woman didn't miss the slight.

"No cabbage?"

"Not tonight, Mrs. Wilson. I don't think it will aid my digestion." Of that I was certain — burned cabbage wouldn't aid anyone's digestion.

The older woman wrinkled her forehead, and her eyebrows slid into a cascading downward dip. "Oh, dearie me, no. Cabbage and an upset stomach don't mix — not at all. Josef can have double portions tonight." She beamed a smile at Josef as though she'd bestowed a special award.

I slapped my napkin across my mouth before Josef could hear me giggle. Given his sour disposition, I didn't think he'd look kindly upon my laughter or the fact that I'd managed to avoid eating the cabbage.

Mrs. Wilson picked up the plate of chops and passed it to me. "Your letter, Carrie. You were going to tell us about your letter from Miss Galloway."

"Yes. And there's some very exciting news, although I wonder whether there's been some mistake."

Her eyes wide, Mrs. Wilson leaned across her plate. "Oh, do tell us," she begged. "Has Miss Galloway gotten engaged — or perhaps she's already wed. Is that it?"

Mr. Lundgren speared a pork chop and dropped it onto his plate. "If you give her a minute, she's gonna tell us, Minnie."

Mrs. Wilson clapped her palm across her mouth and motioned for me to speak.

"There were some people attending a party in the Thousand Islands who had recently returned from France, where they'd purchased one of my father's paintings."

"Oh, that's simply delightful, dear."

I could see the disappointment in Mrs. Wilson's eyes. She would have been happier to hear about a wedding announcement. "That's not all," I said.

"Do tell us." Her enthusiasm had waned, and she was now more interested in carving her piece of meat than hearing about my father's paintings.

"Augusta's letter said that my father's paintings have recently received great acclaim and are fetching high prices. She said people are scouring the shops looking to invest in them."

Once again the older woman perked to attention. "You'll be wealthy, Carrie. Why, that *is* wonderful news. You'll be able to do all the things you —"

"Other than the carousel picture hanging in my bedroom, I own only two of my father's paintings. Father sold most of the others to pay expenses. And as I recall, none of those canvases sold for much." The thought of how little still confounded me, for I had always known my father was a talented artist.

Mr. Lundgren looked across the table at me, his expression thoughtful and kind. "Hearing all this still makes you proud, don't it?"

I bobbed my head. "Of course — very proud. But I wish it would have happened before his death. So much of his time was spent giving art lessons to untalented students." I shrugged my shoulders. "But that was what put food on our table."

"But if your father hadn't been giving untalented students those art lessons, we would never have met you. And that would have been a terrible loss." Mrs. Wilson patted her heart. "Maybe one day your paintings will be worth a great deal of money, too. When that happens, I can say that you lived in my boardinghouse as a young woman." Mrs. Wilson straightened her shoulders as though I'd gained special stature in the art world.

"I think there are already those who are willing to pay for her drawings," Josef said. The tablecloth fluttered and the floorboards bounced, synchronized to the jiggling of Josef's leg.

"Do tell!" Mrs. Wilson's mouth dropped

open, and she stared at Josef, waiting to hear the news.

I spread a spoonful of applesauce atop my pork chop, hoping to give the dry piece of meat a little moisture — and a little flavor. "Josef is worrying overmuch. He thinks some businessmen are interested in purchasing my sketches of carousel animals." I turned my attention back to Josef. "And those may be my drawings, but they are designs we developed together."

"What *are* the two of you talking about?"

Mrs. Wilson was clearly confused and clearly eager to hear the details. Josef pushed away from the table, his food half eaten. "Carrie will tell you. I think I'll go upstairs. My digestion, it isn't very gut this evening, either."

CHAPTER 24

During our walk to work the following morning, Josef apologized for his behavior the previous evening. "You are right that my worry will not change things. No matter what happens, God is in charge. This, I must remember. He will see us through these problems."

My heart warmed at his use of the word *us* rather than *me.* Knowing Josef considered me a friend and an ally would make the blow easier if and when it came. And though I hadn't expressed my innermost thoughts to him, there was little doubt something was afoot regarding the factory.

We'd departed earlier than usual that morning so that Josef would have time to go through his paper work in case Mr. Galloway arrived without warning. "I want everything in order so he can find no fault with my work," he'd said.

I'd agreed to come along and help, but I

hadn't expected to leave quite so early. Had it been wintertime, we would have been walking to work in the pitch-darkness. I couldn't imagine Josef had permitted any of his duties to fall very far behind. But I didn't argue.

When we neared the front door, Josef removed the key from his pocket and grabbed the heavy lock with his right hand. The handle disengaged, and the door creaked open before he'd even slipped the key into the lock. His eyebrows shot up on his forehead. "The door is open!" He leaned forward and examined the lock. "This has been pried open. Look."

I bent forward and examined the broken hasp and lock. Someone had been very determined to enter the building during the nighttime hours. But why? I considered the men who had visited the factory the previous week. Surely they had nothing to do with this. They were, after all, reputable businessmen — at least they had given that impression.

All color vanished from Josef's face, and I fleetingly wondered if men ever fainted. If so, Josef looked like the perfect candidate as he waved me forward. "Let us pray no mischief has occurred."

I followed him inside and waited a moment until my eyes adjusted to the dim light. All appeared to be in order in the office. Josef pointed toward the paint shop. "I will check the storage area. You make sure all is fine in the back." I nodded and strode toward the door that divided the carving and paint shops. I hadn't yet made it to the exit when Josef called, "You would please look to see if the back door is still locked?"

I waved my agreement and continued walking. Nothing appeared amiss thus far, but a knot formed in my stomach when I thought of young hooligans wielding paint-brushes or knives. In no time they could ruin work that had taken weeks to complete. I uttered a silent prayer as I entered the room. I held my breath and scanned the room. Everything appeared to be in order. I continued walking and let out a whoosh of air once I'd arrived at the back of the building. There was no indication anyone had been in the building. Josef would be greatly relieved.

I returned to the front and called out to Josef, "All is well in the paint shop!"

When he didn't respond, I peeked into the office, but he wasn't there. Stepping to the other side of the room, I checked the storage room, where the lumber and supplies occupied most of the space. I caught sight of Josef and stepped forward. He looked up at the sound of my footsteps, his face contorted in pain or fear — I couldn't be certain which, but I quickened my step.

"What is it? Has something been damaged or stolen?"

He pointed over his shoulder, and no words were necessary. My father's paintings were gone — I didn't need to ask. I could see it in his eyes. A stirring deep inside my stomach made me thankful I hadn't eaten breakfast. Wrapping my arms around my waist helped settle my stomach, and for some odd reason, the touch of my arms around my midsection offered comfort. Maybe because it felt like a hug — even if it was my own.

"Both of them?"

His grim nod confirmed my apprehension. "Your inheritance, it is gone. A new life for you, those paintings could have given."

"They were my father's artwork. I'm very sad that they are gone, but I wouldn't have sold them." I touched Josef's arm. "As for a new life, I began that the day I moved to Collinsford."

"I must contact the police."

My stomach roiled and dipped in a violent lurch. "The police? Is that really necessary?"

I didn't want another encounter with Detective Lawton. The man would surely think I'd had something to do with stealing my own paintings!

His frown made it evident he thought I'd lost touch with reality.

"I haven't gone mad," I said. He didn't appear overly assured.

"You stay here. I will catch the next streetcar and go to the police station."

"What about the office paper work? I thought you wanted to be sure everything was in order if Mr. Galloway arrived."

Josef pinned me with another strange look. "I think Mr. Galloway would overlook unfinished paper work before he would excuse an unreported crime."

Unable to counter with an intelligent rebuttal, I waved a halfhearted good-bye. Once Josef was out the door, I returned to the storage area. Part of me wondered if someone had simply moved the paintings to another spot; another part of me thought this was all a bad dream and I'd wake up to find the paintings back inside their shipping crate. Neither turned out to be true. The paintings were gone. Before long Josef would return and likely have Detective Lawton in tow. No need to stand here staring at the empty space. The paintings weren't going to miraculously reappear. It would be better to occupy myself with work.

I plodded off to the paint shop, donned my apron, and continued painting the leopard. Today I planned to complete much of the animal's shading. Perfecting my technique would keep my mind on painting rather than the missing canvases or the police — at least that was my hope.

When Mr. Tobarth arrived, he was impressed with my technique as well as my progress. He rubbed his chin while he circled the animal. "I don't think I've ever seen a more beautiful carousel animal. This even outshines the ones produced at the Philadelphia Toboggan Company." Moving to survey from a distance, he gave a nod. "Yep. That's fine work. Josef will be proud of that one. And so will Mr. Galloway."

"I still have to complete the eyes, and I want to shade the paws."

"How'd you get so much done before I got here? You been working all night?" He chuckled, but his narrowed eyes meant he expected an answer.

My explanation was brief. "Don't say anything to the other workers. Since it's my paintings that are missing, they'll probably hold that against me, too."

Mr. Tobarth slapped his forehead. "I'll bet

that's it, Carrie." His whispered voice sounded like gravel rubbing on sandpaper.

"What's it?" I whispered back.

He stooped down beside me with a look that reflected I didn't have the brains God gave a goose. "The men are playing a trick on you. I bet they got together and decided to take the paintings just to see you get all upset."

Maybe Mr. Tobarth was right — and maybe he could find out if the men were involved. "Would any of them tell you?"

"Don't know, but it's best to wait and watch. Let's see if any of them come back here — ones who don't normally come into the paint shop."

It wasn't long before one of the apprentice carvers sauntered through the door and headed straight for Mr. Tobarth. I'd seen him in the paint shop only once before, and that was to carry some horses to one of the drying racks when Mr. Tobarth was ill. I strained closer. He was asking about Josef's whereabouts.

"He's off to fetch the police. Seems Miss Brouwer's paintings are missing from the storage room. What did you need him for?"

"The wife is in a bad way and needs to see the doctor. I was hoping he could give me a little advance on my pay."

After the two men had talked a few minutes longer, I saw Mr. Tobarth reach in his pocket and hand the man some money.

"Why did you tell him? I thought you said we were going to wait and watch."

He tugged his apron over his head. "My mouth got ahead of my brain. I'm sorry. Maybe he won't say anythin'. He's worried about his wife."

None of the other men came into the paint shop. Either the apprentice had warned them or Mr. Tobarth's idea didn't hold merit. I was disappointed. To have the paintings so easily recovered seemed unlikely.

At midmorning Josef returned. He'd been gone so long I'd begun to wonder if the police had locked him up. He strode through the door with a determined step. My breath hitched in my throat when I glimpsed Detective Lawton following him. The two of them marched directly to my work area.

Josef smiled broadly — as though he'd brought me a special treat. "The detective is very eager to speak to you, Carrie."

"We meet again, Miss Brouwer." Detective Lawton stepped forward, his eyelids lowered to half-mast while he scanned the room. "And again our meeting is in regard to missing valuables."

"Only this time they are *my* missing valuables," I said.

"Insured?"

"Excuse me?"

"Were the paintings insured? Can you collect insurance money due to the loss of your paintings? It's a simple question, Miss Brouwer."

His arrogant manner offended me. Perhaps that was his desire — to anger me so I would incriminate myself. "I have no insurance. Even if I had considered the paintings valuable, I wouldn't have had the financial means to pay for insurance."

"What do you mean *if* you'd considered them valuable? Mr. Kaestner reported that the paintings are of considerable worth." The detective looked to Josef, who nodded.

I explained that Josef's reasoning was based upon Augusta's recent letter. "I really have no way of judging the value of the paintings. But because my father is deceased, they are of great sentimental importance to me."

The detective paced the short distance between my leopard and Mr. Tobarth's gray elephant. As my attention settled on the elephant, it became obvious the giant pachyderm would benefit from highlights of umber, deep gray, and black. I decided several places could use a touch of silver, as well.

"Am I boring you, Miss Brouwer?"

Startled by the detective's loud voice, I lost my balance and took a giant sideward step. I nearly toppled into the elephant. "No. But Mr. Kaestner and I entered the building at the same time. I don't know any more about this matter than he does."

"But they are your paintings. And you're the one who received the letter from Miss Galloway, so there are a few differences." He took a step closer. "And there's the missing jewelry, as well."

I gritted my teeth. "I've told you all I know about the paintings *and* the jewelry."

Mr. Tobarth hiked his paintbrush into the air. "I'm thinkin' you might want to check with some of the men in the carvin' shop, Josef. They might be playin' a trick on Carrie. You know — like the problem with the paint."

The detective arched his brows. "There have been other problems?"

I sighed and looked at Josef. "Why don't you explain? I want to complete this leopard so I can begin work on the panther tomorrow."

Josef motioned the detective toward his

office, and the two men strode off. They were near the door when the detective stopped and turned. "I'd like to see that letter from Miss Galloway. I'll stop by the boardinghouse this evening."

He didn't wait for a reply. I clenched my jaw, annoyed by his overbearing attitude. The detective certainly hadn't learned any manners during his police training. It would serve him right if I didn't go home after work. But then, he'd probably take my absence as an indication of my involvement in the theft. The man was determined to find me guilty.

By late afternoon I finished the leopard and went to the far rack to check the panther. The animal appeared perfect, and I was eager to begin work on him. Josef had done an exceptional job carving the muscular body. The animal looked as though it were flying through the air, prepared to pounce upon its prey.

Fear prickled my skin. I leaned against the panther's wooden body, longing for answers that would erase my mounting apprehension. But the panther was too much a reminder of the obsessive detective and his determination to make me his prey. I pushed away from the carving and trudged back to my work station, glad the day had finally come to an end.

As usual, Josef stood by the front door until I arrived. The hasp and lock had been replaced with a sturdier variety. He checked the door two times to make certain it was tightly locked. When he attempted to turn the knob for the third time, I touched his hand and grinned. "It is locked, Josef."

"Ja, too late I am careful. A stronger lock we should have had on the door." He jammed his cap atop his head.

"Blaming yourself is not going to change things. If the paintings are never found, I will remain thankful for the one I have in my bedroom. It was the most important, after all."

"Your forgiveness is gut, but I want to know who has done this. The men say they had nothing to do with it, and the detective believed them." Josef touched his index finger to his heart. "In here I believe them, too. There has been no trouble since I fired Louis. I think they learned their lesson from that."

I agreed with Josef. Although the men weren't warm or inviting, there had been no other incidents during the past months. No new employees had been hired, and most of the men at least greeted me each morning. I didn't want to cast blame on the workers unless there was convincing evidence. Such accusations would only reignite disharmony.

Conversation during the evening meal included a retelling of all that occurred during the day. Josef's patience as he answered Mrs. Wilson's endless questions amazed me, and I was thankful to be relieved of the duty. We'd just completed our dessert when I heard a knock at the front door.

I pushed away from the table. "It's probably the detective. You go ahead with your dishes, Mrs. Wilson. I'll speak to him on the front porch."

"Now, don't you act like we don't know how to properly entertain company in this part of town. Invite him inside. That's why we have a parlor."

I didn't reply — not because I didn't appreciate Mrs. Wilson's hospitable offer, but because I wanted to keep the detective's visit brief. Given half a chance, he'd probably settle in and remain the entire evening.

The detective stood on the other side of the screen door looking into the foyer. Had I shoved open the door, I could have rendered him quite a blow. The idea gave me some satisfaction even though I knew such behavior wasn't an option — at least not one I'd really consider.

"Good evening, Detective," I said from

behind the screen door. He pulled open the door, but before he could gain entry, I took a forward step that forced him aside. "I'll join you out here, where it's a bit cooler."

From his expression, I knew my move surprised him, and for a moment he peered longingly toward the interior of the house. "I want to review the letter."

I patted the pocket of my skirt. "And so you shall." After a quick perusal, I handed him the pages that mentioned my father's paintings. While he reviewed the contents, I leaned back in the wooden chair and enjoyed the evening breeze. The scent of Mrs. Wilson's climbing roses drifted toward me like a sweet perfume. The evening would have been lovely had it not been for the detective's presence.

He rattled the pages and I opened my eyes. "Finished?" I extended my hand to retrieve the pages.

"I'd like to read the rest of the letter," he said.

"I think not. The remainder of the letter speaks of personal matters, none of which have any bearing upon your investigation." I was doing my best to maintain my decorum, but the detective was making it extremely difficult.

He exhaled a loud sigh. "I need to know

what she says about Tyson Farnsworth in that letter, Miss Brouwer."

"Why?" The detective had managed to arouse my interest. Did he suspect Tyson of taking the jewelry?

"You're the one who asked that I continue to watch him. I'd think you would want me to know anything regarding his whereabouts."

"Fine!" I gathered the remaining pages and shoved them into his hand.

Once he'd finished, he returned the letter. "Guess I'll be on my way."

"That's it? You have nothing else to say?"

He slapped at a mosquito that landed on his neck. "I can't comment on a case that's under investigation, Miss Brouwer, but I do need the full cooperation of folks who have information. I trust that if you hear anything more about the paintings or Mr. Farnsworth, you'll let me know."

A nod was my only reply. Now that I'd made it clear I didn't intend to invite him inside, the detective didn't linger. I wasn't certain if it was the biting mosquitoes or my lack of hospitality. Either way, I was glad to bid him farewell.

CHAPTER 25

Once I'd finished my lunch, I strolled to the front of the building to see why Josef hadn't joined me. On our way to work, he'd made it clear he planned to meet me outside at our usual spot behind the paint shop. And Josef was known for his punctuality. When he didn't appear, I assumed something of importance had occurred, so before returning to work, I decided to locate him.

Rounding the corner near Josef's office, I stopped in my tracks, surprised by the sight of Mr. Galloway. I hadn't expected to see him so soon after his recent visit with the businessmen. Since the arrival of summer, his visits had been sporadic, and I assumed he'd been spending time with his family in the Thousand Islands.

One peek in the window on the door was enough to reveal a distinct sheen of perspiration glistening on Josef's forehead. Telltale patches of red splotched his neck and cheekbones, as well. Both were signs this meeting wasn't going well. From the movement of his upper body, I knew his legs were bouncing at breakneck speed behind his desk.

Hoping to duck out of sight, I took a sideward step, but not soon enough. Josef caught a glimpse of me and jumped up, his chair tumbling backward in a chaotic somersault. I could hear the crash of wood on cement as the chair landed upside down. With surprising speed, Josef vaulted the chair and charged to the door.

"Carrie! Wait!"

I didn't want to become involved in a meeting with Mr. Galloway, but one look at Josef's contorted features brought me to a halt. He needed help, and I couldn't refuse. I inched inside the doorframe, not wanting to offend Mr. Galloway, for he hadn't invited my presence.

"Good afternoon, Mr. Galloway." I forced a thin smile and ignored Josef's gesture to step closer.

"Good afternoon, Carrie. I trust you are well."

"Yes. And you?" The exchange seemed trite, given the tenseness that permeated the room.

He shifted in his chair, as though the

inconsequential question had caused discomfort. "To be frank, I am not well at all. That is why I am here."

I glanced at Josef, who had returned to his desk. His color remained ashen, although the splotches of red had mostly disappeared.

Stepping further inside the room, I said, "Not well? I hope it's nothing of a serious nature." But the sadness in Mr. Galloway's eyes revealed something more than a simple head cold afflicted him.

"The doctor tells me my condition is very serious."

I grabbed for an empty chair to steady myself. Unable to ease my disbelief, I circled around and dropped into the chair with an unladylike thud. "How serious?" Like a flash of lightning, memories of my own father's unexpected death returned to haunt me. My heart quickened when Mr. Galloway tipped his head forward and stared at his shiny black shoes.

"Suffice it to say that upon my doctor's sound advice, I will be liquidating my business interests so that I may be relieved of the pressures they place upon me. Then I will need to relocate to a different climate. He tells me some people have been cured with complete rest and a move to the mountains. No guarantees, of course, but it is my best option, and it's better for the family if I liquidate everything before we move. Just in case." He cleared his throat. "This includes the sale of the carousel factory. Unfortunately, all of this must take place as soon as possible." I saw a slight quiver of his lips before he clenched his jaw.

"But how can you sell the factory? Josef owns a portion of the business, doesn't he?" I looked back and forth between the two men.

"He does." Mr. Galloway fidgeted with several pieces of paper he held in his hands, finally rolling them into a tube. "But the terms of our contract specify that I need only give Josef a first option to purchase. If he can't make the arrangements to buy my share, or if he doesn't elect to purchase, then he loses his rights."

"That doesn't seem fair." I looked at Josef.

Mr. Galloway's eyes glistened. "Life isn't always fair, Carrington." His grief-stricken words dangled in the air like a hangman's noose.

My lungs constricted as I watched him fight to maintain his composure. Still, my allegiance was to Josef. "Do you have someone in mind if Josef can't arrange the necessary financing?"

I wasn't surprised to hear his answer. The men he'd taken through the factory recently had expressed a great deal of interest.

"I dislike doing this to you, Josef, but if I must sell, I believe these men will be fair. They've agreed to keep you on as manager." He glanced in my direction. "And the other employees, as well."

"What they say to you and what they do once the papers are signed — that could be very different," Josef said.

"There is always that possibility." Sounding a bit more hopeful, he added, "Yet it is your designs for the new carousels that have influenced them that *this* factory is their best choice."

"They've looked at another?" I asked.

"Yes. A factory in Brooklyn, but the owner has changed his mind several times over the past year. They came here because they'd wearied of waiting for his decision. And now that they've seen the new designs, they are eager to move forward."

Hope faded with Mr. Galloway's explanation. These men weren't casually interested — they were *eager*. If they knew of Mr. Galloway's health problems, they'd likely be able to strike an excellent bargain. And Josef was correct. Who could say what they would do once they took control? Words were cheap, even those printed in contracts.

And to think our new designs had been a contributing factor in the proposed deal made it all the worse. My stomach ached in protest. How I wished I hadn't eaten my lunch. "How long does Josef have to arrange for the purchase?"

Josef stared at me as though I'd taken leave of my senses. "What do you mean, *arrange?* There is no way I am able to do such a thing. What banker is going to loan me money?" He turned toward Mr. Galloway and said, "I have been living in a cheap boardinghouse and saving every penny possible because you promised I could one day buy more of the company. But what I have saved is not near enough. I have not had enough time to save so much money."

Ignoring Josef's outburst, Mr. Galloway said, "Our contract states thirty days." He traced his finger along the row of numbers on Josef's desk calendar. "That's a Saturday. Why don't we just wait until Monday, August 18."

Josef doubled forward as if he'd been punched in the stomach. Thirty days was barely enough time to gather ideas, much less acquire funds. "Impossible." The one strangled word sounded as though it had lodged in his throat.

"I am sorry, Josef. I will do my best to gain you additional time if you think there's some way you can obtain a loan." Mr. Galloway tapped the rolled-up papers on the edge of the desk. "If I weren't ill . . ."

"But you are, and that cannot be changed. I will do what I can." Josef brushed a lock of damp hair from his forehead.

My head reeled at the many questions skittering through my mind, and I wondered how his family had accepted the tragic news. "Does Augusta know? About your illness, I mean."

Mr. Galloway's shoulders sagged. "She knows I am ill, but she doesn't realize the gravity. Only my wife knows the full extent of my illness — and now the two of you. I trust you won't write and tell —"

"No, of course not. I would never do such a thing."

"In due time I will speak with Ronald and Augusta." Mr. Galloway pushed up from his chair. "I am so very sorry, Josef. I will be praying you arrive at a solution that will permit you to keep the factory." Shoulders slumped, he crossed the room and disappeared from sight.

A wellspring of pain filled Josef's eyes, and I struggled to find words that might soothe him. Instead, despair pumped through my veins. A suffocating fear permeated the room, and I reached out and covered Josef's hand with my own. "Somehow we'll find a way," I whispered.

He shook his head. "There are times when there is no way. This is one of those times."

"Don't say that! You have worked too hard to give up on your dream. We'll go to the bank. Maybe Mr. Tobarth or Mr. Lundgren will have an idea. You have thirty days. We must use the time wisely."

He looked out the office window into the carving shop. "The men, they are watching us. You should go back to work before there is talk that I am showing favors."

I leaned back in the chair and crossed my arms across my waist. "I will not go back to the paint shop until you promise me you will fight to keep this factory."

The thread of a smile lurked behind his sullen look. "I will give you my promise, but only because there is work that must be done."

"And because you want to own this factory," I said. "Should I tell Mr. Tobarth, or will you speak with him?"

"With the pushing, you never stop, do you? I will speak to him later. Now return to your work."

■ ■ ■ ■

August 7, 1890

Three weeks had passed since Mr. Galloway's appearance at the factory. After a visit to the bank and receiving the discouraging news Josef had expected, I had helped him pen letters to all of his old acquaintances in Philadelphia. We had hoped that maybe, just maybe, one of them would have enough money and a desire to become a partner in the carousel factory. Except for his friend Reinhold, all of the replies had arrived containing the same message: *If only I had the money, I would be very pleased to invest in the business.*

We were on our way home from work on what should have been an exciting day. Josef had completed carving an elaborate rocking gondola — a first for any factory in this country. All of us had raved over the intricate details and beauty of the piece, but his mood continued to remain glum.

He kicked a small stone out into the street. "I may decide to return to Philadelphia when the new owners take over."

I couldn't believe my ears. "Why would you ever consider such a thing? Mr. Galloway said —"

Josef interrupted me with a flick of his wrist. "I know what he said. They want us to stay so they can use our talent for their own gain. I'm not interested in such an arrangement. If I cannot be an owner, I do not want to stay." He gestured for me to keep walking. "You can remain and help them. It is your choice."

My choice? What did that mean about us, I wondered. Not long ago he'd spoken of his affection for me and plans for the future. Distant plans, of course, but he'd led me to believe he cared for me, even loved me. "So you plan to cast me aside?" I came to a stop in front of Mrs. McDougal's house.

"I am not casting you. I am not even sure what it means to cast you. I am telling you what I must do. If you want to leave Collinsford, I think I could help you find work in Philadelphia."

"I don't want to live in Philadelphia." I hadn't meant to shout, but I couldn't subdue my anger. His decision to give up wasn't acceptable, and he needed to know it.

Mrs. McDougal inched forward on her chair and rested her forearms across the porch railing. She peered down at us as though preparing for an evening of entertainment. I glared in her direction. You would think the woman would be inside fixing her husband's supper!

Josef grasped my elbow and propelled me forward. "We should not discuss this in front of the neighbors. Mrs. McDougal repeats everything she hears." He clacked his fingers and thumb together like a quacking duck.

I smiled at the gesture. "Fine, but I want to talk when we get home."

Josef didn't agree or disagree, but the discussion was forestalled by Mrs. Wilson's flurry to greet us the minute we entered the house.

She held an envelope in each of her hands and waved them overhead like miniature banners. "One for each of you."

I glanced at mine. "From Augusta."

"From Reinhold," Josef said.

We walked back outside and sat down on the front porch. "You first," I said, staring at his missive. Reinhold was Josef's final hope; the remaining friend he'd written to in Philadelphia; the last possible investment partner in the factory. I held my breath while he ripped open the envelope and extracted the letter. There was no need for Josef to tell me the contents. His crumpled features said it all.

"Your turn." Instead of waiting, he stood

up and gestured toward the door. "I will go in and clean up for supper while you read."

I didn't try to stop him. There was nothing I could do or say that would make the news he had received any easier to bear. "I'll see you at supper." I traced my finger beneath the envelope's seal and unfolded the two pages. The first page was news that Augusta's father had developed a medical problem and the family would return home on August 11. Next Monday! I wondered if Mr. Galloway would bring word from the investors that they wished to move forward at the earliest opportunity. I would wait until later to tell Josef. He didn't need more bad news before supper.

Near the bottom of the first page, Augusta lamented the fact that they would depart the Thousand Islands prior to one of the grand parties scheduled for the end of August. From the tone of her letter, I could only assume Mr. Galloway hadn't yet disclosed the depth of his medical condition. Perhaps he wanted to wait until the family returned to Fair Oaks.

Turning the page, I continued scanning the page until my breath caught in my throat. Near the bottom of the letter, Augusta said her Mother's necklace had been recovered and that Detective Lawton hoped to have the crime solved very soon. The letter ended with a promise to explain more fully when next she saw me. I folded the pages together and replaced them in the envelope. Augusta's comments made no sense. If the necklace had been recovered, didn't that mean the crime had been solved?

CHAPTER 26

Time passed over the next few days much too quickly — and much too slowly. While I had wanted time to stop so that we could formulate a plan for Josef to purchase the factory, I'd also wanted the days to hurry by so Augusta would return home. I had anticipated hearing from her yesterday, but when bedtime arrived and there'd been no word, I assumed their train had arrived late. Since early afternoon today, I'd been eagerly contemplating the end of the workday.

I'd already cleaned my brushes in preparation. At the sound of the buzzer, I yanked off my canvas apron and, with a hefty toss, smiled when it landed on the hook.

Mr. Tobarth chuckled. "You're becomin' quite accomplished at hittin' that hook."

"Lots of practice," I called over my shoulder.

With a wave I raced toward the front door. I'd already decided to take the streetcar to

Fair Oaks if there wasn't any word from Augusta when I returned to the boarding-house. I could wait no longer. If I didn't soon receive answers about Mrs. Galloway's necklace, I would burst with curiosity. Josef was still sitting in his office when I skidded to a halt outside his door.

He glanced up and tapped the papers on his desk. "Go ahead without me. I have to complete these records."

I didn't argue. Even though I knew he'd appreciate my help with the figures, Josef was more than capable of finishing the task on his own. He'd been doing it without my help long before I arrived in Collinsford. I glanced up and down the street on the chance I might see the Galloways' carriage but quickly determined it was nowhere in sight and hurried onward.

When I turned the corner and saw the car-riage sitting in front of the house, I hiked my skirt and raced down the sidewalk at full tilt, my lunch pail clunking my leg with each step. I hoped I wouldn't discover Ty-son waiting to fetch me to Fair Oaks. I squinted against the harsh descending sunshine that shone in my eyes, and the mo-ment I spotted Augusta standing on the front porch, I wanted to shout for joy. Ever the lady, she leaned across the porch rail and waved her handkerchief instead of calling out to me.

I inhaled a giant breath and bounded up the front steps. Augusta held her arms open, and I breathed heavily as we embraced. "I'm so happy to see you." I panted for air and collapsed into one of the chairs. She sat down opposite me.

"And I'm every bit as delighted to see you, although I hadn't expected to have our vacation cut short." She snapped open her fan and wagged it back and forth with little conviction. "This summer wasn't at all what I had hoped for." She sighed and touched a hand to her high-crowned straw hat. Fancy bows of green ribbon adorned the brim and matched her dress to perfection. "Do you like my hat?"

"It's lovely."

Augusta didn't seem herself, but I told myself we'd been separated for nearly two months and we'd need a short time to reacquaint. She'd become accustomed to discussing fashion and attending parties with her wealthy friends, while I'd remained busy with my life as a factory worker. We'd been living in different worlds with nothing but a couple of letters to connect our lives.

"Mother and I managed a few shopping trips before we departed for the Thousand

Islands. I don't think you've ever seen this dress or hat." She smoothed the luxurious silk skirt.

I thought it a fancy choice to wear when calling in The Bottoms, but I didn't say so. "Would you care to join us for supper? I'm certain Mrs. Wilson can set another place."

Augusta wrinkled her nose. "I haven't forgotten that woman's lack of culinary skill. You should know I'd never dine at her table. I'd likely be sick for a week."

"I've managed to survive, and you'll hurt her feelings if you refuse."

"Then we shall take the carriage and go to the tearoom downtown. They serve a light evening meal. Run upstairs and freshen up. I'll wait."

I didn't argue. I wouldn't win. Besides, I wanted to hear about the returned necklace. I performed my toilette as quickly as possible and stopped downstairs long enough to advise Mrs. Wilson of my plans.

"But I've made cabbage rolls for supper, and you're going to miss out." She rubbed her hands together. "I know they're one of Josef's favorites, and I hope to cheer him."

I didn't think Mrs. Wilson's cabbage rolls were going to cheer Josef. Perhaps the ones his mother had made when he was a young boy had been a favorite — but not the ones prepared in Mrs. Wilson's kitchen. "I hope you all enjoy them," I said.

"I'll save one or two for your lunch pail tomorrow."

The thought of cold cabbage rolls, especially Mrs. Wilson's cold cabbage rolls, was enough to send me skittering out the door without comment. Augusta hooked her arm through mine, and soon we were on our way. When I tried to quiz her about the necklace, she interrupted and said we'd discuss the necklace over supper.

Once the waiter had delivered a cold chicken salad and warm rolls, I reiterated my question. "Who stole your mother's necklace?" I bit into the warm roll, the fragrance reminding me of the bakery beneath our apartment back in France.

"As I mentioned in my letter, the detective said he's still in the process of investigating. I'm not supposed to be discussing this with you, but we are best friends. Besides, I don't believe the detective."

The bite of roll stuck in my throat. "About *what?*" I croaked.

"Well." She whispered the drawn-out word and leaned across the table, her gaze darting around the room. Did she think Detective Lawton might peek out from beneath one of the linen-clad tables?

I pictured the detective with one of the freshly starched tablecloths draped across his bald pate, his beady eyes trained upon us, and burst into a fit of giggles.

"Oh, do stop, Carrie. This isn't funny. If my parents discovered I was telling you any of this, I'd find myself in a great deal of trouble."

I thought Augusta's parents had much more worrisome problems to focus upon, but her recrimination and thoughts of Mr. Galloway's medical malady did bring my laughter under control. I covered my mouth with my fingers. "I won't laugh. I promise."

Augusta fixed her lips in a prim, tight line that matched the ramrod frame of her shoulders. I realized that during the past two months she'd become the socialite daughter her mother so desperately desired. I knew we would never again walk barefoot in the grass or stroll down the sidewalk eating warm bread. My old friend had disappeared, just like my father's paintings. Had the detective mentioned the missing paintings to Augusta or her family? I'd said nothing to Mr. Galloway, though Josef may have reported the theft to him.

At my encouragement, Augusta finally continued. "This truly is an exciting happening. That's why I wanted to tell you in person." Once again she looked around the near-empty room. "At a recent party hosted at the home of — well, it doesn't matter where it was hosted; you won't know the people. Anyway, I was standing with some of my friends waiting for the orchestra to begin, and the butler announced Mr. and Mrs. Summerly, people I'd never before seen. They entered the room, and that's when it happened." She paused and stared at me.

"What happened?" I asked, becoming increasingly annoyed by Augusta's theatrics.

"Mother screamed, and I went racing to her side. She appeared to be frozen with her outstretched index finger pointing at the woman who'd entered the room. Mrs. Summerly was wearing Mother's necklace." Augusta clasped her hand across her neckline.

"No!" I could barely contain my excitement. My ravenous appetite had completely disappeared, and I pushed aside all thoughts of my earlier exasperation. Had we not been in the tearoom, I would have jumped to my feet and danced with delight.

"Indeed!" Augusta's eyes shone with excitement. "Isn't that the most amazing thing you've ever heard?"

Who could argue? The news was more

than amazing — it was very strange. Why would a woman wear a stolen necklace to a party where she might encounter the owner? My enthusiasm dissipated. "There's more to this, isn't there?"

"Yes, of course. Mrs. Summerly didn't steal the necklace — nor did her husband. Though I must admit he was served a giant slice of humble pie."

"How so?"

"He had presented the necklace to his wife for her birthday and said it had cost him a fortune." Augusta winked. "He purchased it at a pawnshop in Cincinnati."

Realization dawned like a blazing sunrise. "So the thief pawned the necklace, and the detective still hasn't been able to discover the identity of the actual thief."

"This is the part he doesn't want you to know." She lowered her voice to a whisper. "The owner of the pawnshop said a woman brought the necklace and two rings to him. He gave a description, and the detective thinks it is *you.*"

"*What?* That's ridiculous! He needs to do his job and find the true thief. From the very start, he's been determined to make me the guilty party. Surely you know I would never do such a thing, Augusta. I've never even been to Cincinnati."

She patted my hand. "Of course I know you didn't take the necklace. And my parents continue to believe it is someone else, as well. As far as we're concerned, all is well. Fortunately for Mother, the couple agreed to return the necklace without a fuss, though I think Mr. Summerly will now be out even more money." Augusta took a sip of her water before she continued. "His wife insisted upon a new necklace — and this time she said she would accompany him to the jeweler. Isn't that delicious?" After taking a bite of chicken salad, Augusta grinned. "Almost as delicious as this chicken salad."

The chicken salad held little appeal now that I knew the detective still held me in his sights. "Do you think Detective Lawton will search for the real thief, or do you think he's going to appear one day soon and take me off to jail?"

Augusta giggled. "Father would never permit such a thing. He wouldn't bring charges against you." She spread a teaspoon of jam on a bite of her roll and popped it into her mouth.

"From what the detective told me in one of our earlier conversations, the charges are filed by the attorney who represents this district in Ohio. Your father's consent isn't needed."

"Why, that's absolutely dreadful. I'm going to have Father talk to that detective and set things aright."

Mr. Galloway had more pressing problems to contend with at the moment, yet I didn't discourage Augusta. I feared she would question why I wouldn't want Mr. Galloway's help, and I might misspeak about her father's health. In truth, I wanted any help I could get, and I'd let Mr. Galloway decide if he was physically able to meet with Detective Lawton.

"Tell me what has been happening where you and Tyson are concerned." Had the two of them become engaged, Augusta would have immediately shown me her ring. Besides, I'd looked the moment she removed her gloves. Her ring finger remained bare.

She feigned a look of indifference and batted her lashes. "He has become somewhat a bore of late. I thought he'd be the perfect companion while in the islands, but his business interests keep him much more occupied than I'd realized." Holding her little finger at the perfect angle, she sipped her tea.

"So you're seeing other gentlemen?"

Augusta settled the cup on the matching saucer. "No one in particular. Tyson remains my favorite suitor, but he is most difficult to figure out. One minute I believe I know him quite well, and the next he's a stranger. Have you ever known anyone like that?"

"Only you." I chuckled. "You've become a bit of a stranger over the summer."

Augusta's eyebrows dipped low, and she tightened her lips into a pout. "That isn't kind at all, Carrie. After I've gone against my parents' wishes and told you about the necklace, how can you say I've become a stranger?"

I reached across the table and patted her arm. "You're right. I am deeply indebted that you've taken me into your confidence. It's just that you *act* so different — so proper and refined."

Her shoulders drooped into a slump. "Mother insists. She says if she hears even a whisper that I'm not behaving in a genteel manner, she'll force me to attend Mrs. Bogart's Finishing School again in the fall. I couldn't bear another three months of classes with Mrs. Bogart."

I remembered Augusta's description of the classes she'd been required to complete before coming to France. "Then I'll forgive you," I said.

"Good!" She lifted a strawberry from the plate of fruit the waiter had recently placed on the table. "I'm surprised you've said nothing about your father's artwork. Weren't you excited? I think Father could find a buyer for your pieces, and at a handsome price."

Apparently no one had mentioned the missing paintings to Augusta. It took only a moment to explain the loss. "Thankfully the one of me on the carousel horse remains in my bedroom. I doubt I'll ever locate the others. Detective Lawton is working on that case, as well."

"Mmm. You may be right. That man's ability to solve crimes hasn't been stellar thus far. I'm surprised he worked for the Pinkerton Agency. Let's hope your paintings will be found. With money from those paintings, you could quit your job at the factory. Wouldn't that be grand?"

"You believe they would fetch that much?"

"Father said there were art dealers in New York City clamoring for them. Two dealers went to France hoping to locate some of them."

Such furor. And to think that only a year ago, the money from one of Father's paintings would barely cover our rent for a month. How did people decide art was worthless one day and worth a fortune the next? Who made these judgments? And why did others abide by their decisions? Such a mystery.

"They may find several pieces hanging in Madame Leclair's bakery," I said. "I'm sure she would rather have money than the paintings. Maybe she'd use a few coins to purchase Stormy a nice piece of fish at the market." I smiled, remembering the fat silver-gray cat I'd left with Madame Leclair. Had he ever missed me? He was an independent sort, but I liked to think that on occasion he wondered where I'd gone.

"I don't know if you'd ever consider selling the carousel painting, but I'm sure it would fetch a huge price. I think the art dealers would find it the most beautiful of all."

"My father painted that when I was a young girl." I shook my head. "It brings back fond memories of my childhood. I could never sell it."

Augusta forked a piece of melon onto her plate and sliced it into small pieces. "If you change your mind, you need only tell me or Father. He will see to the arrangements."

I couldn't meet her gaze. Augusta took for granted her father would live forever, yet his death lurked around the next corner.

Josef was nowhere in sight when I returned home, but a note on the foyer table stated that Mrs. Wilson and Mr. Lundgren had gone down the street to visit with the neighbors. I waited on the porch for a short time but finally went upstairs. No light shone beneath Josef's door. He'd either gone to bed or returned to the factory to finish his paper work.

I'd been excited to tell him that Mrs. Galloway's necklace had been recovered. In retrospect, it was probably better to keep that news to myself. Had the thief been apprehended, there would be no reason to withhold the news. But I was still considered a suspect — and Josef would ask far too many questions.

I prepared for bed and then opened my Bible. I'd been reading it every night. Mrs. Wilson said reading the Bible every day was a good habit and the best way to learn what God wanted us to know. I didn't doubt her word, but I figured I'd forget what I had read in Genesis by the time I finished Revelation. She said not to worry about that because when I finished, I should start all over again. Apparently Mrs. Wilson had high hopes for how much I'd accomplish each evening.

I continued to read until the sound of Mrs. Wilson's chattering voice drifted up from the sidewalk below. Mr. Lundgren laughed at something she said, and soon the front door opened and closed. I placed my Bible on the small table and stared at the painting hanging on the opposite wall. A little girl sitting on a beautiful carousel horse. What was more important: a painting hanging on the wall, or a factory that crafted carousel animals? Which would my father choose, I wondered.

CHAPTER 27

Two days later Detective Lawton met me outside the factory at lunchtime. Had he come to arrest me? I looked over my shoulder, hoping to catch sight of Josef, but I remembered he'd gone to the train station to check on a shipment of lumber. My mouth felt like a drought-ridden prairie. When I tried to swallow, a dry breath of air caught in my throat. I coughed until tears trickled down my cheeks.

I didn't detect any compassion in the detective's eyes. I swiped away the tears and tried to calm my escalating fear. I didn't want to go to jail, especially for something I hadn't done. But it seemed Detective Lawton was determined someone must be punished. I didn't think he cared if he had the proper person or not — just so someone paid the price for committing the crime.

He waved me toward the tree where Josef and I usually sat. "Good afternoon, Miss

Brouwer."

"Detective." That was as much as I could manage without suffering another coughing spasm.

"I find myself in need of your assistance, Miss Brouwer."

I sat down on the bench and told myself to breathe.

The detective was staring at me. I opened my mouth, but my voice refused to co-operate. I signaled for him to continue.

He sat down beside me and finger-pressed the brim of his hat between his fingers. "I don't know how much information Miss Galloway has divulged." When I didn't comment, he continued. "I know the two of you enjoyed a lengthy dinner at the tearoom a couple of nights ago." He waited.

"We did." I hoped he didn't notice my surprise — or fear. My hands remained steady, but my insides quivered like Mrs. Wilson's grape jelly. He'd obviously been unable to hear our conversation or he wouldn't be quizzing me.

I didn't want to betray Augusta's confidence. Now I wished I'd stopped her before she'd divulged the secrets. Instead, I'd clung to every minute detail and even longed for more. I massaged my throat with my fingertips and hoped the detective would take the cue. If he wanted to talk, I'd listen. Otherwise, I had nothing more to say.

"Sorry you're having problems with your voice," he said. "I'm going to tell you what I need from you, and if you still haven't regained your voice, you can just shake your head to let me know if you agree or disagree." He grinned. "Unless you have a speedy recovery. In that case please don't hesitate to use a verbal response."

Almost word for word, the detective's information matched what I'd heard from Augusta. He rested his forearms across his thighs and looked over his shoulder at me. "I need your help, Miss Brouwer."

I touched the tip of my index finger to my chest. "Me?"

"Yes. If I'm to absolve you of the crime, I'll need the owner of the pawnshop to see you. He says he can identify the young woman who brought him the necklace and rings."

I stared at him, stupefied by the request. "You want me to travel to Cincinnati so this man can look at me?"

"Not exactly. Do you by any chance have a recent photograph or drawing of yourself?"

I shook my head. Sending a photograph certainly made more sense than traveling to

Cincinnati, but photographs had been an unknown luxury in our home. Other than the painting of me on the carousel horse, I had nothing to offer. And that picture would be of no help in making a proper identification.

Detective Lawton tented his fingers beneath his chin. "Would you object to having a likeness drawn? We have a policeman who does an excellent job. And since you're an artist yourself, you could help with any changes before I'd send it off."

The proposal held little appeal, but if I objected, the detective would think I had something to hide. "If this man says I'm *not* the woman, will you then eliminate me from your list of suspects?"

He smiled and gave a firm nod. "I know this isn't pleasant, but I'm required to follow every lead."

"I hope you've followed the leads I've mentioned as closely as you've followed me, Detective. When am I required to sit for this drawing? It must not interfere with my employment."

Before the detective departed, we agreed to meet outside the police station the following evening.

Time dragged the next day. While working

on the carousel animals, I considered how I would react to seeing my likeness drawn by someone other than my father. I'd painted portraits of others. But except for the painting hanging in my bedroom, no one had ever drawn or painted me. Until now I'd not given the matter much thought, but it did seem somewhat strange — much like the cobbler's children needing their shoes repaired. By the end of the workday, I'd begun to look forward to seeing the completed drawing.

After supper Josef excused himself and returned to the factory. He'd been following this same routine each day, determined he would leave everything in perfect order for the new owners. My pleas that Josef continue to seek financial backing had fallen on deaf ears. He'd accepted defeat. And though he'd not mentioned moving to Philadelphia again, I worried he might make plans that didn't include me.

While Mrs. Wilson and Mr. Lundgren performed their nightly ritual of washing and drying the supper dishes, I retrieved my bonnet and reticule. "I'm going out for a while." I hurried down the front steps before either of them could question me.

Detective Lawton stood outside the police station as promised. He whisked me through a side doorway and into a small office with only enough room for a small table and several chairs. The detective introduced me to the artist, Mr. Feldham, a paunchy man who appeared far too soft and old to perform much police work.

Detective Lawton pointed to one of the chairs. "You can sit there. I'll stand." He rested his back against the door, with his legs crossed at the ankle and arms folded across his chest. I didn't know if he'd chosen to lean against the door in order to keep others out or to keep me in, but I believed it was probably both.

Mr. Feldham wasted little time. Before I settled in the chair, he had his sketch pad open and had begun to draw. His eyes flitted from my face to the sketch pad and back again. He never requested that I sit in any particular position or even that I sit still. Before fifteen minutes had passed, he slid the sketchbook across the table.

"Close enough, or do you want some changes?"

He'd used soft, short strokes, but the likeness was remarkable — except for my eyes. "Are my eyes that wide set?"

He peered at me and then at the picture. "Whaddya think, Lawton?" He shoved the sketch pad toward the detective, who pushed away from the door and picked it up.

Holding it at arm's length, the detective looked back and forth between me and the paper. "She's right. Her eyes need to be a little closer together."

The police artist grunted and grabbed the pad. After one final look, he shrugged and set to work. His adjustments didn't take long, and once I'd given final approval, Detective Lawton escorted me outside. He hailed a carriage, and once I was inside, he said, "I'll pay you a visit when I hear back. I don't expect it will take too long."

I didn't know if that was a promise or a threat, but it had an ominous ring. I'd need to complete my plan as soon as possible.

When the police station had disappeared from sight, I signaled the driver. "Fair Oaks," I said.

His bushy brows dipped low on his forehead. "I thought the detective said The Bottoms."

"He did. But I want to stop at the home of the Galloways. It's a new house at the —"

"I know where it is. Just finished building it not long ago. Big enough for ten families," he muttered.

If Mr. Galloway succumbed to his illness,

I wondered if Mrs. Galloway would remain in the huge house. I silently chastised myself for the morose thought and forced it from my mind. Right now I needed to prepare a convincing plea.

I asked the driver to wait. "I shouldn't be long," I said.

"You'll owe me extra."

I nodded the comment aside and, with a determined stride, marched to the front door. Frances greeted me with a frown. "Mrs. Galloway and Miss Augusta are out for the evening. You weren't expected, were you?"

"No, but it's Mr. Galloway I wish to speak to. Is he here?"

Frances glanced over her shoulder. "He's in his library. I s'pose I could ask him." She peeked over my shoulder toward the driveway. "Your driver going to wait?"

"Yes. I won't be long."

She trotted down the hall. Soon she reappeared and waved me forward. Mrs. Galloway would be aghast to see the maid behave with such informality. But now that I worked at the factory, Frances considered me more an equal than a guest.

"Go on in," she said.

"Thank you." I entered and closed the door behind me in case Frances decided to linger in the hallway.

Mr. Galloway stood to greet me and beckoned for me to sit down opposite him. "What brings you to Fair Oaks, Carrington? Something to do with the factory, I'm guessing."

"Yes. I'm hoping we can strike a bargain."

"Josef has secured financial investors?"

"Possibly." While I detailed my plan, Mr. Galloway listened without interruption. "What do you think? Are you agreeable?"

"I don't know. I fear you'll live to regret your decision, and I wouldn't want to be responsible."

"But the decision is mine to make. I suppose I could seek someone else, but this seems the most expedient method. And I trust you."

"If you're certain, I'll have my lawyer prepare the paper work."

"I'll see that the painting is delivered tomorrow. Thank you, Mr. Galloway."

"It's I who should be thanking you, Carrington. I believe I've struck the better bargain."

In my heart I wasn't persuaded he believed what he said, for it could take many years before my carousel painting would equal the value of the factory. Yet thankful he considered it a wise investment, I remained silent. Only time would tell, and I hoped Mr. Galloway would have enough time to discover whether he'd made a wise decision.

Either way, by placing the painting in Mr. Galloway's possession, I would provide myself with a level of protection.

When we rounded the corner near the factory on Monday morning, Josef stopped midstep. "Mr. Galloway's carriage." It was August 18. Josef's time had expired. "He didn't waste any time." Bitterness shaded his comment, but I decided against a response. Instead, I continued onward, and he soon caught up and matched my stride. "I don't see any other carriages, so he's come to deal the blow before the new owners arrive."

"Who can say why he's here," I said.

Josef reached for the latch. "We both know why he is here."

"He's ill, Josef, and he's doing the best he can under the circumstances."

"You are right, but that makes it no easier for me." Head lowered in obvious shame, he yanked open the door.

Mr. Galloway's warm smile provided a welcome sight. He waved Josef forward.

"Come in. Both of you. I have some good news."

Josef stepped inside, his gait cautious and his shoulders rigid. It was clear he didn't intend to let down his guard for a moment. After stepping to the side, he waited until I entered. He closed the door, and at Mr. Galloway's signal we both sat down.

"Well, Josef, I'm pleased to announce that you will become the proud owner of the Collinsford Carousel Factory if you're willing to agree to a few stipulations."

Josef's jaw dropped at the announcement. He stared across the table, disbelief darkening his eyes. "How can this be true?"

"A benefactor has stepped forward to assist you. I am not at liberty to discuss any of the details with you. However, you will be expected to make monthly payments until the loan is paid in full."

Deep lines creased his forehead. "Who would do such a thing? I have contacted all my friends, and they could not loan the money. This is impossible."

Mr. Galloway tapped his pen atop the papers. "You wish to refuse the contract?"

"No! But this is a very big surprise. A wonderful surprise. Tell me what I must do."

Josef's excitement continued to mount while Mr. Galloway read the terms of the contract. When he'd finished, the older man looked at Josef. "Do you agree?"

"Ja! With a thankful heart I will sign, but still my head wonders who would do this thing for me."

The men signed the contract, a copy for each, and shook hands. "For now, be thankful that someone cares enough to extend such generosity. Maybe one day your benefactor will realize it is better to come forward and personally speak to you."

Josef clapped a hand to his heart. "That would be very gut. You will give my thanks to this benefactor?"

"I will be most pleased to do so, Josef. And since I know you have orders to fill, I will leave so that the two of you can begin your workday."

"Can you believe this, Carrie? I am the owner of this place." He spread his arms wide and turned in a circle. "God has answered my prayer."

"And one of mine," I whispered.

CHAPTER 28

After church on Sunday I decided the day much too beautiful to sit indoors. I had hoped to spend the afternoon in the park with Josef, but he insisted he must first complete the ledgers and prepare the lumber orders. So gathering up my sketchbook and pencil, I established myself on the boardinghouse porch. Across the street two young girls sat chattering on the front steps of their house, providing me an enchanting picture to capture on paper. I sketched a quick outline of their oval faces, flowing hair on one, braids on the other with a hand cupped to hide a whispered secret to her friend.

I'd made little progress when the sound of clopping horses' hooves gained my attention. I stretched forward and squinted against the afternoon sun. Was that the Galloway carriage? Surely not — Augusta wasn't one for unexpected visits. And she would be with her family or with Tyson on a Sunday afternoon. Yet it looked like Thomas. Shading my eyes with one hand, I stood and looked down the street again. It *was* the Galloway carriage!

Closing my sketchbook, I stepped to the edge of the porch. The carriage hadn't even come to a complete stop before Augusta pushed open the door and motioned me forward. "Hurry!"

Augusta's pinched features and unexpected arrival could mean only one thing: Something had happened to Mr. Galloway. Bunching a handful of skirt in each fist, I raced down the steps. Agitated when I paused at the carriage door, she shouted, "Get in!" I didn't hesitate to follow her order.

My breath came in short, panting spurts. I wanted to remain calm. I wanted to offer the proper words of condolence and reassurance. Words of comfort that I had never received when my father had died. I wiped my perspiring palms on my skirt and waited to hear the sad news.

"To the park, Thomas!"

I startled at the shouted command. Augusta's behavior was bizarre in the extreme, but I knew reaction to death could create odd behavior. "The park?" I was careful to maintain a quiet, calm demeanor.

"I want to speak to you in private." She folded her arms across her waist and pierced me with a cold stare.

This was not the conduct of a grieving daughter. Something was terribly amiss. I decided to dip my toe into the icy waters. "I trust your family is well?" My voice quivered.

"My family is fine."

I wasn't sure what created more fear: Augusta's answer or her behavior. The clipped response closed the door to further conversation. If her father hadn't died, what on earth could cause such abnormal behavior? I culled my memory for the slightest remembrance of what could create this unexpected animosity. The distance to the nearby park seemed interminable. For the remainder of the ride, Augusta maintained a dagger-filled glare directly above my head.

When we finally entered the park, she ordered Thomas to stop the carriage near a stand of trees. I was thankful she hadn't opted for the duck pond. I feared the ducks would be forced to swim for their lives while Augusta shoved me into the water.

Hiking her skirts, Augusta marched toward the trees like an opponent preparing for a duel. She wheeled around and faced

461

me. "How dare you betray me!"

Confounded by the outburst, I stared at her like a complete ninny. I didn't know whether to laugh or cry. What had happened to my friend? And what was she talking about?

"Well?"

I took a backward step at the high-pitched demand. "I don't know what you are talking about. How did I supposedly betray you?"

"Don't you dare feign ignorance, Carrington Brouwer. I know you've been seeing Tyson behind my back." As she clenched her jaw, I saw the veins in her neck protrude like thick, pulsing cords.

Tyson. How could Augusta possibly think I would ever be interested in Tyson Farnsworth? Yet her anger was genuine. "You know I don't care a whit about Tyson. I've even discouraged your relationship with him."

"And now I know why! All the time you were telling me he was a selfish cad, you were plotting against me. You wanted him for yourself."

My stomach lurched at the accusation. "This is ridiculous. I have not nor will I ever be associated with Tyson. And I think I have a right to know how you've come to believe this nonsense."

"It isn't nonsense. Mary Flinchbaugh and her mother saw the two of you together here in Collinsford when I was in the Thousand Islands."

I clenched my fists in an attempt to abate my anger. "It's not true. I haven't seen Tyson since before you departed for your summer vacation. If he was in Collinsford during that time, I had no knowledge he was in town."

"So you're saying Mary and her mother would simply make up a story to hurt me? Is that what I'm to believe?"

"I don't think they would intentionally hurt you, but they couldn't have seen me with Tyson. He may have been in town, but I was not with him. Perhaps he was with another woman, but it wasn't me."

"Another woman who looks exactly like you and entered a carriage with him near the carousel factory."

I wanted to ask what Mary and her mother were doing near the factory but didn't think that would further my cause. "I can't force you to believe me. Their allegation is false. The only way to disprove what they've said is through Tyson." I doubted my suggestion would prove helpful. If Tyson had been with another woman, he'd not admit such an indiscretion to Augusta. Still, I had nothing else to offer to counter the accusation, and I felt an urgent need to reinforce my plea of innocence.

"Tyson seems to be keeping otherwise occupied these days. The last I heard from him was while we were vacationing in the islands. He returned to assist his father with business in New York City. To date, my letters to him have gone unanswered."

"Doesn't that prove that there is no liaison between us? He would be in Collinsford if he'd developed any interest in me."

She shook her head, unwilling to believe the truth. "Now that I'm home, he's not going to come around until he believes I've accepted losing him." She tilted her head to the side and curled her lip. "Surely you know his family will never approve of you."

I couldn't believe the jealousy and anger that raged in her terse words. "Of course they won't. Which is all the more reason why you should believe me."

Her eyes softened for an instant but soon returned to a hardened glare. She didn't want to believe what I said — it was easier to blame me for Tyson's absence. She wouldn't face the fact that he was exactly what I'd told her — a philanderer and rogue of the worst sort.

"Mary said you would deny her claim."

"She did? And exactly why is that?"

"She told me she called out to Tyson when she saw the two of you. He turned her way. She got an excellent view of him, but you immediately covered your face."

"And did Tyson acknowledge her?"

"No. Once he saw her, he sped off in the carriage — but you already know that."

I shook my head. "I'm going home. I hope you will soon realize the foolishness of these accusations and come to your senses."

"You were supposed to be my friend," she shouted as I walked away.

I turned and stared at her. "I am still your friend, Augusta."

While I walked toward home, Augusta's accusation replayed in my mind. I had met both Mary Flinchbaugh and her mother at several of the parties in Fair Oaks. They hadn't seemed the type to spread malicious rumors. Yet who could know why people did such things. Perhaps Mary hoped to win Tyson's affections. Many of the young socialites thought him quite a catch. If Mary could create a rift between Tyson and Augusta, it could work to her advantage.

I tried to recall the various Fair Oaks parties and whether I'd seen Mary with any particular fellow — or if I'd seen her fawning over Tyson. Unfortunately, I couldn't remember much of anything about Mary except for the hideous plum and sea green dress she'd worn one evening. She'd resembled a green-stemmed eggplant.

Lost in my own thoughts, I startled when Josef called out. He loped down the front steps to meet me. "I've been worried. Where have you been?"

Only now did I realize the concern I'd caused him. I'd taken off in such a hurry I'd failed to tell anyone I was leaving. "Augusta stopped by and wished to speak to me privately. We went to the park."

He glanced over my shoulder as if he expected to see her appear. "She is still at the park?"

"No. She went home, but I wanted to walk."

"Mr. Galloway?"

"Mr. Galloway's health remains unchanged." Josef's first thought had been the same as my own. "Augusta wished to speak to me in regard to another matter — of a private nature." I hoped he wouldn't quiz me. "I apologize for causing you to worry."

He smiled. "My work is now finished, but I have agreed to help Mr. Lundgren repair the trellis in the backyard. After that we can go to the park."

I didn't argue. By the time he finished, he'd be tired, and I had no desire to return to the park. "You go ahead. I believe I'll work on my sketching." The girls who'd been sitting on the porch across the street had long departed, but I worked from my outline and the memory of two young friends sharing a secret. A stab of betrayal pierced me as I recalled Augusta's fiery words.

I didn't have to wait long for my meeting with Detective Lawton. He appeared at lunchtime on Tuesday. Fists jammed into his pockets, he stood leaning against one of the huge old elms behind the paint shop. He tipped his hat as I strolled toward him. Hoping he came bearing good news, I offered an enthusiastic wave in return. Had he come to tell me the pawnshop owner had finally responded?

"You've received word from Cincinnati?"

He nodded toward the bench. "Don't let me keep you from eating your lunch. I know you need to keep your work schedule."

Was he giving me an opportunity for my last taste of freedom before hauling me away? Surely not. I lifted the lid from my lunch pail and removed the sandwich. I glanced at the sandwich and then at him.

"I'm sorry. I wasn't expecting company."

"Thanks." He wrinkled his nose. "I think I prefer the diner near the police station."

I chuckled. "I won't tell Mrs. Wilson you said that."

He lowered himself onto the bench. "I finally got word from the owner of the pawnshop. He says he can't be certain if the sketch is the same girl who came in with the jewelry."

The bite of ham sandwich hit my stomach like a rock. "*Now* what?" I despised the fact that my voice quivered. Over and over I had practiced what I would do if the detective returned with such a response. My plan had been to appear either brave or completely nonchalant. I'd done neither.

"I know you are disappointed with the news. So was I. I'd hoped to cross your name from my list of suspects."

He had a list? It was a relief to know I wasn't the only person he'd been investigating. "The shop owner took a great deal of time to respond. Did he say why?"

The detective shook his head. "No, but he is passing through Collinsford at the end of the week on his way to visit a relative. He offered to stop at the police station and speak with me — and you."

"Me?" Was this a scheme to ensnare me? I

didn't know what to think. One minute I thought Detective Lawton supposed me innocent. The next I thought he believed me guilty and hoped to see me in jail. My mind whirled with possibilities as I awaited his response.

"Yes. He believes if he can see you in person, it will be easier to rule you out as the woman who pawned the jewelry."

Rule me out? Had the shop owner said he wanted to disqualify me as a suspect, or was it the opposite? There was no need to ask. I'd already learned the detective divulged only what he wanted me to know — nothing more and nothing less.

"You don't object, do you?" His brow furrowed. My hesitation seemed to place him on the alert. "If you're concerned about missing work, I'll schedule our meeting during the evening hours."

"After work would be best." I stared at the ham sandwich, my appetite gone after only one bite. Placing the sandwich on my napkin, I carefully surrounded the uneaten remnants between the folds. Mrs. Wilson would scold when she discovered how little I'd eaten. No doubt she'd insist upon feeling my forehead and sending me to bed. At the moment, the woman's tender care would be a welcome respite from the detective and his determined stance.

Detective Lawton pushed up from the bench and nodded toward my lunch. "You better hurry and eat or you'll be mighty hungry before day's end." He plopped his straw hat atop his bald head and glanced toward the carousel factory. "I'll send a message about our meeting once Mr. Charleston arrives."

"Mr. Charleston is the shop owner?"

"That's right. Charleston and Sons." He fixed his gaze on me. Maybe he expected some sign of recognition when he uttered the name. If so, he'd been disappointed. I'd never heard of Mr. Charleston, or his sons, or their pawnshop. And I'd certainly never set foot in Cincinnati. At least this meeting should remove my name from Detective Lawton's list. But instead of elation that I would soon be vindicated, I trudged back to the factory feeling a sense of defeat. Each step in this process seemed to lead to another. Would it never end?

CHAPTER 29

When I stepped outside the factory Friday afternoon, Detective Lawton was waiting across the street. He waved me forward, and I heaved a sigh of relief, thankful that Josef wasn't by my side. I'd been disgruntled earlier in the afternoon when he'd mentioned remaining late to finish his paper work. Now I was grateful, for the detective's presence wouldn't require an explanation.

After glancing over my shoulder to make certain Josef hadn't wandered to the door in order to bid me farewell, I darted between two carriages and across the street. Somehow I managed to remain upright while skidding to a rather unladylike halt in front of the detective. "Mr. Charleston has arrived?" Clutching one hand to my bodice, I panted for breath.

He tipped his straw hat and grinned. "That was quite a run. If I had to give chase, I believe you could lose me."

"I do hope that won't be necessary," I said.

A hint of admiration shone in his eyes. "Agreed. Mr. Charleston is waiting for us at the police station. Are you free to come with me right now?"

It seemed all was working out. Mrs. Wilson and Mr. Lundgren were to join friends for supper, and Josef and I had agreed we would fend for ourselves this evening. I murmured my agreement, and the detective immediately hailed a carriage. We made the journey mostly in silence, although the detective did mention the dry weather and the need for rain several times. I didn't know if the silence bothered him, or if he was genuinely worried about his wife's failing crop of garden vegetables. I tended to think it was the latter, since he peered heavenward when we arrived at the station and said, "Our green beans could sure use some rain."

"Is that a prayer or a comment?" I asked as he assisted me down from the carriage.

"A little of both, but I think the good Lord already knows we need the rain," he said with a grin. He lightly grasped my elbow and guided me toward the entrance we'd used on my previous visit. "Let's use the side door."

Within minutes we were in the same room

where my portrait had been sketched. Mr. Charleston wasn't at all what I'd expected. I had envisioned a sleazy sort of man with greasy hair, beady eyes, and disheveled clothing. Instead, I was introduced to a refined gentleman who could rival any of Mr. Galloway's associates. Mr. Charleston possessed a commanding presence that seemed to fill the small room.

He muffled a faint chuckle as we were introduced. "You were expecting someone less respectable?"

I didn't know if he was attempting to trick me into admitting I'd previously seen him, but perhaps he had truly observed my surprise. The fact that he'd so easily detected my inner thoughts both embarrassed and disturbed me. There was no use denying the obvious. I gave a firm nod.

He squinted his eyes and drew a circle in the air with his index finger. "Please turn for me," he said. "Slowly." Mr. Charleston made it clear that he wasn't afraid to take command. And it seemed the detective had acquiesced power to the shop owner. Once I'd completed my pirouette, Mr. Charleston said, "Please step to the other side of the room." I edged around the table and faced him. "No. Turn sideways." I did as he commanded while still attempting to see if he was sending signals to the detective. He sighed and dropped into one of the chairs. "I don't think this is the woman, but I can't be absolutely certain until I hear her speak."

The detective dipped forward and rested his palms on the table. "Say something for the man, Miss Brouwer."

I arched my brows. What did one say to a man attempting to identify you as a criminal? I didn't wonder for long.

Mr. Charleston once again took command. "I'd like you to ask me if I'd be interested in purchasing a valuable necklace."

The detective signaled for me to comply.

"Would you be interested in purchasing a valuable necklace?" I said as naturally as possible.

"No." He shook his head. "Not her. The woman I dealt with had a deep, raspy voice with a southern accent."

The detective slapped his palm on the table. I don't know who was more startled: Mr. Charleston or me. "I wish you would have mentioned her voice earlier. I could have confirmed that Miss Brouwer doesn't have a southern accent or a deep voice."

The shop owner shrugged. "Still, it's probably better to verify in person, don't you think? Criminals are always disguising themselves in various ways — or so I've been told."

The detective merely grunted.

Mr. Charleston didn't appear to notice the detective's irritation. He tapped his fingertip on the table. "Yes. She had a very distinctive voice. I made note of it both times she came into the shop."

The detective jumped to attention. "*Both* times? The woman was in your store more than once?"

"I thought I mentioned that to you when I wrote that I would be passing through Collinsford. I must have forgotten that, as well." His eyebrows matted into knotted ripples. "The woman returned with two lovely paintings and asked if I could find them a good home in another country." He grinned. "Her way of advising me the paintings might be stolen."

The detective directed a wary look at me. "And you bought them anyway?"

Mr. Charleston edged his finger beneath his collar. "I deal in fine art and jewelry. I am one of few brokers in the state who can properly value such items. Most of my inventory comes from wealthy people who have fallen upon hard times."

"Still, she told you —"

"Not outright," Mr. Charleston replied.

"People come to me because I understand the value of their items, and I'm willing to pay them more. My shop bears a fine reputation. You'd be surprised at the number of wealthy men who visit my business. When an item is brought to me, I don't question the ownership. That's not a requirement of my business."

The detective didn't appear impressed with Mr. Charleston's defense, but he didn't argue, either. If he was going to gather further information, he'd need Mr. Charleston's cooperation. "So this woman came in and asked you to find a home for the paintings. I believe you said two paintings. Is that correct?"

"Yes."

Unable to squelch my excitement, I leaned across the table. "Were they signed?"

"Yes. I'd become aware of this artist only recently. Leland Brou—" His jaw went slack. He looked at the detective and then at me. "*Your* name is Brouwer, isn't it?"

I nodded. "Yes. And I hope you have the two paintings of mine that were stolen from the Collinsford Carousel Factory."

Mr. Charleston listened intently while the detective explained the circumstances surrounding the theft. When the detective had finished, Mr. Charleston rubbed his jaw. "So that young lady stole both the jewelry and the paintings. And she closely resembles Miss Brouwer? Am I understanding this correctly?"

"I'm not certain she's the actual thief," the detective said. "She may be an accomplice selected merely because she closely resembles Miss Brouwer."

"This thief had a well-thought-out plan," Mr. Charleston said. "Not many men would contemplate such an idea."

The detective curled his lips in disgust. "If criminals would use their time and energy for good, this would be a much better world."

Mr. Charleston removed his pocket watch and snapped open the lid. "I must soon be on my way, Detective. About the paintings . . ." He looked in my direction.

"I have no money to reimburse you," I said.

Mr. Charleston chuckled. "I believe the detective will inform you that I am not entitled to reimbursement for stolen property." He stood and turned toward the door. "Besides, I had not actually purchased them. I was to receive a percentage of the sale price once I located a buyer and settled on a price. Now I must inform my prospect that our arrangement must be canceled."

I could barely believe my ears. "You had a buyer?"

"In London. He was most eager. If you are interested in selling them . . ."

I shook my head. "No, but if you could tell me their value, I would be most appreciative."

Glancing at the table, he returned and picked up a pencil. After scribbling on a sheet of paper, he folded it in half and shoved it toward me. "This bears my signature and the estimated value of the paintings. If you decide to sell, you should show this to the art dealer. Don't sell for any less."

I unfolded the page and gasped when I saw the figure. "This can't possibly be correct, can it?"

"Trust me, Miss Brouwer, it is correct. I have investigated and know the worth of those paintings." He extended his arm and shook hands with the detective. "Keep me advised, and I will do all in my power to see that the thief and his accomplice are punished."

The detective didn't release Mr. Charleston's hand. "If I can detain you for only a little longer, I believe I may have a plan that will help accomplish that purpose."

"Talk quickly. I don't want to miss my train."

Mr. Charleston and I listened while the detective quickly detailed his plan. When he'd finished, he said, "All we need to do is set a date."

"I'll return to Cincinnati the third of September. Any time after that would be fine with me." Mr. Charleston was reaching for his hat.

The detective arched his brows. "Miss Brouwer?"

"I'll speak to Josef and make arrangements to be away from work once you tell me the date."

The detective hesitated for only a moment. "We can be at the shop on Saturday, the sixth of September. That way you won't be required to miss too much work, Miss Brouwer. I'll try to arrange for a train late Friday afternoon. With any luck, we can return Saturday afternoon." Detective Lawton agreed to write out the details and mail them to Mr. Charleston. The three of us walked out the side door, and Detective Lawton hailed a carriage.

"To the train station," Mr. Charleston called to the driver as he tossed his bag inside. He turned toward me. "Nice to make your acquaintance, Miss Brouwer." Giving the detective a mock salute, he said, "I look forward to our future meeting in Cincinnati."

Once Mr. Charleston was on his way, I tapped Detective Lawton on the arm. "Does this mean you will now remove me from your list of suspects?"

He grinned. "Indeed it does, Miss Brouwer. And I extend my apologies for any difficulty this investigation has caused for you. Nothing personal was intended. I was merely doing my job."

Now that I no longer had to worry about going to jail, it was easy to accept the detective's apology. After agreeing on our arrangements, he waved for a carriage. "You sure you don't want me to come to the factory and explain to your employer?"

I shook my head. "There won't be any problem. I'll speak to Mr. Kaestner myself."

Settling against the warm leather carriage seat, I closed my eyes. So much had occurred, it was difficult to digest the complete depth of it all. When my stomach growled, I realized it was nearly eight o'clock and I hadn't yet eaten supper. If Josef was at the boardinghouse, I wanted to speak to him and clear the air. Keeping secrets and telling half-truths had proved more difficult than I'd anticipated.

The semidarkness provided a hazy shroud as I approached the boardinghouse. Someone said my name, and a strangled scream escaped my lips. I hadn't seen Josef sitting on the front porch.

He jumped to his feet. "I am sorry. I did not mean to frighten you." With three long strides, he was at my side to offer comfort. Leading me to one of the chairs on the porch, Josef patiently waited until I regained my composure.

"I have so much to tell you," I said. He offered an encouraging smile and proved to be most understanding when I explained the circumstances surrounding the theft of Mrs. Galloway's jewelry — and the fact that I'd been the primary suspect. But it was the news of my missing paintings that particularly aroused his interest. He listened intently to that portion of my recital. However, he wasn't quite as tolerant when he heard of Augusta's condemning behavior or the fact that the detective wanted me to accompany him to Cincinnati.

"A lot you have told me this evening."

"Yes, and that's not even the most important part."

He stared at me as though he didn't know if he was up to hearing anything more. "There is something else?"

"Yes. While I was riding home in the carriage, I realized that God had answered my prayer." I tapped my fingertips against my chest. "*Me.* Can you believe it? God truly listened when I prayed. He saved me from a jail cell. I am so thankful I didn't have to suffer like Paul or Daniel. It's amazing. God answered my prayer in the way that I asked." The words gushed from my lips uninhibited.

"You had faith," Josef said.

His response settled in my heart like a cold stone. How I wished I could agree with his statement, but in truth my faith had been nearly nonexistent. I hadn't expected God to act. In fact, I'd expected the opposite. "My faith wasn't strong at all. I think it's probably because God knows I couldn't withstand such punishment. I'm not nearly strong enough to be a martyr."

"Maybe it's true that you are not strong enough for living in a jail, but you have changed. Your faith in God, it has increased since first you came to Collinsford. And God, He knows how much your heart has changed, too. Is gut God agrees you should be free. I am pleased all is settled." He exhaled deeply and leaned back in his chair.

Only the sound of chirping crickets and the rustling of a light breeze through the tree branches interrupted the quietude. Josef must not have understood all I had told him. I shifted forward on the chair. "All is not yet settled, Josef. Remember, I must go to Cincinnati."

When he bobbed his head, several strands of hair fell across his forehead. Brushing them aside, he said, "Ja. And I am thinking such a journey might be dangerous. I do not know why the detective cannot go by himself to apprehend this thief. This is his job. Why must you be there?"

"I'm not supposed to discuss any details. I've already told you more than I should have." I knew Josef wasn't pleased with my response, but he finally agreed that I could leave work early on the appointed Friday. He stood and paced back and forth in front of my chair. "I hope I will not regret my decision."

I grasped his hand and pulled him to a halt in front of me. "You won't. I promise. Thank you, Josef."

"If something should happen to you . . ." He took my other hand and helped me to my feet. Cupping my chin in his palm, he stared deep into my eyes. "I could not bear to lose you, Carrie." Lowering his head, he covered my lips with a gentle kiss.

I melted against his broad chest, enjoying the warmth of his embrace and the strength of his arms encircling me. Had I ever experienced such love and protection as I felt with this man? Maybe as a little girl when I had walked hand in hand with my mother or father. But since that time I'd buried any longing for love and convinced myself I would live a life without strings or attachments. Now it seemed Josef had changed those ideas. Now I wanted to shed the life of a solitary soul; now I wanted to share my life with another — I wanted to share my life with Josef. Tears pooled in my eyes and trickled down my cheeks.

"What is this? You are crying?" Using the pad of his thumb, Josef wiped away one of the tears. "My kiss makes you sad?"

I shook my head. "No. Your kiss makes me very happy." My thoughts were far too complicated to explain at this time, but one day I would tell him what had created the staggering mixture of emotions. For now, I simply said, "Sometimes ladies cry when they are happy."

"Ja. My mother, she did this sometimes, too." His eyes shone with pleasure, and I knew my answer had been enough for the moment.

Lost in our conversation, neither of us heard Mrs. Wilson and Mr. Lundgren approach. "You two will be the talk of the town come morning." Mr. Lundgren chuckled as he assisted Mrs. Wilson up the porch steps. With his free hand he pointed toward Mrs. McDougal's house. "Saw Mrs. McDougal leaning over the porch railing that faces this direction. Wondered what she was gawkin' at." His grin widened. "She must be taking lots of pleasure in watchin' the two of you out here."

"Now, Ralph. Don't tease the young folks." Mrs. Wilson plopped down in one of the chairs. "Think I'll sit out here for a minute and catch my breath. That ought to be enough to send Mrs. McDougal back inside."

Mr. Lundgren laughed and dropped into the chair beside her. "She might stay out there to see if I'm gonna kiss *you*. Ever think of that?"

"Ralph!" Mrs. Wilson gave his arm a playful slap. "You shouldn't talk that way."

"Don't know why not. Kissing is a good thing, right Josef?"

Before Josef could respond, Mrs. Wilson waved at me. "How was your day, Carrie? Did you and Josef find enough for your supper?"

Supper! In all the excitement to tell Josef what had happened, I'd completely forgotten about supper. I looked to him for a response, for I had no idea if he'd eaten.

Thankfully he patted his stomach. "I am still full," he said.

Mrs. Wilson's shoulders drooped. I wasn't certain if she was tired or if she had hoped to hear we'd had difficulty getting along without her.

"Mrs. Finley insisted upon sending me home with several pieces of her peach cobbler." She pointed to a basket beside her chair. "I told her I'd left plenty of food for the two of you, and you wouldn't be hungry."

My stomach rumbled at the mention of food. Both Josef and I strained toward the basket, but I was the first to speak. "I think I could manage to eat a piece. She might ask on Sunday morning, and I wouldn't want to hurt her feelings."

"Ja. We would not want to insult her." Josef picked up the basket. "No need to get up from your chair. I will take it inside."

Following close behind Josef, I glanced over my shoulder. "And I can dish it up."

"You'd think neither of them had eaten a bite all evening." Mrs. Wilson's comment drifted through the screen door, and I slapped my palm across my mouth to keep from giggling aloud.

CHAPTER 30

On the way to work in the morning Josef
and I had agreed we would walk to the park
after supper. Though summer was still upon
us, it wouldn't be long until there would be
a chill in the morning and evening breezes.
Living near Lake Erie meant long cold
winters with a great deal of snow; at least
that's what Augusta had told me. And
recently both Mrs. Wilson and Josef had
confirmed that fact. Already there were
fewer hours of daylight, and I wanted to
take advantage of the beautiful day.

Sitting on the front porch, Mrs. Wilson
waved to Josef and me when we arrived
home from work. "Supper's ready and waiting," she said.

Pleasure surged through me — an exciting sense of anticipation. Usually, Mrs. Wilson didn't have supper prepared until at
least a half hour after our arrival. Josef and
I could eat a quick supper and be on our

way to the park. We would have even more time to enjoy the summer evening. I wondered if Josef had told her of our plans. However, I quickly dismissed that idea. We hadn't decided to visit the park until after we'd left the house. Before I could mention my delight, she leaned forward and pushed herself up from the chair.

"I wanted to get supper finished early. Mr. Lundgren promised to move some things up to the attic." She beamed at Josef. "I think he's going to need your help. I hope you don't mind."

My spirits plunged, for I knew how Josef would respond. He wouldn't refuse the boardinghouse owner's request. Shifting from one foot to the other, he gave me a sideways glance. "Carrie and I, we were going to the park this evening. Could this wait until another time for me to help?"

Mrs. Wilson's shoulders drooped, and she slowly shook her head. Motioning toward the interior of the house, she said, "Ralph took off work an hour early today, and the two of us managed to move most everything into the hall before you came home."

Josef and I stepped to the door and peered through the screen. They'd left only a narrow path between the trunks, boxes, and crates. Mrs. Wilson offered an apologetic smile. "That's Mr. Wilson's old chair and a few of his other things that I want to pack away."

I eyed the belongings lining the walls and concluded there was a lot more than a few of Mr. Wilson's personal effects. Where had all of it come from? "This is all yours?" I couldn't contain my wonder.

She tipped her head to the side and gave me a sheepish look. "Not exactly. There's some folks who belong to the church, and they needed a place to store their household goods for a time. They're going off to look for work elsewhere, and I said I'd help out. Once they find work, they'll return for their things, but they thought it would be a while. I can't leave all of this sitting around."

I wondered why the older woman hadn't insisted the owners lug their belongings to the attic before leaving town. She hadn't even thought about the imposition upon Josef. She was always prepared to help others and assumed the same of everyone else.

"Let's eat and then we will see how long this will take," Josef said. "There still may be time to visit the park if we work quickly."

I didn't reply. I knew Josef was already weary from a long day at work. After moving trunks and furniture up two flights of stairs and then into the attic, he'd be exhausted. Silently the two of us followed Mrs. Wilson into the house. After taking only a few minutes to wash up, we each hurried downstairs. I was surprised to see Mr. Lundgren had nearly finished his supper by the time we entered the dining room.

He pushed back from the table and stood. "I got home early, so I'm gonna go ahead and get started, Josef. There's lots of smaller crates I can take upstairs while you're eatin' supper. You take your time."

Planting a hand on each side of his waist, Josef arched his back. "Do not lift anything too heavy or your back, you will hurt."

Mr. Lundgren grinned. "I'll do my best."

After a hasty prayer of thanks for our food, Josef downed his supper in record time. Mrs. Wilson fretted that he would develop digestive ailments, but I thought the tough meat and underbaked rolls would likely cause more stomach problems than his hasty consumption. Of course I wouldn't say such a thing, but the thought stuck in my mind.

Although I offered to help with some of the smaller boxes, the men shooed me away. "Sit on the porch and draw me some new carousel animals," Josef suggested. He winked, and my stomach catapulted into riotous motion. I could feel the heat rising up my neck and rushed outside before he could see my cheeks turn crimson. "You forgot your sketch pad," he called after me.

"I'll get it after you've taken your first load upstairs." I sat down on the porch and waited until I heard the men climbing the stairs. Each upward step was accompanied by a grunt from Mr. Lundgren, and I wondered if he would survive the many trips that would be required to clear the hallway.

Once they'd begun their work in earnest, I returned inside and gathered my sketch pad and pencils. Josef had suggested I draw him a new carousel animal, and I'd been considering one of the dragons I'd seen in a book that my mother had read to me when I was a child. In the past the Collinsford Carousel Factory had used authentic replicas of animals in their carousels. Never before had I presented the idea of a fictitious creature, but an entire carousel of make-believe animals might be fun. I wondered what Josef would think of such an idea. Picking up my pencil, I drew careful strokes until the form of a dragon took shape before me. I smiled at the whimsical eyes and mouth I'd given him but decided he needed something more. I held the sketchbook at a distance and studied the animal.

"Carrie!"

Dropping the sketchbook to the porch, I jumped to my feet. Josef's frantic tone was a sure sign something had gone wrong. My insides churned as I hurried inside.

Josef stood on the first landing, his face ashen. "Come quick." He pointed up the stairs. "Your painting, it is missing!" I could see the panic in his eyes.

The churning ceased, and my stomach plummeted. I'd completely forgotten that the narrow stairway leading to the attic was located in my bedroom, which Mr. Lundgren and Josef had been required to enter in order to carry Mrs. Wilson's items to storage.

He continued to wave me forward. "Come! You will see for yourself."

I remained at the bottom of the stairs. "I *know* it is missing, Josef."

His features twisted into a jumble of confusion. "But you said nothing to me? The detective, he knows about this?"

"Come downstairs, Josef. We need to talk." Although I hadn't planned to speak of the painting unless absolutely necessary, the time had arrived — far too soon. Foolishly I'd thought I could hide the part I'd played in purchasing the factory. Now I hoped Josef could push aside his pride and accept what I'd done as a gift from my heart.

He followed me into the parlor, and we sat side by side on Mrs. Wilson's upholstered divan while I tentatively explained the whereabouts of the painting. His features changed from a look of surprise to one of utter disbelief. He cupped his palms on his cheeks and shook his head. "Nein, nein." He repeated the words over and over. It appeared the revelation had created greater distress than I had imagined. "This, you should not have done, Carrie. We will change the papers. Mr. Galloway will return the painting to you. I will beg him."

I grasped one hand and tugged it away from his cheek. Holding tight, I said, "Don't you have faith that we can make the factory a success?"

"Ja, of course, but not this way. Is not gut."

"Mr. Galloway promised he would return the painting to me when you have repaid the selling price for the factory."

"He is a sick man. After he dies, then what will happen? You think his wife will give you back the painting?" Once again he shook his head. "She will learn the value and never return your inheritance. You have made a great mistake."

The heat in the parlor now seemed stifling, and I reached for Josef's hand. "Come outside." I pulled him along behind me, and we sat down on the front steps. "Let me explain how this will work. Mr. Galloway added a codicil to his will that stipulates the painting must be returned to me. The lawyer assured me this addition to Mr. Galloway's will, along with our contract, will protect my ownership in the painting."

"I am sorry, but I worry this will go wrong for you."

I leaned closer and placed my hand atop Josef's. "The family can't sell it. Unless the factory fails and the payments are not made, the painting will be returned to me one day. I have been reading in the Bible about trusting God."

"It is not God I am worrying with — it is the Galloways. I know Mr. Galloway to be a man of his word, but even with *my* contract, you see what happened."

"Your contract provided an escape for him, Josef. The contract I signed does not. Don't you see that Mr. Galloway wanted you to have the factory? Even if he should die, this is the one way he could make it happen without a risk to his family."

Josef stood and jammed his fists into his pockets. "Maybe he has no risk, but you have taken a serious gamble with your beautiful painting. It is all you had left to remember your father."

"That's not true. I remember him every time I paint a carousel horse, Josef." I tipped my head and smiled up at him. "I won't deny that the painting is very dear to me — but not as dear as you. We are building a future with the factory. And who can say for sure? I may yet regain possession of my other canvases."

He gave a firm nod. "But even if your other pictures are not returned, your painting on the carousel horse will one day be returned to hang on your wall. This I promise to you."

I had no doubt he would regain the carousel painting for me, but I hoped it would hang on a wall in our own home and not in Mrs. Wilson's boardinghouse. Of course I would never be so bold as to say such a thing, but when he looked into my eyes and thanked me for my faith in him, I believe he knew the longing in my heart.

I had hoped to hear more from him, but Mr. Lundgren meandered onto the porch with a box of knickknacks under his arm. "You 'bout ready to take that trunk up, Josef?"

"I'll be along in a moment," Josef said.

He waited until Mr. Lundgren returned inside, and then he turned to me. "I am not so gut with words, but this I want to say."

I held my breath and waited.

"I have told you before of my feelings for you. Today I feel such love in my heart for you." Bright pink splotched his cheekbones as he clasped my hand in his. "I know we do not know each other for long enough to speak of such a thing, but I want to say that it is my wish to one day make you my wife." The anticipation in his eyes begged a response.

"One day I would be honored to be your wife."

Josef jumped to his feet and let out a whoop. The moment I stood, he swept me into his arms and twirled me around the front porch. "You have made me a happy man this day."

"Mrs. McDougal is watching us. You should put me down," I whispered.

He set me down and cupped his hands to his mouth. "One day she is going to marry me, Mrs. McDougal."

The old woman looked away and pretended she hadn't been watching, but Josef wouldn't be deterred. "Did you hear me, Mrs. McDougal?"

With a dismissive wave, she called, "People get married all the time."

"Not like this — this time is different," he said. "This time it will be *us.*"

CHAPTER 31

September 5, 1890

All morning I'd been fretting about the trip to Cincinnati. What would people think if they saw me departing on a train with a strange man? Not that many people in Collinsford knew me, but there was always the possibility that someone who had attended one of the Galloway parties would be making a trip to Cincinnati. The very thought of such a happenstance caused me to shudder. What would I say if one of those very proper ladies should approach me?

"Not makin' much progress." Mr. Tobarth was looking at the huge jumper I'd been working on all day.

I couldn't offer any argument. "My mind is elsewhere today."

"Well, you better get it back, 'cause we got a lot of work that's needin' to be finished before Monday mornin'."

I nodded and swallowed hard. Clearly Josef hadn't told Mr. Tobarth I'd be leaving work early today and that I wouldn't be at the factory tomorrow, either. It would be another hour before I left for the train station, and I immediately decided I would wait to inform him. If he became angry over the turn of events, he could discuss it with Josef once I was off to Cincinnati.

Although I tried my best to remain focused, I accomplished little over the next hour. Thankfully, Mr. Tobarth was busy working on the far side of his horse, where he couldn't see how little I had managed to complete. At fifteen minutes before my departure time, I began to clean my brushes and clear my work area. Unfortunately, it didn't take long for Mr. Tobarth to take note of what I was doing.

He stepped around the back of his horse and tapped my shoulder. "What do you think you're doin', Carrie?" With the tip of his paintbrush, he pointed toward the clock. "It's not time to go home. You forget how to tell time?"

Instead of looking up, I continued to clean my brushes. "I have an appointment and need to leave early. Josef has given me permission."

His eyebrows dipped low on his forehead. "He didn't say nothin' to me about you takin' off early. We've got lots of work that needs to get done. You gonna be here early tomorrow to make up the time?"

I had hoped to slip out without explanation, but Mr. Tobarth wasn't going to let that happen. "You should speak to Josef. He knows my schedule."

"I'm your supervisor. I should know your schedule, too. If we don't get the work done, I'm responsible." Generally soft-spoken and kind, Mr. Tobarth was clearly annoyed with my unexpected plans to leave early, and his voice assumed a sharp edge.

"I'm terribly sorry, but this is a matter of great importance. I'm not able to discuss it with you, but I can explain when I return to work on Monday. And I'll work late all next week if you need me."

"It'll be too late to do me any good on Monday. I just hope Josef plans to get back here and help. Since he's the one givin' you permission, I figure he oughta be willin' to help out."

I removed my apron and carried it across the room. Today wasn't a day that Mr. Tobarth would appreciate my ability to fling the canvas covering onto a hook. I picked up my straw hat and strode toward the door leading to the front of the building. "I'll tell Josef you're in need of help back here."

Mr. Tobarth didn't respond. Not even so much as a wave. If all went according to plan and I returned by Saturday evening, I could come to the factory and work on Sunday afternoon. Josef was in his office when I arrived at the front of the factory. I could see a carriage waiting outside. Likely it was the detective waiting to take me to the boardinghouse to retrieve my traveling case before heading for the train station.

Josef walked me to the front door. "I still do not like this idea. Promise me you will not let them put you in danger."

"I promise," I whispered. He leaned forward and brushed my cheek with a kiss. "Josef! One of the men might see you."

He shrugged. "I do not care what they see. Besides, once we get the papers changed, you will be owner of this company."

"*We* will be owners of this company. Equal partners," she said. "And we're going to make it the grandest carousel factory in the world."

"But you must come back safe from Cincinnati so we can do that, ja?"

"Yes." I glanced toward the street. "I better hurry or we'll miss the train."

Josef grinned. "Would not bother me if you missed the train."

"I know," I said, hurrying out the door.

Fortunately Mrs. Wilson wasn't at home when I stopped for my baggage. Though she was aware of my plans to be gone until the following evening, I knew she had mistakenly assumed I would be visiting the Galloways, and I'd done nothing to dispel her conjecture.

Conversation between the detective and me remained minimal during our ride to the station. I waited at a distance while he purchased our tickets. He suggested we remain in the same coach, but he would sit a few rows behind me. To avoid any possible embarrassment should we be seen or recognized, he'd said.

I agreed but couldn't help but tease him. "Afraid someone might tell your wife he saw you with a young woman?"

He didn't appear amused. "I was thinking of protecting *your* reputation rather than my own. My wife understands I might be seen in the company of a woman from time to time, Miss Brouwer."

So much for my attempt at levity. I boarded the train and selected a seat in the middle of the car. I didn't speak to the detective until we arrived in Cincinnati several hours later. Our rooms were on separate floors of the hotel, and arrangements were made to have a late supper and our breakfast delivered to our rooms. The detective was unwilling to take any chance that I might be seen.

The following morning my heart pounded as we entered Mr. Charleston's shop through a rear entry. Beads of perspiration dotted the detective's forehead, and he yanked a handkerchief from his pocket and swiped his face. Detective Lawton's obvious anxiety did nothing to settle my nerves. "When are they expected?" the detective whispered to Mr. Charleston.

"Nine o'clock. The note I received said my offer had been accepted."

The detective sighed. "I'm thankful for that!"

A bell jingled in the other room, and Detective Lawton clicked the catch on his pocket watch. "Nine o'clock. Right on time. Leave the door ajar," he said, careful to keep his voice low.

I sat on an old wooden chair and scanned the storeroom that Mr. Charleston used for his excess inventory. We were surrounded by a plethora of artwork. Some framed, some not. Some lovely, some quite ugly. I would have enjoyed going through the stacked canvases but dared not make a noise. From my position across the room, I was scrutinizing a beautiful still life when

Mr. Charleston returned. His face contorted in either fear or anger while he hissed a message to the detective. Clearly he was worried, but I couldn't hear what he said.

I didn't have to wait long. The detective waved me forward. "I'm afraid we will need to put our plan into motion. I'm going out front and arrest the woman. You'll need to change clothes with her. I'll bring her back here shortly."

When the woman entered the storage room with Detective Lawton, I gasped. It was like seeing a duplicate of myself. Her reaction mirrored my own. Eyes wide, the woman clutched her throat and stared at me. "*What?* Am I seeing a doppelganger?" she croaked, her words barely audible.

The detective shook his head. "She's no ghost. She's as alive as you are."

I don't think she believed him, for she proved exceedingly cooperative. Fear shone from her eyes, and she couldn't do my bidding quickly enough. Thankfully she was wearing a skirt, and her cloak covered her shirtwaist. I offered her my clothing in return, but she refused. Instead, she yanked the muslin cloth from several paintings and covered herself before retreating to a far corner of the room.

I pointed to her hat. "I'll need that, as well."

She unpinned the chapeau, and I shoved it firmly atop my head. "Where is Tyson?" I asked.

"In the carriage across the street, but I do not think he will come in."

Mr. Charleston was correct. The woman had a raspy southern drawl, and I prayed I wouldn't have to speak in order to lure Tyson into the shop. Mr. Charleston took charge of the woman while the detective edged along the wall toward the front door. "Do your best. I'll be watching from here. If anything goes amiss, I'll be at your side before you can call out."

I doubted that, but I didn't want to think about the possibility of peril. After inhaling a deep breath, I opened the front door and walked to the corner. I hoped the detective could still see me. The carriage was parked where the woman had told me. The minute I appeared, Tyson leaned forward. I motioned for him to come.

He shook his head. Using my palm and forefinger, I mimicked signing a paper. When he didn't move from the carriage, I motioned more frantically. Again I pretended to be signing my hand. Surely he understood. Even from a distance I could see he was annoyed. I turned toward the shop and once again waved.

I could only hope he would consider my performance tempting enough to join me. I glanced over my shoulder. He had jumped down from the carriage and was loping across the street at breakneck speed. If I didn't hurry, he'd catch me before I could get back inside. And I desperately wanted the detective's protection.

My heart pounded in my ears and drowned out all other noise. Had Tyson called to me, I wouldn't have heard. Arm outstretched and afraid to look back, I grasped the door handle and shoved my way forward. I'd barely cleared the threshold when a hand clutched my wrist. A shrill howl escaped my throat; the detective lunged forward, and the fingers wrapped around my wrist clawed to maintain a hold. I twisted around and broke free.

Before he said a word, I saw the hesitation in his eyes. Recognition immediately followed. "Carrington!" His eyes darted about the room like an animal seeking escape. "Georgia! Where are you? Why have you betrayed me?"

"She didn't betray you, Farnsworth. She had no choice but to cooperate."

"Women! You can't trust any of them."

Tyson spat the words at me.

I took a step forward. "How *dare* you speak of trust or betrayal! You stole my paintings and have wreaked havoc upon the Galloways. A family who has shown you nothing but kindness and goodwill."

He glowered at me, his lips curled in anger. "Kindness and goodwill? I think not. Mrs. Galloway was seeking a husband for Augusta — one from a socially prominent and wealthy family. And Augusta was no better. She is so enamored by the idea of marriage, she would fawn over any man offering the slightest attention." He shifted his weight and leaned forward. "It would have served them right had I married her. And if it weren't for my friendship with Ronald, I would have taken her for my wife."

I stared at him, dumbfounded. "Whatever do you mean?"

"Because I haven't lived up to my father's standards, he has disowned me. He cut me off — from his money and from the family." His eyes shone with anger. "Don't you see, Carrington? Had I married Augusta, both she and her mother would have become the laughingstock of Collinsford. I saved Mrs. Galloway from herself. Stealing her jewelry was a small price to pay when you consider she maintained her place in society."

"And why did I deserve to have my paintings stolen?"

He shrugged one shoulder and tipped his head. "Because art can't be appreciated when it's hidden away."

Not only was Tyson Farnsworth a thief, he was also a scoundrel of the worst sort. He even lacked the courage to admit his wrongdoing. Instead, he pointed a finger at others. Thankfully, he hadn't pursued Augusta any further. How sad her life would have been if she had married him.

A short time later, Detective Lawton escorted me to the train station, even though he wouldn't be accompanying me back home. Tyson and his friend, Georgia, were being detained in Cincinnati, and the detective needed to return to the police station to complete paper work for their transfer to Collinsford. "I'm sorry you must make the journey home alone," he said.

"No apology is required. I'm pleased to return knowing the crimes have been solved and the true criminals will pay for their misdeeds."

The detective handed my bag to a porter. "I owe you a debt of thanks. There's no way to repay you for your assistance."

"You've already repaid me. Have you

forgotten? You recovered my paintings," I said. "It's Mr. Charleston who ended up with a financial loss."

The detective nodded. "I'm thankful for the help he gave me. Yet he had a strong suspicion he was dealing in stolen goods. I think he's learned an expensive lesson. I doubt he'll make that same decision again." He tipped his hat. "Have a good trip home."

It was well after bedtime when I'd finished relating the day's overwhelming events. Had Mrs. Wilson not interrupted quite so often, my explanation would have been completed at least an hour earlier. But I couldn't fault her. I'd furnished her with more excitement than she'd experienced in her lifetime — at least that's what she told the three of us.

When I'd told how Tyson had wrenched my arm during my hasty return to Mr. Charleston's shop, Josef tensed. He clenched his teeth and growled, "It is probably gut I was not there. I would still be using my fists on him." We all laughed, but later I told him that his protective words had warmed my heart.

Once Mrs. Wilson and Mr. Lundgren went off to secure the house for the night, I moved nearer to Josef. "Tomorrow after church, I must go and speak to Augusta.

She deserves to hear from me what has happened."

"I will go with you," Josef said. "We both need to speak with Mr. Galloway, as well." Josef placed a fleeting kiss on my cheek. "All day I prayed for your safety, and God protected you. I am most thankful." His eyes glistened in the dim light. "Now we must go to bed, or tomorrow we will fall asleep during the preacher's message. Would not be gut to do such a thing."

Josef followed me up the stairs. When we arrived on the second floor, he bid me goodnight, and I continued upstairs to my room. It was late, but after I'd prepared for bed, I dropped to my knees and thanked God for the safety He'd provided me. I also thanked Him for the safe return of the two paintings. But mostly I thanked Him for sending Josef into my life: a good man, a man who loved God, a man I could trust.

When I rose from my knees, my eyes were drawn to the empty space on the wall — the place where my picture had hung. "And thank you for giving me the opportunity to help Josef," I whispered before I slipped between the fresh sheets and buried my nose in the sweet-smelling pillowcase.

The following morning I awakened to Mrs. Wilson rapping on my door. "Carrie!

Are you awake? You better hurry or you'll be late for church."

I jumped out of bed and prepared in such a rush that I forgot my Bible and had to race back up the two flights of stairs. Then I realized I'd forgotten my reticule and again scurried up the steps. When next I discovered I'd forgotten my gloves, I decided the Lord would forgive the oversight. I lacked the fortitude to manage even one more flight of those wretched stairs.

Mr. Lundgren and Mrs. Wilson led the way on our walk to church. Since that first day when Mrs. Wilson had ordered Josef to escort me, it had become our accepted pattern, and I held tight to his arm. Rather than focusing on the Lord, I could think of nothing beyond Augusta and the sad news about Tyson I would soon give her. I glanced at Josef. His dark eyes reflected sympathy, and he patted my hand. How had he sensed my anxiety? I once again offered a prayer of thanks that God had sent Josef into my life, but this time it was a silent prayer.

Throughout the church service, I did my best to listen to the preacher. I had hoped to hear something that would help me when I later approached Augusta. Unfortunately, my mind wandered during the sermon. If the preacher said anything that would have provided guidance, I missed it.

"Was a gut sermon the preacher gave us, ja?"

I lifted one shoulder and let it drop. I didn't want to lie, but I didn't want to admit I hadn't been listening.

Josef grinned and touched his forefinger to his head. "Your thoughts, they were on the Galloways instead of the preacher."

I nodded. He knew me so well. Rather than turning over my cares to the Lord, my worries had grown to magnificent proportion. Even if Augusta had given up on Tyson as a marital prospect, she'd still be devastated by the news of his criminal behavior. And who could say whether she'd given up on the idea of Tyson and marriage. If she'd found no other love interest, she might still be pining for him. She'd made it clear she remained enamored of him when we met in the park. The thought made me cringe, for I'd be the one to deliver the appalling news.

"We should return home and eat before going to the Galloways'. Otherwise we'll interrupt their meal," I said.

Josef didn't argue. Although I'm sure he realized I wanted to delay our visit to the Galloway home, my suggestion also contained some merit. Neither of us would want to dine with the family and then present them with unpleasant news.

When we arrived home, I slipped upstairs to my bedroom while Mrs. Wilson completed preparations for the noonday meal. I opened my Bible and searched for something that would sustain me through my encounter with Augusta. Following Mrs. Wilson's instruction, I'd been doing my best to make my way entirely through the Bible, but I had skipped over a number of passages where there seemed to be more *begats* than anything else.

Josef had told me he'd learned much from the Psalms and Proverbs, and they were near the middle of the Bible. I'd try that first. Inserting my finger between the pages, I opened to Proverbs 27. My gaze dropped to the sixth verse. *Faithful are the wounds of a friend; but the kisses of an enemy are deceitful.* I leaned back in the chair. Would Augusta accept the wounds I would impose upon her today? Would she believe they were inflicted to protect her? Would she believe Tyson to be her enemy, or would I forever be assigned that role? Surely she would realize that Tyson was not the man God intended for her.

When I walked downstairs, Josef was standing outside his bedroom door with his

Bible lying open in his hand. His eyes softened with kindness, and he stepped forward. He tapped his forefinger on a Bible verse. "To speak to Augusta is a hard thing. God has given me this passage for you."

"From Psalms."

He nodded. "Ja. Psalm 121. This you must read."

As we hurried from the house to catch the streetcar, Mrs. Wilson bid us farewell with a bravado that made me wonder if she had sensed my apprehension. Josef had suggested a carriage, but I thought the cost too extravagant. He didn't argue. Obviously he wanted me to remain calm. That's exactly what I wanted, too.

Far too soon for my liking, we strode up the wide walkway leading to the expansive porch that bordered the front of the mansion. Silently I murmured the words from the psalm Josef had given me. *I will lift up mine eyes unto the hills, from whence cometh my help. My help cometh from the Lord, which made heaven and earth.* There were some verses in between that I couldn't recall, but I did remember the one that said, *The Lord shall preserve thee from all evil: he shall preserve thy soul.* I didn't believe Augusta was evil, but I might need to be preserved from her wrath.

A maid I'd never before seen rushed to the door before Josef could strike the brass knocker against the door. Her eyes shone with disapproval. Though no carriages lined the driveway, I wondered if we might be intruding.

"Would you please tell Miss Augusta that Carrington Brouwer and Josef Kaestner are here to speak with her?"

"Are you expected?"

"No, but if you would tell her I have a matter of importance to discuss, I believe she'll see me."

The maid permitted us entry into the foyer and made it clear we should await her return. She made Frances seem like a gentle saint. I glanced about and hoped either Frances or Thomas might appear. A glimpse of either would have lessened my anxiety. The disquieting feelings I'd experienced during my initial arrival at the Galloway home returned with a rush. At least back then I'd known Augusta would be pleased to see me. Now I wondered if any member of the family would welcome my visit. Before I could further contemplate their reaction, the unpleasant maid returned, with Augusta following close on her heels. I struggled to relax my clenched fists. Inhaling a deep breath, I forced myself to smile.

Her formal greeting was as icy as a frozen pond. "You wish to speak with me?"

"Yes. I apologize for calling without an appointment, but . . ."

She sniffed. "I wouldn't expect *you* to abide by rules of etiquette."

Her comment struck like pellets of sleet, and I instinctively took a backward step. "This is a matter of great importance, Augusta. News I wish to deliver in private." I glanced toward the maid, who appeared to be enjoying our exchange.

"Is that why you brought Josef along? Because you want to speak to me alone?" She cloaked her anger with clipped, controlled words.

Before I could respond, Mr. Galloway entered the foyer. "Look who's here! Josef! Carrington! Why didn't you tell us we had company, Augusta?" Her father stepped forward to grasp Josef's hand. "What brings the two of you to Fair Oaks? Augusta didn't mention you were going to pay us a visit."

Once her father arrived, Augusta's mood lightened, and she immediately suggested the two of us visit in the music room. Josef motioned for me to go along. "You go and talk. While you are with Augusta, I will speak to Mr. Galloway about the contract."

Remembering the verses from Proverbs, I silently followed Augusta to the music room.

Lips tight and shoulders rigid, she sat opposite me. "Well? What do you wish to tell me?"

My words flowed with surprising ease and tenderness. I relayed all that had occurred: Tyson's thievery, the lookalike he'd used as a decoy, his capture in Cincinnati, and his lack of remorse for those he'd injured. "I know you cared for Tyson, and it's difficult for you to hear these things. I only hope you know that it causes me great pain to bring you this news." I reached forward and prayed she would accept my hand in friendship. Though it seemed an eternity, only a few seconds passed before she leaned forward and grasped my fingers.

"I didn't want to believe Tyson was a scoundrel, but deep in my heart I knew he didn't truly love me. I became angry when I knew he'd never commit to me. When Mary Flinchbaugh told me she'd seen the two of you together, I thought it impossible. But I wanted to blame someone else for his lack of affection. Can you ever forgive me?"

Her apology washed over me with a cleansing relief. "There is nothing to forgive. I told you that day in the park that I was still your friend. That has never changed —

not for me."

"You've changed, Carrie. You're not the same person who came to Collinsford. I can't put my finger on it, but there's been a change. What is it?"

"Thanks to Josef and Mrs. Wilson, I've been reading the Bible, and I've discovered there is much more to being a Christian than attending church on Sunday. It's a very difficult thing to live as a Christian. I'm trying my best, but I certainly don't have the attributes of the martyrs I've read about."

Augusta tipped her head, and her lips curved in a half smile. "I think what you experienced with Tyson might qualify you for martyrdom." We embraced, and then Augusta spoke of her father's illness. "We've not yet sold the house, but we're going to move next month — to Colorado. We're told the climate may help restore Father's health, although there's no promise from the doctors. Mother is beside herself with worry."

"Will Ronald relocate, as well?" I wondered if he'd gathered the courage to tell his parents about the young woman who had captured his heart.

"No. He's met a young woman and plans to live near her home in Boston. He's secured a position with a bank. I don't think Mother approves. The woman's family isn't on the social register, but Ronald says he's going to marry for love."

"Good for Ronald. I hope that he'll be happy with his new position and the young lady proves to be a good match."

Josef tapped on the doorframe. Mr. Galloway stood behind him. "We can join you?" I nodded and motioned him forward. "Mr. Galloway says he will change the contract so that the factory will belong to us as equal partners."

Mr. Galloway sat down on the brocade sofa. "And I'd like to exchange paintings with you."

"Exchange paintings? Whatever do you mean?"

"Josef explained that you own two other paintings that your father completed before his death. I'd prefer to return the carousel painting to you, and I'll choose one of the others as collateral for your loan. That painting of you on a carousel horse should be hanging on *your* wall, not mine."

Mr. Galloway's generosity amazed me. "You are too kind," I whispered.

"A person can never be too kind," he said. "Besides, there is great pleasure when I see the results of my kindness. It gives me immense joy — perhaps even more joy than that of the recipient."

Not caring what anyone would think, I rushed forward and embraced him. "I don't think that's true in this case." I stepped back and placed my palm on my heart. "In the short time since we've met, you have shown me great kindness. Where would I be without my job at the factory? And now, your willingness to return my painting . . ." My voice cracked with emotion, but this time it was not an urge to giggle. Instead, I forced back tears: tears of joy and tears of thanks. Although I was grateful for the things he'd done for me, mostly I was thankful I'd been given the opportunity to observe him living a godly life. Mr. Galloway transcended mere talk and exhibited his faith through example. Even when faced with a bleak medical diagnosis, he'd continued to treat others with love and benevolence.

As Josef and I prepared to depart, I hugged Augusta and promised one more visit to Fair Oaks before her family left for Colorado.

"And you must send us an invitation to your wedding. I promise to return and be your bridesmaid at the ceremony." Augusta grinned at me. She'd spoken loud enough for all to hear.

I didn't fail to note Josef's look of surprise, but he remained silent until we were waiting for the streetcar. "So this wedding of ours, when will it take place, *Miss Brouwer?*" His eyes twinkled with amusement.

"I didn't . . . There isn't . . . She only meant . . ."

Josef tilted his head back and laughed. "To Augusta, you said you want to marry me, ja?"

My cheeks blazed with embarrassment. "I told her *someday* . . ."

In broad daylight, in front of the strangers who stood waiting for the streetcar, Josef boldly pulled me into an embrace and kissed me. When he lifted his head, he smiled and said, "For sure we will marry someday. Someday very soon."

THANKS TO . . .

. . . My editor, Sharon Asmus, for her generous spirit and excellent eye for detail.

. . . My acquisitions editor, Charlene Patterson, for encouraging me to step out of my comfort zone and write this story in the first person.

. . . The entire staff of Bethany House Publishers, for their devotion to making each book they publish the best — it is a privilege to work with all of you.

. . . Rae Proefrock, Trustee, Herschell Carrousel Factory Museum in North Tonawanda, New York, for a tour of the factory, a behind-the-scenes look at repairs and painting of carousel animals, sharing her painting expertise, and reading my manuscript for technical accuracy.

. . . Jerry Reinhardt, Director, C. W. Parker Carousel Museum, Leavenworth, Kansas, for sharing his carving and painting expertise.

. . . Mary Greb-Hall for her ongoing encouragement and expertise.

. . . Lori Seilstad, Michelle Cox, and Kim Vogel Sawyer for their honest critiques.

. . . Mary Kay Woodford, my sister, my prayer warrior, my friend.

. . . My husband, Jim, my constant encourager, supporter, and advocate, and the love of my life.

. . . And, above all, thanks and praise to our Lord Jesus Christ for this miraculous opportunity to live my dream and share the wonder of His love through story.

ABOUT THE AUTHOR

Judith Miller is an award-winning author whose avid research and love for history are reflected in her novels, many of which have appeared on the CBA bestseller lists. Judy and her husband make their home in Topeka, Kansas.